BOOK OF BLOOD

JAYA FARRER

Copyright © 2025 by Jaya Farrer

All rights reserved.

No part of this publication may be reproduced, distributed, or transmitted in any form or by any means, including photocopying, recording, or other electronic or mechanical methods, without the prior written permission of the publisher, except as permitted by U.S. copyright law. For permission requests, contact the publisher at jayafarrer.com.

ISBN 979-8-218-75635-2 (paperback)

ISBN 979-8-218-75637-6 (ebook)

The story, all names, characters, and incidents portrayed in this production are fictitious. No identification with actual persons (living or deceased), places, buildings, and products is intended or should be inferred.

Cover design by Rhonna Farrer

Edited by Lily Edgerton

First edition 2025

For my sister, Tali.
This wouldn't exist without you.

A shriek echoes through the plaza.

Conversations quiet, and the flurry of movement ceases as heads swivel, whipping around in search of the source.

There. At the northwest corner of the square.

Four soldiers enter the bustle of the market. Two of them grip the arms of a woman, her face lined with age, and drag her with them. Gray hair escapes her loose hairstyle with every step as she struggles against the men beside her.

My blood runs cold at the sight of her panicked expression, fear evident in her misty eyes.

"I'm not a witch! *No soy bruja!*"

Her voice is high and raspy, and the old woman's cries pierce my skin, grating along my bones. I can feel her words in my teeth, along my fingertips, and at the back of my neck.

Following close behind, a priest wrings his hands beneath the wide sleeves of his robe. I cannot see his face, but the thought that one of the brothers from Santa Maria dels Turers has caused this scene makes my throat thick with contempt.

Next to me, Inés stands unmoving, limbs stopped in midair, her position a mirror of mine. But she only freezes for a moment.

My sister turns away from me, as though to move around our table. I snatch her wrist.

Inés looks back at me, her face contorted. "We have to do something, Catalina," she grits out.

I shake my head, tightening my grip on her arm.

"We can't just let them take her." Inés's voice drops to a whisper.

Loud, clattering footsteps join the hurried group, and my sister looks across the plaza once more.

Through the crowd, I catch a glimpse of another man, his strides sure and confident. His long black coat flaps behind him, and I spy a leather satchel hanging from his shoulder. He is not from our town.

"Witch hunter," I whisper. I have never seen a witch hunter before. In fact, I have never seen a witch hunt. Our town has only heard the rumors—rumors I prayed were only hollow words.

Inés nods slowly, confirming my suspicions.

She tugs against me, and I realize my fingers are still wrapped around her wrist. She pulls again, but I do not let her go.

"Inés," I plead with her, my voice breaking. "We can't."

She glares back at me, her eyes filled with unshed tears.

"Wouldn't you want someone to do the same for you, Catalina?" Inés clenches her hands, curling them into fists. "If it were you, wouldn't you want someone to stand up for you?"

I shake my head at her again, not as an answer to her question, but to communicate to her once more to stay.

She is right, of course. Completely right. Yet I cannot find it in myself to act, to move, to endanger myself when fear has taken such a hold on my heart, squeezing it in a vice that makes it impossible to breathe.

Inés wrenches her arm from me, and I look away from her, searching for the woman.

But she has already been taken out of the plaza. Peering through the market crowd that has started moving once more, I see no sign of the screaming woman. Nor the stoic soldiers, the holy priest, or the smug witch hunter. No, they have completely disappeared. And the only evidence that the woman existed at all is the way my hands cannot stop shaking, the way my knees threaten to give out at any moment.

Though an anxious energy lingers around me, the market is once again busy, full of bartering, exchanges, and people continuing with their lives.

I know this is not the last we have heard of it. I know the whole town will be buzzing, worrying, gossiping, and plotting about this most recent development. Yet, their world spins on.

I cannot understand. Do their ears not ring with the woman's screams?

Inés elbows me in the side, and I realize the customer perusing our wares asked a question.

"Yes, I painted that one, too," I hear Inés say as she takes the *talavera* bowl and inspects it.

I struggle to focus as the sounds and scents of the main square penetrate my consciousness. I close my eyes, trying to ground myself in the moment, in hopes I will be rid of the shivers that crawl up and down my spine in the hot sun.

With the slight breeze, I smell the subtle indication of Josefina's fresh flowers next to us. We always try to set up near her booth. Her plants dilute the square's odor of humans, animals, and sweat that grows stronger through every sun-soaked hour.

I hear a young woman gasp in distaste at what I can only assume is the price of the embroidered textiles at Beatriz Maria's booth, and my eyes open to see children along the borders of the plaza, laughing with glee, squealing as their mother weaves in and out of the dark stone arches in an attempt to catch them.

"Cuánto cuesta?"

The woman in front of me catches my attention again, her hands clutching a different bowl. It is one I painted last week. One of my favorites. The bright blue swirls and flowers stand out against the stark white of the bowl, thick lines that make the design easy to see rather than many of our tediously detailed patterns.

Banyoles may not be particularly well-known for our *talavera* pottery, not like Toledo or Andalucía, but I know that our tiles and dishes—our abstract patterns and scenic paintings—make their way around this northeast region of Spain.

I love being a part of it, creating it, being the one to sell it. Mamá learned pottery from her parents. It was her family's business, and thankfully, she was able to take over. That is what kept us afloat before Mamá found the courage to make money from her true gift.

Inés responds to the woman and, to my surprise, instead of arguing with the price set, she hands over a few coins in exchange for the bright blue bowl.

I thank her and her companion, watching Inés place the money into her canvas pouch.

"Oh, Catalina," she says. She clears her throat, not meeting my eyes, and I know she is still just as shaken as I am. "Guess what Agustin told me yesterday."

I suppose Inés is planning on ignoring the scene we just witnessed. And she does so with the worst possible distraction.

I try not to roll my eyes, but it gets harder and harder with each passing day she spends with her beau. At twenty years old, my older sister seems desperate to find a husband.

Mamá never pressured either of us into marriage. In fact, she often actively scared off potential husbands. And I certainly did not mind. Even if I will one day be considered an old spinster, I would rather be alone than trapped, and I am forever grateful my mother will never force me into something I don't want.

But I guess Inés does not feel the same way.

"I'm sure you will tell me whether I want to hear it or not," I say.

"You would be right," she says, shuffling the bowls and tiles around on the little table in front of us. "A new group of soldiers is coming in today."

My shoulders tense, and I glance around the plaza in reflex. At the opposite corner, I spot a band of soldiers at ease, talking and laughing with each other loudly.

"Great," I mumble in response. "Not like we already have too many." My voice is quiet, but Inés hears me.

I have never liked soldiers. They are always ready for a fight and for violence, walking around with swords strapped to their belts like a disaster waiting to happen. It makes me nervous.

Now, the idea of a new surplus of soldiers has my stomach in knots. Especially after what we just witnessed. The Inquisition is cracking down on their witch hunts, arresting and executing women all throughout the country.

You are not a witch, I tell myself. But every day it gets more difficult to convince myself we are safe.

After all, were any of those women really witches? Or were they only disliked? Sometimes, I think witch hunts are simply an excuse for those in power to eradicate the social outcasts.

Perhaps I am being dramatic.

Next to me, Inés waves enthusiastically, and I follow her line of sight to see Agustin across the square, his hand raised in greeting.

I manage to keep my groan to myself, but apparently my eye roll is enough for Inés to read my thoughts. She folds her arms over her chest and turns to me, shifting her weight to one leg and popping her hip, her long blue skirt swishing with the movement.

"Why do you hate him so much?" A few strands of hair have escaped from her dark braid, and she hastily brushes them back out of her face, revealing the light blue eyes that are a copy of mine.

Though our features are similar, Inés's skin is somewhat fairer than mine, and her cheeks flush pink when she blushes. Or when she gets angry. Which is more likely to be the case when she is with me.

"You know why," I answer.

She just groans in frustration. "You can't judge people just because you looked at them once and got a bad feeling about them."

"I can, I have, and I will keep doing it," I say, nodding my head with every statement. "I'm telling you, Inés. There is something off about him. He doesn't seem like the best choice."

"Look, I will admit that sometimes you are right. But that doesn't mean you are a prophet." Inés throws her hands up. "And so what? He is nice to me and he is interested. At this point, what else could I want?"

I don't tell her that she can remain single like Mamá. Like me. We have had this conversation too many times in the past few weeks alone.

"He's a soldier, Inés," I hiss at her. "How can you look at him without thinking of the woman we just saw dragged away?"

Her face falls and she turns away stiffly. "Papá was a soldier. They can't all be bad."

She doesn't need to remind me. I know it.

I also know he isn't around.

"That doesn't change the way I feel, Inés," I say with a sigh. She pinches the bridge of her nose with her thumb and forefinger. I pull her hands away from her face and hold them in mine. "You know it is because I care about you, right? I just want you to be happy. And safe."

"But this will make me happy," she says, her voice nearly a whisper.

I don't protest. It is not worth another fight.

I am spared from needing to answer when the devil we spoke of rushes toward us.

"Inés!"

His sword swings with his movement, and nausea grips me. Perhaps Agustin wasn't one of the soldiers to take that woman, but it does not matter much when he appears in front of me with the same weapons strapped across his chest, the same insignia on his clothes.

Yet, my sister embraces him.

"What will happen to that woman?" Inés asks him after pulling away.

Agustin frowns. "What woman?"

"The woman that was just screaming in the plaza, getting dragged away by four soldiers," she says, throwing her arm in that direction.

Agustin blinks. "Oh, I didn't pay much attention."

"A woman was accused of witchcraft." My anger rises in my throat, and it takes everything in me to keep my voice from shaking. "She was screaming, terrified, and you didn't pay attention?"

Agustin glances away, looking between my sister and me. He opens his mouth and closes it again as Inés shifts away from him, just an inch, staring at him with her jaw tight.

How could he not pay attention? It was likely his friends who hauled the old woman off, people he knows. And he didn't pay attention?

But a voice scratches at my consciousness. *You, too, did nothing. You may have noticed her, but what good did that do?*

"She will be imprisoned while she awaits trial," Agustin states, pushing forward to answer my sister's original question.

We have no time to react as another commotion erupts down the road, and I jump, rattling the *talavera* in front of us.

At the north end of the plaza, a new group of Spanish soldiers enters the square. It is nearly the same place where the old woman vanished, and the ground sways as I watch them replace her.

Through the stone arches, I spot ten soldiers or so, led by two on horses. Agustin leaves us without another word, hurrying off to the two groups now greeting each other. Inés and I relax, the tension dissipating.

"I guess they're here," Inés says. She clears her throat with a cough and wipes her hands on her skirt. "Supposedly, there are a few soldiers that are good friends with some of the men here. They grew up together in a small town somewhere."

I hum in response. What does she expect me to say? Are we supposed to welcome them with open arms when we know it will only result in a greater threat to our safety?

I turn my attention to Agustin as the troops meet, clapping each other on the back. Some pull one another in for a quick embrace.

Out of habit and a new need for self-preservation, I stare at each new soldier, eager for visions or impressions about any of them.

They all look the same to me, wearing frilly shirts and silly pants, weapons hanging from their belts while their tall leather boots clap on the stone of the square. Dressed as a man ready to arrest someone for nothing more than a pointed finger.

As my eyes glance over the group, all I feel is distaste and apathy. I know those are my own emotions clouding my judgement. I have never understood why someone would choose to be a soldier. Mamá raised Inés and me with a strong aversion to violence, aggression, and any ill will.

Not that I don't have any ill will toward anyone. I do. I have a lot.

But she taught us that these feelings and actions have serious consequences from the universe, and that humanity means forgiving, healing, and helping others.

After watching their counterparts cruelly capture an old woman, my hatred for these soldiers feels especially poignant.

Is that why this new group has come?

My scrutiny comes to a halt. This new soldier is young, perhaps only a year or two older than I am. He is dressed the same as the others, but he is clean shaven, his light brown olive skin glowing in the setting sun. His brown hair curls at the ends, creating waves that move with him as his head swivels to search the crowd, looking for someone.

His eyes land on one of the soldiers, Agustin's friend. I believe I met him once before. What was his name? Mario?

The new soldier's face lights up in a blinding smile, his eyes crinkling at the edges, and my stomach drops. My mouth goes dry. There's something about this soldier—something I can't quite see. And I can see *everything*.

I squint, zeroing in on him as he embraces Manuel, or whatever his name is. I can't decipher what it is that I am feeling. A shiver sweeps through my body despite the warm weather. It isn't unpleasant, but it sets me on edge all the same.

The soldier pulls back, and his eyes immediately find me from across the plaza. For a moment, I am frozen, unblinking.

Even from this distance, I can see his rich brown eyes are framed with long lashes and eyebrows so dark they are almost black. It makes his gaze even more intense.

But I quickly recover. Eyes down, I focus on gathering our remaining *talavera*, stacking and organizing. Every cell of my body vibrates, and I shake my head in an attempt to rid myself of the tingles blanketing my skin.

I have never felt anything like it. Nothing like when I look at Agustin and dread spreads within me, an uneasiness sticking in my throat. Nor when I look at Mamá and know the bad news she is about to tell us before she even opens her mouth.

The pottery clinks quietly as I carefully set each piece on top of another, and I am so concentrated on my task that I don't hear them approach.

"This is the girl I told you about. This is Inés." It's Agustin. Back again. *Dios,* will I ever be rid of him? "And this is her sister, Catalina."

I hardly see him. Instead, I look up into the same eyes that I was trapped in just a moment ago. My mind starts spinning, whirling, trying to make sense of what I'm seeing.

He is just a man, a new soldier. *Calm down.*

He studies me intently, yet his face appears remarkably passive. I notice a small birthmark right beneath his lip, the only inconsistency in his otherwise unnaturally symmetrical features.

Unfortunately, Agustin continues with the introductions. "This is Diego Tremiño, and you know Marcos, of course." Oh, right, Marcos. That's his name.

"Of course," Inés says with a nod in his direction.

Marcos turns to me with a smile, his lips pointed in a sharp curve. "I don't think we've actually met," he says, extending his hand.

I don't take it. Nor do I correct him. We were introduced once before, but I am oddly relieved he does not remember me.

Marcos recovers quickly from my rejection and throws his arm around Diego's shoulder. I can tell he is an inch or two shorter than Diego by the way he lifts his elbow in an exaggerated reach.

"We actually grew up together. In a small town in Navarre," Marcos says.

At first glance, the two could be brothers. Alike in coloring, their skin tone is closer than mine and Inés's, though Marcos looks like he's spent more time in the sun. Both have dark hair, yet Diego is clean-shaven while Marcos has a short beard and his hair is long enough to tie into a small ponytail at the base of his neck.

However, where Diego's gaze makes me sweat, my skin chills when I see Marcos's icy blue eyes. They are piercing, even lighter than mine, and I look away quickly.

Diego doesn't take his eyes off me. Observing silently, he stares down at me through dark lashes. His scrutiny feels dangerous and secretive, like he is privy to every hidden thought in my head and matches each with one of his own.

Marcos and Agustin keep talking to Inés, but something behind them catches my attention.

Past the three men now blocking our booth, our neighbor Maria Luisa gives a small wave in our direction, causing me to lean over and peer between Diego and Marcos to see her properly.

I return the wave as my face lights up. I am excited for her. She is only a few years older than Inés and me, and I know she has always looked forward to being a mother—to having a family and home of her own.

"Congratulations!" I call out to her with a wide grin. I hope she knows I mean it.

But Maria Luisa pauses and her smile falters, a crease appearing between her brows. She tilts her head, considering me. I keep my grin painted on, hoping confusion does not creep into my face as a reflection of her expression.

Next to me, Inés goes silent. She moves closer to me and catches sight of Maria Luisa.

"Congratulations for what?" My sister asks, her gaze shifting from Maria Luisa to me and back again, waiting for one of us to answer.

Her question gives me pause. How is it possible I know about Maria Luisa's pregnancy before Inés? Usually, she is the one with news and gossip around Banyoles.

Hesitating, Maria Luisa gives a subtle shake of her head, keeping her eyes on me. *"Sí,"* she says, "congratulations for what?"

I have suddenly become very aware of my skin as the tiny hairs on the back of the neck stand on end. Glancing around, I find the entire group looking at me, faces blank. All save Inés, whose frown deepens.

"What are you talking about, Cata?" she whispers, leaning close.

Of course. Once again, I have seen what no one else has. And once again, I have foolishly spoken without thinking.

This is what gets people killed.

Releasing a shaky breath, I force the corners of my mouth up into an apologetic smile. "I am sorry, Maria Luisa. For a moment, I thought you were Antonia." I swallow hard in an effort to speak casually despite my tightening throat. "I have yet to congratulate her on the engagement."

It is a terrible lie. Though cousins, Maria Luisa and Antonia look very different: one is short while the other is tall, one wears her hair in a tight bun while the other wears hers loose around her shoulders. And I know Maria Luisa does not believe me.

But she offers me a gracious smile. "I will let her know," she says with a nod. Taking a slow step forward, Maria Luisa looks back at me once more, the same crease in her forehead.

My eyes shut with relief as she rushes off, getting lost in the evening crowd.

"Are you okay? What was that?" Inés grabs my elbow. "Is Maria Luisa...?" She trails off and her eyes widen, flicking her gaze around nervously.

I glance at Diego and Marcos, both of whom haven't taken their eyes off me, looking just as confused as Maria Luisa.

Affecting a laugh, I wave my hand. "I'm fine. I must be tired from squinting in the sun all day long."

Agustin catches Inés's attention once more, but as her head turns toward him, her eyes stay locked on my face for a moment.

I try to shake off the anxiety that so quickly took hold of me and stare down at my hands, which hold a stack of painted tiles.

Out of the corner of my eye, Diego picks up one of our dishes to take a closer look. It is one of Mamá's—a plate with green and yellow fruits and flowers, with an intricate border of blue swirls.

"I like this," he comments quietly, switching it from one hand to the other. Marcos is laughing with Agustin and Inés, and I realize it's me he is talking to now.

I sniff, another wave of irritation washing over me, amplified by my lingering adrenaline.

I reach over and snatch it from his hands, placing it in our basket. "If you aren't going to buy it, give it back," I say.

I focus on stacking our *talavera*, but I can feel Diego's eyes on me.

"You don't like me," he states. His voice is full and deep, quiet yet strong enough to permeate my core. After a pause, he continues. "You don't like Agustin, either. Even though he is courting your sister."

I grind my teeth together.

"Why?" he asks.

I would like to think I have more self-control. But apparently, I do not. After the shock of seeing the old woman's arrest and the panic from my interaction with Maria Luisa, my head snaps up at him.

"I don't like soldiers," I mutter.

Diego nods slowly, squinting at me.

"Don't worry," I say with a humorless laugh. "It is nothing personal."

"Oh, but it is," Diego says. "You dislike us based on our occupation, our appearance. That feels a little personal to me."

It suddenly occurs to me that I should not be making enemies with the very people I fear. With a deep breath, I try to center myself.

"I just don't like violence, that is all," I say. I keep my voice high, sweet and innocent. "And you go around with swords on your belts."

"A few of us even have guns."

I gaze up at him, giving him a saccharine smile. "You can see why that would make me nervous."

Diego arches a brow with a dubious look. "So, you don't like violence."

"It is unnecessary and ineffective," I say, shaking my head.

"Yet, violence is often necessary for our protection."

"I disagree."

"Without it, you are weak, vulnerable. It is dangerous," he says. "You would rather people walk all over you?"

I shoot him a look. "Passivity does not mean you let people walk all over you. It doesn't make you weak."

"And violence doesn't make you evil."

As I glare at him, I notice Marcos, Agustin, and Inés are watching us silently.

I break eye contact with Diego and clear my throat. "Inés, isn't Andrés Carlos coming by this evening?"

"Oh, right," she says with a snap of her fingers, as though she had completely forgotten until that moment. She probably had.

"Andrés Carlos?" Agustin asks, his brow furrowed.

Inés joins me in carefully filling our baskets as the three soldiers hover near us.

"Andrés is our neighbor who has kindly agreed to take our wares to Girona to sell. He is coming by to pick up our *talavera*," she explains. "We have to get back home to meet him."

Inés turns to Agustin. "I'll see you tomorrow?"

He smiles at her, bringing her hand to his lips. "Tomorrow."

I pick up two of our smaller *talavera* baskets, leaving the big one for Inés.

"*Adiós*," I say without looking at any of the men.

I take a few steps toward the edge of the square, but I hesitate. I can feel his eyes on me.

I turn back to see Diego studying me, and I pause to do the same with a scowl, not bothering to hide my annoyance and frustration.

No aura, no vision, no discernible feeling. I haven't had this much difficulty reading somebody since I was a child.

But there is something there. A vibration from Diego that sends a shudder down my spine.

2

"Catalina!"

Inés's voice is more of a growl than a yell. It is enough to make me stop.

I started walking before she even picked up her basket and I listened to her steps hurry after me in an attempt to catch up.

She called to me once or twice, and I slowed down a little, but now I feel sorry.

I come to a stop in front of Santa Maria dels Turers, the church only a few blocks from the plaza, and I hear a huff down the street as Inés approaches.

Moving closer to the massive stone building, I look up at the warm, brown stone wall that stretches down the long side of the church. I lean against it near the end of the church where the walls curve to create the heptagonal room I know lies inside. The large doorway takes the shape of a peaked arch, framed by Gothic columns that make the entrance seem bigger and the stone darker, graying with age.

The streets are not at their busiest, but there are still plenty of people rushing around. In and out of the church, crossing the streets, carrying food or children. The faint sound of horseshoes echo down the street, coming from around the corner.

"Why did you have to leave me like that?" Inés comes up beside me, a little out of breath.

"Come on, I didn't leave you," I argue, pushing off the wall of the church to continue our walk. "You are being a little dramatic."

"Rude," Inés comments. I grin at her—whether to pacify her or aggravate her, I am not sure. Either will feel like a success.

Right as we pass the front door of the church, a loud clanging reverberates through the street and I jump.

The bells at the top of the church swing from side to side. I have rarely ever been right beneath them when they ring, and I am shocked at how the sound shakes my chest.

I guess it startles Inés too, because she nearly drops her basket. *"Mierda!"*

I let out an exaggerated gasp. "Inés, language." I draw out her name like Mamá does, slightly raising my voice to be heard over the bells.

She laughs as I shake my head sadly with a *tsk*. I try to keep a straight face, but my smile breaks through.

"So," Inés begins, her words quiet as we move forward, "Maria Luisa." She doesn't say it like a question, but I know she is asking nonetheless.

I heave a sigh. "What about her?"

"Is she, like, pregnant or something?"

"Why would you say that?"

Inés shoots me a look. "Because you obviously did not think she was Antonia. No one believed that."

My stomach twists tighter. "Really?" Instantly, I think of the old woman's face as she was arrested in front of us.

My sister must sense my anxiety, because she revises her words. "I mean, I don't think anyone is suspicious or anything. They probably just think you are a little strange, and Maria Luisa will consider it for the rest of the evening before forgetting it forever."

I make a sound in the back of my throat, unsure whether her words are comforting or disconcerting.

We walk together past the front of the cathedral and up the street that leads to the monastery. The Sant Esteve monastery is as big—if not bigger—than the church. I find the design to be simpler, and we can see it even from down the long street. Its light stone creates a flat, clean wall with a small door and a circular window above it. The tower stands on the north end of the building, but it does not look as grand as the church tower. It looks almost like an afterthought. I know, of course, it was not. The monastery itself is older than the church. And though it has been rebuilt, it certainly feels ancient.

As we move farther from the town square, the smell of fish fades. Everyday I leave the fishermen behind in the town square, I am grateful we do not live closer to the lake. The obnoxious smell of fish and mud makes my skin feel tight against my bones, like the world is pressing in on me. I can handle it for a few hours, but if the smell were constant, I think I would go mad. On this end of town, the sweat and salt are not as strong, cut by dust and dirt that somehow smell fresher.

"Are you going to tell me what you saw?" Inés asks before adding a warning. "I won't stop asking until you do."

"Fine," I acquiesce. "Yes, I think Maria Luisa is pregnant."

"Ha! I knew it!"

For some reason, the idea that Inés believes me makes me panic. "I could be wrong, though," I hurry to say. "I am right sometimes, but that doesn't mean I am a prophet." I echo the words she said to me less than an hour ago.

Inés frowns and opens her mouth, as if to protest. She trusts me, and I know she wants to say that I am right most of the time. But that would mean admitting that I may be right about Agustin. That he may not be who she thinks he is, or who she wants him to be.

On our street now, the small buildings stand close together, several stories leering over us. The design and architecture are plain, but the white walls burn bright in the fiery glare of the setting sun.

"Are we going to talk about what we both saw?" I ask quietly.

Inés's blue eyes flicker over to me, and she shifts the large basket in her arms. "What is there to say?"

To that, I have no response. A part of me wants Inés to reassure me, to tell me it was nothing to worry about. Another part of me wants to tell Inés she was right. We should have done something to help the woman. But what? How could we possibly help?

Neither of us has the answers we want to hear, so we do not say much as we move closer to our home, and I have to hurry my pace to keep up. Inés isn't much taller than me, but it is enough to give her a longer stride. I end up walking a bit behind her, watching her deep brown hair swing in its long braid across her back.

Inés and I arrive home just as the sun sets behind the houses. I can instantly feel the lack of warmth and shiver in the cool shade.

We enter through the front door, carefully placing our *talavera* right inside so it is ready for Andrés Carlos.

"*Chicas?*" I hear Mamá call to us.

"*Hola*, Mamá," I say.

"Girls, can you come here? Inés, I want to see what you think," she says.

Someone else is in the other room with Mamá. Someone who came to her for help.

I hoped the house would be empty, but it was not a realistic wish. Mamá is always busy.

I follow Inés farther into our house and forget the dusty smell from outside. My senses are overwhelmed by the fresh and colorful scent of herbs and flowers, mingling together in a comforting chaos. I take a deep breath, and my body relaxes as it recognizes home.

The walls of our house are plain, roughly painted with a white plaster to allow the space to glow even from the single window next to the front door. Our small sitting area is complete with a plain worn sofa, a faded rug, and an old wooden rocking chair from Mamá's mother.

Our hearth keeps the room warm—sometimes unbearably so—though it is cozy at night. But we always keep the fire going with a pot of water heating above it, ready for cooking and creating mixtures for healing.

Between the fireplace and the kitchen, the square wooden table sits with chairs on three sides. The surface is covered in herbs, tinctures, bowls, and jars. Out of habit, I check that none of the items will soon slide off the sanded wood. Until I remember Inés folded up an old handkerchief and shoved it beneath the uneven table leg, keeping the rickety piece of furniture steady.

Mamá sits on the side closest to the kitchen, the small back window softly illuminating her silhouette, while her guests sit facing the door so we are able to see them the moment we walk in. It is Margarita and her little daughter, Juanita, at our table. Mamá pats the girl's hand before holding it out to Inés.

I slow my steps, hanging back in the doorway. I feel so out of place, even in my own home.

"What is wrong?" Inés asks in a soft voice. She looks at Juanita, but I know the question is really directed to Mamá.

"She is hot, dizzy, and has been sick three times since last night," Mamá answers quietly.

Inés nods and closes her eyes. I watch eagerly, my eyes flicking around every part of the scene in front of me. I don't want to miss any detail.

Mamá is the neighborhood *curandera,* welcoming countless people into our home throughout the day in hopes of healing whatever ails them.

Since we were young, we have watched Mamá calm and reassure the sick, the injured, and their families with a gentle touch and an almost magical presence. She can see what is wrong with someone by sight and touch. And sometimes she doesn't even need that.

However, contrary to what many of our neighbors may think, Mamá does not actually heal them. She simply discovers what will heal them. She can read the body like a book, and she knows the blessings of nature inside and out. With those skills combined, Inés and I have barely been ill a day in our lives.

As I watch Inés hold Juanita's hand, a whirlwind of emotions wars in my soul, ranging from awe to jealousy.

Inés possesses the same gift. I try not to envy her, especially because I can occasionally heal like she and Mamá do. But it is not the same. The way my mamá and my sister help people is incredible. The way families arrive at our home in distress and leave with hope is a testament to the good they do.

Inés exchanges a glance with Mamá and then leans down to whisper in her ear. I know what they are discussing without needing to hear them: whether Juanita has been cursed.

It is common. More common than people realize. Particularly because curses generally come from someone you know, though it is often only subconscious.

"I think an infusion of *hinojo* for tonight," Inés says for everyone to hear. "And a poultice of *hipérico* and *lino* tonight and tomorrow."

Mamá nods. "That is what I was thinking. Catalina, would you retrieve *hinojo* and *lino* from the back room so I can make the mixture?"

"Do you need the *hipérico*, too?"

"I have some here," Mamá says, shaking her head.

Our entire home feels like a greenhouse, herbs growing and drying in every room, especially the kitchen. Once we started growing our own herbs, we didn't have to go out and buy them, nor did we have to search the fields and forest in the hot sun and pick what we needed. It is better to be sent to the back room than to a pasture a mile away.

As the largest room in our house, the kitchen is always packed full. One end of the room is dominated by our stone oven. Next to it, a pile of pots and pans is stacked neatly, ready for use. The floor on the other side of the oven is taken by newly picked herbs, laid out on old handkerchiefs. Their proximity to the heat of the oven is ideal for the drying process. Though as I get close to the oven, I notice it hasn't been heated up—I'll have to do that later.

The other end of the room has a small window like the one behind our table. This space is lined with pots and planters filled with plants at different stages of growth. Rosemary, fennel, flax, spearmint, basil, mugwort.

Along the north wall, bundles of dried herbs and flowers are strung up, hung like banners and layered to fit as many as possible in one space.

The south wall is the smallest and closest to the door, its space taken up entirely by two chests of drawers. The wooden furniture pieces are not particularly fancy or well-made, but they serve their purpose. Each chest contains five drawers, and each drawer is further divided to hold seeds, leaves, flowers, and branches, as well as previously prepared mixtures and poultices.

I quickly retrieve a small bundle of fennel leaves that has been drying near the window and a little jar of *lino* seeds that have already been powdered. I return to find Mamá grinding the *hipérico*.

"Thank you, *mija*," Mamá mutters. She takes the *lino* from me and blends it with the *hipérico*.

Inés disappears for a second and comes back with a small cup in one hand. She retrieves the kettle from over the fire, pours some boiling water on the powdered herbs, and Mamá then turns it into a paste.

Inés takes the *hinojo* from me and places some of the dried leaves into the cup of still-steaming water.

"Do you have a jar or a bag, Margarita?" Mamá asks.

Margarita holds out a jar she has brought from home, and Mamá fills it with the poultice of *hipérico* and *lino*.

"Put it on her back twice before bed tonight," Mamá instructs her, "and once more in the morning."

As Margarita nods seriously, Inés sits next to Juanita, bringing the hot water with her.

"If she drinks this right now, it will help with her symptoms immediately," Inés explains.

Juanita shakes her head hard and tries to push her chair away from the table.

"I don't want it," the little girl whines.

Margarita looks up at Mamá with an apologetic, if not slightly panicked, expression.

"Oh, but we aren't done with it, Juanita," Inés says with a smile.

Juanita raises a skeptical eyebrow at Inés, and it takes everything in me not to laugh at the young girl's serious face.

"Take out the leaves, Inés," I tell her, turning around to retrieve a few dried pieces of *naranja*. The hot water should have enough of an infusion from the *hinojo* by now.

I drop the peels into the newly leaf-free cup of water. Mamá hands Inés a clean spoon, and my sister begins stirring the elixir.

"Does your mamá make you tea, Juanita?" Inés asks. The girl nods slowly. "This tea is my favorite. It is what my mamá makes, and this one will make you feel better."

Juanita turns her attention to the cup on the table, her little eyebrows coming together in determination. She takes a cautious drink.

Mixed with the strong flavor of *naranja*, the *hinojo* should be nearly undetectable, but children will imagine any taste once they know medicine is present. Inés should not have put the leaves into the cup in front of Juanita.

She takes a few more sips from the tea before pushing it away. Fortunately, a little girl like Juanita won't need much to stop the stomach pain and vomiting.

"You did great, Juanita," Inés says, taking the cup away from her.

Margarita stands. "*Gracias,* Soledad." She embraces Mamá and offers her a few metal coins, her other hand clutching the tiny jar filled with the herbal paste.

"Will I get better now?" Juanita asks Mamá.

Mamá smiles. "Very soon."

Margarita passes Inés and presses her hand to her cheek with a warm smile.

Juanita waves at me as she leaves, her hand in Margarita's. Mamá follows them out and checks that no one else is waiting to see the neighborhood *curandera.* She shuts the door and locks it when she sees no one.

"Why put the tincture on her back?" I ask.

"That is where the curse is attached to her. That is where she is weak," Inés says, gathering up the mortar and pestle as well as the remaining herbs.

"Who was it?" I cannot help myself. Even if they do not tell me, I know I will ask every time.

Inés looks up at Mamá, who shakes her head. "That is not important, *mija.* We should not talk about such things."

I leave it at that. I know how Mamá is about curses. And I know the cost it has on someone who has cursed. I am sure if I look close enough in town, I could find who it was that placed this affliction on Juanita.

But I won't. Mamá is right. It's not important.

What I need to focus on is becoming a better healer.

"How did you know what to do to help her?" I ask Inés, moving around the table to stand closer to her.

She just shrugs. "I don't know. It just came into my head."

"Okay, but how?" I ask, trying to keep the whine out of my voice. This frustrates me. I am looking for answers. "Was it an image? The names of the herbs? What?"

This time, Inés stops what she is doing and actually takes a moment to think.

"I can't explain it. I just know it," she says. Before I can argue with her, she questions me. "How do you know when something is about to happen? How do you know someone has bad intentions? How do you know when our neighbor is pregnant?" She raises her eyebrows and looks at me meaningfully.

I stop short. "Well, sometimes I get a dream, but most of the time..." I trail off.

"Most of the time, you just know," Inés finishes for me.

I nod.

"It is the same for me." My sister comes over to me and puts both hands on my shoulders, facing me fully. "You will get better at it with practice. Keep following your intuition. The more you act on it, the more you will feel it."

I know this is true from experience. Once I stopped questioning and doubting the things I knew or the dreams I had, I started getting even more premonitions.

"You already have the gift for healing," Inés continues. "More than most people."

I swallow a lump in my throat and give her a small smile. I know she is trying to help and I know she means it, but it only makes me feel worse. More than most people is not good enough. I want to help like she and Mamá do.

"How's this? The next time I feel unwell, I will ask you for a reading. You tell me what you see and feel, and we can both get better."

I give her a real smile this time.

M amá goes to the bedroom to change her clothes. As her footsteps pat up the stairs, Inés and I begin the daily ritual to clean and cleanse.

"Sweep or salt?" Inés asks me.

She holds out the broom with her elbow half-bent, ready to extend it to me or claim it for herself.

"Sweep."

I take the broom, and Inés goes back into the kitchen to retrieve a bundle of dried *romero*. She lights the herbs on one of the candles on the table, quickly blows out the flame, and sets the smoking leaves in a small bowl.

All the while, I move around her, broom in hand, starting in the kitchen where the most energy gathers. Then I sweep near the hearth and around the sofa, ending at the door. I go outside and brush off the three steps that lead into our home, knowing many bring their troubles to our doorstep.

Behind me, Inés sprinkles salt into a cup of water and swishes it around with her pointer finger, mixing the solution. She sticks her fingers into the water and flicks them in the air to scatter saltwater in every corner of the room.

We move as though in a trance. I don't even have to think about it; this is as routine as much as Mamá cooking for us or Inés snoring at night.

Though, if I am honest with myself, I do not know if sweeping truly makes a difference. When we burn *romero* to cleanse the energy, I can feel a distinct shift, but I am unsure if sweeping has anything to do with it.

But Inés and I have learned not to argue. Sweeping the house is a tradition passed down through Mamá's parents, so I don't question.

It doesn't take Inés long to salt the room, so she follows me as I finish up, waving the *romero*-scented smoke around each doorway and corner to target stagnant and harmful energy, looking for anywhere it might be hiding.

I'm glad she let me sweep today. I am in no mood to chase spirits around the house.

Once I finish, I stand in front of Inés so she can pass the smoking herbs over my body.

"Right at the back of my neck," I tell her. She makes a humming noise in her throat, indicating she senses what I do. She waves the *romero* over my head more than the rest of my body—that is where I have a weakness today, where someone could be trying to curse me.

Once she is done, I take the bundle and do the same to her, paying close attention to any heavy energy I find on her. I hesitate at her left side, spending more time where I can feel an enervation in her aura.

"You want to cleanse, Mamá?" I ask when she comes back downstairs. I hold up the smoking herbs in a gesture to her.

Mamá's olive skin glows in the firelight as she approaches us. Her complexion is more bronze than Inés's and mine, and her round eyes are a warm shade of brown that always makes me feel seen and secure.

Though I see the allure of our blue eyes, I envy Mamá's golden features. She says that we look a lot like Papá, save for our dark hair we inherited from her. She says we are lucky to have gotten the best of each parent, and it makes me wonder if she knows how exquisitely beautiful she is.

She stands in front of me, waiting for me to wave the *romero* around her. I take my time, paying more attention to her than I did to Inés, simply because I know Mamá normally has more spirits hanging onto her.

After her quick trip upstairs, Mamá's dark hair is still in the braided bun she wears at the base of her neck. She has changed out of the blue dress she wore earlier and into a simple white blouse and flowing skirt.

She insists on washing her clothes after a day of *curandismo*. The energies from her visitors, both good and bad, stay on her dresses and skirts, so she changes once she has finished for the day. Of course, this means Mamá's outfits get less than one full day of wear, but I do not blame her. I wouldn't want to walk around drenched in the energy of everyone in the neighborhood.

"Did you sweep, too?" Mamá asks, stepping away from me once I have finished with the *romero*.

I want to roll my eyes. When was the last time we forgot to sweep? "Yes, I swept."

The herbs are only smoking a bit now, a single stream of wiggling smoke slithering up to our ceiling. I place the bundle into the bowl in which Inés had set the other herbs earlier. The burned tips fall off the bundle, and the ash blackens the bottom of the dish.

A musical knock at the door causes Mamá to stiffen, her weary eyes growing bigger.

"It is just Andrés Carlos," I assure her. I do not think she has it in her to deal with any more healings today. I must be right, because I see her shoulders droop, visibly relaxing.

"Well," Mamá says, "don't keep Carlitos waiting." She nods toward the door.

I smile. Much of the neighborhood calls him Carlitos. I suppose it began when he was young, but it always strikes me as funny when a mountain of a man is called *Carlitos*.

"Catalina, will you do it?" Inés has a whine in her voice that grates on me. "Don't you like talking to him?"

I do. And I could easily go help Andrés Carlos load our *talavera* into his cart. But her grumbling irritates me.

"No! I did everything at the market today, and all you did was talk to your idiot boyfriend," I snap at her. "It's your turn."

Mamá looks at Inés. I cannot see her face, but Inés lets out a sigh, slumping in her chair before getting up to answer the door.

Mamá turns back to me, a tiny line in between her brows. She searches my face in a way that makes me squirm in my chair.

"What is on your mind, *mija*?" She asks.

What *is* on my mind?

Nothing. Everything.

I think of the old woman from the market and her desperate screams, and of the ever-lingering threat of being arrested that hangs over me.

No soy bruja!

I think of Inés's relationship with Agustin and how I am certain it will not end well; of the new soldier, Diego, and why I cannot read him the way I read others; and of my mother's innate gift to heal and what I have to do to become as she is.

Can I say this to Mamá?

Sure, she has always been there for me. Always listened to me, never judged me. But this feels different somehow. Everything feels different lately, as though my mind is being poisoned over time. My thoughts seem to be burdened by fear, anxiety, anger, and jealousy.

Shoving my doubts aside, I let out a breath and shrug. "I am just feeling frustrated because of you and Inés." I had not planned on saying that, and the instant I say it, I know it did not come out right.

"What about us?" she asks me calmly, but I see the nearly imperceptible way she draws back in surprise.

"I want to help people," I hurry to clarify. "Heal people the same way you do. But it doesn't come to me like it does for you and Inés."

Her face softens. "Catalina, you have other gifts."

I can't help it now. I roll my eyes and groan. Not the *you-have-other-talents* routine again. This must be something every mother says to her children.

Mamá reaches out to me and takes my face in her hands. Her fingers are soft and warm, and I can smell the subtle, earthy scent of *hipérico* and *albahaca* still on her hands from the day's work. "It is true, *mija*. You are sensitive to the energy of others, the energy of the universe. You know things that Inés and I can only dream to know."

"I guess," I say, purposely mumbling in a way that makes me feel like a pouting teenager. Although, I guess that is exactly what I am right now. "But that doesn't help people."

"It helps me. It helps you. It helps your sister."

"It is not the same, and you know it."

Mamá releases me and sighs, leaning back in her chair. "Listen to me, Catalina. You can cultivate the same gifts that Inés and I have. You can acquire different ones, too. But it will take time. And you need to accept your own power to make the most of it."

My chest swells with hope. "Really? You think I can be like you?"

"I do not want you to be like me. I want you to be like you, whatever that may look like," she says. "But yes, you can get better at healing if that is what you want. It just takes practice."

"Inés says she will help me."

Mamá smiles. "And you will help her."

I scoff. "With what?"

"Anything, everything. That is what you have been doing since you were born. That is what family does."

I consider her words, and even though I still feel disappointed that I don't know how to heal like Mamá, her confidence that I can learn is encouraging.

"All loaded up?" Mamá asks as Inés walks back into the kitchen.

"Yep," she says. "No thanks to Catalina."

It never ceases to amaze me how quickly I can switch from love and adoration to resentment and indignation, and back again. It is a power only a sister can have.

"You owed me," I counter.

Inés waves a hand wearily, swatting away the impending argument.

"So," Mamá starts as Inés slumps back in her seat, the wooden chair creaking under her weight, "you saw Agustin today?"

"Yes, and a bunch of new soldiers that just arrived," Inés says.

"That is exciting."

"*I* thought so," my sister says, eyeing me. "But Catalina wasn't very friendly. Not that she ever is."

"I am friendly to people I like," I mutter.

"And that doesn't include Agustin."

"He is not right for you, Inés. If you would just listen—"

"Oh, here we go again," she says, her voice rising.

"Perhaps you should listen to your sister, Inés," Mamá says.

My mouth falls open, and we sit speechless, staring at Mamá. She has never interfered before when we start arguing about Agustin.

Inés recovers first. "What? Why? Are you serious? She doesn't have a say in my relationship with Agustin."

"Of course, we will respect your decision," Mamá says. I huff. "But Catalina has a gift. A gift we have seen many times over."

"This isn't her gift talking." She says *gift* like the word has offended her. "She hates all soldiers. Even though Papá was one."

"We are not discussing Papá right now," Mamá responds firmly. A line appears between her eyebrows, but only for a moment before she smooths her expression again.

"Alright, well, maybe if Catalina could explain why she thinks Agustin is so bad, I would listen to her."

They both turn to me.

Mierda.

"I don't know how. I just know." When Inés rolls her eyes at me, I continue. "Just like you said when I asked you how to heal someone. It is not always something you can explain."

I know that doesn't help, nor does it answer her question. But it is something she can understand. She just refuses to.

"Well, I will not break this off just because you have a bad feeling about it," Inés says quietly. "This is my chance. Agustin asked me to marry him."

Mamá brings her hand to her mouth in a silent gasp, and I give an incoherent yelp.

"Don't act so surprised. I am basically an old maid at this point. It is a miracle someone wants to marry me at all," she says bitterly. "I have to think of my future, and the world is not kind to single women. The only reason we have survived is because you are the *curandera*."

The three of us are silent for a moment. It is true. We have been lucky.

Mamá sighs, bringing a hand to her lined forehead and massaging her temples with her thumb and fingers.

She suddenly looks older to me, more weathered. The lines around her eyes are deeper. How long has she been this tired? This worried?

"Inés is right," Mamá says. "Maybe this marriage is a good idea."

"Mamá!" I cry out, scandalized and betrayed.

"You know I will never pressure either of you into a marriage you do not want. But things are changing, and we need to be able to survive."

Inés and I share a glance. "What do you mean?" I ask.

"Help me make the meal," Mamá says instead of answering my question. When neither of us moves, she tells us, "I will explain while we eat."

4

ut Mamá doesn't explain.

All through dinner, she asks about our day, and Inés nervously prattles on about Agustin, with the occasional sidelong glance in my direction.

By the end of the meal, my uneasiness has spread, and I cannot stop bouncing my leg.

"Stop that, Catalina," Mamá says. "What is wrong with you?"

"I am anxious, Mamá," I explain, trying my best to keep the irritation out of my voice.

"Do you want *tilo*? Or we could do an infusion of *toronjil*?"

"No, I want you to explain what you meant." I know Mamá is just trying to help. And perhaps it would be good for me to have some of my favorite calming herbs. But, believe it or not, it isn't my top concern right now.

Mamá stands and retrieves the warm kettle from the hearth. It should have just enough hot water for our nightly herbal tea.

Inés gets up to help her, but I stay put, arms crossed over my chest in protest.

I watch Mamá pour three steaming cups, and Ines places dried *manzanilla* and *naranja* in the water. This is the good tea—the tea we save for ourselves for pure enjoyment, rather than remedies for injury or illness.

Once Inés places the herbs into each cup, Mamá slowly stirs the herbal mixture. Inés grabs the first two finished teas and brings one to me, sitting down at my side.

With a cup in front of each of us, Mamá takes a drink from hers and squeezes her eyes shut. Inés looks at me, and I widen my eyes at her. She shrugs with a shake of her head.

"Today, Señora Diaz came to see me," Mamá starts. She opens her eyes and gives us both a hard look. "She is not ill. But she had some news."

"*Mamá*," Inés groans, "out with it already! You are killing us. Look at Catalina." She says it with a straight face, but I can see a glint in her eye when she gestures toward me.

"*Ay!* What does that mean?"

"Hush," Mamá says, her voice quiet. "Listen to me. Señora Diaz told me that the Inquisition is making their way out from Girona."

Inés catches my eye, all signs of mischief gone from her gaze.

"They are arresting anyone they think is sinful or threatening. Sometimes even executing them. Anyone against the church. There were a few arrests in Terrassa recently, and some in Viladrau, too," Mamá continues, her voice lowering to a whisper. "They are looking for witches, *mijas*."

I wish Mamá wasn't telling us. I don't want this to be a serious matter. I want to forget the woman we saw at the market today. I want to ignore all of this.

I remember the stories Mamá told us when we were younger: the history of the Inquisition. It was before I was born, before Mamá was born. But at their height, the Holy Inquisition arrested and imprisoned many witches and women. Whether or not they were truly witches is unknown, but I do not think it mattered to them. Some women were executed; some even burned at the stake.

Of course, that was almost a hundred years ago. But it is no longer history.

"We know, Mamá," Inés says quietly, glancing at me again. "We saw…"

I swallow hard. "We saw a woman get arrested today at the market. She was screaming that she was not a witch."

No soy bruja!

Mamá tries not to show her fear, but I see the color drain from her face.

"Who was it?"

Inés shakes her head. "I don't know her. An older woman. But she must not be from this neighborhood."

"So," Mamá says, almost to herself, "it is here already."

I can hear the blood pumping in my ears. Wave after wave, louder and louder. I want to convince myself this means nothing. But my subconscious itches with an anxious anticipation, and my stomach sinks.

It is not nothing. We saw the woman today.

My breathing comes faster and harder, like when I walk to the plaza carrying all our *talavera*.

This isn't fair. How dare they make us afraid?

"We are not witches," I protest. I clench my fists. "We don't do magic. We just work with the energy that is already there. We just see what is present."

"Cata." I can hear the impatience in Inés's voice, and I bristle.

"Just because we do things differently, does not mean we are inherently evil. Does it? To whom are we a danger? Mamá is helping people, healing people. But we are not witches," I repeat.

"Maybe not," Mamá says. "But we are witch enough. And it will not matter what we say if we are accused of witchcraft."

"You don't think anyone will accuse us, do you?" Inés asks. Her face is stoic, but her voice wavers. "Everyone in the neighborhood knows who you are. They all come to you when they are ill or injured."

"I hope not, but we cannot be sure."

Thinking of the neighbors, I feel no trepidation. But there is a threat.

I lean back in my chair, crossing my arms over my chest. "It won't be anyone in the neighborhood. They are not the enemy."

Inés looks at me once, then away, and her head swivels back to me quickly when she understands that I am talking about her new fiancé.

Her eyes widen before she rolls them, cursing under her breath. "Seriously? I'm not doing this right now."

"This isn't why I brought it up, Catalina," Mamá says. "I just want you girls to be careful. Okay?"

Inés nods solemnly. I take another drink of my tea. They both look at me.

"I'll be careful," I say with a sigh, the fight slowly leaving my body. My heartbeat slows, and exhaustion creeps in.

I stare at my cup, slowly spinning it in my hands as I watch the tea swirl within it. We sit in silence, but I can almost hear Inés thinking. I feel her body tense next to me, bracing herself to speak.

"We didn't do anything," she says quietly.

Mamá looks at her inquisitively, tilting her head to one side. But I know what my sister means.

"We didn't do anything to help. When the old woman was getting arrested. I wanted to, but…" She looks down at her hands instead of at me. "Cata grabbed me."

"That may have been for the best," Mamá replies.

"But—"

I push my chair back harshly and set down my cup. "I am going to bed."

Without waiting for a response, I leave the table, my cup sitting in the ring it left on the wood.

I pad up the stairs, listening to the whispers of Mamá and Inés in the kitchen behind me. They are nearly silent, if not for the penetrating hisses of every "s" sound they make.

I cannot face my cowardice again today. Though it occurs to me that running from my own fear makes me more of a coward.

But I am too tired to care. I'm tired and I'm scared and I'm angry.

I'm angry at the world, at the people hunting for witches. Angry at the soldiers who carry out these arrests. Angry at Inés for her bravery, her talents, her condescending tone. Angry at myself for not having that same bravery or those talents.

I think of Diego's words today. *Violence is often necessary for our protection.* I told him I disagreed, but sometimes I can feel violence coiled inside me. Sometimes, it is the only thing I feel.

Perhaps I cannot heal because I have this desire to hurt.

Tears clog my throat, and I hurry to get settled into bed. Inés will not be long in joining me, I am sure.

We have one bedroom in the house. Though all three of us keep our things in the dresser here, only Inés and I sleep upstairs.

We used to sleep in the bed with Mamá when we were little, but as we got older, there wasn't room for all of us, and Mamá began sleeping on the sofa downstairs by the fire. She said it was because she could not sleep with me kicking her, but I know it is because she wanted to give us our own space. Besides, I don't kick anymore.

I change out of my clothes in the dark, blindly feeling for the handles of the dresser drawer as I put my skirt away and fumble with the ties on my stay. I didn't bother bringing a candle upstairs with me, which proves to be a mistake when I slam my big toe into the heavy trunk at the foot of our bed.

It is the last straw, and the tears finally spill over, burning my eyes. With a frustrated growl, I kick the trunk again for good measure.

The trunk is the only thing we have of Papá. Or, more accurately, the things in the trunk.

Mamá would take things out and read us his letters or show some of his old clothes. She gave each of us one of his flowing white shirts when we were little. We wore them as nightgowns until they no longer covered our knees.

Cheeks wet and foot throbbing, I climb into bed and squeeze my eyes shut, wiping my face and nose as I try to erase the evidence of my tears.

Ignoring the conversation my mother and sister are surely having downstairs, my aching foot reminds me of the summer I turned thirteen, when I wanted to read one of Papá's letters. As I reached into the trunk, a gasp sounded behind me, making me jump.

Mamá stood at the top of the stairs, her fingers twitching at her sides.

She told me not to touch anything. Her voice was low and measured. I can still hear it echo in my mind. I know she was trying to be calm, but she could not hide it from me. I could see it in her eyes: she was angry.

She told me she would get whatever it was that I wanted to see, but I couldn't bring my voice to work through the lump in my throat. I was too embarrassed. So I just shook my head and ran past her.

I was nearly down the stairs when I doubled back. I wanted to apologize, though I wasn't sure what for. I only knew Mamá was upset, and it was my fault.

Three steps from the top, I saw Mamá in the bedroom, on her knees, crying into one of Papá's shirts.

I watched her for only a few moments, but it felt like hours. I was overwhelmed by guilt, knowing I was the one who caused this scene. I wanted to help her—needed to help her—but I didn't know what to do. I felt helpless and useless.

What is a little girl supposed to do when her mamá cries?

I remember my heart racing when she let out a yell and threw one of his shirts across the room. I ran back downstairs as quickly as I could.

I never touched the trunk again.

My cheeks are sticky with drying tears, and I wipe at my face when I hear Inés walking up the stairs. I keep my eyes closed as she comes in, the covers pulled up to my chin.

"I know you are not asleep," she whispers.

"You don't know that," I whisper back.

She laughs and bounces on the bed next to me. She turns on her side to face me, but I open my eyes to stare at the ceiling.

"Are you scared?" I ask her.

She lays there for a long time without answering me. She flips onto her back and huffs out a breath.

"I don't know," she finally says. "I was at first, but I am feeling braver now."

I nod to myself in the dark.

"I think it will be better once I marry Agustin." She breathes the words, and a tremor passes through her.

I don't respond. I do not want her to marry him, but she does. She wants this, and I won't ruin it for her. I just stay quiet.

"I am worried most about Mamá," Inés says.

"Me too."

"But she will be okay, right? I mean, none of the neighbors are going to accuse her. If anything, they will protect her. They need her."

"I hope so," I say.

"Maybe we should go to that weird cliff town," Inés says with a smirk. "What is it called?"

"Castellfollit de la Roca," I reply, rolling my eyes.

All of Banyoles—and probably all of Spain—has heard rumors of the tiny town miles north of us. It is said that there are no soldiers there, that it is a refuge and a sanctuary for witches from all over Spain. The witch town.

Of course, Inés and I have never been far from our hometown, so we have no firsthand knowledge. And most people agree it is only a rumor.

"Right, Castellfollit. We could run off to the witch town—"

"There is no evidence of that," I cut her off.

"—of Castellfollit de la Roca." She pauses. "You never know," my sister says with a shrug that rocks the bed.

"I suppose that's true, but maybe we shouldn't put stock into it."

She makes a face. "You know I was joking. But enough of that," Inés transitions, a smile growing on her face. "What did you think of that new soldier today?"

I open my mouth in shock, only to close it again. I cannot believe that, of all the topics, she wants to discuss the new soldiers.

"We saw a woman arrested for witchcraft today, Inés," I hiss at her, incredulous.

Her eyes close briefly, face turning stony, and she looks at the ceiling.

"I don't want to think about that," she whispers.

I suppose I can understand that.

"Besides," she continues, "you clearly thought something of that soldier, Diego, or you wouldn't have gotten into such a heated discussion with him."

I scoff, sputtering in an attempt to respond, and I realize when my sister starts laughing, she just wanted to get this reaction. I hit her arm as she giggles, and she rolls onto her other side, her back to me.

I don't know what to make of Diego.

The feelings, impressions, and premonitions that I usually sense are noticeably absent when it comes to him. In their place, I only sense a constant vibration.

It makes me anxious.

Dios. Is this what everyone feels like all the time? Not knowing who to trust, not knowing what is going on in someone's head. Maybe my premonitions aren't as inconvenient as I sometimes think.

We do not say anything else. Inés's breathing evens out as she begins to drift off.

"Inés?"

She grumbles.

"Mamá put *tilo* in the tea tonight."

Ines hums in a way that tells me she disagrees. "No, she didn't. She wouldn't do that without asking, you know that. Besides, it is tasteless, Cata. You wouldn't know it even if she did," she mumbles, her face pressed against the pillow.

"I don't need to taste it. I just know it."

5

I wake early the next morning, the sun shining through our tiny east-facing window, right onto my face.

When I try to pull the blanket to cover my eyes, I cannot tug it free of Inés's death grip.

With a sigh of defeat, I lay there for a moment, blinking the sleep from my eyes and squinting in the sun.

I lick my lips, suddenly thirsty. My mouth tastes of bitter oranges, and the flavor brings the previous night rushing back to my memory. My stomach drops, feeling uncannily like the dreams I have where I fall out of the tree behind our house, causing my body to jerk awake.

But I am already awake.

I tell myself it is nothing to worry about. Just because there are rumors of the Inquisition hunting down witches, it doesn't mean that it is true. Or that they will come to our town. Or that they will accuse and arrest us.

There is no reason to twist myself into knots, worrying about something that isn't a current threat.

I indulge in these thoughts a few minutes more before swinging my feet out of the bed. I rifle through the dresser, trying to stay quiet. It is still early.

I find a dark blue blouse and pull out my favorite skirt, the one Inés embroidered for my birthday last year. It took her months to finish, and Mamá helped her hide it from me. It is a veritable work of art and the most beautiful thing I own. Red and pink flowers adorn the bottom of the cream colored skirt. The hem has a subtle red border that looks like swirls. But if you look closer, it says *Gonzalez* over and over, each letter connecting to the next.

Gonzalez is Mamá's name. Soledad Isabel Gonzalez Moreño.

Even though Inés and I both have Papá's family name, Navarro, I think we both consider ourselves more Gonzalez than anything.

Papá isn't here. He has never been here. Mamá is our family.

Once I am dressed, I lace up and tighten the light blue stay over my blouse, and sneak downstairs, careful to skip the second stair from the top so I don't wake Mamá.

But I find her already sitting at the table with a steaming cup in front of her. The short blue curtains of the windows are pulled open, letting bright morning light shine into our house.

A fire burns in the hearth, small but warm. I peer into the pot hanging above the fire before going into the kitchen to retrieve a cup and some herbs.

I see Mamá has lit the fire in the oven as well, and by the temperature, I can tell it has been burning for at least an hour. A ball of dough sits atop of our herb cabinet, waiting for the oven to be hot enough to bake the bread.

Quickly placing leaves into my cup, I pour hot water to steep my *manzanilla* tea. As I move around her, Mamá says nothing. She is deep in concentration, painting one of our *talavera* bowls.

Mamá taught us the art of *talavera* when we were young, and before long, we could make the clay on our own, drying and forming the tiles and dishes. When we had the occasional extra or broken piece, she would let us paint it.

I tried so hard to copy her colorful flowers and smooth lines, the detail she could put into it so effortlessly. But it never quite looked like hers. As we got older, Mamá taught us that if we want our painting to look just like hers, it will never work. We had to find our own style and our own designs. We had to put our heart into them as she did.

By the time we entered our teenage years, Inés and I could paint them on our own and then go to the market to sell.

Mamá doesn't do the *talavera* much anymore. That is our job. These days, Mamá is busy being the best *curandera* in town.

I sit down next to Mamá, but she doesn't look up. She concentrates on the blue flower she is painting on the center of the bowl.

"How did you sleep, *mija*?"

"How did *you* sleep?" I ask. I have an inkling Mamá didn't sleep much.

She glances at me with a crinkle in the corner of her eyes. The hint of a smile. She sighs. "You know too much, Catalina."

I wish I could laugh, but I don't. Instead, I get up and retrieve a few wood-fired, finished tiles from our stack under the stairs, the pottery clinking together.

"I know," I finally respond. "Yet, I want to know more."

Mamá makes a *tsk* sound against her teeth, and I fight a smile.

I sit down and watch her work for a few moments. Her hands move effortlessly as she paints. That is how she does everything. In a graceful, unbroken motion.

I remember watching her mix the *talavera* clay, her gentle fingers steadily kneading the blend of dirt and water. Everything she did was so fluid, it was hard to decide where her hands stopped and where the clay started.

I pick up a brush and start painting next to her.

With a slow, smooth motion, I watch the brush glide across the *talavera* tile, spreading dark blue paint with it.

I do not make the conscious decision, but I find myself striving to recreate the bold blue swirling pattern I sold yesterday.

Though the small and exquisitely detailed patterns are always beautiful, I like these bigger designs. They may appear to be simpler, but they are actually more difficult for me to paint. They require concentration and precision in order to get the perfectly smooth line. Any mistake will be easily noticed, unlike the small designs, where little slips can be covered or hidden.

We sit in comfortable silence, the only sounds coming from our paintbrushes. It has been at least half an hour before Mamá speaks again.

"Do you want to marry, Catalina?"

I pause in my painting. I want to give Mamá a real answer, give her the truth. I answer with a question. "Do I have to?"

Out of the corner of my eye, I can see Mama's smile. "You know my answer to that," she says.

"And I know everyone else's answer, as well," I comment.

"A single woman is a woman who has not conformed," she explains. "To many, that is a threat."

"A single woman has more power," I say.

Mamá hums. "In some ways, perhaps."

"And in other ways?"

"In other ways, single women are punished, targeted, and attacked. It can be dangerous."

I know this is true. But I am also afraid of being trapped in a marriage that becomes a prison.

"So, you do not want to marry," Mamá continues after a few minutes of quiet.

I shake my head.

"Not even for love?" she asks me.

"Did you love Papá?"

Mamá doesn't react for a moment, and I feel silly for asking. I feel silly for assuming my mother and father married for love.

With my words echoing in my head, I frown. I don't like the way I said it. *Did you love Papá?* I know how it sounds—like I criticize those who do not marry for love.

Do I judge others who marry because their parents desire it, or they want it for some other reason besides love? Most marriages happen that way.

"Yes," Mamá finally whispers. "Yes, I did love your father. And he loved me."

The creak of the second stair from the top rings through the house, and Inés appears moments later.

Inés is not marrying for love. I am sure of it.

"*Buenos días*, Mamá," she says, leaning down to give Mamá a kiss on the cheek.

Inés takes a seat next to me.

"Oh, I love that. Let me see, Cata," Inés says. She reaches toward me, palm facing up.

I extend the nearly finished *talavera* tile in her direction, but I stop mid-motion, the back of my neck tingling. I pause, waiting for more. Something prickly licks up my spine.

"Mamá," I say. "Someone is coming." It is not just someone, though. It feels as though something big—something danger-ous— is happening.

Mamá and Inés look at me. My sister seems confused, but Mamá has a serious, searching look on her face.

"There is a knock at the door," I say.

"No, there isn't," Inés says, looking between Mamá and me. Her hand is still stretched toward the *talavera*, but her fingers begin to curl inward.

Mamá doesn't take her eyes off mine.

I listen to the knock echo in my head, but my ears hear nothing.

It is not an ill neighbor. It is someone else, someone I have never met. I do not know how I know. I never know how. I just *know*.

I swallow hard, my fingers drumming on the table with excess energy.

After a moment, Mamá nods and starts toward the door. She swings it open to find a trio of men. The one closest to the door has his hand raised in a fist, as though about to knock.

The three of them appear startled, stepping back.

"Señora Gonzalez?" the soldier at the front asks. He is taller than both Inés and Mamá. His black hair is pulled back into a ponytail, making his features seem sharper. His round eyes are dark green, and they flit around between Mamá, Inés, and me.

"Can we come in? We want to ask you a few questions," the green-eyed soldier says.

Mamá does not move, just stands in the doorway "You can ask me out here."

The two men behind him exchange glances. The one on the left is a soldier as well. His build is shorter, and his chest is nearly twice as wide as mine. He looks like he would need to turn sideways to get in the door.

My eyes almost pass over the man on the right. He is not a soldier. In fact, he is perfectly average. Nothing sets him apart, from body size to facial features.

But I recognize his long, dark coat. I remember it flowing behind him, leaving shadow in his wake.

The witch hunter from yesterday.

His crooked nose is turned down at the end, and he sniffs loudly, his beady eyes shifting from side to side, looking around our home past Mamá.

Taking them in, I have a visceral reaction, my breath becoming shallow. The air around them darkens, just barely. Like they're pulling it into themselves. Perhaps it is a trick of the light.

"We want to talk to your daughters, as well," the witch hunter says. His voice is deep, and every sentence sounds like a command, like he is used to being listened to. But his oily words slide across my skin uncomfortably.

Mamá stands there for a moment before she steps to the side, motioning for the group to come in.

"Thank you, Señora," they repeat quietly, one after another, as they walk into our house. Their heavy boots slap loudly across the floor.

"You may call me Soledad. And these are my daughters, Inés and Catalina."

They bow their heads briefly in acknowledgement.

"What do you want?" I ask brusquely. Inés kicks me under the table, and I grit my teeth.

"Would you like something to drink?" Inés asks, standing up from her chair. "I can make some tea. Please, have a seat."

The two soldiers fidget, shifting from one foot to the other, as though nervous.

"No, no, thank you," the witch hunter says quickly and coolly. A smile spreads on his face, but it does not reach his dark eyes. "Please, do not bother. We won't take much time."

A pregnant pause permeates the house, each of us waiting for another to speak.

Finally, the silence is broken by the green-eyed soldier. "What is it you do, Señora Gonzalez?"

"Soledad," she corrects him. "My daughters and I make *talavera* pottery. We sell it at the *plaza mayor* and in larger cities as well."

The soldier stares at her. She stares back.

He nods to the men behind him, and the wider man moves forward, walking into the kitchen.

"Excuse me," I say, rising from my seat at the table. "Can I help you?"

"What are all these herbs for?" he asks as his giant fingers pick up one of the bundles hanging in front of our window.

"Cooking," Inés says smoothly. "*Romero, albahaca, menta, hinojo*. We like to grow our own."

I snatch the bundle of *romero* from his hands.

"You are unmarried, señora?"

Mamá sighs. "Yes."

"Whose house is this, then?"

I see Mamá's throat working as she swallows. "My husband died before Catalina was born. It was his house."

That is not entirely true. He hardly lived in this house. It was actually Mamá's parents who lived here.

"So, you were married?"

"Yes. He was a soldier, like you."

The soldier narrows his eyes, looking Mamá up and down, before doing the same to my sister and me.

"Your daughters are not married, either," he comments stiffly. "Do they intend to join the church?"

I scoff out a laugh in disbelief. When he turns his gaze to me with a serious expression, my mouth falls open.

Joining the church is not the only option for an unmarried woman. Why is it that the entire world divides us into those two groups, pressuring us to choose between the prison of marriage or the restriction of a convent?

Before I can argue back, Inés jumps in. "I am actually engaged to be married."

My anger rises in my throat. Perhaps Inés is smarter than I am. I cannot control my emotions like she can.

She shakes her head at me, eyes wide.

I bite my tongue so hard I taste blood.

It strikes me how differently Inés approaches this scenario, when it was only yesterday that she was ready to risk everything for a woman we have never met. Where is that fire in her eyes, that desire for justice? Now, she simply keeps her mouth shut, silently pleading for me to do the same.

The witch hunter looks around again while his counterparts move to stand behind him, their hands at their sides. His black eyes stop at the *talavera* tiles on the table. He picks one up.

"Whose work is this?" he asks, inspecting it.

I clear my throat. "Mine."

He glares at me and sets the tile down.

"You do excellent work," he says, looking now at my sister and Mamá. Not me. "I would suggest you stick to it. Especially as an unmarried woman. This business must be profitable for you."

Mamá nods. The tension is thick. No one moves.

Until the green-eyed soldier's face splits into an unsettling grin.

"Thank you for welcoming us into your home, Señora Gonzalez," he says. "It was a pleasure to meet you both, Inés and Catalina."

He doesn't wait for us to respond. The soldiers turn on their heels and walk out.

The witch hunter hesitates for a moment. Without the soldiers blocking my view, I see a worn leather satchel hanging on his shoulder. Barely visible is a small book, its pages and cover yellowed with time and use.

But the corner of the book is enough for me to know. *Malleus Maleficarum*. The Hammer of Witches.

My stomach twists at the thought that a centuries-old bit of Latin could influence this man enough to put my life in danger.

He catches me looking at the book and smiles. A real smile, this time. His teeth are as yellowed as the pages of his book, broken up by the black space between the front two. The cruel curl of his lips makes me shiver.

He finally inclines his head toward my mother before following the other men, leaving our front door open behind him.

Inés rushes to shut the door and collapses against it.

"What was that?" she whispers. "Were they the Inquisition? Looking for witches?"

Mamá stares blankly ahead of her, slowly lowering herself into a chair.

"I don't know," she says quietly.

"That was the man from yesterday." I let out a shaky breath. "He had *Malleus Maleficarum*."

"So, he is a witch hunter, then," Inés says.

Mamá shakes her head. "We cannot know for certain."

"Either way. It's not like they found anything," I say, in an attempt to soothe my nerves.

"Except our herbs," Inés adds.

I roll my eyes. "Everyone has herbs in their kitchen. It is nothing."

Inés lowers her eyelids in a way that looks condescending despite her fear, a face only an older sister could make. "But not everyone is a single *curandera* woman with two single daughters."

We sit in silence for what feels like minutes, but is probably only a few seconds.

"It is good I'm getting married, isn't it?" Inés asks quietly. "It will make us less of a target."

"I do not know, *mija*," Mamá answers. "That does not change the fact that Catalina and I are both unmarried women who have not dedicated our lives to the church. Though having a man in our family may help. But if they find out about my *curandismo*…" She trails off.

Inés doesn't respond. She has a faraway look, and I hope she is reconsidering this marriage.

"No use fretting about it now. We need to move forward and continue our day as usual," Mamá says, clapping her hands together.

She begins to gather a few herbs from our kitchen, preparing for any visitors today.

Then someone knocks at our door for the second time this morning, and Inés jumps.

6

Inés opens the door to reveal our neighbor, Señora Isabela Sosa.

She stands stiffly, still as a statue, her hands clasped in front of her. She takes off the scarf covering her head to reveal dark hair slicked back into a tight bun at the nape of her neck, streaks of gray adorning her temples. Her thin lips are pinched together, adding to the severe look she always wears.

With her home across the way and down the road, Señora Sosa has never been my favorite neighbor. She used to yell at us for singing too loud in the street, and it seems her husband is the only one who can ever calm her. Good for him, I suppose.

"Señora Sosa," Inés says, gesturing for her to come inside. She enters with short, quick steps that are impossibly loud, like her heel is slamming into the ground as she walks. "What can we help you with?"

Mamá comes out of the kitchen, her arms behind her back to tie her apron, and Señora Sosa turns to her.

"My husband is ill," she explains. "Coughing all night. Pale, weak, sweating. He is at home in bed now." She clears her throat and lifts her chin a bit higher. "Can you help him if he is not here?"

She tries to appear cold, unaffected. But I can see her falter. The energy around her ripples with her nervousness, and I see a flicker of disquiet in her deep black eyes.

"We can certainly try," Mamá says with a warm smile, her voice as smooth as her movements. "Have a seat, Isabela. *Chicas,* will you help me?"

I do not know how much help I will be, but I nod anyway.

Inés takes a seat, and I stand at Mamá's shoulder. Inés reaches for Senora Sosa's hand. "May I?"

She hesitates, her eyes shifting between Inés and Mamá. I sense her frustration and confusion that it is my sister who will read her, not my mother. Señora Sosa almost protests, but after a brief pause, she nods once and extends her hand, fingers rigid.

Inés takes it, closing her eyes. Though I don't know exactly what Inés is looking for, I am confident she will know it when she finds it.

"Hmm," Inés hums. She furrows her brow in concentration. "Mamá?" She opens her eyes and turns to our mother, who nods in return.

She takes her turn holding Senora Sosa's hand, which has relaxed only slightly.

It is much more difficult to find out what ails someone when they are not present, but it is possible. Often, we use someone or something to bridge the gap, as Inés and Mamá do now with Señora Sosa. Though sometimes we do not even need a bridge. With enough concentration, you can find what you need. If you know where to look.

"*Hipérico* and *amapola*?" Mamá asks Inés.

She nods in agreement. "An infusion of both."

I nod as well, unsurprised. *Hipérico* is one of the herbs Mamá uses and prescribes most often. She used it with Juanita last night. The leaves and flowers can be used alone or mixed with other plants, and it can be taken orally or applied externally. It has marvelous physical benefits, helping with injury and inflammation. But it also has powerful metaphysical qualities: breaking curses, uncrossing spells, calming anxieties, and soothing the spirit.

"But I think they should both take it," Inés continues, her voice low. Her bright blue eyes snap to Señora Sosa for a split second before looking back at Mamá.

"Why would I need to take it?" Señora Sosa asks. "I am not ill."

Mamá smiles in her direction, but does not answer right away. "Will you girls go into the kitchen to get dried *hipérico* and *amapola* leaves?"

Inés and I leave the women. It is not a big space, but we turn the corner so we are out of sight. We can at least give them the illusion of privacy.

The moment we can no longer be seen, Inés and I press ourselves against the wall next to the herbs, the corner of the wooden cabinet digging into my back. But we do not dare move. Mamá's voice is quiet. We can hardly hear her. Inés and I stand perfectly still, holding our breath to listen.

"...partially energetic. Occasionally, family members can be a part of the problem," Mamá says. "I believe you are both hurting each other."

"That is ridiculous," Señora Sosa hisses. "How could I possibly be hurting my husband?"

Silence. "My mistake, Isabela. I just want to make sure you are both well, alright?"

Señora Sosa mumbles something I can't make out.

Inés shuffles to the side and thrusts a bundle of *amapola* leaves into my hands.

We bring the herbs to Mamá, and she picks the leaves off each bundle, mixing them together in a bowl.

"Make a hot tea with these leaves," she instructs. Señora Sosa stands up and holds out her apron pocket. "Your husband should take it twice before bed tonight and three times tomorrow. After that, both of you should have it every morning until it is gone."

Señora Sosa just grunts in response. Her face is red and angry, but she takes the herbs nevertheless. And I know she will follow the instructions. She may be angry at Mamá, but she isn't willing to risk her husband's health.

She digs her hand into her other pocket and pulls out a few coins. She slams them on the table and spins around to leave.

Mamá follows her to the door, a sweet smile on her face, but Señora Sosa stops on our doorstep and turns around to Inés and me. She looks back at Mamá.

I know it's coming before it happens. Bitterness seeps from Señora Sosa's body, and instead of letting it go, she clings to it. She feeds it.

"These girls should be married by now," she says. "It is unacceptable that they are single at this age. How old are you, Inés?"

It is as though she can hear the echo of the green-eyed soldier's words. *Your daughters are not married, either.*

Before Inés can answer, Mamá speaks firmly. "You have no say in the lives of Inés or Catalina. Nor do I. If, when, and who they marry are up to them."

"If?" Señora Sosa looks appalled. She brings her hand to her chest like someone has shot her with an arrow. "*If?* You aren't encouraging them to end up like you, are you?"

"We could be so lucky," I call out.

Senora Sosa's eyes flash. "A young woman should not be living alone. How do you expect to survive?"

Do they intend to join the church?

"We seem to be doing just fine," Mamá says pleasantly. She steps closer to the sputtering woman. Her voice grows quiet but firm, the pitch dropping in a way that sends chills up my arms. "Remember: you need to take that tea, too."

The corners of Senora Sosa's mouth pull down slightly.

"*Gracias,* Soledad."

We watch her kick up dust as she walks down the road.

"What a witch," Inés says.

"Language, Inés," Mamá admonishes, closing the door on the sight of Señora Sosa getting smaller and smaller.

"She is, though," I say, smiling at Inés.

"Yeah, she is kind of the worst," my sister comments to me.

"I cannot wait for the next time they get sick and show up expecting our help."

"And we will help her," Mamá says.

I gasp, looking at my sister. Inés's shock is painted on her face.

"After what she just said to you?" she asks Mamá.

"Our help is not contingent on how people treat us," Mamá says. "If someone needs help, we help them."

"But, Mamá—"

Mamá cuts us off with a wave of her hand. "What do you think will happen if we start refusing to use our gift to help people?" She looks between us. I just shrug, dreading becoming an unwilling participant in Mamá's lecture. "You know what happens when you curse someone, don't you?"

"You get cursed yourself. By your own hand or the hand of another," Inés says, her tone bored.

"So, I am sure you can figure out what would happen if we started keeping our gifts to ourselves."

Personally, I do not think it would be that bad. But I am not about to say that to Mamá and Inés. And definitely not right now.

So, I just nod.

After a moment, Mamá smiles. "But she is kind of the worst, isn't she?"

Inés looks at me with wide eyes, and my mouth drops open. Mamá keeps the smile in her eyes as we erupt into giggles.

But we are interrupted by yet another knock at the door.

Inés freezes. "She's back?" Her voice is a hushed whisper.

"No, it is not her," I say. I tilt my head, confused. This morning seems especially busy. "Whoever it is, they are here for something else."

Mamá opens the door to a different neighbor. This time, a middle-aged woman I do not recognize.

Her wispy brown hair hangs down around her face as she slouches forward, a shawl covering her shoulders. She must be as tall as Inés, but her posture and slight frame make her seem smaller, more fragile.

"You're scary, Catalina," Inés says quietly, shaking her head in disbelief.

"You are Soledad, yes?" the woman asks. "The *curandera*?"

"Yes, you are in the right place," Mamá says. I can hear her smile. "I am Soledad. Why don't you come inside?"

The woman moves slowly, filling the seat that had been Señora Sosa's just moments ago. But, where Señora Sosa tried to make herself seem bigger than she is, this woman looks like she is shrinking in on herself. She wrings her hands together, her fingers twitchy and shaking.

"What can I do for you?" Mamá's voice is soft and quiet, the way you might speak to a frightened child.

The woman looks around, her gaze darting here and there. When her deep blue eyes meet mine, my stomach turns. Fear-filled nausea nearly overtakes me, but I cannot take my eyes off hers.

My nervousness is different from what I felt with the soldiers or with Señora Sosa. It is not from my mind or my body, nor from this woman's words or the situation I am in. Whatever I am feeling, it is *her* fear.

"I need your help," the woman whispers. "Please. It's my husband."

"Is he ill?" Inés asks.

The woman shakes her head jerkily. Inés wrinkles her forehead as her brows come together, perplexed. But I begin to understand.

It does not happen often. Maybe once or twice each year. Visitors come to our door asking for more than to be healed. They ask for potions or curses—ways to entice lovers or spurn enemies.

And each time, Mamá has to explain that she is a *curandera*, not a *bruja*. Sometimes, they leave embarrassed and dejected. Other times, it is difficult to get rid of them, as they try to persuade Mamá to do some sort of spell.

That is what is happening here, isn't it?

"He..." The woman hesitates. She swallows hard. "He hurts me."

I hear the words after I see her mouth move, as though the sound is delayed. Her voice sounds faraway, but it pierces my heart and unravels our home all the same.

My head spins, my stomach churns, and my knees knock together.

She still has not told us her name.

No one says anything and a sense of dread blankets my being, starting with the realization that Mamá has to turn this woman away. I know she must. But I do not want her to. I do not want this woman to have to go back to the monster she calls husband.

"Inés, Catalina," Mamá says in a clipped voice. "Go."

Inés's head whips in her direction so harshly, I can hear the bones in her neck crack.

"Mamá—" That is all I can get out.

"I will not tell you again. Go. Now." Mamá's voice is hard, unyielding. I don't think anyone could argue with her if they tried.

The chair scrapes against the floor as Inés rises from her seat.

Walking past the woman at our table, I follow Inés out the door in silence. Almost in a daze.

We turn down the street, but we have nowhere to go. It isn't until we have walked an entire block that Inés breaks the silence.

"Mamá is going to do something to help that woman," my sister says. It is not quite a question, but she also doesn't sound completely confident.

I nod solemnly.

"How, though?" Inés asks. I don't know if she is talking to me or to herself.

I respond anyway, "How would you do it?"

She doesn't answer right away, and I know she is thinking about it. Making a plan or a potion. Just like I have been.

"How would *you* do it?" Inés turns the question on me as we make our way toward the *plaza mayor*, our bodies working on habit.

I don't answer.

And we walk in tense silence.

7

The question haunts me for days. *How would you do it?*

When we got home, the woman was gone, and Mamá made it clear she wouldn't say anything about it. But that has not stopped me from thinking about it every day since.

How *would* I do it?

I would make some sort of herbal mixture to slip into his drink, but it would take more than that. A blessing. Or a curse. Some sort of energetic intention.

I am certain Mamá did something akin to it.

And as I ponder the question, I cannot help but wonder if I could do the same thing to another. Not a potion to stop him from violence, of course, but perhaps a spell of protection.

Whatever it is, I know I must do something about Agustin. My unease grows more with each passing day my sister spends with him.

After arguing with Inés for so long over the subject, I know she will not give up, and I refuse to do anything to harm their engagement, regardless of how much I want to.

Instead, I will ensure Agustin trusts Inés. He will protect her, maybe even truly love her. And I can make sure she is protected from him, that he will be no harm to her.

Fortunately, I know my mother's herbs inside and out, whether or not I have the same gift she does. I come to the conclusion that the mixture should be simple: *manzanilla* and *serbal*.

The *manzanilla* will act as a relaxant to ease Agustin's spirit. It is one of the more common teas, and his body will surely be familiar with it.

The *serbal* will be the main power source. Beyond its physical benefits, the tree is an impressive plant for energetic protection, and it can also promote honesty and truth. However, I have difficulty deciding whether to use the bark, the leaves, or the berries of the tree.

Over the days I spend planning my potion, my nerves are restless, and I feel ready to startle at any moment. Mamá even comments on my jumpiness and distracted energy. But I simply tell her I'm excited for the upcoming festival.

The festival. San Juan Eguna.

That is where I will slip the mixture into Agustin's wine.

Each day, I take leaves of *manzanilla* from the table or a hanging bundle. We always have an excess of it lying around. It is the *serbal* berries that I must slowly pilfer. I think berries will be less noticeable in the flavor of wine, so I open the third drawer in the cabinet closest to the door, sneak them into my apron, and let them dry out.

It would be so much easier if I did not have to hide it all from my family. And for a moment, I debated simply telling them that I was experimenting. But I cannot. It is better that Mamá and Inés have no suspicions or questions.

The evening of the festival arrives and Mamá comes home after her mysterious errand with a basket of fresh flowers.

"I thought we could put them in our hair for tonight," she says with a grin.

Inés claps her hands in delight. "They are beautiful. Should we make crowns or weave them into braids?"

"A braid," I say, wanting my hair out of my face for this evening. I am already sweating, knowing what is coming and what I plan to do.

"Go get the hairbrush," Inés tells me.

I run upstairs, my heart pounding. When I step into the bedroom, I glance over my shoulder, making sure my sister hasn't followed me.

I reach under the mattress on my side of the bed, where a dark blue handkerchief holds the dried ingredients. They are crushed, but I know they need to be powdered. As fine a powder as possible.

Without the mortar and pestle we normally use, I retrieve a hairbrush and use the flat wooden back to grind the herbs on top of the dresser. It takes much longer than I thought. And the powder isn't nearly as fine as I would like.

I keep at it for a bit longer, my senses heightened as I listen for that creaky step on the staircase.

"Cata, what is taking you so long?" Inés calls to me.

"Un momento más!" My heart drums in my throat.

This will have to do.

I brush the powdered herbs from the dresser into the handkerchief. I carefully wrap it up and stuff it into my stay, between my breasts.

Snatching the hairbrush, I hurry downstairs.

"What were you doing up there?" my sister asks with an impatient sigh.

"I wasn't sure if this is what I wanted to wear," I lie through my teeth.

"Oh, *mija,* you look beautiful," Mamá says. "You both do."

Inés ushers me into a seat at the table and takes the brush from me, slowly running it through my tangled hair.

I look down and smooth my skirt. I never once questioned my outfit choice today. I am wearing my favorite skirt again, with a white blouse to match, covered in my light blue stay.

"Ouch, Inés!" I wince as she rips through a knot in my hair.

"Your hair is so much harder to brush than mine."

"That doesn't mean you can't be gentle," I mutter.

Inés has smooth, shiny hair that lies flat. I have always envied it. She takes my frizzy hair in her hands and slowly creates a thick braid down my back. She ties it with a ribbon before sticking little red flowers into the plait.

"How does it look?" I ask, my fingers smoothing over the back of my head.

"It is perfect," she says. She pats me on the shoulder and motions with her hand. I stand, and we switch places. "Will you do just a little braided crown? But keep the rest of my hair down?"

I begin working her soft locks into a halo, tucking the end into the beginning.

Mamá hands me a hair pin and spreads out the flowers on the table. I pick out the pink blossoms, wiggling them into the braid.

"Mamá?" Inés stands when I finish her hair.

Mamá sits in her place, and my sister braids the sides of her hair, wrapping it into Mamá's signature bun. I stick red, pink, and white flowers into the bun, leaving enough of the stem that they will stay all night.

Inés brushes the rest of the flowers back into the basket and places it on top of the chest of drawers in our kitchen.

With that, we shut the front door behind us, and the evening begins. San Juan Eguna.

As we approach the plaza, I hear the droning buzz of the San Juan bonfire excitement, conversations accented by loud laughter and the occasional joyful squeal. Music is barely discernible, and I don't know from where it is emanating, but it tickles my mind as it becomes the backdrop for the scene before us. Lamps line the walls and arches surrounding the square, flickering as they are lit for the low light of the evening.

I follow Mamá and Inés to the right, sticking to the edges of the plaza while we search for familiar faces in the sea of people. The square is positively humming, even busier than market days.

At the center of the square, an enormous fire rages, the flames flickering and dancing as sparks fly up into the night air. On the other side of the courtyard, a few men throw in more logs and a long wooden board. The smoke distorts my view of them, and their silhouettes ripple like a mirage.

Around the fire, I catch glimpses of dancing, with twirling skirts and clapping hands. In the east corner, a group of men and women pour wine for one another, the group quickly evolving and re-forming as wine cups change hands and cheeks redden contentedly.

It doesn't take long for Agustin to approach us.

"Inés," he greets my sister with a smile, kissing her hand. He bows his head in our direction. "Soledad, Catalina."

"*Buenas noches*, Agustin," Mamá says pleasantly, her lips curving up in a kind smile.

"Let's dance," Inés says. She grabs Agustin's hand and the two disappear before he even has the chance to reply.

The sun sets quickly, and Mamá tightens the shawl around her shoulders. My skin feels warm despite the cool breeze. The crowd heats the space, and their frenzied energy only raises the temperature.

"Soledad!"

The woman appears out of nowhere, and Mamá jumps with a laugh.

Mamá has always been close with Josefina Valverde. She was one of Mamá's first patients and one of the first to discover her talent. She helped Mamá not to be afraid of sharing her gift to heal people. Truthfully, she is the one who got the entire neighborhood on board.

Mamá embraces the woman, kissing her cheek as she greets her. "Josefina, *comó estás?*"

"*Hola, mi amor,*" Señora Valverde replies. Her eyes light up when they reach me, and she brushes past my mother to take me in a tight hug. "Catalina, *mija,* you look beautiful! Let's go get us some wine."

"Actually, Mamá, I think I will keep looking around."

I want to keep an eye on Inés and Agustin. I need to know the perfect time for my plan. I cannot lose them.

Meandering over to a small patch of flowers, I sit down on the short stone wall around them. I take a deep breath and enjoy the mild breeze here, away from the crowd and fire. It is the perfect temperature. Not cool, but not hot, hardly even warm. The air simply melts into the people and music and food, blurring the edges until it is one mass of vibration.

Mamá talks with Señora Valverde and her teenage daughter. I watch them laugh at something Mamá says, their drinks spilling as they shake.

I smile. It is nice to see Mamá look so unburdened and free-spirited. Especially after the past few days. And I am glad she is talking to women who will never question her decisions or judgment.

I move my focus to watch the group dancing in the square, twirling and laughing.

It is not hard for me to find Inés. She dances with Agustin, but she looks subdued, not laughing so readily as I know she can. She smiles at him, and he returns the look before spinning her under his arm.

I should not be worrying about how she is not laughing. That does not mean anything, does it? People aren't supposed to be laughing all the time.

But, the more I stare at them, the more agitated I get. The way I always feel when I look at Agustin.

They slow down enough for me to really see his face. His smile looks like a grimace to me. Just for a moment. But I blink, and it's gone.

I shake my head. If Inés is going to marry this man, I have to be okay with it. I need to be supportive.

And this powdered mixture will help me do that.

I'm lost in thought, about to retrieve the handkerchief from my dress, when I sense someone near.

I glance up to see the soldier from the market. Diego.

He watches me and walks in my direction, his face unreadable. His hair is mussed, messier than it was that day. And, like most of the soldiers here this evening, he has taken off his awkward vest-coat to let the white shirt flow in the breeze.

I stare as he approaches, taking the opportunity to catalog his features.

His long lashes make his brown eyes look darker as he lowers them, framed by thick eyebrows. Diego has a prominent chin and a strong jaw, and when he tips his face down, his hair falls into his eyes. But instead of brushing it out of his face, he keeps his gaze on me.

My skin tingles, my body rushing with adrenaline as my feet fidget. My fingers twitch with the thrill.

Diego stops in front of me, clearing his throat and pushing his hair back.

"We met at the market," he says. His thick eyebrows come together as though in concentration. "It is Catalina, isn't it?"

I nod. "Diego."

He sits next to me, and I try not to flinch.

"I am glad you remember," he says. "I would have thought you burned the name of a soldier from your mind as quickly as possible."

I frown. No sign of apology nor civility, just another dig.

"Why are you here?" I ask.

"In Banyoles? They wanted to bring in more soldiers, and I didn't want to stay in Navarre."

"No," I force out. "Why are you sitting here, talking to me?"

His dark laugh is barely audible.

"I wanted to get to know you," Diego says.

My stomach churns. I do not want him to know me. I am not naive enough to think that a man wants to learn about me without wanting something in return.

I have made that mistake before, and the only reason I didn't end up in a marriage is because Mamá stood by me.

It was last year. I thought Mateo and I were friends. I liked spending time with him, and when we talked, I felt like we had a real conversation, like he valued what I was saying. But I only wanted friendship, nothing more.

Apparently, that isn't what he wanted. I refuse to allow myself to fall into that trap again.

"Catalina?"

Diego brings me back to the present moment.

I look over at him, trying to force either the dislike I have for Agustin or the ease I feel around Andres Carlos. Anything.

But I do not get either feeling.

I feel something else. Something I cannot identify. And that won't help me now.

"My apologies. What did you say?" I ask, clearing my throat.

He stares at me, probably gauging whether or not I am actually listening.

"Your family makes *talavera*, right?"

"Yes, we make *talavera*." I may as well tell him. I try to keep my face pleasant and placid, my voice light. This conversation doesn't need to be painful.

"I saw your work," he says softly. "It was beautiful."

"Thank you. That one you picked up was Mamá's."

"And what about your sister? Inés," he says. "Do all of you paint?"

"It is mostly my sister and me now," I say with a shrug. "Mamá is a *curandera,* so she is normally too busy."

The words slip out of my mouth, but the moment I say them, I know it was a mistake.

Diego's face shutters closed, his eyebrows lowering, and his jaw going stiff.

"*Curandera*?" he repeats.

It is not unusual or abnormal. *Curandismo* is everywhere. But some people like it more than others.

My face flushes. I panic. What do I say?

"*Sí,* she just gives people herbs. That is all, really." My words rush out, and my tongue trips over itself.

"Gives people herbs?"

"When they are sick, you know," I say.

"If they are sick, they should go to a real doctor," Diego comments. "Or see a priest."

My skin itches as a wave of irritation brushes up my spine. "A real doctor?"

"I just mean that a *curandera* is not going to help a serious illness."

"How would you know? Are you a real doctor? A soldier, a man of violence, ready to whip his sword out at the smallest sign of trouble. Is that how you help a serious illness?" My voice rises, but I am shocked at the way my words escalated so quickly. I squeeze my nails into the meat of my palm in an attempt to calm down.

Diego turns his body to face me, his mouth open and his eyebrows drawn together.

"What is your problem with soldiers?"

"What is your problem with healers?"

"At least I have a real profession," he huffs.

I hear a sound that is a cross between a scoff and a laugh, before realizing it came from my throat.

"A real profession is something that enriches the world around you—something that helps people," I say. "What you do is the opposite of a real profession."

"You speak of enriching the world, yet here you sit, looking down on me and acting as though you know better."

I want to hit him, but I manage to limit myself to a frustrated groan.

"I refuse to have this discussion with you again," I say. "I told you at the market, I do not believe in violence." My words do not have as much bite as I hoped.

"Don't you?"

My stomach drops, but I hide my alarm and roll my eyes at him.

"Violence is necessary for protection. You will learn that for yourself sooner or later, Catalina." Diego's low voice makes the hair on the back of my neck tingle. It feels dangerous. Like a threat.

That is when I realize I have taken my eyes off Inés and Agustin. One glance toward the dancers in the middle of the square, and I know they have gone.

I have to get out of here.

"You know what, Diego?" I ask, standing and brushing my skirt off. "You win. You are right, I am wrong."

"What happened to not letting people walk all over you, Catalina?"

I swallow the scream threatening to rip from my throat.

"Thank you for the enlightening conversation," I say. "Regrettably, I don't see my sister in the crowd, so I must find her."

Diego grins, raising his eyebrows. "The pleasure was mine, Catalina. I look forward to getting to know you better."

Yeah, right. Keep dreaming, *chaval*.

I waste no more words on the dark-haired soldier and turn on my heel to rush off toward the bonfire and into the crowd.

After asking around, I determine Inés and Agustin have ventured out of the main square and into the darker, quieter streets. Where people become more spread out and the crowd dwindles as the loud celebration becomes muffled with distance.

Weaving through the courtyard, I walk with determination to the corner I know holds the wine. I grip the sides of my skirt and try to wipe the sweat from my palms. But the moment I do, sweat covers my skin again, smelling of smoke and anticipation.

I spot Josefina, but I do not see Mamá with her. She's talking to the mother of Maria Luisa, the girl we saw at the market.

"Catalina," Josefina greets me with a wide smile. "Oh, Rosa, tell Catalina the good news."

Rosa claps her hands together, beaming at me. "Maria Luisa is pregnant!"

My lack of surprise makes it difficult to react properly, but I swallow my anxiety and offer the two women my most charming grin and a giddy laugh.

"That is such wonderful news! Maria Luisa has always looked forward to being a mother," I say. "She must be so happy."

Rosa nods, getting a little misty-eyed, even as her smile grows.

"You looking for wine, Catalina?" Josefina asks me. "Your mamá said only one glass."

"But you won't tell her if I take two, will you?" I look at her with a wink. She frowns at me, and I chuckle. "I am actually getting a cup for Inés. It's not for me." I hold my hands up in surrender.

She eyes me, feigning suspicion. It doesn't last long.

Josefina sets a gentle hand on my elbow and pulls me closer. "If you wait a little, Melchor is going to bring out his good wine," she whispers, winking at me conspiratorially.

With a laugh, I shake my head. "I don't care for the good wine. I just told Inés I would grab her a cup, so I should hurry back."

Josefina nods before pouring. "Don't you dare tell your mother I gave you more than one cup," she says as she hands them to me.

I grip the wine so tight my fingers ache. But I am scared Josefina and Rosa will see me shaking if I let up.

"*Te prometo.*" I give her a kiss on the cheek. "Thank you, Josefina."

Slipping away quickly with wine in hand, I wander into the streets, following after my sister and carefully carrying the two cups.

I pause when I find myself alone in the alley. It isn't too dark, lit by lanterns with a soft glow. It is enough to see. But I am *alone*.

Heart racing, I place one cup into the crook of my arm and reach into my bodice with the other hand. My fingers brush against the dark blue handkerchief. Energy dances across my skin in time with the exaggerated shadows writhing on the walls. Everything feels heightened.

I try to convince myself it is nothing more than nervousness left over from being so close to Diego.

But as I remove the package of powder, blood pounds in my ears. I can hear my heartbeat—a drum, beating loud enough that I fear I will be discovered in this dark alley.

My trembling hand hurriedly removes the handkerchief, and I sprinkle most of the powder into one cup. I swish the wine. I know the mixture won't completely dissolve, but I can only hope it will go unnoticed. Perhaps it will settle at the bottom of the dark cup.

I close my eyes and repeat the same ritual I have done with the herbs every day this week. I do not think it is a spell or a hex, or whatever it is the Inquisition thinks *brujas* do. This "ritual" is the only thing I know to do: imbue the herbs with my pure intention, commanding them to live up to their power and carry out my desires.

May these herbs and berries bring honesty, truth, and love to Agustin. May they build trust for their marriage. May they offer protection for my sister.

I hope it is enough.

I stuff the empty handkerchief back into my dress. Admittedly, I still don't quite know how I will get Agustin to drink the wine. I just know I have to do it.

Turning the corner, I remember the small square on the next street over and make my way along the buildings, walking quickly and quietly as I search for the couple.

Soon enough, I can make out the silhouettes of Inés and Agustin, barely outlined by the low light of the lanterns. Even so, I know it is my sister.

They are close, their heads together. They don't see me.

Dios, I hope they are not kissing. I consider stamping my feet in warning, but I then hear Inés's hushed and hurried voice.

"...terrifying. I have been so on edge all week," she says. I strain to listen. "They just came in, asking questions and insulting Mamá."

"I am sure it was nothing," Agustin says, but there is an undercurrent in his voice. Something nervous and stiff. "You don't have anything to hide."

"No, we don't, but I am worried other people won't see it that way," Inés whispers. "Mamá is *la curandera*. She heals people."

"I know that."

Inés takes a deep breath, and my heart stops. "But it is more than that. She knows *how* to heal people."

Agustin shakes his head. "I don't understand."

"Mamá, she can see what is wrong with people. And then she sees exactly what they need in order to fix their situation."

With every syllable from Inés's mouth, my stomach twists tighter and tighter. After my encounter with Diego, I know this is not a good idea.

"It is hard to explain, but," Inés pauses, and I can see her wring her hands from here, "I can do it, too."

Mierda, mierda, mierda.

I hasten forward, coming out of the shadows toward them, but Inés keeps going.

"And a few days ago, a woman came to see Mamá. Not about a healing. She—"

"Inés!" I call out to her as I finally step into the light near them. Agustin jumps so high I would laugh if I weren't worried about what my sister just said.

"Goodness, Catalina," Inés exclaims, pressing her hand to her chest. "What are you doing, sneaking up on people like that?"

I hold up the cups. "Melchor finally brought out some of his good wine. I wanted to make sure you guys had a chance to taste it." I force the lie out of my mouth with a smile.

"Oh, thank you, Catalina," Agustin says. He seems hesitant, although to be fair, he has never liked me.

Hell, he *should* be nervous.

I take care to hand him the cup with the herbs, giving my sister the other cup.

"No wonder Melchor hoards it," Inés exclaims, moaning as she takes a taste.

But Agustin doesn't drink his. He just watches her.

Drink it, you bastard.

I clear my throat. "What were you guys talking about?"

Standing above him, I look down on his dark blond head. His hair is cut short, the ends barely touching his ears, and it is nearly the same color as his tanned skin. It looks unnatural. I hate it.

Agustin glances at me with his soft hazel eyes, then looks back at Inés. His eye color, too, matches his hair.

It strikes me how different he looks next to my sister. She is a natural beauty, with dark eyebrows that emphasize her clear blue eyes, and long brown hair that frames her delicate features. Though she is self-conscious about the size of her nose, it is perfectly sloped, coming into a point that adds to her striking features, like her smooth lips with their distinct cupid's bow. And, as if that wasn't enough, her tall body always seems so graceful and feminine to me. I can only hope to be as beautiful as her.

All the while, here sits Agustin, looking like the ghost of a man, his dull, monochromatic appearance fading more and more with every blink.

"I was telling Agustin about those soldiers that came to the house," my sister says.

He shifts on the bench. He stares down at his cup and brings it to his soft, hooked nose. My stomach drops as he sniffs it.

"Yes, that was strange. What do you make of it, Agustin?" I ask.

He takes that moment to take a big drink of wine, trying to avoid my question.

Perfecto.

"Agustin, would you mind if I spoke to my sister?" Inés asks him, laying a hand on his arm. I feel her eyeing me.

Agustin nods quickly. "Of course. I will find Marcos and Pedro. Get some food." Agustin doesn't look me in the eye, shuffling past me.

As soon as he is out of earshot, I whirl around. "What the hell are you doing?"

"What are you talking about?" she asks, leaning back defensively.

"Telling Agustin about Mamá, about you, about what you can do. The Inquisition is already asking questions, and you are telling a soldier that you can heal people."

Inés narrows her eyes at me. I narrow mine right back, mimicking her expression.

"He is not just some soldier," she argues. "He's Agustin. He is my fiancé."

"You need to be careful."

Inés shakes her head, her mouth open in disbelief. "Really, Catalina? Will you stop at nothing to ruin things with Agustin?" She tries to move past me.

I grab her elbow to stop her. "This time, it isn't about Agustin."

"Like hell it isn't!" She wrenches her arm from my grasp. "I thought you had finally accepted it."

"I have. I promise! Inés, you can marry Agustin a hundred times for all I care. But you are putting all of us in danger."

"You don't understand, Catalina! I am not doing this for me," she yells, her voice breaking. "I am doing this for all of us. I am doing this to save us—to protect us."

I feel as though she has slapped me across the face. *For us?*

Why would she do that? Why would she sacrifice herself, marrying such a fool? He will do nothing to protect us. Whatever she may think, Agustin is not the way. He is not our savior. I can only hope he will be loyal to Inés after drinking this wine.

"You really think Agustin can save us?" I ask. "You think he even cares?"

"He cares about *me,* Cata. That will have to be enough."

"Does he love you? Do you love him?"

Her face twitches when she clenches her jaw. "I am doing the best I can, Catalina."

I stay silent, shocked by her confession.

Inés turns from me and follows the path Agustin had cut back to the center of the square.

I don't stop her.

With a heavy sigh, I sit on the hard stone bench the couple occupied previously. I drop my head in my hands.

I shouldn't have said anything about Agustin.

Inés and I used to be so close. We used to tell each other everything. Agustin ruined that.

Or, perhaps, I did.

Every time I bring him up, I am only putting a wedge between us. I cannot imagine what she would say if she knew what I have done.

And to think, she's doing all of it for us.

Being married will certainly offer some protection for her, and at least one of us would be married. We might even move in together. That would take the heat off of us a little, being under the same roof as a man. Having someone to watch our every move.

I groan, shaking my head.

That might have worked in the past, but this? This witch business? This is different. My family is truly in danger.

That is why I had to do it.

I am acting out of fear, I know that. But I am afraid.

I am afraid of everything and everyone. My body winds up tighter and tighter everyday, waiting for the moment my world unravels.

Maybe Inés has the right idea. Maybe she will be safe. Maybe I should follow her lead. Maybe I was right in slipping something to Agustin.

But no matter what I tell myself, I cannot get rid of the heaviness sitting deep in my stomach.

The rising sun is bright as I squint my eyes, but the air isn't too hot. Not yet.

My thick hair forms a single loose braid that falls down my back. It swishes as I walk, brushing between my shoulders along the fabric of my white dress.

I smell it before I see it. Banyoles Lake.

With a smile, I cross the uneven dirt path—the one used by wagons and horses—and get closer to the lake, eager to feel the water on my skin.

Green trees, bushes, and all kinds of plants line the shore. I run my hands along the top of the tall grass, the blades tickling my palms in the most delicious way.

After last night, I need a moment to ground myself, to calm down, to be alone. Although, in all honesty, I did try to convince Inés to come with me.

The lake used to be our sanctuary. It is still mine.

Filled with beautiful blue water, the lake of Banyoles is bright turquoise when the sun shines, and though I've never been any-where else, I know there is something special about this place. I know it looks like a paradise. As I gaze out on the lake, I notice parts shaded by trees where the water looks darker, grayer, and greener all at once.

When we were younger, Mamá would take us to the fields on the outskirts of town to collect any wild herbs and flowers we could find that might be useful in *curandismo*. She taught us what each plant looked like and their benefits, both physical and mystical. It wasn't long before Inés and I knew enough that we could gather medicinal herbs without her explicit instructions.

On the way home, we would stop at the lake, and Mamá let us play in the water. None of us knew how to swim, so we only waded out amongst the water grasses, skimming our fingertips across the water's surface and watching it ripple around us.

I do the same now, bending down to unlace my boots and pull up my skirt to step into the cool, blue water. It is colder than I expected, and the temperature sends a chill up my spine. The wind passes through the tree branches above me, and I shiver again.

I glance around. I can see no one but the fishermen out on the lake. I hike up my skirt higher and go deeper, farther away from shore. Soft mud squishes around my toes as I walk carefully, probing for stones and sticks with every step.

Breaking away from the shade, I step into the sun and have to squint again, the light reflecting off the water and shining in my eyes like a mirror.

The breeze smells like lake—fresh and filthy at the same time. The scent of decay mixes with the smell of dirt and fish. But the smell of the water and wet plants makes me feel clean and new, despite the muck of grime and death.

With a sigh, I deliberately make my way back to shore, shaking off the water from my legs. I sit on the grassy land and notice a length of the hem at the back of my dress dipped into the water. I ignore it, and I begin picking the small flowers next to me.

Years ago, Mamá would pick wildflowers along the edges of the lake and build a little pile that we sat around. She taught us to make flower crowns, just like her mother taught her. We never came out here without leaving with a flower crown on each of our heads, laughing and dancing like we were *hadas* in the forest.

They are some of my favorite memories of Mamá and Inés.

As we began growing our own herbs at home, we no longer had the need to go out to the fields and the lake to gather plants in the sun. But Inés and I still found refuge here after the work and chores were done. Sometimes even before then. We liked to quiz and test each other on the properties of certain plants, reminiscing on the times Mamá worried that one of us might confuse a useful plant with a poisonous one.

Even years later, we made flower crowns every time. And we always brought one home for Mamá.

After Inés's twentieth birthday, she began rejecting my offers to go to the lake. Instead, she spent her free time with Agustin.

I could see the change in Inés a year ago, as her birthday approached. She was on edge, irritated, and always felt like she was in a rush. She began talking about how old she was, how she couldn't be single forever, and how difficult it would be to find a husband.

It confused me, seeing this new version of her. We had never felt the need to find a husband before.

Now, I know a lot of that stress came from her feeling a need to protect us, and she thought this was the best way she could do that.

Instead, I dosed her fiancé in order to protect her.

Did I do the right thing? I know not to give anyone anything without their consent—Mamá always emphasized that. But I did it anyway.

I take a deep breath and close my eyes, my eyelids turning fiery against the rays of sunlight coming through the leaves. I press my hands into the ground, feeling the solidity of the earth beneath me. The stability.

Just as Mamá taught us, I ground my energy and allow nature's life and power to flow into me.

With my eyes closed, I focus on seeing with my soul. I sense the flowers several feet to my right. I sense the trees beyond them and the lake in front of me. I even sense the deadened grass far behind me, the place where carts and horses trample out of town.

I reach out farther, looking into the town, trying to sense human life.

Diego.

My eyes snap open. Where did that come from?

No, thank you.

Bringing my attention back to my body, I lay down. My head swims with the vibrant energy of the living things around me.

I need a distraction.

I sit up and begin picking flowers out of my pile, focusing on getting the longest stems to make it easy to braid, white wildflowers flashing in the sun.

I braid the three flowers about an inch before adding another flower into the braid. I do it over and over, the movements familiar to my hands. It soothes me, and I hardly realize I have gone through all my flowers until my hand feels around on my lap and comes up empty.

I shorten the leftover stems, cutting through them with my thumbnail, and then tuck them into the beginning of the braid, creating the perfect floral halo.

Once I have secured the glowing flowers on my head, I carefully look through the field, collecting shades of white and yellow to create crowns for Inés and Mamá.

I am nearly finished with the last crown when a tremor runs through my hands and nervous energy settles in my stomach.

I groan with frustration. I came out here to forget the Inquisition, to forget Agustin. But, even with the comforting crowns, it seems I cannot escape it. My fear has followed me, and I cannot outrun my sense of dread.

Is this what I will feel for the rest of my life? The constant need to look over my shoulder, to never trust anyone, to live with the anxiety of being accused of witchcraft?

There must be more to life.

I will make sure there is more to life. I won't let this fear consume me.

Gathering the crowns in my hands, I make my way back into town. I step around short green bushes that stick out of the ground like tufts of hair, and weave through crooked, knotted trees.

It isn't long before my feet transition from the soft dirt to the unyielding stone. Short homes grow into taller buildings, the walls covered in yellowed plaster chipping away to reveal the rock beneath.

High in the sky now, the sun bakes down on the town, and its heat warms the road under me. I brush my hand along the wall next to me, and as I turn the corner, I feel the warm stone turn cold in the shade.

I try to enjoy my walk, but my anxiety swells as my feet slap against the ground, the sound irritating me. Every one of my steps that reaches my ears gets louder and louder, sounding like a drum leading me to my execution.

What is wrong with me?

I quicken my pace. Inés will distract me when I get home. And I can ask Mamá to give me *toronjil,* or perhaps *rosa silvestre.* I just need to leave this fear behind me.

With all my haste, I run right into Andrés Carlos. As my body slams into his, I hear the tinkling shatter of *talavera* pottery.

"*Caracoles,*" Andrés mutters. His eyes widen as he looks down at the broken clay, but when he glances at me, it is as if he doesn't recognize me. He takes a step back, though his jittery movement looks more like a jump. "Catalina!"

"Andrés, I'm so sorry," I apologize, reaching out to him. I see the basket he carries. "Were those some of ours?"

He stares at me with his mouth hanging open.

"Andrés?"

"*Sí,*" he says, shaking his head. "*Sí,* these are yours. I sold most in Girona, but I brought back the remaining pieces."

I sigh in relief and offer him a smile. "Well, if I was going to break something, I am glad it was mine to begin with." I hold my arms out, my fingers spread wide, ready to carry the pottery. "I can take them from you."

Andrés shakes his head again. "Catalina, I was taking them to your house, but..." His voice trails off, and he swallows hard. "I didn't make it. There is something wrong. Soldiers in front of your house."

He is still talking, but I am already running past him, leaping over the broken pottery fragments.

It isn't far, yet it feels like miles. I cannot run fast enough. My hands curl into fists, and I know I am crushing the crowns for Mamá and Inés.

But as I turn the corner onto our street, my fingers release the flowers, and they drop as fast as my heart.

10

S oldiers stand in front of our house, just as Carlitos said.

I stop short, my fearful feet refusing to take me any farther. My upper body sways forward as though anticipating the remaining distance.

Just down the street, I am close enough that I can recognize a few of them.

The green-eyed soldier that came to our house last week is talking to Marcos and another man. Next to them, I see Diego standing incredibly still amid the blur of action. And behind him, Agustin, shifting from one foot to the other on the gray stone street.

I am far enough away that they haven't seen me, but I cannot manage to make myself move forward or take a step back. I cannot even press myself against the walls on the side of the street. I can only watch the scene in front of me unfold, my muscles stiff.

Our neighbors appear in their doorways, drawn outside by the commotion. A wave of mutters and gasps emanates from their lips, sounds of shock at something I cannot yet see.

Then, there they are.

I watch as my mamá and my sister are pulled from our home, two soldiers on either side of each.

My blood runs cold.

Inés is red in the face, her twisting expression somewhere between tears and fury. Mamá whips her head from side to side, but her braided bun holds tight, even as she yells at the soldiers holding onto her.

"She has nothing to do with it! She doesn't know anything about the *curandismo*. It's just me," Mamá says. "Let her be."

One of the soldiers smacks her across the face.

A sob catches in my throat.

"Enough," Marcos says calmly. "There is no need for that, Juan."

The soldier from last week steps forward. "We have testimony that you and your daughters perform *brujería*."

The group of uniformed men turns toward Agustin, and when my sister's gaze lands on her traitorous fiancé, tears spill onto her cheeks. Though now, I see the fire in her eyes, and I know: these are tears of anger not sadness.

"What we do is not witchcraft," Inés says in a low voice. I can barely hear her, but her words echo down the street.

Agustin lifts his head and clears his throat twice.

"This woman and her daughters work in witchcraft. They work with the devil. They perform rituals and claim to heal people with supernatural power. They make love potions and poisons to give people without their knowledge."

Inés barks out a laugh.

Agustin won't look at her, but he continues, his voice weak and shaky. "This girl gave me a potion in the form of my wine to make me marry her. Just as we have heard happening in other regions."

His wine.

A chill washes over my skin. My head spins, and my lungs squeeze tight. I can't breathe.

"I did nothing to any drink you have ever consumed," my sister bites back.

It is true. She didn't. But I did.

"I was sick last night because of it, but I suspect... I suspect she has been cursing me for weeks," he stutters. "They are *curanderas,* after all."

He was sick last night. He shouldn't have been sick.

What have I done?

Agustin will not look at her. He shuffles to the side, half hiding behind Diego again.

Inés screams at him. A scratchy, angry scream that claws up her throat and scrapes in my ears. "Look at me! Look at me, you coward!" She struggles against the soldiers at her sides, but they hold her tight.

Marcos walks forward, standing in front of Mamá. She looks so small as she raises her head to face him.

"Where is the other one? Catalina?" Marcos asks.

Mamá lifts her chin an inch higher, pressing her lips together. They stare at each other for a second longer, and when Marcos realizes she will say nothing, he turns away.

"We will find her," the leader says. He looks at the soldiers on either side of Mamá and Inés, then jerks his head to the side in instruction.

They start dragging my mother and sister away from me.

And it is my fault.

My vision blurs. As the ground tilts beneath me, I run toward them without a thought.

My movement draws attention. Mamá catches sight of me, and I watch her eyes grow wide with panic.

"Catalina, no!"

Following her gaze, Inés lets out a strangled sound. We lock eyes for just a moment before she is pulled away behind the group of soldiers.

"Run, Cata, run!" Inés screams at me. She tries to twist back around to face me.

"Diego," Marcos says his name in a command.

That is all it takes.

I watch as the man I argued with last night sets his sights on me. His eyes darken, and his eyebrows lower into a scowl.

He moves quickly, but not quickly enough to close the distance between us.

I spin on my heel and nearly trip over myself.

Standing before me is the witch hunter that came to our house. The man gives me a mocking grin, and the gap between his front teeth grows wider and wider, nearly swallowing me whole. But my gaze snaps to where he holds his hands out in front of him, gripping a small book: *Malleus Maleficarum*.

With my brief hesitation, Diego's heavy boots slam into the stone street behind me.

I am trapped.

But it only takes a moment for me to realize that I fear the soldier behind me more than I fear the devil in front of me.

I charge toward him, and it catches the witch hunter off guard, surprise and fear flickering in his eyes. Fear.

He is afraid of me. My heart leaps at the idea that I have any sort of power over him. If he thinks I'm a witch, I can use his fear.

Raising my hands toward him as I run, I open my mouth, intending to yell some obsolete curse. Before I can utter a word, the witch hunter jumps out of my way with a strangled cry, clinging to his papers like the book is his salvation.

As I run past him, the flower crown on my head catches the wind and flies off behind me. I do not look back.

I can't think, can't see. My feet retrace their steps, taking me on the path back to the lake and the fields at the edge of town, zigzagging through the streets.

I hear Diego get closer, but I make the last turn toward the lake. I can lose him. Once we are out of town, I can lose him. I know the terrain better than he does. That has to be enough.

The stone turns to dirt beneath my feet. I follow the trampled horse path for only a minute. I turn, break through the grass, and finally glance back.

Even as he tries to maneuver around the flora, Diego's long legs carry him fast. His hand grips his sword at his left side, preventing it from swinging as he runs.

"Catalina," he calls to me. He isn't even breathing hard. "Stop running!"

I reach the tree line around the lake and duck beneath a branch. The trees block out the sun, and the sudden shade seems dark to my eyes. But I keep going, moving toward the end of the lake and the northern border of Banyoles.

How long can he chase me? How long can I keep running? If I keep going, I will be farther than I have ever been from my town.

Just as I have that realization, my foot catches on a protruding root.

My hands shoot out in an attempt to break my fall. My palms slam into the dirt just in time to stop my face from hitting the ground. I don't feel the sting that I expected to accompany my fall.

Before I can scramble away, my head is jerked back, and my hair is yanked hard enough that I slide along the dirt.

Diego pulls again, and the hair at the base of my neck sends shooting pain down my spine. I bite back a scream.

His large hand grips my loose braid, pulling me up. I clamber to my feet, and he wraps my hair around his fist.

"I don't want to hurt you, Catalina." His breath is hot in my ear.

I try to take a step, but he holds me tight against his chest.

"*Cabrón,*" I spit. "Arresting my family? Chasing an innocent girl and holding her by her hair? Yet, you say you do not want to hurt me? Forgive me if I don't believe a thing you say."

Diego's body stiffens. "Witchcraft is seen as a threat to the Crown." His words sound austere and monotone, like he is reciting a mantra—the words of someone else.

I clench my fists at my sides. "There are no witches. There are only women you cannot control," I say, thinking of my mother.

He laughs and releases me. I stumble forward, my hands flying back to my hair as though I need to ensure it is still there, attached to my head.

"The girl who doesn't believe in violence? You will be easy to control. You are nothing but a witch. A sinner." Diego grins. He truly does not see me as a threat, only a nuisance. He views this encounter as an amusing play before hauling me back to my fate. "And I will have you begging for mercy before we are done."

I take slow steps backwards, trying to put more distance between us, but he matches each step with one of his own.

"I didn't do anything wrong, Diego," I say. I hate the way I sound. Pleading. My voice, barely a whisper, the words catching in my throat.

It's a lie, a voice whispers. *This is your fault.*

And perhaps it is a lie. Perhaps I did do something wrong. But not wrong enough to be hunted down like this, surely.

We look at each other, our eyes locked, waiting for the other to break first.

My breath hitches in a gasp. "Just let me go."

He chuckles with a stiff smile and drops his head, running his fingers through his hair before rubbing the back of his neck.

When he looks back up to me, his brown eyes look black.

His right hand flies to the sword strapped to his belt, drawing it in a blur of motion.

At the metallic swish of the steel, I crouch to the ground, swinging my hand along the dirt and grabbing a handful. I fling it in Diego's face in the same movement.

I watch with heart-pounding pleasure as the dirt dusts his face and he shuts his eyes with a growl of pain. Knowing I have hit my target, I turn to flee again.

"Run, *brujita*! Run as fast as you can," he yells after me. "I will make you regret every move."

I gulp air into my lungs as I pass the clear water of Banyoles lake. I break out of the edge of town and stick close to the trees, winding in and out of them.

I do not hear Diego behind me, but I can hardly hear anything over the sound of my blood pumping. So I grip my dress in my hands, and I keep going.

11

I run and run and run until my lungs are screaming for relief.

The voice in my head chants with each step: left, right, left, right. *Your fault, your fault.*

Branches claw at my legs. I stumble onward, struggling to keep my eyes focused. The plants become more and more dense as they rush past me.

I don't know how long I run, but it is too long, and when I finally look behind me, I see no one. No sign of Diego. No sign of anyone.

I come to a stop, and my stomach lurches.

Holding my hair behind me, I double over and vomit my breakfast into a large green bush. I stand heaving until I have nothing left.

Then the heaves turn to sobs.

This girl gave me a potion in the form of my wine.

I gasp for air as my legs buckle and I collapse to my knees. Bringing the back of my hand to my mouth, I bite down, and I scream.

Run, Cata, run!

I scream and scream, muffling it as best I can, tasting salt as tears flow down my face onto my lips. I try to stop crying, but I can't.

I will have you begging for mercy before we are done.

I see Inés's hair sticking to the tears on her cheeks, and Mamá's pinched expression when Agustin accused us of witchcraft.

I was right about him. Never have I wished to be wrong so much. I wish the man Inés had chosen to trust wasn't a coward, a traitor. A self-serving bastard.

And then, there is Diego. I feel just as betrayed by him, though I have no reason to be. He owes me nothing. We are not friends. We have spoken twice, and we only ever argued. But it was just last night that he told me he wanted to get to know me, and even though I did not want that, I still feel betrayed.

You will be easy to control.

I want to blame them. I want to blame the Crown and the Inquisition and the soldiers who took my family away.

But I did this, didn't I? I am the one who made Agustin sick with the herbs I slipped into his wine.

The herbs. *The berries.*

All the air leaves my chest in a *whoosh* as I realize. The *serbal* berries must be boiled. They are not supposed to be consumed raw for fear they will make you sick. I did not think to boil them because they were dried and powdered.

My stomach sinks.

I tried to protect my family. I tried to help, and all I succeeded in doing was getting my mother and sister arrested.

I scream again, gripping the roots of my hair as I double over on my knees once more.

After a final choking sob, I think I have cried out every drop of water in my body. I let out a shuddering sigh that gets lost in the breeze moving through the trees.

What do I do?

I ran from Diego. My body tells me to keep running.

If I keep running, I do not have to think. None of it will be real. I will live on adrenaline.

But I cannot leave my family. I can't leave my mamá and my sister to face this on their own. I can't leave them to their fate in jail, especially when it is my fault they are there.

Do I go back?

It is after noon, and I do not know how much longer until it grows dark.

With nowhere to go, I aimlessly walk onward, moving farther away from everything I know, doing my best to numb my pain.

I walk for perhaps another hour or so before I come upon a narrow path that I hope will eventually lead to a road or trail. The trees are growing farther apart. I feel like that is a good sign, but I cannot be sure. I don't know where I am.

I hear something in the trees ahead of me. My heart jumps to my throat. At first, I thought it was a person, but the heavy and cadenced footsteps tell me otherwise.

A horse. Even worse.

I rush to the side of the path, hiding behind the biggest tree I see.

I squeeze my eyes shut and listen.

It sounds like there is only one. Perhaps I can convince the rider that I am a lost girl, a damsel in distress.

Or perhaps Diego did not give up. He may have returned to retrieve a horse and then continued after me. There will be no outrunning him now.

The horse gets closer, its hooves making soft, patting sounds on the leaf-covered ground.

Hidden behind the tree, they will pass by me.

And they do.

I hear them pass my tree, but then I hear nothing. Are they gone? Did they stop?

"I know you're here."

I nearly gasp at the deep sound of a man's voice. A new wave of adrenaline floods my body, and my hands shake against the rough tree bark.

"I can feel you."

Still, I do not move. He cannot see me, he cannot hear me, he cannot know I am here.

The horse starts moving again, its footsteps getting closer and closer, louder and louder. But I keep my eyes screwed shut.

Until warm breath envelops my face.

I open my eyes to find the horse's nose right in front of me.

With a yell, I fall back and slam my hip into the tree trunk.

"Are you all right?" A man hops off the horse—a man I am relieved to see who is not Diego—and comes to my side, extending a large hand to help me up. "I did not mean to scare you."

He is not a soldier. That much is obvious, and it gives me a touch of relief. He appears to be a regular man, a farmer perhaps. He wears a simple black shirt and plain brown pants, and I see no sign of weapons. Though, one can never be sure.

He is a handsome man with a strong jaw covered in a shadow of stubble. His rich, dark hair falls in thick waves past his ears. His fair skin is smooth and young, but his brown eyes are lined, making him look older. Though he is certainly younger than my mother. Early thirties, perhaps?

His smile wavers when I do not take his hand.

I slowly get to my feet on my own, eyeing him. Who is this man? Where did he come from? What does he want? Can he help me? I have so many questions.

But I start with the least important one.

"What is your horse's name?" I ask.

The man laughs. A real, deep laugh, his white teeth gleaming and his shoulders shaking.

"What's so funny?" I cross my arms over my chest defensively. "I am only trying to be civil."

The brown-eyed stranger sobers, but a smile still graces his face. "Yes, you're right. His name is Caballo."

My eyebrows shoot up. "You named your horse *Horse*?" I ask.

But he just shrugs. "What can I say? I am awfully creative."

"Creative," I smirk. "And so far from the road. What are you doing out here?"

"I could ask you the same question. Far from both Banyoles and Serinya."

I had not realized I had run so far, ending up somewhere between the two towns.

"But to answer your question," he explains, "I heard the Inquisition was closing in, and I came to help." At my confusion, his grin widens. "I come from Castellfollit."

My arms fall to my side, and my mouth drops open. "Castellfollit de la Roca? The witch town?"

He shrugs. "I suppose it depends on your definition of witch. But yes, Castellfollit de la Roca, the witch town. I take it you know the place."

My unease is eclipsed by curiosity. "I know of it. How could I not? I have heard much about Castellfollit. How far away is it? Do you live there? Are there really witches in Castellfollit?"

He holds up a hand to stop me. "Let's get a few things out of the way before I answer any of your questions. My name is Rafael."

"Oh, right," I say, my cheeks warm. I smile at him. "I'm Catalina. From Banyoles."

"And what are you doing out here, Catalina from Banyoles?"

My smile drops. It seems like it has been ages since I ran this morning. But it hasn't.

I clear my throat once, trying to swallow my tears. "My mother and sister have been arrested."

"And you ran," Rafael finishes.

I nod.

"Of what were you accused?" His question is quiet, but his voice sounds strong. It is the kind of voice you cannot help but answer.

"*Brujería,*" I mutter. I suspect he already knows the answer. He mentioned the Inquisition before, but I cannot stop the fear that moves through my blood at the idea of admitting it to him.

Witchcraft is seen as a threat to the Crown.

He looks at me, his eyes frozen in a squinting expression. "And are you? A *bruja*?"

Am I a *bruja*? Those soldiers certainly seemed to think so. And who knows? Maybe some of our friends and neighbors felt the same way. If they didn't before, they probably do now.

I hesitate too long before shaking my head. I watch his face, waiting for any indication of surprise, fear, or disgust.

But he just gives me a sad smile.

"There are many so-called *brujas* that have found refuge in Castellfollit," he tells me. "I was on my way to Banyoles. We received word that a witch hunter had arrived in your town. I was going with the hope of aiding any who require sanctuary."

"Require sanctuary," I repeat. More questions struggle in my mind, vying for my attention.

"And it seems that is you," Rafael says. His eyes bore into mine. "Come back with me."

Come back with him? To Castellfollit? I cannot do that.

"And do what?" I ask, staring back at him.

He chuckles. "Well, for starters, you would have a place to stay rather than wandering in the forest. A safe place, an asylum. There are no soldiers in Castellfollit. It is outside the reach of the Inquisition."

He has a point. I could find safety in Castellfollit.

"I can't leave my family back there," I whisper.

Rafael sighs and brings his hand to his chin, rubbing the short facial hair there. His eyes concentrate on a spot on the ground, lost in thought.

"You know, because we have so many refugees in Castellfollit, we have actually created a bit of a community," he says.

"We?"

He smiles, but does not answer my question. "We have begun teaching each other *hechicería*."

I frown. "You mean *brujería*?"

"If you like."

My frown deepens in confusion. He chuckles.

"*Brujería,*" he explains, "has a certain negative connotation, as determined by the Holy Inquisition: devil worship, human sacrifice, nighttime cult rituals."

"But I don't do any of that," I say in frustration.

"Exactly. According to their definition of a *bruja,* you most decidedly, are not one."

"I am an *hechicera,*" I say slowly, sensing the difference between the two words.

"Though I don't know anything about you," Rafael says, "I am confident in assuming that you are, indeed, an *hechicera.* Someone who uses the energy of nature."

"Yes! That's what we do. There is nothing magic about it. At least, in the way I understand it. It is energy that is already there."

He nods in understanding, and comfort washes over me in a way I have never felt with another person outside my family. He understands. And he has been able to put it into words better than I ever have.

"Thus, we have begun to teach each other *hechicería,*" he repeats. "We share our gifts and knowledge, helping one another develop their understanding and abilities."

I picture a school for *hechicería,* and I wonder what he could teach me. I wonder if the witches in Castellfollit could help me become a healer like Mamá and Inés.

"Mamá is a *curandera,*" I explain. "My sister has the same gift."

"*Curanderas* are easy targets for witch hunts. It is easy to misunderstand the process and power of *curandismo,* misconstruing it as witchcraft rather than something of nature." Rafael hums deep in his throat. "And what about you?"

"What about me?"

"What gifts do you possess?"

I try to find the words, but it has always been difficult to define. Especially to the people who have never experienced it.

But Rafael has understood so far.

"I'm not sure what it is exactly," I say. "I can see into people, I guess. I can tell what their intentions are. Whether they are wholesome or they harbor ill will. Sometimes, I know what will happen, what is to come to pass."

He is already nodding before I finish speaking.

"A *vidente,* or *clarividente,*" Rafael says.

"A seer? No, no, I wouldn't call myself a seer."

He smiles kindly. "Whatever you choose to call it, there are many *hechiceras* in Castellfollit who possess the same gift. And many more who are learning."

"So, you can really learn other gifts? I could become a *curandera?*"

"Everyone has their natural propensities—things that come easier than others, things that they will always be better at. But, yes, it is very possible to learn other forms of *hechicería.*"

My head is spinning. I want that. I want to meet more people like me. People who understand and accept the part of me that lies invisible under my skin.

How terrible is that? My mamá and sister have been arrested, and I am thinking about a new adventure for myself.

I shove the guilt away. I don't plan on leaving my family behind, and I cannot bring myself to tell Rafael to take me to Castellfollit.

"I will not abandon my family," I say it almost to myself.

"I understand," Rafael says. "But what will you do?"

I don't have an answer. How can I help Mamá and Inés?

You will be easy to control.

"Listen, I can bring you to Castellfollit. You will be safe. And you needn't stay forever, just long enough to plan your next move. Long enough to evade the witch hunters." Rafael takes a step closer and places a hand on my shoulder. "But if you would rather figure out something else on your own, it is up to you."

When he puts it like that, it doesn't really sound like it is up to me. I don't have many other options.

Eyeing his horse, I ask him, "How far is it?"

"Not so far," he says with a smile. "And it won't take nearly as long on horseback. We can make it before nightfall if we leave now."

I swallow hard. "I have never ridden a horse."

"All you have to do is hold on. I will do the rest."

I bite my lip. What other choice do I have? I certainly cannot stay here on my own. And I do not know if Diego is still out there somewhere, looking for me.

"Let's go."

12

Rafael and I ride for hours, but it feels like days.

And he severely downplayed what I would have to do when riding a horse. He failed to mention how painful it would be. Sure, all I'm doing is holding onto him from behind, but my entire body aches.

We take a break for the horse—Caballo, I remember he called him—and I can hardly slide off. My legs are so stiff. When we get going again, it is even worse. After the brief relief, getting back on that horse is like pouring hot water on sunburned skin.

We don't talk during the ride. I just cling to his waist. He is a tall man with broad shoulders, and he feels solid as I hold onto him. It makes me feel safe for the first time in what seems like an eternity.

We ride north until we pass through a town called Besalú, and Rafael tells me we are halfway there. We don't stop, but I see enough to know it is a beautiful town, and I find myself hoping Castellfollit is as lovely.

We turn and begin heading west, following the river and entering a small valley, with mountains on our left covered in dense foliage. We have mountains like these on the other side of Banyoles Lake, but it is different riding next to them, observing the beauty while being among it, instead of gazing across the lake.

Following the river, we pass by a few small towns nestled in the emerald hills, but we do not stop there either.

A few more hours pass, and I think my legs are numb. No, I just wish they were.

The sun shines in our eyes as it approaches the horizon. The air is cooler here among the lush trees and plants. I thought Banyoles was green, but the farther we ride, the more I realize Banyoles cannot compare to these mountains.

Soon, there are green hills on both sides, acting as a border along the river, and as the valley gets narrower, Rafael gets my attention.

"Look up there," he says, pointing his finger ahead of him.

Straight ahead of us, I spot a sheer cliff that juts out from the rock, creating a pointed crag that must be over fifty meters high. On top of this magnificent mountain, I see a church tower reaching for the sky.

"Is that it?" I ask. "Castellfollit de la Roca?"

"Castle cliff of the rock," he says with a nod.

"I understand the name now."

"Amazing, isn't it?" He smiles as he says it.

"How do we get up there?"

"With the cliffs on all sides, there is only one way into the town. We have to go along the south side of the river in order to circle around to the entrance." Rafael turns to look at me. "You ready?"

I smile at him. Anticipation coats my tongue. I do not know what to expect. Fear and excitement war for dominance in my mind, but my skin tingles, and a chill runs down my spine.

The horse slows as he carries us up a gradual incline on the south side of the town. I watch the cliff that leads up to the church get shorter as we climb the mountain, until the ground levels out.

We turn right onto a dirt road, and before I know it, we are entering Castellfollit de la Roca.

The sun is low on the west horizon, casting an orange light over the scene. It feels like a dream. A tiny part of me wishes it was.

Rafael takes us into the town. It is really only two small streets lined with homes and buildings packed together like they're holding onto each other to keep from falling over the edge.

Castellfollit is a great deal smaller than Banyoles. The entire town is probably as big as our neighborhood at home. There is only so much space on this narrow bit of land above the river, and they have certainly made the most of it.

People we pass nod or wave at Rafael, greeting him with familiarity, and he smiles back, often calling them by name.

I am too distracted to remember anyone we see.

I am shocked at the countless cats meandering through the streets, weaving between pedestrians and tiptoeing atop walls. Brown and orange, spotted and striped. I have never seen anything like it.

I am no stranger to stray cats, to be sure. There are plenty in Banyoles, but not like this. Here, the people seem unbothered by the cats, and the cats, unbothered by them. The animals seem well-fed and friendly, though obviously free. They keep their distance from us on the horse, and I watch them dash away or hop onto windowsills.

The two roads converge, becoming one that continues to the tip of the rocky cliff, and I can see the church tower in the distance.

At this converging point, Rafael slows to a stop. He dismounts the horse and helps me down, my sore legs protesting. I vow never to get on a horse again.

This single road is even narrower than the one we came down. I thought we were living on top of each other in my neighborhood, but this is something else.

I glance to my left and see a rare space between buildings where the two roads turn to one. At the sight of the sky, I gasp and rush over to see the edge of the cliff. I realize the street is so narrow because two rows of homes have so little room to stay on this cliff.

"Welcome to *hechicera* Castellfollit."

"Everyone here practices *hechicería*?" I ask, marveling at the idea.

He shakes his head, leading the horse by the reins as I walk beside him. It isn't long before we reach the church at the end of town. It is not as big as Santa Maria dels Turers back home, but it has a tall bell tower as well as a large open space in front of it that looks over the river and the valley.

"Not everyone," he says. "And not every *hechicera* in Castellfollit lives right here. But this is the general meeting place. It is also where we have extra space for those seeking refuge."

"Like me," I say softly.

"There are many families in town, but there are plenty of children and young people who are on their own as well."

He ties his horse to a fence post in front of the church and looks around in the fading light as the sun dips below the stone buildings around us.

"What do you think?" Rafael asks, his arms gesturing wide. He grins at me—he knows I cannot help but be amazed. Castle cliff, indeed.

From fifty meters up, I look down to the river, my eyes following the same route we traveled minutes ago. The valley is already getting dark, the raised mountain town blocking the sun as it sets. But I can still see the deep green of the land and the flow of the river.

"It is unlike anything I would have imagined," I exclaim in awe. "I did not know a place like this could exist."

"We are lucky to live here. A place that is not only beautiful, but unfailingly safe," Rafael says. He takes a moment to look over the valley with me before clearing his throat. "I need to get Caballo into the stables. But first, let me introduce you to Kosia. She can help you get settled and find you a place to sleep."

I nod silently, suddenly nervous. I feel displaced and I have no idea what awaits me.

We approach the house nearest the church. The windows are bright against the darkening street, and laughter floats out into the haziness of the evening.

Rafael gives a loud knock before opening the door and entering. He motions for me to follow.

"Kosia!" he calls out.

It is even warmer than outside, and the home smells of cinnamon. We round the corner into a cozy sitting area, so filled with people that many of them sit on the floor.

"Rafael, you've returned!"

A beautiful woman stands from her chair, holding her arms out toward us. She has a red scarf wrapped around her hair, stacked atop her head. Her smooth, ebony skin glows in the candlelight, making her look more like an angel than a woman.

She catches sight of me, and her full lips stretch into a welcoming smile. She weaves through the people sitting on the floor to get to us. I cannot help but notice they are all women. I relax slightly.

"You've brought someone with you, I see," she says.

"This is Catalina," Rafael says, gesturing to me.

The woman grabs my hands in a gentle grip. Her hands are warm and dry, worn but smooth. "Catalina. My name is Kosia."

"Kosia. A beautiful name."

Kosia's smile wrinkles the corners of her eyes. "You are from Banyoles?"

I nod and open my mouth for an explanation, but a knot in my throat keeps me from speaking.

"What happened, *mija*?" Kosia whispers, her voice soft and understanding.

Her sweet tone nearly sends me over the edge. I swallow hard and try to compose myself.

"My mamá and sister have been arrested for *brujería*." I keep my voice quiet. Even though Rafael claims Castellfollit is a welcoming place, I feel nervous announcing witchcraft, for fear someone will look at me with suspicion.

"And you weren't."

She doesn't phrase it as a question, but I can see it in her eyes and the crease of her forehead.

"I wasn't home when they came to take us," I answer her. But I can barely get the words out. "I ran."

Her bright eyes look at me with kindness and empathy. It makes my heart ache at the thought of my own mother.

My own mother is in jail because of me.

"Well, we can talk more tomorrow," Kosia says, patting my hand. "Let's get you settled. I'm sure you are exhausted."

I give a sighing laugh. "You'd be right."

She ushers Rafael and me out of the house. Rafael unties his horse and waves at me without another word. I don't think I could have said anything anyway.

"This way, honey."

Kosia leads me to a large *residencia,* one of the buildings I spotted at the converging roads.

The outside is covered in a reddish-brown color, making the top portion of the building glow like a dying ember in the last of the day's light. The wooden door creaks as we enter the home. A small courtyard extends through the length of the house, but Kosia takes me directly up a staircase to the left.

"What's your full name, dear?" she asks me as we walk. "To make a record of you here."

"Catalina Navarro Gonzalez."

"Alright, Catalina Navarro," she starts. "Let's get you settled."

I falter in my next step, and Kosia looks back at me with a frown. I shake my head vehemently.

"Gonzalez," I correct her. "If you are going to call me by only one name, it will be my mother's. Catalina Gonzalez."

She nods slowly. "Catalina Gonzalez," she repeats.

I am surprised by my strong reaction, but I simply couldn't let her think I was Catalina Navarro. I don't know who Catalina Navarro is, but I have never been her.

We land on the second floor, which overlooks the courtyard. From up here, I can hear talking and giggling coming from downstairs. Or maybe it comes from the rooms we pass as we move down the hallway. Though the doors seem to be made of a dark wood, they must be thin enough that the sound of evening chatter floats out to anyone willing to listen.

We slow as we reach the end of the hallway at the corner of the building, and Kosia knocks at the last door, the sound echoing in time with my heartbeat.

"Adanna? It's Kosia."

I hear a shuffling on the other side.

The door creaks open. A young woman looks at Kosia with a smile, but her face quickly morphs into surprise when she sees me.

"Oh, hi," she says. Her mouth opens and closes like she wants to say something else.

Kosia puts a hand on my shoulder.

"This is Catalina," she says. "Rafael found her after she fled from Banyoles."

Found her. Though it is technically true, it makes my skin crawl. She makes it sound like I am a stray dog. Or a cat.

Perhaps all the cats of Castellfollit were found like me.

"More Inquisition arrests?" the girl asks, turning her attention to Kosia.

Kosia nods.

The girl turns back to me with a sympathetic smile. "I'm sorry you had to run, but I'm glad you made it here."

"Me, too. I think," I say.

Adanna grins.

"Adanna, would you mind if Catalina were your new roommate? I know you have had the room to yourself, but this is the easiest solution," Kosia says. Her voice is assertive, but her soft tone puts no pressure on Adanna, like an understanding mother. "And I think the two of you may be good for one another."

Adanna nods enthusiastically. "Of course! I have always wanted a roommate." She winks at me.

"Wonderful. Thank you, Adanna."

"No problem. I'll show her around and get her bedding and everything. I can take it from here," Adanna says.

Kosia turns to me. "I will talk to you more tomorrow. For now, Adanna should be able to answer any of your questions."

"Thank you so much, Kosia." My voice cracks a little. I clear my throat to cover it.

"*Buenas noches,* girls."

Kosia gracefully walks down the hall the way we came. Her feet don't make a sound, and her skirt flows after her in a *swish*.

"Come in, come in," Adanna says. "I've got a cot over there on that wall. And I think I have an extra blanket somewhere."

I follow Adanna into her room.

The room is already dark, with only one small window facing north. It is a bit smaller than our room at home, but not by much. Adanna's bed is along the wall on the right side, and a mirror hangs above it, reflecting the edge of the cot on the opposite wall. It's bare, but it looks to be in good condition. A small table sits underneath the window to complete the simple space.

"I'm Adanna. Adanna Farias Cepeda," she introduces herself with her full family name.

"Catalina Navarro Gonzalez," I say. "Sorry to impose on you. You've had this room all to yourself."

Adanna waves her hand. "No need to apologize, Catalina. I'm the oldest here, so I have just had a room to myself for a while."

"You are the oldest?"

"In the *residencia*. This is where all the kids without families stay."

"Oh," I say. Kids without families. I'm here. I do not want to think too much about that. "How old are you?"

"Turned nineteen last week," she says with a smile.

"Me, too," I exclaim. "I mean, I'm nineteen, too. Not that I turned nineteen last week."

Adanna laughs. It's a full, musical laugh, her white teeth such a contrast to her deep ochre-brown complexion.

I take a moment to study her. She's tall—much taller than me—and her limbs are long and lithe. Her hair is tied up at the top of her head, creating a big puff, like a soft cloud right above her. She is utterly beautiful.

She looks over at me with a smile.

I sit down on the edge of the cot and I remember how sore I am. I let out a loud groan.

"Are you okay?" Adanna asks quietly.

"Yes, just sore from riding with Rafael," I mumble.

She is silent for a minute. "That's not what I meant."

I look up at her. She sits on the edge of her bed, facing me. Her eyebrows are pinched, almost like she is in pain. But I can see true sympathy in her eyes.

A lump settles in my throat, threatening to rip out of me in the form of tears. I don't trust myself to speak, so I just shake my head.

Adanna moves to sit next to me. She hesitates for a moment, then wraps her arms around me.

"I'm sorry," she whispers.

Every emotion of this never-ending day rushes to the surface, and my eyes drown in it.

I lean into her body with a sob. Her arms tighten around me, like she is trying to keep me from falling to pieces. I don't think she can.

She holds me until I have no tears left.

I finally pull away, wiping my face with the back of my hand, my eyes puffy and cheeks burning.

"I'm sor—"

Adanna holds up a hand before I finish my apology.

"Don't. There is nothing to be sorry for," she says. She squeezes my hand in hers. "I will go get you some water, okay?"

I lay down as she closes the door behind her, making the same soft creak as when she opened it.

Adanna probably isn't gone long, but sleep takes me before she returns.

13

From an eternal, dreamless sleep, I wake all at once.

It is late in the morning, already getting warm. Sunlight shines through a small window I don't recognize.

My heartbeat triples, hammering against my throat. Panicking, I sit up and rub my eyes. I look over to find Adanna's bed empty, the blankets carefully folded.

Then I remember.

It wasn't a nightmare. It was all real. Mamá and Inés and Diego and Rafael and Kosia and Adanna.

Before I completely fall into hysteria, I hear a quiet scraping sound from the door.

"Oh, you're awake."

Adanna is wearing a blue blouse and a muted red skirt, her hair in that same puff. She carries a carafe into the room, setting it down on the table underneath the window.

"You were already asleep when I came back last night," she says, sitting on her bed. "And you didn't even stir when I was getting dressed this morning. I was worried you might be dead."

I laugh quietly, my smile feeling forced. "Nope, just exhausted and traumatized."

"Yeah, that'll do it."

"Is that water?"

I get up and cross to the table, realizing how thirsty I am. When was the last time I had something to drink?

"Yes," she says. "We can go downstairs and get you something to eat, too. Everyone else has already eaten breakfast and left, but I am sure we can find some food for you."

"Thanks, Adanna," I say. My heart swells with gratitude as my panic subsides. Adanna reminds me that I am not alone.

She gets up and pulls a trunk out from under her bed.

"Let's get you something clean to wear. We can wash your clothes later today."

Pouring the carafe, I fill and drain the cup twice, while Adanna rifles through a pile of fabrics, skirts, blouses, and dresses.

"I'm definitely taller than you, so let me see if I have something I have grown out of," she mumbles, almost to herself. "Oh, this is perfect."

She pulls out a dark blue skirt. The bottom of the garment is embroidered with large flowers, plants, and birds in golden thread. It is absolutely beautiful.

"Here you go!" She hands it over to me without hesitation.

I pull back and hold my palms out to her, refusing to take it. "Adanna, I can't wear this."

She frowns, looking genuinely confused. "Why not?"

"It's gorgeous! It is not the kind of skirt you just hand out to someone," I say, chuckling.

She rolls her eyes. "Catalina, I never wear this skirt anymore. I grew out of it years ago. I don't even know why I keep it."

Adanna holds it out to me again, waiting for me to take it. When I do, she dives back into her trunk.

I run my hands over the gold thread, watching it glisten in contrast with the dark fabric.

"And you can wear this blouse, too." She hands me a simple white top. "It's nothing fancy, but it'll do. And you can wear your stay, right?"

"Yes, of course. It is perfect, Adanna. Thank you."

"You can keep them."

"What? No, no, I cannot keep—"

"Catalina," she whines. "I already told you. I never wear these. Just keep them, so you have something else besides the dress you brought with you."

I look down at myself. I am filthy, my white dress smudged with dirt and dust I accumulated from my escape.

I think of the skirt Inés made me, sitting in the middle drawer of our dresser, and my heart breaks again.

"Let's get you washed up."

Adanna leads me to a cramped washroom downstairs and fills a bathtub for me to clean myself. When she leaves me, I take a brief moment to sink down into the water, letting it fill my ears with deep silence. It isn't a large tub, just big enough for me to submerge. My lungs ache, but I don't surface. My eyes burn with tears under the water.

I have found refuge in Castellfollit. I have found people who will help me and keep me safe, while Mamá and Inés have been accused and arrested for witchcraft because of something I did.

Water splashes over the sides of the tub as I push myself up, heaving a breath. This guilt is eating me alive. But I mustn't let it. I have to move forward, or it will destroy me.

I finish my bath, scrubbing hard and washing my hair to get rid of the horse smell.

Adanna returns with a bowl of fruit as I dress in her clothes.

"Here's what I managed to scrape up in the kitchen."

I rip open the piece of pomegranate and hear my stomach growl. I hadn't realized how hungry I was either. I grab an orange, too, feeling greedy.

"Do you want help braiding your hair?" she asks.

I just stare at her. Gratitude warms my chest. Adanna gave me a place to sleep, food, water, and clothes—things I had not even realized I was starving for. If she weren't here, would I be able to take care of myself?

I suppose it does not matter. She is here, and she is helping me.

Adanna smiles when I don't answer. "I just noticed your long braid from before. If you wanted to do that again, I could help you. I have really nimble fingers." She wiggles her fingers in front of me.

A real laugh comes out of me, starting in my belly and ending in a loud guffaw.

Adanna grins. She comes up behind me and takes the ribbons I had in my hair the day before, weaving them in like Inés does. Did.

I try to shove down my feelings as despair threatens to take hold. Without thinking, I shake my head.

"Hey, I'm not done," Adanna complains.

"Sorry," I whisper. My fingers lay woven together on my lap, and I grip them tight to keep from fiddling.

Though my hair is long, it doesn't take her much time.

"Alright, all finished," she says, placing her hands on my shoulders. "Let's get going."

"Get going? Where?" I turn around, and she puts one hand on her hip.

"To find everyone else and join them for classes." She turns to leave, and my mouth goes dry.

Not two days ago, the thought of learning more of *hechicería* would have sent a thrill down my spine. But now, my overwhelming exhaustion and fear cripple me. My left knee almost buckles, but I hide it, shifting my weight.

"Adanna," I start. "I appreciate everything you're doing, but I just don't think I'm up for it."

She threads her arm through mine, guiding me out into the courtyard of the *residencia*.

"I hear you," she says, "and I ignore you." Adanna says it so bluntly, so confidently, it makes me laugh.

"You ignore me?"

"Correct. We cannot have you wallowing and panicking all day long. This will be a good distraction."

She leads us out of the *residencia* toward the church at the end of town, and I assume we will meet in the courtyard behind it. In the daylight, I can see how simple and modest the building really is, yet at the tip of the cliffs, everything looks so much bigger.

It isn't far, but we manage to pass three cats along the way. A brown cat runs along the road at the bottom of one of the building walls, its light feet making no noise. Another, an orange cat, skitters in front of us, crossing the street. And the last, a black cat, spots us and circles us as we walk along. It only circles us twice before going on its way, but I'm fascinated. I have never seen cats behave this way.

Adanna doesn't seem to notice.

"Besides, I want to see what you have to teach us," she says. "What *hechicería* does Cata have up her sleeve?"

The hum of chatter grows as we approach the church, and I smile even as my heart aches at the nickname that reminds me so much of Inés. "Don't get your hopes up, Adanna. My knowledge and experience are minimal. I will be doing all the learning here. Trust me."

"We'll see about that."

Adanna pushes open the heavy wooden doors of the church. Before she can go inside, I grab her arm.

"They let us teach *hechicería* in a church?" My whispered question is frantic. It has suddenly hit me that we are studying witchcraft—or what some may consider to be witchcraft—in a church.

She laughs. "It is the *escuela*, Catalina. Besides, it is not like we're summoning the devil, are we?" My mouth falls open at her cavalier attitude, but she just passes through the doors with easy steps.

I steel myself and follow her inside. The air in the stone building is cool on my skin. Voices bounce off the walls and high ceiling, and rows of benches fill most of the space, with a center aisle giving access throughout the room.

Toward the front, a group sits among the benches. The class seems to be made up of mostly women of all ages, though I spot a few men scattered throughout the space, including Rafael.

Kosia stands in front of the group, her head wrapped in a pale blue scarf today. She looks up when Adanna and I enter.

"Oh, good! I'm glad you girls could make it," Kosia says.

The group turns in their seats, and my face involuntarily heats at the number of eyes staring at me.

"This is Catalina Gonzalez from Banyoles," Kosia announces, her hand stretched toward me. "Rafael brought her last night. She will be joining us for the foreseeable future."

Instead of the shocked gasps or hushed whispers I expected, children smile at me, while many of the women nod in understanding.

I give a small wave and follow Adanna to sit in a row behind a cheerful band of girls.

"We are just reviewing some healing herbs, and then we will break before this afternoon," Kosia explains to us as we get settled.

Warmth floods my face once more, but this time, my anxiety calms a bit. I am familiar with herbs, plants, and healing. It feels like home.

"I'm sorry, Leonor," Kosia says, turning to a teenage girl at the front row. "Will you repeat your question?"

The girl I take to be Leonor asks her question, waving her hands as she speaks. I can only see her from behind. A thick, smooth braid falls down her back, ending between her shoulder blades.

"Well, I was just wondering if you know any good plants for treating stomach issues," she says. "You know, like something that would keep someone from vomiting."

Instead of answering, Kosia looks at the group. "Anyone have any suggestions?"

It is quiet for a moment, and I whisper to Adanna under my breath, "*Hinojo*."

Adanna elbows me in the ribs. "Say it out loud," she whispers.

I shake my head, and she rolls her eyes.

"*Hinojo*," Adanna announces. It's my turn to elbow her.

Leonor turns in her seat to look at Adanna. She looks younger than me, her thin figure making her movements jerky. Her elbows and shoulders stick out as she twists to face us. Her tawny face is long and skinny, with a wide forehead at the top, tapering into a pointed chin. Her full lips open as she stares back at us with a shallow crease between her brows. Her features, though sharp, appear young. Yet her wide hazel eyes look wise and worn, and I see something in her gaze that draws me to her spirit.

"In what form?" Leonor asks.

Adanna looks at me and raises her eyebrows.

I have to clear my throat twice before I find my voice. "Any part of the plant will work: leaves, seeds, flowers. I find it easiest to have the leaves dried and then infused into a tea."

Now, most of the group has turned around to look at us again. I am confident in my response and in my knowledge of medicinal herbs, but I still shift nervously in my seat.

"It depends on the need and the person, of course," I explain. "Other plants work, too, like *ajenjo* or *artemisa*. But I find *hinojo* to be the most accessible, as well as the most effective."

I see Leonor flick her golden eyes in Kosia's direction, looking for confirmation.

Kosia smiles at me from the front of the room. "Catalina knows her herbs."

She keeps talking, but Adanna whispers to me, "How do you know all that?"

"My mamá is a *curandera*," I whisper back.

Adanna leans back and looks at me with wide eyes, her smile growing. "Damn, *prima*. You're the real deal."

I shove my shoulder into hers with a laugh, and she shoves back.

Kosia goes over a few more herbs: *albahaca, saúco, escaramujo, olivarda.* Another adult in the group, a woman named Rita, talks about her experience with healing and how she learned to sense what someone would need.

"It started as thoughts that seemed completely random," Rita explains. "Words and images that appeared in my mind. But as I listened to the inklings in my head and my heart, I found I could heal myself and my children with ease. After that, it came naturally, as effortless as breathing."

It is very similar to the way Inés explained it to me.

They both make it sound so simple. So why doesn't it come easily for me?

I understand exactly which plant can be used for what. I have learned and memorized, but it isn't enough. Anyone can do that. The true gift comes in being able to read the human body, tailoring the healing to the person in need.

As my frustration grows, so does my homesickness.

Luckily, we don't sit there for much longer before Kosia excuses the group. Chatter starts up again as everyone stands.

"We normally have a formal class like this in the mornings," Adanna explains to me. "Then we break for lunch, and we have the afternoon to do whatever we feel we need to."

"Like what?"

"Most of the kids and teenagers will still study, but we do it in smaller groups. Sometimes Rafael helps us to ground or meditate to become more in tune with our power. Some people will help their families with their business or their farm. It varies," she says with a shrug.

"Meditation?" I ask.

Adanna nods. "Meditation is probably the most important thing you can do to become more prolific in *hechicería*. Of course, that's just my opinion, and what do I know?"

"I have never really meditated," I admit.

"I doubt that," she replies. When I look up at her in surprise, she laughs. "I just mean, you seem like you know your stuff, and you're in tune with nature. Have you ever grounded?"

"Of course. Mamá taught us how to feel the energy in nature when we were really young," I explain. "She used to tell us that if we could draw power from the earth, then we could use that power to help people."

"Sounds like meditation to me."

I had never thought of it as meditating. It was just something we did. Now, I wonder what else my mother taught me that is more valuable than I know. And what else does she still have to teach?

Most of the group has filed out of the church by the time Adanna and I stand to make our way out.

"So, Rafael helps sometimes?" I ask.

"Most days," she says. "He and Kosia are the ones that have really formed this community—the unofficial leaders. And they have both kind of taken it upon themselves to help teach this younger generation."

I have more questions, but Kosia approaches us with a warm smile.

"It looks like you two are getting along well," she says. "Thanks again for your help, Adanna."

"Thanks for bringing me a fun roommate."

I chuckle. I couldn't agree more. Already, Adanna feels like a sister.

My chest constricts at the thought. Not my sister, not Inés. But close.

"Catalina, I would like to talk to you a bit more, if that is alright," Kosia says to me.

I nod quickly. "That would be great."

"I'm going to study with a few girls, but you need to teach me everything you know about healing later, okay?" Adanna says to me, already walking away.

"I will do my best," I call to her.

Adanna waves before hurrying to catch up with a group of students.

"You are already an asset to Castellfollit de la Roca," Kosia says softly. "Come with me. Let's talk."

14

I follow Kosia back to the home Rafael and I visited last night.

In the daylight, I can see more of the building. It isn't very different from the buildings surrounding it—the walls made of a gray stone and thick stripes of mortar between each block. Some portions of the wall are covered in a warm beige plaster, but in other places, it has been chipped away.

Kosia opens the thick wooden door, and we enter the sitting area that had been so occupied the night before. It doesn't have the same warm cinnamon smell, but the energy is just as comforting.

She guides me through the house and picks up some items on the kitchen table before we make our way to the back door. A few steps descend from the door to the ground, the top stairs shaded by the slight overhang of orange roof tiles.

The space is small and slightly crowded, but welcoming. A large potted plant sits at the bottom of the stone stairs. A string is tied at the door and stretches across the little patio to the thin tree near the house, covered in laundry. Blankets, towels, and clothes ripple in the breeze, and I can tell which ones are still damp as they hang heavier than the others.

Across from us, a tall stone wall protrudes out of the ground only a few feet from the home. I find myself wondering why you would build a wall so close, especially when the space is already small. If you have a back door, wouldn't you want to take advantage of it?

Unless the town is at a dizzying height.

"Is that the cliff?" I ask in shock.

She sits on the steps and reaches into a basket, pulling out pieces of fired *talavera*. Now I see what she gathered from the kitchen: paints and brushes. She sets them down next to her.

"Yes, right on the other side of the wall," Kosia says with a smile. "Most of the homes are at the edge. We have to fit as much as we can on such a narrow strip of land."

My mouth drops open. What a terrifying, beautiful place.

Over the stone wall, the mountain dominates our view. All I can see is the green of leafy trees, pressed close together, making the mountain look like it is covered in a soft moss that I want to touch with my fingertips.

"I figured we could talk while I work," she says. She dips her brush into a bright blue paint.

My heart twists. Homesickness fills my chest at the sight of pigmented paints and brown clay.

"Would you like help?" I ask.

She glances up at me. "Do you know how?"

I grin. "I have been painting for years. If there is anything I know in this world, it is *talavera*."

Kosia laughs, handing me a tile and a paintbrush.

I get right to work, letting my fingers move from muscle memory, lulling me into a familiar peace as I feel the smoothness of the clay against my skin.

"Rafael filled me in this morning, but he didn't know as much as I would like," Kosia starts. "You told me your mother and sister have been arrested."

I watch my brush glide on the tile, fluid white lines appearing before I answer. "They haven't even done anything wrong," I say bitterly.

"You really do know what you're doing," Kosia says, a smile in her voice.

I can feel her looking at me, but I stay focused on the *talavera*. "I should be there with them. It's not fair that I escaped."

"No, sweetheart," Kosia says. "Your mamá is glad you did. Mothers care more for the safety of their children than their own."

I stop painting as my vision blurs with tears. "It is my fault they were arrested."

Kosia sets down her work and turns toward me. She gently takes my face in her hands.

"No, *mija*," she whispers. I shake my head, unable to form the words that reveal my guilt. But she just tightens her grip, staring into my very soul. "Whatever you think you have done, I promise you: it is not your fault. Strong women who refuse to conform are a threat to the way this society functions. Healers, leaders, storytellers. They are all challengers and, as such, they will always be a target."

It may be the truth, but it doesn't take away my guilt. It only fuels my anger. The anger that eats away at my insides, eroding my soul one day at a time.

This anger feels better than the guilt.

"Are all the refugees here accused of witchcraft?" I ask, swallowing the lump in my throat.

"No, but many are. Some in our *hechicería* classes were accused. Some ran before they could be. A few here in Castellfollit de la Roca were accused, but they have no experience in *hechicería* or *brujería*."

"I saw that the class mostly consisted of women this morning," I comment.

"Most accused of witchcraft are women," Kosia replies. She gives me a sad smile and concentrates on her own tile. "Some refugees were targeted by the Holy Inquisition for practicing Judaism. Or other things not looked on kindly by the church."

I frown. "Is that a punishable offense? That doesn't make sense."

"The Inquisition is not always consistent. Some may be executed for the same crime others were granted a pardon for," she says. "But one thing that is consistent is that the Inquisition uses these so-called crimes, whether true or not, as a way to attack and eliminate anyone they deem to be a threat."

"Anyone who is different," I conclude.

She nods. "And anyone who has more power than they think is appropriate."

"Like my mamá."

"It appears so."

"She never remarried after my father," I explain, the words coming easily. "And she never pressured my sister or me to get married. In fact, she stopped it from happening if she knew we didn't want it. My sister is twenty, and I am nineteen. So, for some people, that was a big deal."

"Your mother sounds like a strong woman."

"She is," I say.

"Then you know she will be okay," Kosia says gently. She places her hand on mine, giving it a comforting squeeze.

I cough in an attempt to clear my emotion, refusing to cry again in front of this woman.

"We will keep an ear to the ground about anyone who has been arrested in Banyoles, alright, dear? Messengers and travelers are always coming through here with news," she says. "Even without them, Rafael finds his way to different cities quite often."

I try to smile, but it feels more like a grimace. "Thank you, Kosia."

She finishes her tile and picks up another, making the same pattern as the previous one so that the design fits together when the tiles are placed beside each other.

"Now, as for your experience in *hechicería*, I think you can be quite helpful in our little school," Kosia says. "It is obvious you know a great deal about healing herbs. Your mother taught you well."

"I know the concepts," I explain, "but I don't have the healing gift that my mother and sister have. I would say that is more important than memorizing a catalog of plants."

She looks at me thoughtfully. "I agree. And the fact that you recognize that shows me how much you understand the value of listening to the energy of nature."

"I suppose. Everyone is different—every illness, every injury, every body. It is important to listen to the body to find the proper way to heal. And my mamá can see what people need. My sister, too."

"And you can't?"

"Not really. Not in the same way Mamá and Inés can. It comes so naturally for them."

"Well, it is as you said: everyone is different—every illness, every body, and every talent."

I pause and tilt my head to the side. I had never thought of it that way. When it comes to healing, I understand the uniqueness of individuals so readily. Yet, I find myself frustrated when I cannot do the things my mother and sister can.

"We all have our own gifts that come easier than others," Kosia continues, "but you can work to develop others, as well."

I laugh. "That's what Mamá always says."

"She understands the way of *hechicería*," Kosia says with a smile. "So, what does come naturally to you, Catalina?"

I hum, trying to determine the best way to explain. "Sometimes I know what is going to happen or when something is going to happen. I can also look at people and see their intentions, their energy."

"Ah, I see. You're a *vidente*."

"That is what Rafael said."

"A seer. You can see the present and the future," she says. "I would not be surprised if you have also seen the past, or perhaps you will soon."

A seer. Again, I am not sure how I feel about that label. I don't know if that is who I am or if I can live up to that expectation.

"You're not happy with it?" Kosia asks, carefully analyzing my expressions.

"I am," I hurry to say. I know better than to deny the gifts of nature. "I just wish I could help people like my mamá."

"You do not think being a seer is helpful?"

"I don't know," I answer honestly. "I mean, it's a cool trick, but in my experience, it does little good. Sometimes it even *causes* problems."

"Well, perhaps we can change your mind while you're here," Kosia says. "And perhaps you can strengthen your other skills, too."

As I watch Kosia speak, movement catches my attention out of the corner of my eye.

A brown cat tiptoes on tiny paws, balancing easily atop the stone wall. Knowing the steep cliff and long fall that lie on the other side of the wall, my paintbrush stalls. Of course, the cat does not have the same fear I do.

It pauses and sits, turning its yellow eyes to me. I forget where I am. Peace settles in my soul. Something stirs in my chest, a connection with the creature in front of me as it licks the fluffy fur on its paw.

After its brief respite, the cat stretches, arching its back and yawning, its long tongue flicking out to taste the air. It hops up and gracefully darts across the wall and down into the town.

"Can I ask you something, Kosia?" When she nods, I continue. "What's with all the cats?"

She chuckles quietly. "I suppose this must be odd for someone who has not lived with so many cats."

"I mean, there are plenty of strays in Banyoles, but not like this. Where do they come from?"

Kosia nods. "A lot of them are simply drawn here to us. Many were brought by refugees, and many were brought back when we found them outside of town."

"Why?"

"Why do we bring them back? Cats protect our energy. They are sensitive to the life force and spirits around us. They know the bad energy from the good, often lending their power to us as we do to them. Does that make sense?"

I shake my head. "I am not sure, to be honest."

"Well, you will get used to them. Next time you encounter one, try to get a feel for their energy," she says. Kosia offers me a mischievous grin. "They're also great for getting rid of mice."

"Mamá!"

I turn to see a young boy come through the back door. He may be taller than I am, but his face still looks young, cheeks full and round.

"Preko," Kosia says, standing. "This is Catalina. Catalina, this is my son, Preko."

I wave at him.

"Preko just turned thirteen," she says. "And he is always very eager to meet newcomers."

"I know who you are," he says brightly, sitting on the step above me. "I saw you come into class this morning."

Preko looks so much like his mother, his flawless skin the same rich umber that makes his brown eyes seem warmer. He runs his hands over his short black hair, his limbs long and thin, his joints sticking out awkwardly, as though the boy has gone through a growth spurt and doesn't yet know how to move his gangly form.

"When did you get here?" he asks. He rests his sharp elbows on his knees.

"Last night."

"Where are you from?"

"Banyoles."

"How long did it take to get here?"

He shows no signs of stopping this line of questioning. It makes me smile. I don't have a younger brother, but I imagine it would be something like this.

"Most of the afternoon and evening. On horseback," I say.

"How long do you think it would take to get here on foot?"

"Alright, Preko, enough." Kosia's voice is firm but loving.

I laugh when he sighs in frustration, shoving his hands through his curly hair again.

"I don't know how long it would take, Preko," I answer him anyway. "Maybe a full day?"

He nods seriously.

"Where are you from?" I ask him.

"Well, I was born somewhere else, but Mamá brought me here before I can really remember," he says. "So, I would say here."

"Do you like Castellfollit?"

"Oh, yes. There is always something happening here." He opens his mouth to say something more, but freezes, his eyes shifting to the side. He holds up a hand, as though to stop Kosia and me from talking.

I stiffen, my mind replaying my chase with Diego yesterday. Does Preko sense danger?

But the boy just smiles, flashing his teeth at me as he stands slowly. He turns and faces the side of his home, looking up.

"Come on down," he calls softly.

Before I can question him, a brown cat appears on the roof, and it looks to be the same cat I saw just moments ago. Silently, it leaps onto the tree branch closest to the roof, though it looks like the cat should be too heavy for it. Then it jumps down, landing in front of Preko.

The fluffy brown feline approaches him, meowing loudly, and Preko laughs, reaching down to pet it.

"You see?" Kosia says with a cheeky grin. "Cats know who the good ones are."

Preko sits back down, and the cat hops onto his shoulder.

"That is bizarre," I mutter.

Preko shrugs, the cat bobbing up and down with his shoulders.

"Well, Preko has a gift," his mother explains.

"What? Can you, like, talk to animals?" I ask with a disbelieving laugh.

"I wouldn't put it that way," Preko says. "But sometimes I can feel them. I can feel when they are near, and I can tell what they want or need. One time, I thought I managed to tell a cat to steal a sweet roll for me." His full lips stretch into a youthful smile as my eyes grow wider with each word from his mouth. "But the cat took it for himself and ran off."

Kosia presses her lips into a thin line. "Speaking of gifts," she says, "aren't you supposed to be studying with Rafael today?"

He shakes his head. "Rafael said he's busy. He will help me tomorrow."

Kosia levels him with a look I can only describe as motherly. "Then you should be working on something with Adanna or Teresa. You know that."

Preko groans. "I'm tired of studying with all the girls. Can't I just help you with the *talavera*?"

"This is with the girls, too," Kosia points out, gesturing to me. Preko shrugs.

"I have never studied with everyone," I say. "Or anyone, really. Can I join your group?"

Preko narrows his eyes at me. "You're just trying to get me to study."

"Partially," I admit. "But I'm also curious to find out what I don't know by studying *hechicería*. And I am a little nervous."

"Take her with you, Preko," Kosia tells him.

He heaves a dramatic sigh. "Fine. Let's go." He lifts the purring cat off his shoulder and sets it down, nudging it softly with his foot. The creature rubs its head against his legs once more before deftly climbing onto the wall and out of sight.

Mirroring him, I stand and turn to Kosia, who is already looking up at me.

"Thanks again, Kosia," I say. "For everything."

"No need to thank me, child. I'm here for you. We all are."

15

Preko leads me down the street, back towards the church. He stays quiet while we walk, kicking up dust as we go, but he seems content, if not a little resigned.

"Why don't you like studying with everyone else, Preko?"

"I don't know," he says with a shrug. "I like it most of the time. I like learning, I do. But sometimes I just get tired of it."

I nod, staying in step with him, which has proven difficult because I can now see that he is definitely much taller than me. "That's understandable. I think that happens to everyone."

"I get bored. Not all the time. But I have never been anywhere else, and when I hear where everyone comes from, I want to leave Castellfollit. When I stay and study, sometimes I feel stuck."

"I'm sorry," I say. "I haven't been anywhere else, either. I mean, until today. I always stayed in Banyoles."

"Will you tell me more about it sometime?" he asks me. His round eyes are wide with hope, but he blinks and glances down like he is hesitant to ask me.

"Of course. You can ask me anything you want, and I'll tell you all about it."

His face splits into a grin, reaching from ear to ear.

"But you have to help me with this studying stuff," I say. "I have never done anything like it."

He nods quickly. "No problem! I've been doing this my whole life, so I know what to do. Don't worry."

I roll my shoulders as a pang of jealousy runs down my neck. His whole life. I cannot imagine the things he has learned. He understands things that I never will.

We approach the courtyard in front of the church, and I see a group of girls sitting in a circle, Adanna among them.

"Here we are," Preko announces.

Adanna looks up and smiles when she sees me.

"Catalina! Come sit by me," she says, patting the ground next to her. "Kind of you to finally join us, Preko."

He makes a face at her and sits down across from us, between two teenage girls.

"Let's make some quick introductions so Catalina can learn your names, okay?" Adanna pats my knee.

"I'm Araceli." It's the girl on the other side of Adanna. She leans around her to smile at me.

They continue around the circle: Andrea, Constanza, Juliana.

"I'm Leonor," says the girl sitting next to Preko. She gives me a small wave. "Thanks for answering my question today." When I frown in confusion, she clarifies. "About *hinojo*."

"Oh, right! Yeah, no problem," I say. "It was a good question."

"Are you a healer, then?" It is the girl next me.

"That's Rosa, by the way," Adanna says.

I shake my head. "No, not really. But my mamá is, so I know a lot about it."

"So, what *do* you do?" Constanza asks, the corners of her mouth tugging down in a slight frown.

The girl is about my age, but she acts much older, like she isn't a child and has never been a child. Her deep blue eyes are a color I have never seen in someone's gaze, and her soft olive skin only makes her eyes more intense, making me shift uncomfortably. Her dusty brown hair falls around her shoulders, and she promptly pushes it behind her ears as she waits for my answer.

"I guess I'm a seer. I don't know, that is just what Kosia and Rafael said." I don't know why I hesitate now. Just saying that I am a seer makes it seem more real. And it makes it seem like I know what I am doing.

"Cool, me too!" Rosa smiles at me. I smile back. Her tight bun reminds me of Señora Sosa back home, but the light in her eyes is the opposite of the old woman's bitterness.

"Are the rest of you healers?" I ask.

Adanna laughs. "No, definitely not. Well, Juliana is, but not the rest of us."

"Are there other things in *hechicería*?" I feel silly asking, but I begin to realize how little I know.

Adanna nods. "Some things are a little harder to label and define, but everyone has their own strengths."

"Like Preko and animals," I say in an effort to understand.

"Preko does a lot more than that," Constanza says with a scoff.

"It's true," Adanna says next to me. "Preko is very talented. He is like a witch prodigy."

I raise my eyebrows at the boy, but he just lifts a shoulder at me, his eyes on the ground.

"So, what else is there, then?" I ask.

"Well, I, for example, can communicate with the dead," Adanna answers.

I gasp. "*Dios!* How did you figure that out?"

I think of the first time I knew something would happen, the first time I experienced this seer gift. I felt such a shock. But that doesn't hold a candle to finding out you can speak to the dead.

"It started gradually, you know? Seeing things," she explains. "Then one night, I woke up and found a man leaning over me in bed."

I bring my hands to cover my mouth.

"That was my reaction. I screamed so loud, thinking someone had gotten into our house, but when my mamá came into my room, there was no one there. After that, I started sensing other spirits around me. Sometimes I saw them, sometimes I didn't. But I could talk to them."

I think of my father. I never even knew him. He died right before I was born. If I was like Adanna, maybe I could talk to him.

"Can people gain that gift? Develop it?"

Adanna looks at me, her eyes becoming sad. "You lost someone important to you." It isn't a question.

My face heats, and I nod.

"I think so," she says, smiling. "We can at least try."

"Rafael says he learned how to talk to the dead," Preko offers.

"Everything is learnable," Constanza says. She claps her hands together to get everyone's attention. "If we are all finished, let's continue, shall we?" She shoots me a look, her eyebrows lowered.

I flinch at her harsh gaze.

"Don't worry about her. Constanza has a tough time with new people," Adanna whispers to me. "And she doesn't like to be interrupted."

"She is teaching us about stones," says the girl next to Adanna.

I must not have heard her right. "Stones?" I echo, but immediately regret it when I am once again on the receiving end of Constanza's glare.

But her bristling attitude doesn't deter the other girls.

"Like how we can use plants to help us," Leonor explains to me, "certain stones have properties that can be healing or strengthening."

I don't know why I had never thought of it before. It makes sense that we can use the energy of nature in any form. I draw on the strength of the earth—stones are merely an extension of that.

I clear my throat and turn my attention back to Constanza. "Where did you learn all of this?" I ask her with a smile.

"Señora Vargas," she says stiffly. "She knows everything."

"Because she is absolutely ancient," Leonor comments.

"Leonor!" Juliana admonishes her with a gasp.

She presses her hand to her chest, her long fingers spreading up toward her collarbone. Her soft, russet-brown complexion is a stark contrast to the white blouse and faded green stay she wears. To match, she has a green handkerchief tied around her hair, pulling the dark twisted locks into a thick ponytail that cascades down her back.

Despite her scolding, Juliana's warm brown eyes glow with affection toward Leonor, and I hide a smile as I watch their interaction.

Leonor holds her hands up in defense. "I'm just saying, she has been around for a while, okay? So, she knows her stuff. And she has learned from a lot of people over the generations."

"Let's just continue the lesson," Constanza says. Her thin lips become thinner as she purses them, and she taps her fingers on her knee with impatience.

"We were just talking about the ultimate stone: *cuarzo*," Leonor says, looking at me. "It can heal, strengthen, and protect. It can purify and promote love. It can even amplify your abilities and energy. Will you pass that to Catalina?"

Leonor hands something to Preko, who passes it down until Rosa slips it into my hands.

It is a beautiful, clear crystal, the straight edges glinting in the sunlight. One end comes to a point with five sides. The other end is just a raw stone, like it was broken. I press it between my hands, reveling in the coldness of its surface and its comforting weight on my palms.

"So, that's *cuarzo*," Adanna says.

"Can stones be used for anything?" I ask. "Like, are there stones that can help me with healing or communing with the dead?"

Constanza nods solemnly. "Definitely. For example, this stone is great for physical healing. It also protects against fatigue, both physical and spiritual. It's called *apatito*."

She holds up a small blue stone with smooth, rounded edges. I watch with interest as she passes it down, each person taking their turn to inspect the stone. I take it from Rosa and marvel at the bright blue color. It looks like the water of Banyoles lake, with cracks and lines of gray and brown running through it.

I pass it off to Adanna and eagerly look to Constanza, waiting for her next bit of knowledge.

"Do you have any *prehnita*?" Juliana asks Constanza. "I think that would be a good one for Catalina."

Constanza shakes her head. "Not with me, no. But I may have some back in my room that I can show her." She hesitates before turning to address me. "*Prehnita* is a great stone for increasing visions and predictions, which would be helpful for you. But it also awakens spiritual talents and abilities. That is what you're looking for, right?"

"Yes!" I exclaim. I shake my head in wonder. "You are amazing. I had no idea stones could help me with something like that."

Constanza straightens her spine, looking pleased.

"Stones, plants, animals, even the stars. All of nature holds energy that is meant to be used and shared," Juliana says.

"Speaking of the stars," Preko says with a smile. "Full moon tonight. Everyone will be there, right?"

"Of course," Adanna says, nodding. "Wouldn't miss it."

"I really need to cleanse my energy," Leonor says with a groan.

"I'm sorry, what is happening tonight?" I ask Adanna. I keep my voice quiet, feeling like the odd one out.

"Full moon ritual," she says. "The moon, the stars, the sky—they are some of the best sources of knowledge and power. And the full moon is one of the greatest opportunities to cleanse your energy."

"Have you ever noticed that you feel different around a full moon?" Araceli asks me. She doesn't talk as much as the other girls, but I appreciate her trying to include me.

"Mamá told us that emotions are heightened," I say. "That we may feel differently around the time of the full moon. 'It is nothing to be afraid of,' she would say. 'It is only Mother Luna telling us it is time to let go and move forward.'"

"Especially for *hechiceras* who are already so sensitive to nature's energy," Constanza adds sagely.

"On full moons, we have a big ritual and meditation," Preko says. "But we make it fun, too."

"That already sounds fun," I admit.

Preko shakes his head. "No, the fun part is the dinner."

"And the dancing," Juliana adds.

"Wow, anything else?" I ask.

Adanna shakes her head. "It is dinner, then meditation, then dancing. We do it here in the courtyard so we can see the moon rise over the valley." Adanna grins. "You will love it."

Luckily, the afternoon comes to an end quickly, and everyone is eager for sunset.

Adanna tells me that kitchens all over town are being used to make dishes for tonight's meal. Constanza, Leonor, and Araceli are all helping Señora Ayala in the *residencia* kitchen. Juliana and Preko are helping their parents cook as well.

Adanna wanted to help set up this month, so I went along with her. We walk down to the church as a couple of men—Adanna says their names are Felix and Jacinto—begin lighting the street lamps.

We go inside the chapel, heading for the back, where Adanna opens a few closets and a small storage room.

"You girls need any help?"

Rafael comes up behind us, taking a peek inside the storage space.

"Would you grab one of the tables?" Adanna directs him.

He brings out a simple wooden table. It is no more than a few boards of wood nailed together so that it creates a short platform, only a foot or so off the ground. Adanna grabs another long table, and I follow behind her, struggling to balance the awkward wooden piece.

Just as Adanna walks outside, Rafael meets me at the door, taking the table from me.

"Will you go back in and grab the blankets stacked in the closet?" he asks me, indicating with a nod of his head.

I hurry back into the storage space. Thin blankets and a few worn quilts are folded on the shelves inside. I take as many as I can carry, barely able to see over the pile, and make my way back outside.

The night air is cool, and the warm sunset is already dimming. I eagerly look to the east. Just through the valley, I can see the bright white moon coming up over the darkening horizon, creating an enchanting reflection on the river below the cliff town.

Adanna and Rafael are in the plaza outside the church, the same place we studied this afternoon. As I approach, the two reach out to take some of the blankets in my arms, and the three of us lay them out on the ground before carefully placing the low tables on them.

"This is beautiful," I say in awe.

"The view or our moonlight dinner setup?" Adanna asks with a smirk.

I smile back. "Both."

While I'm breathless at the wonder around and below Castell-follit, I am also surprised at the preparation for the full moon.

"Well, it's about to get even better," Adanna says. "Come on, we still need to get the tablecloths."

She turns back toward the church, and I hurry after her.

Soon enough, the blanketed ground is adorned with white covered tables and a few candlesticks. When Kosia and Preko arrive, they bring more candles with them, setting the tall candlesticks on the tables and placing a few bigger candles on the ground around the area.

Adanna, Rafael, and I help them place their food dishes on the table just as Constanza and Leonor enter the courtyard with theirs.

After that, it is a constant onslaught of *hechicera* arrivals. Some carry food, some flowers, some candles. The dark plaza is buzzing with lively chatter.

"Let's take a seat on this side," Adanna whispers. She takes my hand and pulls me to the west side of the table, giving us the perfect view of the valley and the rising moon.

Rafael sits at my other side while Kosia, Preko, and Leonor sit down across from us.

"Before we begin eating, we do a little ritual," Adanna says as she hands me a dried bay leaf and passes a few more around the table.

"We always take a moment to connect with the herb," Adanna explains, referring to the bay leaves. "And infuse it with the things we want to leave behind because—"

"The full moon is all about releasing," I finish for her.

She smiles at me. "Exactly. Then we light the leaf on the candle-sticks and watch it burn."

The group silences quickly, and everyone takes their leaves between their hands, eyes closed as they meditate. I close my eyes and do the same.

As much as I don't want to think about it, I try to be brave. I release the events of the past few days, allowing the energy to flow into the bay leaf that crinkles between my palms.

My chest aches as I acknowledge the suffocating guilt that weighs on me. I want to get rid of it, I do. Or at least a portion of it. Enough that I can breathe.

Though, I don't know if I will truly be able to breathe until I can embrace my mother and sister again.

I open my eyes to see Adanna holding the dry leaf to the candle's flame. It lights quickly, and as it burns, she drops it into a small stone bowl. She hands me the smoking bowl, and I follow her lead.

The bay leaf catches fire and withers. It turns to ash in the bowl and I cannot help but smile. I feel a strange sense of joy as I imagine my fear and guilt burning away.

And the men.

I nearly drop the bowl as my thoughts turn to images of burning the soldiers who took my family. How could I think that? And, more importantly, how could I derive pleasure from it?

Shame settles deep in my gut. I mustn't think these things. But I cannot forgive yet, either.

My hands shake as I pass the bowl to Rafael. I turn my gaze upon the full moon that imperceptibly moves up the sky. I bask in its light, squeezing my eyes shut. I need to focus on the good, the things I love. Like my family.

Mamá always made sure we knew when the moon was full. We never made plans, always stayed in. Though we did not have a ritual as extensive as this one, full moon nights were still special to me.

Once everyone has burned their bay leaf, Preko takes the bowl to the edge of the cliff, dumping whatever is left. We watch the ashes blow away in the wind.

As quickly as it began, the silence ends, and everyone begins talking and laughing, reaching for food.

"How are you doing, Catalina?" Rafael asks with a warm smile. His eyes crinkle at the corners as he addresses me. "This is a lot for your first day in Castellfollit."

"I've loved it, actually," I say. "It is a lot, but it feels familiar. Comfortable, even."

Rafael nods, passing the *tortilla de patatas* to me once he has filled his plate.

"You fit in perfectly here," he says. "You certainly have *hechicera* blood. A lot of us were impressed with you today."

His words warm my heart, and I blush, grateful for his compliment.

"Thank you," I mutter, my lips curling into a smile.

"Tell us about what it is like at home," Leonor says.

My heart sinks a little, but I force the smile to stay on my face. Part of me wants to forget all about Banyoles. Another part wants to keep it alive and cling to my home.

"What do you want to know?"

"Your mother is a *curandera*, right?" Leonor asks me. "What about the rest of your family?"

"It is just me and my sister with Mamá. Inés is a year older than me, and she definitely takes after Mamá when it comes to *curandismo*."

"Your father isn't around?"

I shake my head. "He died before I was born. I never knew him, and my sister doesn't remember him at all."

"Oh, I'm sorry," Leonor says.

I shrug. "What about you guys? I've obviously met your mother," I say to Preko. "What is your family like, Constanza?"

I shift my gaze to her, hoping to make some sort of connection. On the other side of the table, she is a little far from me to be a part of the conversation, but I want to try nonetheless. Especially after our cold interaction this afternoon.

"I have no one," Constanza says flippantly. She scoops some food onto her spoon. "I came here when I was twelve, after my mamá was arrested and my papá got sick."

Perhaps this was a mistake. I do not ask if her parents died. I can tell they are gone by the way she speaks. And when she avoids my eyes, I do not press further.

"My *abuela* and I came here years ago, but she died last year," Leonor says with a grimacing smile, as though trying to hide her grief.

"I'm sorry." I clear my throat and let out a humorless laugh. "Sorry, I didn't mean for this to turn into something so heavy."

"It's alright. I asked you first," Leonor says.

"It is important to get to know one another," Rafael comments. "We are a community—a family—and it won't help to keep everything bottled up. We are here to support one another."

I see everyone nod in agreement, and I am struck once again by the power this little town holds, acting as a refuge and sanctuary for witches everywhere.

I try not to dwell on the fact that there is even a need for it in the first place.

The conversation turns toward lighter topics, and we spend the rest of dinner laughing at Preko's stories and Leonor's impressions of Preko's stories—something everyone but Preko finds amusing.

The moon is high in the sky when Kosia stands to get everyone's attention.

"If you recall," she starts, "last month, we had Rafael lead us through a full moon meditation as a group. So today, we will have the chance to meditate individually."

"We switch off," Adanna whispers to me. "One month, we have a big group guided meditation, then the next, we just do it by ourselves."

"Do we still stay out here in a group?" I ask.

She nods. "Yes, we always do the dinner and the whole event, but some people like guided meditations while others like the freedom to do it themselves."

Many people, including Leonor and Preko, have moved away from the tables, spreading out in the courtyard. Some stay at their seats, but turn around to face the moon.

"Come on," Adanna says. She grabs my hand and leads me closer to the edge of the cliff. The entire courtyard is surrounded by a low stone wall, and we climb on top of it. We have moved away from the candlelit table, but the moon is so bright, I can see everything clearly.

I cross my legs underneath my borrowed skirt as the courtyard becomes quiet, the only sounds coming from the cool breeze and a few melodic owls.

But the more I try to meditate, the harder it becomes. I am exhausted. And I have already spent so much of today meditating and learning, grounding and feeling.

So, I stay quiet and watch the moon.

I wonder if Mamá and Inés can see the moon.

I don't know if they are still imprisoned or where. If they are safe and warm. If they are even still alive.

My throat tightens, and I shake my head hard. I can't think like that. I will fall apart.

Instead, I explore the rage that burned inside me earlier tonight, when the thought came unbidden: the thought of burning the men who took my family. The thought of making them suffer.

Despite my fatigue, my hands shake, anger flowing through my veins and burning my skin.

Rafael told me I have *hechicera* blood. But right now, I feel no love, no connection, no grounding to the energy of the earth. There is only violence.

I'm sorry, Mother Luna.

Saving me from my thoughts, I feel a poke in my side and nearly scream. Adanna shakes with silent laughter as I hit her on the arm.

Looking around the courtyard, I see many are opening their eyes, bringing their meditation to an end, and I wonder how long I have sat here seething. It doesn't feel like long.

"Is there dancing, now?" I ask Adanna, keeping my voice as quiet as possible.

She nods, and relief floods me. Perhaps I can use that to rid myself of this energy, this untamed fury.

When enough people have finished, we move the tables and candles away from the center of the square. Juliana and Leonor run to the newly opened area, Preko following after them, and they motion for us to join them.

As we move toward them, Kosia claps out a beat. Another woman next to her mimics the beat, and everyone follows suit. Kosia and the other woman begin to sing with Señora Ayala, their voices heard even over the clapping throughout the courtyard. We join hands to form a circle and begin moving clockwise and then counter-clockwise, dancing in the middle and weaving around one another.

Adanna laughs with joy as Rafael joins us, and I notice Preko constantly trying to be near Leonor. It isn't long before my cheeks begin to ache—I cannot wipe the smile from my face. Araceli giggles next to a shockingly happy Constanza, and I realize she has dimples.

"Kosia!" Juliana calls. "Dance with us!"

Kosia rushes into the circle, leaving her post on the sidelines, and the rest of us sing out to replace the sound of her strong voice. She joins the circle next to me. Her face glows under the moonlight as she grins, and a laugh bubbles up inside me.

Joy floods my body and my soul. My breathing comes harder, but I don't stop, reveling in the full moon energy.

We dance until the moon is at its peak and our feet slow in their steps. But even then, we laugh and sing as we merrily skip our way to bed.

☽ ● ☾

I don't remember drifting off to sleep. I hardly remember getting into bed.

But I am asleep now, right? I must be.

I am watching Mamá and Inés get taken away, held on either side by a Spanish soldier. Agustin cowers away, hiding his face from Inés. Mamá's mouth moves, telling me to run, but I cannot hear her.

I see Diego lock eyes with me, and I know he is coming. I remember this.

I turn to run, but I feel like I'm moving through water, my knees struggling to bend. I can barely manage to gain any distance as I try to flee through the streets.

Diego's feet pound behind me. How is he moving so fast?

His footsteps get louder and louder until I realize it isn't his footsteps. It is my heart.

I open my eyes, and Diego is gone. Relief floods me.

I whip my head back around to look for my family.

Instead of Spanish soldiers surrounding them, I see iron bars. Mamá and Inés sit together on a dark stone floor, still in the clothes they wore when they were taken. I can smell the damp earth around us, cold and dead.

Mamá closes her tired eyes and she looks older, weary. She leans her head on Inés's shoulder.

I call to them, trying to get their attention as I search for the key to their cell. But they won't listen to me, they don't see me.

I grab one of the oil lanterns hanging on the wall, approaching them carefully, and Inés finally turns to me.

"*Dios*, Inés," I say, a heavy sigh of relief overwhelming me. I reach for her, but she looks at me with fear. "Inés, what's wrong? It's me. It's Catalina. I'll get you out of here," I promise.

She begins to shake, her entire body trembling enough that Mamá raises her head, a line creased between her brows.

"Catalina, don't," Inés pleads with me.

I don't know what she is saying. Don't what? Doesn't she know I am here to save them?

As I look down at them again, I notice they aren't on a dark stone floor. They sit on a layer of gunpowder.

I am overcome with the need to set a fire to the world that burns as hot as the undying rage within me. I want to watch it all burn.

Then, I'm watching my body from above. I see myself throw the lantern to the ground of their cell.

The glass shatters, and the flame quickly lights the gunpowder. The fire spreads out from the lantern, soon engulfing the entire jail in orange flames and gray smoke. Satisfaction blooms in my chest at the sight.

Until I remember my mother and sister. They scream.

I cannot breathe. The smoke is too thick.

"Catalina!"

I wake with a gasp.

Adanna sits on my cot, her hands on my shoulders, shaking me. Her dark eyes are wide, filled with concern.

"Just breathe," she says.

I take a shuddering inhale, filling my lungs with what feels like my first breath of the night.

She doesn't take her hands off my shoulders, but her touch becomes gentle. She breathes with me until I can do it on my own.

"Nightmare?"

I cover my face with my hands. "I'm sorry I woke you," I mumble.

"It's okay," she says. "I used to have nightmares every night when I got here."

I realize I do not know much about Adanna. I do not know how she got here or where her family is.

I watch her for a moment, not wanting to pry. But I think she senses my need for an engrossing distraction. And perhaps she needs to share her story.

"My parents and I fled to Castellfollit five years ago. My mother sensed a witch hunt would be starting in our village," she whispers. "So, we left, following the rumor of an all-witch town. We had been safe our entire journey. Until we were a few miles out."

Her eyes look glassy, her expression faraway, and my heart cracks as I hang onto her every word.

"Spanish soldiers stopped us. Once they discovered we were going to Castellfollit, they lashed out. They felt threatened and claimed they had seen the evil that witches can do," Adanna says, laughing bitterly. "They attacked us."

My mouth drops open. I take her hand in mine and watch her profile. She stares right at the ground.

"They were a little more focused on Mamá and Papá, so I managed to escape. I started running until I realized my parents weren't with me. I stopped and turned back. I even took a step toward them, but Mamá yelled at me to run. So, I did," Adanna says with a small shrug. "I ran and ran until I came to Castellfollit, screaming that soldiers took my parents."

I wait for her to continue. She squeezes her eyes shut, and the tears finally fall. She uses the back of her hand to wipe them off her cheeks and clears her throat.

"They didn't make it," she finally says. "I don't know exactly what happened. Rafael went after them. I wanted to know every detail, but he would not tell me. He said it was best."

I nod. He is probably right, but I don't say that. Just because it is best does not mean she doesn't deserve to know.

"I stopped asking after a while. Kosia took me in, helped me through the first few months. Learning about *hechicería* distracted me, and I made friends," she says, "but it still hurt. All the time."

Adanna looks at me out of the corner of her eye, and the side of her mouth pulls up in an uneven smile.

"What I am trying to say is that I get it," she says. "Don't worry about waking me up. We are in this together."

As simple as it is, hearing her say it makes me feel lighter, yet stronger.

I also want to protect her from every bad thing in the world.

"We are in this together," I repeat back to her.

"Do you want to talk about it? Your nightmare?"

I start to shake my head, but I hesitate. Adanna opened up to me, let me into her injured past. I want to let her in, too.

I tell her everything I can remember about my dream. She lays down beside me as I fall back, our arms pressed against each other on this cot that is far too small for two people.

When I finish, she doesn't respond. She just lays there with me. And after a while, we both fall asleep.

The next days pass in much the same way as the first.

Adanna and I wake early to meet the rest of the students living in the *residencia* for breakfast. Several mornings begin without the sun, clouds covering the sky and rain sprinkling down on the town.

Regardless of the weather, we walk over to the church together for our main class. These end up being my favorite because everyone is there, the adults and younger children. I've met little Tomasina and Ana Clara, sisters who are no older than eight years old. They introduced me to their friend Ignacio, a young boy who claims to be ten years old, but Adanna informs me he only just turned nine.

Though the group is mostly made up of women, I see more men come in throughout the week. Kosia or Rafael normally take the lead for these classes, but they frequently ask other adults to teach us what they know. Like Eugenia, a middle-aged woman who was raised by her *abuela*. Eugenia teaches us more about the heavens: the power of the moon, prophecy in the stars, and other celestial wonders like eclipses.

I have learned more about stones, which are still foreign to me, but I find myself looking forward to using the earth's elements.

And I have also learned about communing with the dead. It turns out it is not as easy for me as it is for Adanna. The dead have to choose to speak, so it is not always up to you. But Adanna gives me tips on how to be available—how to show that I am open and willing to talk.

Most of these tips and tricks are the same ones that we're taught to practice for any form of *hechicería*: meditating, grounding, becoming close with nature. It is all about feeling the nuances of energy, and it is just as important to feel it inside ourselves as it is to feel it in the world.

It's frustrating. Though there is a lot I can learn and so much I am being taught, a great deal of *hechicería* is a personal journey. It requires each individual to work within themselves in order to discover how they can work with the energy around them.

Everyone is different.

I used to get annoyed when Mamá would say that. Now, I cannot count the number of times I have heard it in classes here.

Another thing seems to be universal: cursing.

Kosia warns us against cursing, like Mamá used to warn Inés and me. She tells us that our power, our connection with energy, can be used for good, but it can also be used to harm other people. Sometimes, we don't even realize we are doing it. It can be completely subconscious, which is why it is vital we stay focused on good intentions.

When Rafael talks about the consequences of cursing, I am not particularly surprised. It doesn't deviate much from what Mamá told us.

Curses harm you, even if it isn't directly. Cursing can open you up to negative energy, drawing the ill will of others into yourself involuntarily. Sometimes, it can take immediate effect on your body or mind. Once you call upon the negative energy, darkness can take root in your body, making you ill.

They really try to scare us away from cursing. In some ways, it works. Though, I have never really had much of a desire to curse another person.

At least, not until now.

Now, I want to hurt people. I want to hurt Agustin. I want to hurt Marcos. I want to hurt Diego. I want to hurt everyone who has hurt my family. And it scares me.

Not that I plan on actually cursing any of these people, of course.

On my fourth day in Castellfollit, Kosia teaches us about something called etheric travel. She says that most of us have probably experienced it in some way, even if we haven't realized.

It is when our soul or spirit can travel away from our body, like it's all happening in your mind. But Kosia emphasizes that it is very real.

Apparently, some of the students are already very good at it, like Leonor. She says she has been projecting since she was a little girl.

"I had no idea I was doing it, though," Leonor explains to the whole class. "I thought I just had a very active imagination."

I hear a few chuckles echo in the church. That seems to be a common experience among us. Whatever our natural skills are, it took us a while to realize they were real.

"It wasn't until I projected to the neighbor's farm and saw one of their sheep run off that I started to realize what was happening," she continues. "A few hours later, our neighbor arrived at our door, completely out of breath and in a panic, telling us he had lost one of his sheep.

"When my mother told him we hadn't seen it, I came up behind her and said the sheep had gone north, up into the hills, and that it hadn't gone far. They both looked at me so strangely, and I felt foolish that I had said anything. But our neighbor decided to follow the path I had laid out for him, and he found his sheep very quickly," Leonor finishes with a laugh.

"Can you imagine?" Constanza whispers to no one in particular, awe coating her voice. I glance at her from the corner of my eye and find her staring at Leonor's profile.

"There are different forms of etheric travel," Kosia says. "And most of you won't be able to do it the same way Leonor does, especially when you are starting out. But it is always good to try."

Rafael stands up. "We are going to do a special meditation session today, designed to help you be more aware of your surroundings and, hopefully, help you get used to the feeling of your etheric body being separated from your physical body."

He motions for the rest of the group to rise from our seats. "Follow me," Rafael says. He walks down the church aisle and out the door.

We scramble to follow him, excited for something new. I walk with Adanna, and we hurry to catch up with Leonor and Juliana.

"What does it feel like?" Juliana asks Leonor. I notice she keeps her steps slow so Leonor can keep up with her long legs.

Leonor shrugs. "It's hard to describe. You start feeling almost lightheaded, kind of dizzy. And then your body just goes into some sort of trance."

"Your etheric body or your physical body?" Adanna asks.

"Physical body, I guess," Leonor says with a laugh. "I never knew all these proper terms before, I just knew how to do it."

"That is so cool," Juliana whispers in awe. Her eyes are fixed on Leonor.

"Stop looking at me, Juliana," Leonor says in a bored voice.

"Where are we going?" I ask. We're still walking, following Rafael and the group.

"I don't know. We already passed the courtyard where we normally meditate," Adanna answers.

Rafael leads us to the edge of town. We walk onto a dirt path covered in fallen leaves. It is not long before we reach a green field nearly entirely encompassed by tall trees. Today is a sunny day, so Rafael stops in the largest patch of shade, motioning for us to hurry.

"Quick, quick, we don't have all day," he snaps, not unkindly. "Sit down."

We gather around him in a lopsided circle. The grass tickles my leg through my skirt, and I try to flatten it.

"We are going to start this meditation as we normally do," Rafael explains. "But like I said before, we will work on separating our etheric body from our physical one. Before we start, I want to emphasize that you can do this at your own pace. I will guide you as best as I can, but don't feel the need to go further than you would like. And don't feel discouraged if you can't do it on the first try, alright? Everyone is different."

Adanna and I exchange an amused look, and she rolls her eyes.

"Get comfortable, close your eyes, and take a moment to breathe," Rafael says. His voice is soft but it carries, cutting through the sounds of the birds and the wind. "In through your nose, out through your mouth."

I close my eyes. The sound of everyone's scattered breathing permeates the field.

I press my hands into the ground beneath me, feeling the dirt and the grass. I allow the earth's energy to flow into me.

"Now, focus on grounding yourself," Rafael instructs. "Place your hands or feet flat on the earth and become one with the energy."

Eyes still closed, I smile. This is something I know how to do.

When we did our first group meditation, I was nervous. I had already been frustrated with learning how to commune with the dead and did not want another failure. So I was pleased when I found that meditation is what Mamá has been teaching us since we could walk. It is familiar to me, and I'm good at it. Good at feeling the earth's energy.

"Now, in your mind, picture your space. Visualize the grass beneath you, the people on either side of you, the clothes you are dressed in." Rafael's voice is even softer now. "Take time to imagine every detail around us."

I start right next to me. I see the blades of grass by my feet. I see the dusty dirt on my hands. I see Constanza to my right, sitting cross-legged with her hands on her knees. I see the blue sky and the bright sun.

"When you are ready, envision the top of your head, like you are looking down on yourself from above. Lift your spirit up, out of your body."

My spirit feels light, airy. I begin to float a bit higher, and my head spins from a dizzy sensation. But soon enough, I can see it. I can see myself from above.

I am not far, just barely above my head. But it's something.

It is quiet for a long time before Rafael speaks again.

"If you feel you can go farther, or you want to stay in your etheric state for a moment, feel free to do so," he says. "If you need to be done, slowly come back down to your body. Take a moment to feel the ground beneath you. Feel the touch of your clothes on your body, feel the sun on your skin, and open your eyes when you are ready."

I keep my eyes closed for a moment longer, but I am exhausted. I open my eyes with a sigh and look around.

Adanna meets my eyes and makes a face. I snicker at her, earning a glare from Rafael.

Most of the group have their eyes open. The facial expressions range from wide-eyed excitement to frowning frustration to tired disappointment.

But Leonor still has her eyes closed. I wonder where she is. I wonder if she has gone out of the field, away from the town.

I am surprised to see Preko's eyes still closed as well. His face is screwed up in concentration, and it's cute to see him trying so hard.

Constanza sits next to Preko. She looks like she is about to burst. "Can we—"

Rafael brings his finger to his lips. She hesitates, but when she opens her mouth again, Rafael shakes his head. She sighs, folding her arms across her chest.

Preko opens his eyes and looks at me across the circle. I nod at him and silently clap my hands in applause. He grins, his mouth stretched wide.

If we are meant to stay here until Leonor comes back, I worry we will be here until dusk.

I lower myself and lie on my back in the grass. Countless green leaves shade me from the sun, shaking in the wind and offering little glimpses of azure sky between them, but I notice the dark clouds coming toward us. I think it might rain today after all.

"Rafael."

I sit up, shocked that someone was bold enough to speak when Rafael all but forbade it.

But it's Leonor. Her eyes are open, and she pushes herself to her feet.

"There's a group coming toward Castellfollit," Leonor says.

"You saw them?" Rafael asks.

She nods.

"How far off?"

"If they continue at the pace they're going, they will be here this evening, I would say. Maybe tonight."

"Refugees?"

Leonor shrugs. "It looks like it, but I am not sure."

"Hold on," Constanza interrupts. "You traveled that far? Like, etheric travel?"

"It's not really new to me."

"That is so cool," Juliana says in the same awed voice as before.

"Thank you, Leonor. I will let Kosia know when we get back." Rafael claps his hands. "But for now, how did it go? Does anyone have any questions? Anything you would like to share about your experience?"

It's quiet as we all look around at each other, waiting for someone else to speak.

"Preko," Rafael says. Preko's head snaps up. "Your eyes were closed for a while. How did it go?"

Preko bites his lip. "I'm not really sure if I did it right," he mumbles.

"Tell us about it."

"Well, I saw myself from above, like you told us," he says slowly. He frowns, his eyes trained on the ground in front of him, deep in thought. "And then I saw everyone else, but I am just not sure if it was actually etheric, or whatever it's called. I feel like I was just making a picture in my mind." He shrugs.

Rafael nods. "Any advice, Leonor?"

Leonor looks surprised to be asked, but no one else is shocked. Rafael is right to ask her. "I don't know. I guess... How did your body feel? Like, your physical body?"

Preko shrugs again, making a sort of *I-don't-know* sound. "I didn't really feel anything."

"That's good," Leonor says. "Did you feel detached from your body?"

"Yes," Preko says. "Yes, I guess I did."

"The entire goal of this meditation was to familiarize yourself with the sensation of detaching your etheric body from your physical one," Rafael emphasizes. "I would say you were successful, Preko."

Preko nods slowly, and then starts beaming.

"Anyone else? Any questions or thoughts?"

Adanna raises her hand. "I felt scared."

I can't help but smile. Adanna's raw honesty and vulnerability never cease to amaze me. She is tough as nails but soft, too, and not afraid to show it.

"Scared?" Rafael asks. "Elaborate for us."

"Well, it was slow going at first," Adanna says. "But I finally got to the point where I was looking down at myself, you know? I started to go higher, but I got scared. It freaked me out to feel so far from my body. I panicked, and that kind of broke the spell."

I watch a few students, including Juliana and Araceli, perk up as she speaks. They may have felt the same way, and I understand why Adanna wanted to bring it up.

Rafael flashes his white teeth in a big smile. He is pleased she mentioned it as well.

"That is totally normal, Adanna," he says smoothly. He turns around in the circle, speaking to all of us. "It is normal to feel nervous or scared when you try anything new. And it is amazing that you even tried at all. You should all be proud of yourselves."

Juliana visibly relaxes, her shoulders falling. Constanza breathes a quiet sigh.

"We will try another one of these next week, but if you feel comfortable, give it a try on your own before then." Rafael smiles again. "Don't worry about doing anything else today. Take the remainder of the afternoon to rest."

The group climbs to their feet, some of us swaying a little, heads light and spirits fatigued. We take our time making our way back into town, kicking up dust as we approach the road.

The sky darkens, the gray clouds completely covering the sun and the formerly blue sky.

Ahead of us, I can hear Preko badgering Rafael.

"Is there any way to travel with your physical body?" he asks.

"Yes," Rafael says, "it's called walking."

I snicker. I can hear the smirk in Rafael's voice. I laugh harder when Preko groans with frustration.

"No, you know what I mean," he says. "Like magical transportation or something. If you can do it with your spirit, can you do it with your body?"

Adanna and I hasten our pace, catching up with the two so we are right behind them.

Rafael shakes his head. "No, there is not. That would take something more powerful than the energy of nature."

He keeps walking and Preko huffs. Up ahead, I see Juliana pivot to face us.

"Yes, but there are legends, right?" Leonor asks. She slows, too, as she realizes Juliana is waiting for us.

"Like what?" Preko asks.

"I don't know," Leonor says. "What about that story you were talking about with Kosia? The Book of Blood, I think?" She glances over to Rafael.

My eyebrows jump in recognition. I have a faint memory of Mamá telling us about the Book of Blood.

I am not the only one who has heard the story.

Juliana claps her hands. "Oh, the Book of Blood. I know that one!"

Rafael has paused in his strides, clearly surprised. "You need to stop eavesdropping, Leonor," he says with a sigh.

Preko waves his arms impatiently. "Well? Anything you'd like to share with the class?" he asks, imitating Rafael's voice.

It earns a deep laugh from Rafael, who quickly recovers his pace. Preko looks particularly pleased with himself as Adanna and I giggle.

We turn to look at Rafael, waiting, but he simply rolls his shoulders back and offers us a small smile, shaking his head with a laugh.

With his silent refusal, the group looks expectantly at Juliana. She grins. "Alright, listen closely," she says, dropping her voice dramatically. " I will tell you about the Book of Blood."

"Wait, so what *is* the Book of Blood?" Adanna asks, looking around.

"I am pretty sure that's what we will learn in the story," Leonor says.

Constanza falls into step with us and rolls her eyes with a groan. "It is just a stupid old myth, Adanna. You know, some story that has been passed down and told to children but never actually happened."

I don't bother to mention the fact that she slowed her pace to listen to this stupid old myth.

Leonor smiles and shakes her finger at her. "Ah, ah, Constanza. You don't know whether or not it happened." She winks at Juliana.

"Tell us the story," Preko moans. He turns his attention to Juliana, and our group parts, making space for Juliana to walk in the middle.

"*Vale*. Everyone listening?" she asks before she clears her throat. Her posture and presence shift, her back straightening and shoulders moving back. She appears older than her fifteen years, her voice full and steady.

"Once, long ago, there was a beautiful young woman who fell madly in love with the farmer's son. The farmer's son loved her back, and he soon asked the woman's father for her hand in marriage. The young woman's father refused to give his blessing, claiming that the farmer's son was not good enough for his daughter." Juliana spreads her arms wide, motioning with her hands as she talks.

"But nothing could thwart their love. The couple ran from the town, stealing away in the night. They travelled all night long, and when they came upon the next town they found the priest, and he married them. Now married, the couple decided to make a life in the small town, and the young man was hired on as a farmhand, while his young bride spent their last few coins to buy supplies for *talavera* pottery. Though they were poor, they were happy."

"How is this a story about the Book of Blood?" Adanna asks.

Preko shushes her, and Juliana keeps going. I feel a raindrop hit my forehead.

"Sadly, only one week after they were wed, the young man grew deathly ill. His new wife was a *bruja,* and she did everything she could to heal the man, but despite all her efforts, he died. The young witch was distraught and would not believe he had passed on. She kept administering to him, even as his body grew cold."

Preko is uncharacteristically quiet, completely enthralled. I glance at Constanza and smile when I see her listening to Juliana's account of the legend, eyes focused on her.

We follow Rafael until we arrive back at the church, and I try to remember how we got here, but I am too distracted by the story. Tiny drops of rain fall onto us, misting our skin. I'm afraid we will get wet, but it doesn't seem to be raining harder anytime soon.

And I am not sure it would be enough to deter us now.

"As she began to truly despair, the young witch recalled her mother's many warnings against making deals with the devil. She had always listened to her mother's fervent words, but she found she no longer cared. She could not live without her love.

"So she called to the devil, and a handsome young man appeared before her, coming out of the shadows. The young man knew of her plight, for the devil is always listening. 'You wish to save your lost lover,' the devil said. 'I can help you, but you must give me something as payment. I will return to ask a favor of you.' The young witch knew it was the devil, but his pleasing smile put her at ease, and her desperation urged her to assent.

"Upon her agreement, he presented a large book bound in leather. 'This Book has the spell you need to raise the dead,' the devil said."

"The Book of Blood," I confirm.

Juliana nods. "The devil vanished, and the young witch opened the book. She found it was a true book of sorcery that held the key to many incredible feats, like transformation, transportation, and resurrection."

"There it is," Preko calls out, pointing at Rafael. "Transportation!"

"But the woman did not care for any of the other spells. As she found the one she needed, her heart sank. The only way to accomplish such impossible magic was to take the life of another and drop their blood upon the Book. That night," Juliana whispers, lowering her voice as we lean toward her, "the witch went into town and heard a man bragging about how he attacked a woman in her home. Furious, she slipped a poison into his wine and followed him to his house, where he dropped dead. She cut his throat, collected his blood on the pages of the Book, and went home to complete the resurrection spell on her husband.

"With the death of another man, she had the power to bring her husband back to life, and the two embraced with tears of joy. The next day, the woman went to town again, intent on sharing the news that her husband was not dead. But the townspeople learned of the other man's death, and, knowing she was a witch, accused her without evidence."

"They were right, though," Constanza mumbles.

"They captured her and dragged her to the jail, but before they could imprison her, the witch used the Book and the power leftover to transport herself back home to her husband. Upon her arrival, she found not her husband, but the devil. 'I have come to collect,' the handsome man said. The woman extended the Book to him. With inhuman speed, the devil's hand snaked out and snatched her wrist. 'Your soul is mine.' Fear spread through her at his cruel words. She only just reunited with her love. How could she leave him now? Frantic, she searched her memories, grasping at her mother's stories to find a way to escape this noose.

"'Perhaps a game? A wager?' she suggested. The devil stilled. 'If you win,' she said, 'you keep my soul. If I win, I keep your Book.' The demon shook his head, his smile twisting, and the woman thought he did not look as handsome as he had the night before. He told her, 'If you can find a way to trap me, I will let you keep your soul and the Book. However, if you cannot trap me by the time of the sun's rising, I will take your soul, as well as your husband's.'

"She agreed, and the devil left her. The woman turned the problem over and over in her mind all night long, and she thought through every bit of *hechicería* her mother had ever taught her, but she could not come up with a solution. Just as the sun began to rise, she had an idea and called to the devil.

"'How will you trap me?' the devil asked her with a grin, for he knew he could not be caught. Instead of answering him, the young woman picked up her brush and her pottery and began to paint. The devil laughed at her, eager to claim her soul and her husband's. But he failed to notice that she had painted him into the *talavera* until he was nothing but a blue devil on a white tile."

At this moment, there are several sounds of confusion and a scoff from Constanza.

"How can you paint the devil into pottery?" Adanna asks. "I don't understand."

"Oh, you've never trapped the devil in *talavera*? My sister and I did that all the time," I say, rolling my eyes dramatically. "Come on, everyone has done it at least once."

Rafael laughs with a snort.

But Constanza groans. "It's a fairytale, Adanna. No one understands."

"Is that the end?" Preko asks.

Juliana smiles, her eyes full of mirth as she continues. "Trapped, the devil yelled at her from the *talavera*, 'Fine, you've won. Now free me, and I will let you live.' The woman shattered the tile on the floor, and the devil reappeared. But this time, he showed his true form, covered in darkness. The woman could barely look upon his monstrous face. 'There is a price to pay for cheating death,' the devil spat at her. 'And now, you will have to pay it twofold.' With that, he disappeared.

"Fearful that the devil would return and aware that the witch was wanted by a mob, the young couple gathered what they could and fled the town, just as they had before they were wed. They came to another town and safely settled down, soon forgetting the business with the devil. They lived to have a child and grew old in the town together, happy and healthy," Juliana finishes.

Constanza makes a strangled sort of noise. "That's not it at all."

We turn to stare at her. Her face turns red, but she straightens her spine, tilting her chin up in a jerky movement that reminds me of a hawk.

"You got the ending wrong," she says. "They leave the town and have a kid, yes, but the husband isn't his usual self. His body is weak, pale, and lifeless. As the years go on, his mind goes, too, and soon enough, he is an empty shell. The woman is eaten alive by the guilt of killing a man, and she grows more distraught as her husband loses himself. They both die, but not before the woman gives the Book to her child and seals it, so no one can use it."

Juliana is shaking her head before she is even done speaking. But Constanza nods her head emphatically.

"Where did you learn that?" Juliana asks her, laughing.

She scowls at her. "My mamá. And my *abuela*. That's how the story goes, Juliana. Everyone knows it."

Juliana doesn't respond right away. It starts raining in earnest, and Rafael wipes a drop from his brow.

I hear a small cough and turn to see Araceli clearing her throat. I hadn't even realized she was here.

"I heard it the same way as Constanza," she says. "They die at the end." Her brown eyes are so dark they are nearly black. But her sweet disposition and her round face make them look warm and comforting. Her olive complexion turns pink on her plump cheeks as she supports Constanza's version of the folktale, and she brings the back of her hand to her face, as though feeling the heat on her skin.

"Anyone else?" Juliana asks.

"Oh, my mamá never mentioned anything about them having a child, but she did say the couple died," I say. "And I think that makes the most sense."

"Why do you say that?" Rafael asks. He looks me in the eyes, patiently waiting for my response.

"Well, of course the husband would die. He is not meant to be in this world, right? As for the wife, by killing the man, she was basically cursing him, wasn't she? Killing is like the ultimate curse. So, the woman would face those consequences," I say, shrugging.

"An interesting thought, Catalina," Rafael says, stroking his chin.

Constanza huffs. "It doesn't matter. It never happened anyway." She stands and leaves us in the light rain, her feet kicking up what is left of the dust as she walks down the road.

Rafael smiles. "She is right. It's just a legend, a myth meant for entertainment."

"It is still a cool story," Preko grumbles, clearly displeased with the turn this storytime has taken. "Imagine having the Book of Blood."

"It is said that there were instructions for incredible magic," Juliana answers. She shrugs, leaning back with an amused look on her face. "At least, that was the rumor."

"It was a cool story, Juliana," Adanna agrees, her sweet voice a contrast to Constanza's consensus. "Thank you."

Juliana beams and takes a small bow, practically vibrating with excitement at all the attention she received. "The storyteller is only as good as her audience. I should be thanking you."

"Alright," Leonor says, rolling her eyes. "Let's go, storyteller."

She takes Juliana by the arm, and the two follow after Constanza toward the *residencia,* raising their arms above their heads as the rain falls. Juliana lives with her family in a house near the town entrance, but she and Leonor are nearly inseparable, so they spend a great deal of time in Leonor's room at the *residencia.*

Rafael claps his hands. "Preko, let me walk you back. I have to tell Kosia about what Leonor saw. I will see you girls later," he says to us.

Once we are alone, Adanna clears her throat. "So, do you still want help with the talking to dead people stuff? I know I said I would help you today."

"*Dios*, no. I'm exhausted," I say, shaking my head. I feel a strand of wet hair stick to my face.

"Oh, good! Me, too."

"That etheric travel really takes it out of you, doesn't it?"

Adanna grins. "Let's go back to our room for a nap."

"And then help Señora Ayala with dinner," I add.

"You read my mind." She slips her arm through mine, our skin wet, and we turn toward the *residencia*. "Now, let's get inside."

19

My stomach growls as Adanna and I sit down to dinner with Leonor.

Adanna pesters Leonor with a hundred questions about etheric travel. I try to listen, but I am busy battling my guilt.

Multiple times today I forgot about my family—about Mamá and Inés locked away. Instead, I am laughing with my new friends, excited to learn more about our *hechicería* gifts.

I have found happiness here. And the guilt is eating me alive.

How could I be enjoying myself, even for a second, when my family is suffering? Suffering for which I am guilty, a crime for which I should have been charged.

I cannot let myself forget about them. I must do something to help them. I have been in Castellfollit for almost a week. It is time to return to Banyoles.

I have just had the thought when I feel it.

A swirling in my chest, almost like the breeze through the trees, signaling something is coming. Something has changed.

I freeze, food halfway to my mouth.

Adanna notices the tension in my body and places a warm hand on my forearm. "Cata?"

"I feel something," I mutter.

"Feel something?" Leonor repeats, her mouth half full. Her smooth forehead creases in confusion.

I nod. "I don't know how to describe it. I just know something is happening." I pause for a moment, closing my eyes. My chest thrums, pulled toward the town gate, toward the road I traveled to get here.

I stare back at Leonor.

"You said refugees were on their way," I say.

Adanna and Leonor freeze, realization dawning across their faces with wide eyes.

"They're here," Adanna says.

Leonor grins. "Well, *chicas*, shall we postpone dinner for a few minutes?"

I smile back at her, and Adanna laughs, nodding her head in agreement. The three of us stand and walk in the direction of the town entrance.

The rain has stopped, but it still lingers in the air, and clouds block out the sunset and the rising moon.

"Let's see who is here."

We hurry our steps, giggling along the way as we begin to trip over one another and slip on the wet stone street.

We turn the corner and see a dirty, tired-looking group in the space where the two roads converge. An old woman wipes her brow, leaning heavily on a tall man who looks to be a little older than Rafael. The man has his arm around the waist of the woman at his other side, a woman his age, most likely his wife.

Rafael's hands move as he speaks to them, while Kosia leans down to talk to a little girl clinging to her mother's skirt.

We sober as we lay eyes on them, the three of us reminded of our own arrivals in Castellfollit. We slow down and quietly make our way toward them.

"Hang on," I say. "That man looks familiar."

"You know him?" Adanna asks.

I shake my head. "No, but I feel like I have seen him before. I wonder where they are from."

I break away from my friends, leaving them behind. The woman and little girl see me as I approach, causing Kosia to look in my direction. She straightens to her full height and meets me halfway.

"Where are they from?" I ask.

She is nodding before I finish my question. "The Estrada family. They are from Banyoles."

"I need to talk to them," I say, pushing past Kosia.

She grabs my arms lightly and forces my eyes to her. Her expression is kind, but firm. "Be gentle. They're exhausted. The old woman was arrested for *brujería*."

"Arrested?" My heart races. "So she was released?"

"Yes. She renounced witchcraft and repented of her sins, swearing herself to Christianity and to the Crown. It is not always that simple, though. The Inquisition is fickle, as you know. Her son was worried they would come after her again."

I nod in understanding, my gaze back on the family. "I get it, Kosia. But I need to speak with them," I whisper.

She releases me so I can make my way over.

"For now, we can get you set up in a boarding house," Rafael is saying. "It will be a tight fit, but you will be able to rest until you can find a place for your family."

"Thank you," the man says, exhaustion evident on his face.

"Excuse me," I say, reaching my hand out in a half wave. "You are from Banyoles?"

He nods but doesn't pay me much attention, already turning to his mother.

But his wife stares at me, her eyes studying my face with warm brown eyes. Her face is thin and delicate, framed by light brown hair that she has pulled back. In a graceful motion, she brings a hand to her cheek, softly pressing her fingertips into her skin.

"You are from Banyoles," she says. "Aren't you?"

I figure there is no point beating around the bush. "My mother and sister were arrested for witchcraft."

Her eyes light up with sympathy. The old woman's head snaps up. Unlike the young mother, she has piercing blue eyes that make her look wild. Her gray, curly hair escapes the fabric draped over her head.

"Witchcraft?" the old woman asks me.

"You were arrested, too?"

The old woman nods solemnly.

"But they are releasing people," I say slowly, my voice unsure. "Do you know who?"

She shakes her head. "What is your mother's name, *cariño*?"

"Soledad," I answer. "She is a *curandera*. Have you heard anything about her?" I clasp my hands behind my back to keep them from shaking.

"I have heard of a *curandera* named Soledad," she says. "But not since I was arrested. I don't know if she has been released."

My heart sinks.

It must show on my face, because the old woman steps forward, laying a wrinkled hand on my cheek. "I'm Lucia. What is your name?"

"Catalina."

"I'm sorry, Catalina," she whispers softly.

I nod my head quickly, trying to show my understanding, but a tear escapes. I can't help it.

"Oh, *cariño*, no. No tears," she says. She wipes my cheek as she looks up at me. Her wrinkled hand is dry and warm, and her soft touch calms me. Her movement disturbs the scarf on her head, causing it to slide off her frizzy hair and onto her shoulders. "If they are half as tough as you, I am sure they will be fine."

I release a shaky laugh. "How do you know I'm tough?"

She grins at me and gives me a wink before stepping away to follow her family. "I just know."

I smile at the same words I had just given Adanna and Leonor. *I just know.*

The small old woman walks away, her hand on her son's arm.

She is right. I am tough.

"Well?" Adanna and Leonor appear on either side of me. I'm not sure which one asked the question.

I clear my throat. "They are from Banyoles. The old woman was arrested for witchcraft, but they released her."

Leonor gasps.

Adanna grabs my hand. "Did she know anything about your family? Have they been released, too?"

"She doesn't know," I sigh.

I can see both of them deflate a little, and I want to laugh and cry all at once. They care so much about me and my family. I have never had friends like them.

I will miss them.

"I am sorry," Adanna says, giving my hand a squeeze.

"It doesn't matter," I say. I turn away from them and start walking back to the *residencia*. I can't bear to face them as I say it. "I am going back anyway."

"What?" Adanna stops in her tracks.

But Leonor hops in front of me. "What are you talking about?"

I swallow hard. I cannot let them dissuade me. "I am going back to Banyoles."

"That is way too dangerous, Catalina," Leonor says, shaking her head.

"Maybe they have been released, like that woman," I say.

"And if they haven't?"

I walk past Leonor with a shrug.

Adanna catches up to us quickly. "Cata, you can't just leave here without knowing whether or not they have been released."

"Why not?" I raise my voice, whirling on her. I regret it instantly. I am not upset with her. Or anyone here. I'm just scared.

Instead of looking hurt, Adanna sets her jaw and narrows her eyes.

"I'm sorry," I whisper. "I didn't mean to yell at you. It is not your fault."

She says nothing, but she throws her arm around my shoulders, and we keep walking. I reach my arms around her waist, feeling foolish and thankful all at once.

"Rafael!" Leonor calls out.

He comes up behind us, and Leonor runs to meet him.

"We need to find out if Catalina's mother and sister have been released from jail," she says. "She wants to go back to Banyoles."

Rafael's eyes cut to me. "We have someone arriving tomorrow who will bring news and information on the arrests. Until then," he says, eyes drilling into mine, "don't make any rash decisions, alright?"

I hesitate. "They are coming tomorrow?"

He nods, waiting.

"Alright," I confirm. "I can wait until tomorrow."

"Let's finish dinner, *prima*," Adanna says. "And find a distraction so you don't run off in the night."

She lives up to her promise and invites the girls to our room after dinner.

Now, I sit on my cot, my back against the wall, facing Adanna and Constanza, who sit cross-legged on her bed. Juliana sits on the ground, braiding Araceli's hair, which is apparently one of Juliana's favorite pastimes.

"Well, did you hear that Alonso and Mónica are finally getting married?" Juliana asks. Though I have not had any gossip to contribute, I enjoy listening to the girls talk about their lives and the goings-on of Castellfollit.

"No! Really?" Adanna exclaims, leaning forward with a sharp motion.

"Finally," Constanza comments with a roll of her eyes, throwing her arms in the air. "They have been in love for ages."

"Is Mónica an *hechicera*?" I ask.

Juliana shakes her head. "No, but Alonso is. He is my older brother. You have probably seen him in the mornings."

"I didn't know you had an older brother." I realize how little I know about everyone's family.

"It's me, Alonso, and my other brother, Felix," Juliana says, nodding. "And Papá, of course."

I turn to Adanna. "Felix, the one we saw lighting the lanterns the other night?"

"That would be him," Juliana answers. "Alonso is twenty-two and Felix is twenty-five. He is already married, but they still live with us."

"I don't think I have ever met Alonso, though," I say, trying to remember.

"Alonso hasn't been in class," Adanna says. She smirks and wiggles her eyebrows. "I suppose he has been a little distracted."

"When is the wedding?" Araceli asks eagerly.

"Next week," Juliana announces.

The door creaks open, and Leonor slips through the crack with a cheeky grin. She holds the hem of her skirt up, creating a large pocket in front of her.

"Guess what I brought." She leans down and holds out her hands, revealing three pomegranates in her skirt.

Araceli squeals and pats the floor next to her. Leonor sits and tosses one of the red fruits to Adanna before ripping one open herself.

"We were just talking about how Mónica and Alonso are getting married," Juliana says. She finishes Araceli's braid and ties it off with a ribbon.

"Oh, I know, right?" Leonor looks around at us and pops a seed into her mouth. "Finally, a good party!"

I let out a loud laugh as the girls continue their chatter. Adanna looks across the room, and I smile. *Thank you*, I mouth to her. She winks back at me.

I am not sure how long the girls stay, but by the time they have gone to their own beds, I nearly collapse from exhaustion. Adanna blows out the candle, and the room is plunged into darkness, save for the subtle glow of moonlight.

But that, too, is soon gone as I drift off.

Inés and I work quietly, painting our *talavera* with precision. She drops her tile, and it shatters. Much to my surprise, she begins to laugh. I laugh with her, but when I look over at her once more, I don't see my sister.

It is my papá. Though I never knew him in life, I know it is him now. It doesn't take much for a daughter to recognize her father.

"Take it, Catalina," he says.

Papá holds out a large leather book, his eyes imploring me.

"I do not want it," I tell him.

He shakes his head. "It is yours. Take it before the devil takes you."

I panic and turn away from him, ready to run.

But when I turn around, I fall into a different nightmare—a nightmare that has been my reality.

Mamá tells me to run. Diego chases after me.

I can't move. I squeeze my eyes shut, and he disappears.

Mamá and Inés are behind iron bars. I search for a way to free them. I have been here before.

I grab one of the oil lanterns hanging on the wall, approaching them carefully. Inés finally sees me. She shrinks away when I reach for her.

"Inés, what's wrong? It's me. It's Catalina."

She begins to shake, her entire body trembling.

"Catalina, don't," Inés pleads, her eyes full of fear.

Then, I remember the gunpowder.

I stare at the lantern in my hand, the flame flickering as I move it. Yet, I want more. I want to start a fire, to burn everything. I want to watch everything become engulfed in flames.

Why? I do not want to burn Mamá and Inés. I don't.

But it is too late.

My hand is raised, arm ready to smash the lantern to the ground at their feet. I cannot control it. Panic overwhelms me.

I swing my arm.

And something stops me. Some*one* stops me.

A strong hand is wrapped around my wrist, the grip firm but not painful.

Diego.

He looks at me. Shakes his head. His lips are moving, but I can't hear him. I can't hear anything.

He pries the lantern from my grip, and my body relaxes as realization hits. I almost set fire to my family. Diego saved us.

But I don't trust him. I should not have given him the lantern.

Diego stares at the lantern in his hand. His eyes move to my mother and sister, then back to the lantern again. As though he is realizing what he can do.

As though he is deciding whether or not to burn my family alive.

I try to talk to him, plead with him, tell him not to. But my mouth won't move. I reach out to him, but I can't touch him. He is so far away. How is he so far away? He was right next to me.

My vision darkens around the edges. The jail disappears. Diego becomes blurry, and I can't see what he's doing. Where is he?

I sit up in my cot with a gasp.

I cover my mouth and try not to scream with fear or cry with relief, afraid I will wake Adanna.

My heart continues to race even as I lie back down.

20

I watch Adanna undo the braids in her hair, creating a halo of dark hair around her head.

"Interesting," she comments under her breath, concentrated on her hair.

"Interesting? Why is it interesting?"

She shrugs. "I mean, you are a seer, are you not? Haven't you had prediction dreams before?"

"What are you saying?" I ask her, arching a brow. "You are saying my dead father is going to come back to life and give me the Book of Blood? I am going to light my mother and sister on fire?"

She laughs, though I don't know why. Just saying it makes me anxious.

"No, I am just saying maybe something is happening with that Diego guy, right? Maybe you are sensing his energy, and he is trying to make a decision or something," she says. Her voice goes up at the end, like she is asking a question.

"That isn't comforting," I say. "At all."

Adanna finishes her hair and puts her fingers into it, fluffing her coils. She reaches for the faded handkerchief on her bed before wrapping it around her hair and carefully tying it at the nape of her neck.

"Listen, you're scared. You're stressed. You miss your family. I wouldn't read into it too much."

"So you don't think it means anything?"

"I am sure it doesn't. I was only joking," Adanna says. "Let's go find Rafael and ask when those messenger people are coming today."

That is a plan I can certainly get behind. Though Adanna and the girls did a great job distracting me last night, it hasn't kept me from the constant buzz of anticipation as I await news of Banyoles and my family.

Adanna told me today is market day, and I'm eager to explore the town. We rush down the stairs. We walk into the bright street, and I squint my eyes, screwing up my face as I adjust to the light. The sun is covered in clouds, but the sky is luminous regardless.

Castellfollit is significantly smaller than Banyoles, so their market doesn't have the same busyness I am so used to. But the town still holds a small market in the plaza by the church, selling their wares and their produce. The farmers nearest the town come into Castellfollit to offer their crops, while the townspeople sell what they have made. Sometimes they have merchants from much farther away join the fray.

We walk toward the plaza, though it is not far from the *residencia*. When I see Preko carrying a basket of *talavera* to his mother, my heart aches.

His face lights up as he sees us, and we wave at him.

"Adanna! Catalina!" He tries to balance the basket with one hand so he can wave back with the other.

I shake my head at him because I can see the basket wobble, and Adanna runs up to help him before he can drop it.

"*Mierda*," he mutters. "Sorry. Thanks, Adanna."

"Language," she admonishes him with a snap.

"You're not my mom," Preko says. He has a gleam in his eye when he looks over at me, enjoying his audience.

Adanna narrows her eyes as I bite my lip to suppress my smile. "Just because I am not your mother doesn't mean I won't discipline you."

He rolls his eyes. "Yeah, okay, whatever that means."

"It means," she says, "watch your language, or I will tell your mother."

He blanches. "You wouldn't."

Adanna just smiles and begins to walk in the other direction. I run after her, giggling at the horrified look on Preko's face.

Once we are far enough away, Adanna laughs too. "Oh, I love that kid," she says softly.

"There's no one like him," I agree.

Though the street is busy, the plaza is the true center of the commotion. Tables and booths stand close together around the edges of the courtyard in front of the church, while other sellers carry their wares in baskets, walking from one buyer to the next.

I spot one woman holding out skeins of fabric, her customers running their hands over the deep blue textile. We pass a table of dried herbs and fresh vegetables. Next to them, a couple fills their basket with brown eggs. The smell of sweet breads adds warmth to the underlying scent of imminent rain.

Meandering through the crowd, we catch sight of Rafael on the other side of the courtyard, speaking animatedly with another man.

Anxious to ask him of any news, we cut across the square, weaving in and out of buyers and sellers. But a disconcerting silence ripples through the crowd, and the busy activity quiets.

We pause. I hear the sound of horses, soft at first, but the clanging of their hooves gets louder, and nearly every head moves in the direction of the street.

When they finally appear, I blink over and over. I must be hallucinating.

Four Spanish soldiers enter the town square, each on their own horse. I recognize them instantly. They are from Banyoles.

Marcos leads the group, with two of his friends immediately behind. I do not remember their names, but I am sure I have met them, even just in passing.

Bringing up the rear, Diego slowly takes in the town, his eyes analyzing every detail.

"Do you think these are the guys Rafael was talking about?" Adanna asks, but her voice sounds fuzzy, faraway. Like she is talking to me through water.

I cannot take my eyes off Diego.

I will have you begging for mercy before we are done.

When he finally sees me, he freezes.

"Cata?" Adanna tries to get my attention. "Catalina, hello?"

I break eye contact and turn to Adanna. Her demeanor changes instantly. I try to speak, but my mouth just opens and closes.

"What is it? What's wrong?" she asks in a quiet but panicked voice.

A giant hand is wrapped around my lungs, squeezing the air out of them. My head spins as I hyperventilate, my chest moving up and down rapidly.

"Adanna," I manage between breaths. "I can't breathe."

"Come sit." She rushes me a few feet over to a small stone bench, where she helps me lower myself as I clutch my head in my hands.

"Marcos!"

The loud greeting grabs my attention, and I snap my gaze to the source. It's Rafael.

He throws his arms out, greeting the group with a smile. Marcos jumps off his horse and claps Rafael on the back.

I do not think I could be more surprised, but Rafael's friendliness and familiarity with Marcos has my head spinning.

"Are you okay, Catalina?" Adanna crouches next to me, bending down to look into my face.

In a daze, I nod. I can breathe again. If only from the shock of the scene I watch unfold.

The other soldiers dismount as well, eyes on Marcos.

"Alferez, Pedro," Rafael says, waving at the other two soldiers. "Good to see you. Glad you all made it safe."

Only then does Rafael notice Diego. He pauses. His eyebrows draw together. In concern? Fear? Confusion? Good. He should be wary of at least one of them.

"Who is this?" he asks in a low voice. He keeps his eyes on Diego, but his question is directed to Marcos.

Marcos beckons to Diego, who slowly approaches.

"This is Diego Tremiño," Marcos says. "We grew up together. He joined us in Banyoles a little over a week ago."

"Good to meet you. Rafael, is it?" Diego asks.

Rafael relaxes a bit. He gives him a nod and shakes his hand.

It all looks so normal.

But not to me. I am not so easily won over.

"They are the ones who arrested my family," I say to Adanna. She gasps just as Rafael's eyes find us.

"Catalina, these are the people I told you about last night," he says. "They will have more information about—"

"About who has been arrested and released," I finish for him. I stand and take a step farther into the courtyard toward them. I am shaking, but not with fear. I am suddenly consumed with anger. "They are the ones who took my mother and sister."

Marcos has the decency to look ashamed. Diego simply stares at me.

"Diego here," I say, motioning to him, "is the one who chased me out of Banyoles."

You will be easy to control.

Rafael takes a step back from the two men. He opens his mouth, ready to argue, but Diego beats him to it.

"And you escaped, didn't you?" Diego asks. "I let you go."

"You didn't let me go. You attacked me," I say through gritted teeth. I clench my fists, fingernails digging into my palm. "You chased me through the forest."

Everyone is still. The tension radiates, thick enough to suffocate me.

It is Rafael who finally breaks the silence.

"Catalina," he says softly, "Marcos has been helping us. Alferez and Pedro, too. They give us information; they help refugees get to us." He hesitates, looking at Marcos out of the corner of his eye. "They arrested your family only because they had to. They had to keep their cover."

Because they had to? That is enough to excuse what they have done? I cannot believe Rafael is defending them, and as he does, my faith in him starts to fade.

"And Diego?" I ask.

Rafael's lips press into a thin line. He turns to Marcos.

"I can vouch for him," he says to Rafael. "I trust him. You can, too."

Rafael nods, and I know he is convinced. I have lost.

I spin on my heel and march back to where Adanna stands near the bench. The crowd has started moving again now that they have had a good look at the soldiers.

Her eyes jump between me and the men, looking unsure.

"Apparently, Rafael is fine with them. Happy, even," I say bitterly. She nods once. I swallow hard and lower my voice. "Do you trust Rafael?"

Adanna knows him better than I do. And at this moment, I am hesitant to listen to Rafael.

"Yes," she says clearly and confidently, looking me straight in the eyes.

A cold drop lands on my cheek, and I look up at the darkening clouds. Another one falls on my forehead as the sky begins to sprinkle down on us.

Adanna grabs my arm, and we turn our backs on them. "But that doesn't mean I trust Diego." She glances over her shoulder, and her grip on my arm tightens. "Cata," she whispers.

I follow her eyes.

Diego walks toward us, his gaze locked on me.

As he gets closer, I am reminded of my dream from last night. He may have saved me then, but I don't feel very relaxed in his presence this time.

I refuse to back down.

"Rafael says you want to know about your family," Diego says. His voice is warm and dark, smooth and precise. He speaks without emotion, without intonation. "Your mother and sister are still in jail."

My stomach sinks, and I am falling. I keep falling.

Except I'm not. The world still turns, the town still runs, and the sky still rains. Adanna's hand is still on my arm, but I hardly feel it.

I want to scream, sob, weep. I want to hit him, scratch at his face.

Instead, I lift my chin. "I am going back."

I don't know why I said it. I don't know why I felt the need to tell him.

But, isn't that what I said last night? I told Rafael I would wait until today before making any decisions.

I now have all the information. I have made my decision. I won't leave my family. I can help them.

Diego lets out a mocking laugh. "And do what? They will arrest you, too. You cannot help them."

My anger rises through my chest and up my neck until I feel its heat in my nose. My blood rages, and I try to regain control over my voice despite the emotion erupting inside me.

"Is that what you'll do?" I ask him. "You'll follow me back and arrest me? Make sure I don't escape this time?"

Any indication of amusement is wiped from his face. The muscle in his jaw jumps, and I can see his fingers twitch, his wrist resting on the sword at his side.

The water falling from the clouds comes down a little harder, large drops falling on my blouse and soaking my skin.

"Thank you for your concern," I say with a smirk. "But I can certainly take care of myself."

His eyes darken. In a blur, he has his sword drawn, pointed at my neck. I don't have time to blink, let alone move.

Adanna shrieks. "What is wrong with you?"

I had forgotten she was here. I still don't look at her. My entire focus is on the man in front of me, leveling a blade at my throat.

"You say you can take care of yourself. The girl who frowns upon violence," he mutters. "But you will be taken easily, killed in a minute. Going back to Banyoles is reckless."

I lift my chin even higher. My heart pounds so loud I am sure he can hear it. Perhaps he can see it trying to beat its way out of my chest. He has made his point.

But I won't show it. I will not give him the satisfaction.

You will be easy to control.

I am not the same girl he met in the market.

Instead of backing away, I take a step forward, the blade pricking my neck the slightest bit, but not enough to make me bleed. I blink through the rain and keep my gaze locked on his.

His brown eyes flicker, glancing down to the place where his sword presses into my pulse. His throat works as he swallows.

And then, shouting rings out in the square. People have finally realized this soldier is threatening me.

Behind Diego, I see Rafael and Marcos run toward us.

Marcos grabs hold of Diego, throwing him back.

"No weapons," Rafael commands. "We will not tolerate anyone threatening those under the protection of Castellfollit de la Roca. Is that understood?" His voice is harsh and, though not loud, it sends chills down my spine.

Marcos shoves Diego. "He asked you a question."

"Yes, I understand," Diego says, his eyes dropping to the ground as his wet hair plasters his forehead and neck. "It won't happen again."

"No, it won't happen again," Rafael growls. "Watch yourself, boy."

Rafael holds out his arms, ushering Adanna and me in the opposite direction, away from the church.

I hear Marcos yelling at Diego, but his voice gets quieter as we put more and more distance between us.

We come up to Kosia and Preko's market cart at the end of the plaza. Rafael drags me to the side of their store.

"Rafael, what the hell just happened?" Kosia scowls, her voice harsh and demanding.

He ignores her, standing in front of me and bending down so his face is at the same height as mine.

"Are you alright? Are you hurt?"

I shake my head. "I'm fine."

I can't bring myself to look him in the eye. Not after the display of camaraderie I just witnessed. Rafael knows these men, counts on them, works with them. He trusts them more than he trusts me. And, as such, my trust in him wanes.

Adanna scoffs. "Maybe physically. But he just threatened her. Put a sword to her throat!" The top of her handkerchief has become a darker blue, growing wetter from the rain.

Rafael's brow wrinkles, his eyes hard. He watches me, waiting for me to break.

I half expect it. But I realize I really am fine. A bit shaken up, perhaps. But I don't feel scared. I stood up to him. Diego knows now that I will not give up so easily.

In truth, it feels exhilarating.

"Are you really going to let him stay?" Adanna's voice is outraged.

Rafael straightens and steps away from me, running a hand down his face. "Marcos trusts him."

"And that is enough for you?" I ask.

"For now." He pauses. "I will make sure he stays far away from all of you."

"Rafael, explain," Kosia forces out. "Now."

He sighs wearily, turning toward her. I know a dismissal when I see it.

"We'll go," Adanna says.

"Wait, Catalina," he says softly. "Your family?"

I know what he's asking. And my adrenaline drains all at once as I remember what Diego told me.

He can see it in my face.

"I am sorry," he whispers.

Adanna puts her arm around my shoulders and guides us back into the street.

"*No me digas!*"

Adanna has just finished telling the story of my encounter with Diego. And apparently, it is good entertainment.

"I can't believe he did that," Leonor mutters in awe. *"Dios santo."*

Next to her, Juliana clasps her hand over her mouth.

"Let me get this straight. A soldier had a sword pointed at your throat. And instead of protecting yourself like a normal person, you stepped *into* the sword?" Constanza's voice is laced with disbelief, her eyebrow raised and her eyes wide.

I don't answer, but Adanna nods emphatically.

"That is insane," Juliana whispers. "You're insane."

"Yes, that may be true," I laugh.

I certainly feel a little crazy. It has only been a few hours since I saw Diego this morning, but I feel like an entirely different person. As shocked as my friends may be, I guarantee I am more surprised. The Catalina I know would not have challenged a soldier with a sword. But I did. Whether or not that was the right decision, it makes me feel powerful. I like it.

Word spreads quickly that soldiers have arrived, and soon our entire class is whispering instead of meditating. It isn't long before we give up altogether, and the girls gather around to hear the story, our voices echoing in the church chapel while the sound of rain comes through the roof.

"You're not actually going to leave, are you?" Leonor asks.

I heave a sigh, unsure of how to answer.

"It would be foolish to go back," Constanza says in her matter-of-fact voice.

I try not to roll my eyes at her, but I can't keep the sarcasm out of my voice. "Yes, thank you for your input, Constanza."

She smirks at me. "Always here to help."

"I don't know," I answer. Leonor is looking at me, still waiting for my response. "I need to do something, right? I can't just leave my mother and sister to rot in jail."

"But what can you do?" Leonor asks the question, genuinely wanting an answer. So different from the mocking tone Diego used with me this morning.

What *can* I do?

A blanket of despair falls over our group. Adanna, Leonor, and Constanza have all lost their parents. Araceli lives with her family, and Juliana still has her papá, but her empathy touches me when she reaches out to squeeze my hand. We stay silent.

Finally, Adanna clears her throat.

"I think you should stay, Cata," she states. "I think you should stay in Castellfollit, at least for now. We'll wait for any more news about your family—keep our ear to the ground. And in the meantime, we search for other solutions and ideas. Yes?"

She says the last sentence to the rest of the group, looking each of them in the eyes and waiting for their confirmation.

"If you get better at etheric travel, you may be able to visit Banyoles," Leonor suggests. "Or at least be able to see inside the city." Her voice gets quieter and she shrugs, looking down.

"That's a really good idea," Adanna says. Leonor raises her head, her mouth stretched in a proud grin.

"I mean, it would be harder for me to go there because I have never been," Leonor explains. "I could still try, though. Or, at least help you get better at it."

"That would be great, Leonor," I say.

"I will figure out what I can do, too," Araceli says. Her eyebrows are drawn together in a concentrated expression. "I don't know yet, but I'll think about it." She sounds so determined.

Constanza clears her throat. "As useful as all of you would be, Catalina's gift will be the most helpful."

"What do you mean?"

"You are a seer," she replies. "You know things, and with people as close as your family, you should be able to feel some sort of connection to them."

The corners of my mouth turn down. Why hadn't I thought of that? I have been so focused on gaining other skills, becoming like Inés and Adanna, that I disregarded what comes so naturally to me. But Constanza is right—I have a connection with my family.

"That is true," Juliana says with a smile. She reaches into the pocket of her apron, pulling out a muted green stone. "I wondered why I brought this with me. It's for you."

She presses the cold stone into my hand, but I shake my head.

"I cannot take your *fluorita*."

"Why not? It is the perfect stone for spiritual insights and clear visions. This is exactly what you need!"

I hesitantly close my fingers around the *fluorita* and offer Juliana a smile.

She grins back at me. "We'll help you be ready for Banyoles."

"You will get back to them, Catalina," Constanza says softly. Her normally hard exterior softens, and I see a nearly imperceptible smile of sympathy.

I nod back at her, grateful beyond words for these new friends of mine. It has only been a week that they have known me, yet they are willing to fight with me.

"Thank you." I can only whisper the words, my throat struggling to push down the tears threatening to spill.

We stay inside for a few hours, discussing everything from the soldiers, to the upcoming wedding, to last night's dinner.

A black cat meanders into our circle, rubbing her head against my arm affectionately, and we laugh in shock, wondering how she got into the church. I reach out to pet her head, but she slinks over to Adanna. She flicks her tail into Adanna's face before moving on to Constanza.

Soon, our group is giggling, taking turns petting her soft fur and mimicking her purrs and whines. Leonor pulls a little handkerchief from her dress and jerks it around on the ground while the cat pounces, grabbing for the corner.

We finally clamber to our feet and exit the chapel, stomachs rumbling.

"You go on ahead," I tell Adanna as the girls move toward the *residencia*. "I'm going to find Rafael or Kosia to make sure they know to keep looking out for any news about my family."

"Want me to come with you?"

"No, I'm fine," I say, walking backwards away from her. "It won't take long. Just save me some food, okay?" I wave to her as she laughs.

My steps start out hurried. But the streets are so quiet and peaceful. The sun is setting, and the cloudy sky begins to clear, leaving purples and pinks in its wake, the horizon glowing with the last yellow rays. It is still light enough to see easily without the lanterns.

I pause, taking a deep breath of the evening air, clean and cool from the day's rain. I think of Mamá and Inés. They seem far from me, but they live under this same setting sun.

I will see them soon. I am sure.

I am so lost in thought that I don't notice the tall figure approaching me. The sound of boots on the stone catch my attention.

My body tenses when I look up to see Diego walking toward me, a determined look in his eye.

He stops right in front of me.

Frantically, I look around the street, hoping for witnesses. But we are alone.

"Calm down," he says in a low voice. "I am not going to hurt you."

"Could have fooled me," I say. My hands tremble, but my voice comes out strong and steady. Good.

Diego sighs. Rubbing the back of his neck. He dips his head.

"I want to apologize."

"Pardon?" I must have heard him wrong.

"I'm sorry, Catalina," he whispers. "I don't know why—I don't know what got into me. I never should have drawn my sword. I just..."

His voice trails off. I stare at his face, still looking down.

"Look at me," I tell him. My voice comes out a little harsher than I intended, but it makes him listen.

His head snaps up, and his eyes meet mine.

I study them, searching for the mocking amusement I saw today. But there is no trace. He seems genuine in his apology.

"You really are sorry," I mumble.

Diego nods, his face screwed up as if he is in pain.

I clear my throat. "What are you doing here, Diego?"

"I wanted to say I am sorry, and I wanted to make things right."

"No. What are you doing *here*, in Castellfollit?"

His hands stop moving. His feet stop shifting. It is like he has been frozen. He opens his mouth, then closes it again.

I deserve an answer. I *need* an answer. What are these soldiers from Banyoles doing in the witch town of Castellfollit?

Rafael says Marcos has been helping for years, providing inside information and ushering witches to safety when he can. But that can't be all. And that certainly does not explain Diego's recent involvement.

"Well?" I ask when he stays quiet.

Frustrated, I resign myself to never receiving an answer. I turn away from him, but he stops me with a hand on my elbow.

"Wait," he says, frantic. He heaves a frustrated sigh and squeezes his eyes shut. "I'm not here to hurt anyone, okay? I am here to help."

"Here to help," I repeat. My voice is flat, my eyelids drooping in disbelief.

Diego opens his eyes and straightens his back, pulling himself up to his full height. "Yes. I don't expect you to believe me, but I will prove it."

He takes a glance around the street and gently guides me into the tiny space between two buildings.

I should run. I should scream.

But I am not afraid. I'm curious.

"If you are going back to Banyoles," he pauses, giving me a hard look, "you need to be able to defend yourself."

Diego pulls a dagger from his belt and presents it to me, holding it flat in both hands.

The knife is small, the blade a little longer than my hand.

"This is you proving that you want to help? Giving me a knife?"

"Yes. Well, no," he mutters, taking in my reaction. "I mean, I don't know. But I had to do something."

I sigh. "And your solution is bringing another weapon into the situation."

Diego groans. "Would you just take it?"

"We're not allowed weapons," I say, not taking my eyes off the dagger.

"I won't tell if you won't."

I hear his smile before I see it. The light is dim, but his white teeth match the gleam in his eyes.

Slowly, I grip the dagger by the handle, and my fingers brush his palm. His skin is warm, yet chills run down my spine.

"Maybe I don't want it," I say, even though it is already in my hands. "I don't believe in violence."

"Could have fooled me."

"What is that supposed to mean?" I raise my voice, and he tries to shush me. I see red.

"Well, you seem pretty intent on fighting me every chance you get. Arguing with me, throwing dirt in my face, stepping into my sword."

"You," I volley back, "are the one who pulled your sword in the first place."

"*Por el amor de Dios*. Take the damn knife, Catalina."

Rolling my eyes at his clipped tone, I say nothing. Mamá always taught us to keep the peace, avoid conflict, and never curse in order to keep our energy balanced. Weapons go against everything I know as an *hechicera*. And yet, I want it.

I hold the dagger awkwardly, my grip loose. "I don't know how to use it," I confess.

"Well, that can be easily fixed," he huffs. He removes the leather sheath protecting the blade. "Hold it like this."

Diego's large hands cover mine, carefully repositioning the weapon. He places the dagger so the blade sticks out away from my pinky finger. My hand wraps around the handle. My thumb comes up to cover the dagger's hilt, but Diego slides it around the handle.

"Grip it tight," he says. He smiles when my knuckles whiten. "Good. Now, just..." He frowns, stuttering on his words, and he pauses as though he is unsure how to proceed.

In a fluid motion, he moves behind me, wrapping his arms around my body.

I shove him off, jerking my elbow back into his stomach. "What are you doing?"

I whirl around to face him, and Diego backs away, his hands out in front of him in surrender.

"I just wanted to show you how to use the knife."

"Don't touch me," I spit out. He nods quickly, his eyes wide.

I clutch the dagger like a lifeline, trying to stop myself from visibly shaking. I can still feel the heat of his chest at my back, even though he hardly touched me.

Diego comes to stand in front of me again, approaching me slowly, the way you would a wounded animal. "I'm sorry. I should have asked. May I?" He gestures to my right hand, and when I nod stiffly, he takes a soft hold of the hand with the dagger.

"Slash like this." He moves my arm side to side across my body, my thumb facing my stomach, and the blade facing out. "Stab like this." Guiding my hand slightly above my head, he brings it down slowly, imitating a stabbing motion.

"That is all you need," Diego says softly. He releases my hand like he has been burned, stepping away swiftly.

"That's it?"

He chuckles. "That is all you need to defend yourself, yes."

I study the knife again. The blade is no wider than two of my fingers, coming to a frighteningly sharp point. The handle is longer than my hand is wide, and a small crossguard sticks out perpendicular to the blade. The silver hilt is lined with subtle engravings, giving the grip a textured feel.

I have never had anything like it. I have never even touched anything like it.

"I don't have anywhere to keep it," I say. When he frowns, I clarify, "I don't have a belt, and it will not fit in my boot. I don't have anywhere to hide it." I sheath it and hold it out to give it back to him.

His frown deepens. Diego steps forward and wraps my fingers around the handle once more.

"It is yours, Catalina," he says. "We will just have to find a way for you to keep it on you."

"And until then?"

He grins. "Keep it under your pillow."

With that, he backs out of the small alleyway and disappears into the street.

The night has grown much darker. I feel disoriented as I look left and right, trying to remember where I was going before this encounter.

That does not matter now. I need to get back to my room to stash the knife.

Hurrying toward the *residencia*, I slip inside and race up the stairs, all but running to my room. My right hand holds the dagger at the handle, positioning it vertically along my arm. I keep my arm close to my body in hopes that the weapon won't be obviously visible.

Fortunately, the only people in the house are those downstairs for dinner. I'm glad I told Adanna to go on without me.

I rush into my room and quietly close the door behind me. Letting out a relieved sigh, I remove the leather sheath to take another look at the dagger.

It should feel wrong, having this weapon. I should feel nervous. But this knife gives me confidence and a sense of security, however misguided that may be.

I lift my pillow and carefully place the dagger under it. But that's not enough. I pull the blanket up higher near the head of the bed and hide the dagger within the fabric before settling the pillow on top.

Satisfied it is properly hidden, I take a moment to calm myself. My heartbeat hasn't slowed down since I spotted Diego in the street. If anything, it has sped up, working overtime.

I look in the small mirror hanging on Adanna's side of the room. My cheeks are tinged pink from the cool night air and the hectic run to my room.

My braids have come loose, ribbon slowly untangling itself from my hair. I untie them and run my fingers through my hair. I don't know when it got so long. It brushes my lower back now. I think about braiding it again, but I haven't the patience.

Instead, I stare at my clear blue eyes, wishing I looked more like Mamá. I wish I had her warm brown eyes. I wish I could see her in the mirror in front of me.

But I don't. I only see a naive girl who looks like the ghost of her father.

I swallow my sadness and, carefully closing the door behind me, leave our room.

22

The next morning, we walk to class as a group. Adanna, Constanza, Leonor, Juliana, Araceli, and me, along with little Tomasina and Ana Clara, who follow after us with beaming smiles.

"So, last night," Leonor starts telling us, "Juliana and I decided we wanted to commune with the dead, like Adanna taught us. We were kind of messing around, just having a little fun."

"We were partly serious, though," Juliana adds hastily. "I mean, we definitely wanted to speak with the dead."

"Right, that's true. Anyway," Leonor continues, "we were in my room, and we lit a candle and meditated. We were actually giving it our all. And then it grew deathly quiet." Her voice lowers to a whisper as she faces us with wide eyes. "And we knew a ghost was about to communicate with us."

Juliana nods in agreement. "We were so quiet; we didn't move or even breathe. It was so tense as we just waited."

"Then, bam! Constanza whips the door open, and I swear I have never been so scared in all my life," Leonor says.

"You two screamed so loud, I thought someone was dying," Constanza comments with a smirk. "Juliana fell and almost knocked over the candle."

"Yeah, we screamed so loud that you jumped, too," Juliana says. Constanza scowls at her, but the rest of us cackle.

We laugh loudly all the way to the church, and I feel like a little girl again, giggling over silly things with my silly friends. It feels good.

Once we're within earshot of the school, Adanna hushes us.

On the steps in front of the door, Kosia shakes her head emphatically while Rafael throws his hands out, gesturing wildly. We aren't close enough to make out what they're saying, just the occasional hiss from their agitated whispers.

Rafael sees us and stops mid-sentence. He straightens and nods in our direction, causing Kosia to follow his line of sight.

"Buenos dias, chicas," she calls. Her worried face transforms into a big smile.

"What's going on?" Adanna asks as we approach. She and Constanza lead the group, the rest of us straggling behind.

"Rafael and I simply have a difference of opinion," Kosia says stiffly.

Rafael rolls his eyes. "Well, why don't we ask them?"

"Out of the question," she snaps at Rafael.

Juliana awkwardly shifts from one foot to the other, and Leonor coughs loudly. She is trying to cover her nervous laugh, something I have noticed Leonor does amidst conflict.

"Alright, then I assume you have this covered?" Rafael asks, not looking at Kosia. He starts walking away before she answers. "I have some people to talk to."

Kosia sighs and opens the big wood door, ushering us inside.

"What was that about, Kosia?" Constanza asks.

Kosia shakes her head. "Rafael is under the impression that his soldier friends should be included in all town activities. Apparently, they want to sit in on our *hechicería* studies."

Adanna frowns. "Why?"

"Rafael says they want to get to know everyone better," Kosia explains. "However, I was under the impression they wouldn't be staying for long."

"How long are they staying?" I ask. "They are supposed to go back to their posts, are they not?"

"One would think."

The door opens again, and another group enters the school. I see Andrea, Sofia, and Rosa walk in together, Señora Vargas not far behind. Kosia turns away from us to greet them.

Leonor and Adanna meander up to the front. The rest of us follow, taking seats in the two front rows.

Juliana twists in her seat to face Adanna, Araceli, and me. "I don't think it would be so bad if they came to our classes," she says.

"No, it's ridiculous," Constanza counters. "There's absolutely no reason for them to attend."

"I agree," Leonor says. Juliana whips her head to look at her, affronted. Juliana looks shocked that Leonor disagrees with her. "What? It's just kind of weird, right?"

I am about to agree, but Adanna speaks first.

"I don't know, actually," she says. "It might be helpful for them to understand these so-called witches that the Inquisition is after are no threat. We're just normal people. We have made no deals with the devil." She finishes the last sentence with a dramatic eye roll.

"I didn't think of it like that," I say quietly, humming in thought.

Adanna shrugs. "I am not saying I want them to stay in town, but it could be useful."

"Well, after yesterday," Leonor says, "I don't think Catalina wants them to stay."

Constanza snorts, and Araceli pats my knee, giving me a sympathetic look.

Kosia walks to the front of the class and motions for the girls to turn back around.

"Good morning, everyone," she greets us. "I want to get started today with talking about the skill of seeing and prophesying."

Adanna nudges me, and Constanza glances back in my direction.

"There are many of you for whom this comes naturally," Kosia continues. "So we definitely want to hear your input—"

She stops, and I see her entire body stiffen, her gaze locked on the back wall.

The class turns to see Rafael bringing Marcos, Diego, and Alferez into the chapel. The three soldiers take a seat on a bench farther back and across the aisle from us.

Rafael makes his way to the front, next to Kosia.

"Our friends are curious about *hechicería*," Rafael announces. "I thought it could be a good experience for them to sit in on a few of our classes." He pauses, slowly looking around at everyone. "If anyone has a problem with it or feels uncomfortable, let's discuss it after class. But right now, just give them a chance, alright?"

He takes a step to the side and looks to Kosia.

She clears her throat, jaw tight. "As I was saying, we will be learning more about prophesying. We have several *videntes* among us," she says, looking at me and motioning to a few others. "Even if you don't feel qualified, please feel free to offer your insights."

I nod when her gaze turns to me, knowing her last statement was for my benefit.

"Let's start off with listing some of the ways you can experience sight and prophecy."

"What do you mean? Like dreams and stuff?" Juliana asks hesitantly.

"That is one of the ways, yes," Kosia answers. "Dreams and visions are certainly a common method that many people don't even realize they experience."

"You can also see energy," Adanna says. "Like auras around or inside people."

I raise my hand. "I am not entirely sure if this falls under seeing, necessarily," I start. "But there is also just knowing. I don't know how else to describe it."

Kosia smiles. "That is another way to prophesy. Can you explain what that is like?"

I let out a sigh. One would think that after an entire life of this, I would have figured out a way to explain. I try to take courage in the fact that there are more people here who will understand me, even if I cannot perfectly describe my experience.

"Well, for me, it is more just a thought that comes into my mind. Like, I suddenly think that someone will be at my front door, and then they are. It isn't quite a vision. It doesn't even feel different than any other thought, which is why it can be so hard to decipher your own mind from the premonitions of the future."

"How did you figure out your thoughts were actually prophecies?" Leonor turns in her seat to ask.

"Something would happen, and my sister would comment on how weird or unexpected it was. And then I realized I already knew it would happen, so I wasn't surprised at all. Once I recognized that, I saw it happen over and over, until I knew that a lot of my thoughts were a result of this ability. After that, you just have to trust yourself and your intuition."

"I don't understand."

It's one of the soldiers in the back. Diego.

"How can you just *know* something?" Diego asks, brow furrowed. "Without a spell or a vision or anything?"

I tense at the feeling of being questioned and doubted.

"This isn't witchcraft, young man," Kosia says, glowering at his use of the word *spell*. "At least, not the kind that has been so sensationalized by witch hunters. This is *hechicería*. It is the result of the energy from the earth and from the people around us. This *knowing* is only being perceptive to that energy."

Marcos leans back, arms folded over his chest, face passive. He looks to Diego, observing him and the scene unfolding.

Diego frowns. "But if that was the case," he argues, "then anyone could do it."

"Anyone can." The words rush out of me before I have a chance to think about them.

It is true, though. At least, I believe it is.

"Sure, it comes more naturally for some, but I believe this receptiveness and awareness can be learned," I say. "If you are willing."

Diego stares at me, his rich brown eyes flood my body with warmth. I try not to fidget under the scrutiny.

When I turn away, I realize everyone else is staring at me, too. I look to Kosia, Adanna, then Rafael.

"Was that wrong?" My voice sounds so weak. But I am beginning to think I have spoken some sort of untruth.

Instead of answering, Kosia looks to the group. "What do you think? Do you think Catalina is right in saying that *hechicería* can be learned?"

"Definitely," Adanna says.

"I think so," Leonor comments with a shrug.

A chorus of agreeing hums and nods echo their sentiment, and I relax.

"I think so, too," Kosia says. "Though I also concur with the statement that it comes easier for some than others. We know this from experience, right? As we try to learn a skill that is so natural for someone else."

"And it will always be that way," Constanza says. "But that does not mean we shouldn't try."

Once again, I see the group nod.

"It appears you have already learned something from this class." Kosia offers a tight smile to the three soldiers sitting at the back of the chapel.

Before she can say anything more, the door to the church opens loudly.

It is a young woman, probably in her early twenties. Her thin frame is wrapped in a worn and faded scarf that she pulls tightly around herself as Señora Ayala guides her inside with a gentle hand around her shoulders. The young woman's light brown hair escapes the bun at the back of her head, falling around her pale face in soft waves.

"Oh, Teodora, I'm glad you're here." Kosia raises her voice to call out to the woman. "This is Teodora. She came into town late last night." She holds her hand out, gesturing to the woman in the back.

She looks haggard, tired. Her eyes seem empty and sad. And when she makes eye contact with me, my body goes cold. What has she seen?

"Teodora, will you please come up here and tell everyone what you told me last night?"

The woman hesitates. Señora Ayala pats her hand in encouragement.

"No specifics. Just the general news," Kosia clarifies. "I feel that everyone has a right to know about the developments regarding the Inquisition."

Teodora slowly makes her way to the front.

"I am not doing this to frighten anyone," Kosia says. She looks around the room slowly, and her eyes pause on me for a second too long. "As I said, I feel you should know."

She steps to the side and nods to Teodora.

"Uh, alright," Teodora stutters, wringing her hands. "I just came from Viladrau."

"Where is that?" Adanna whispers to me.

"Way farther than Banyoles," I whisper back. "Mamá said there had been a lot of arrests there."

Teodora continues. "I was accused of witchcraft, like many other women in my town. I saw them coming. I ran." She shakes her head. "But I am assuming Kosia would like me to tell you about the acts of the Inquisition. As you probably know, they have targeted witches, as well as those suspected of homosexual relationships and those suspected of practicing Judaism."

She pauses, and I watch the blood drain from her face. She looks like she may be sick—like she might faint.

"Teodora?" Kosia takes a step closer.

"I'm fine," she says, her voice hoarse. Teodora swallows hard before continuing. "Arrests have turned to executions."

My stomach drops.

"Not many," she clarifies quickly. "But a few of the people convicted have been burned at the stake." Teodora's voice trails into a whisper.

But her voice permeates, striking through the chest of everyone here.

My vision darkens. The floor tilts.

She keeps talking, but I can't make sense of her words.

I stand, nearly tripping over Araceli, and run down the aisle toward the door. I think someone calls after me, but I am not sure.

Arrests have turned to executions.

My lungs heave as I throw myself out the door.

Burned at the stake.

My legs keep going, taking me down the street.

Your mother and sister are still in jail.

I can hardly see; my vision is blurry. Someone grabs my shoulders from behind, spinning me around and into their arms.

Adanna.

I try to shove her off, but it's a poor attempt. She holds me tight, and I finally cling to her.

"Breathe, Cata," she tells me. "Breathe with me, okay? In. Hold. Out. Hold."

I squeeze my eyes shut and listen to Adanna's instructions, inhaling and exhaling when she tells me.

When I open my eyes, she looks right at me.

"That was in Viladrau, Catalina. Not Banyoles."

"That doesn't mean it won't happen in Banyoles, too," I whisper.

"No, but it also doesn't mean we should assume it will."

The two of us walk to the small courtyard outside the church, the end point of the town that drops off at the sheer cliffs.

We sit on the ground, and my mind is already reeling.

"I cannot stay here any longer," I say.

"How many times are we going to do this?" Her voice is a bored drawl.

I turn on her. "This is my family, Adanna. This is not some frivolous conversation."

"No, it's not. Which is why you need to stop playing this game, thinking you can be the hero when you have absolutely no plan," she fires back, her voice stern.

I expect her to apologize. I expect her to hug me or offer comforting words.

But she levels me with a hard stare. It shocks me.

I realize she is right, though. Again.

As if she can see my thoughts, Adanna addresses my next question. "We are not giving up, Cata. We will find a way to get you back, to get your family back. But you need to get smart about it," she says.

I sigh. "You are right."

"I know."

We sit there in silence, leaning back and closing our eyes against the sun.

Finally, Adanna stands.

"Take a minute to process this, okay?" She holds my hand in hers and gives it a light squeeze. "I'm here."

I nod and watch her slowly walk back into the church.

She is right. If I am going to help my family, I need to be ready to really help them. I cannot just go into Banyoles because I feel guilty that I am free while they are jailed.

They will arrest you, too. You cannot help them.

You will be taken easily, killed in a minute.

And then, just like that, I have an idea.

Adrenaline flooding my body, I start walking back to the door of the church. I can do this. I can save myself, my mother, and my sister. But I need help.

Rehearsing the conversation in my mind, I reach toward the door and nearly get knocked down when it swings open.

Diego's eyes widen in surprise. The door falls closed behind him, and I motion for him to follow me as we put distance between ourselves and the church.

I finally turn to face him. "I need your help," I whisper roughly.

He takes a step back, but I grab onto his arm to keep him there. I have to get this out before I lose my nerve.

His tan forehead is lined, and his brows tense as he searches my face. His eyes are much lighter in the sun. They're like liquid gold. I have never seen his eyes look this way.

"I was actually—"

"I need you to train me," I say, "on how to use the dagger. And how to defend myself."

"I already showed you—"

I cut him off again. "No, I need more than the basics. I need to be able to fend someone off."

"You want to learn to fight?"

I nod.

"You?" he repeats. "The girl who judged me for my supposedly violent career choice."

I don't want to think about what he is saying, or about what I am asking of him. If I think, I will back down. I can't do that.

"This is because of what that girl said, isn't it? Teodora," he mutters. His eyes stay on mine, and I try to keep my gaze steady and confident.

He sighs, running his fingers through his dark hair. I notice a large silver band on the ring finger of his right hand, glinting in the sunlight.

"Catalina, I can't do that," Diego finally says. "I shouldn't have even given you the knife." He drops his head with another sigh.

I smother my disappointment and irritation. He will not get rid of me this easily.

"Then why did you?" I ask.

"I don't know. It was foolish," he spits.

My jaw hurts from clenching my teeth together, and I force myself to breathe before I break my teeth.

"You are the one who pulled your sword on me. The one who chased me away from my home." I scoff, my upper lip curling in disgust. "You didn't think giving me a little present would make up for that, did you?"

He won't meet my eye, but I refuse to look away.

"What do you want from me, Catalina?"

"I told you. I want you to train me, teach me," I say, throwing my hands in the air. "I want to not be powerless. I want to be able to do something. Anything."

"You are learning the *hechicería* they teach here," he says, tilting his head as he studies me. "And, based on what you said in there, you are anything but powerless, *brujita*."

I let out a cry of frustration. "Yes, I sometimes know the future and, occasionally, I can help heal people. All so very helpful when it comes to fighting that Inquisition you are a part of."

His shoulders jump an inch, tightening defensively. I see his fingers roll into fists at his sides.

"I am not a part of arresting and killing innocent people," he snarls.

I take a step closer to him, toe to toe. I stare up into his face. "You wear that very uniform, Diego Tremiño."

His entire body is vibrating. I'm not sure if he knows it. But I can feel the confusion, anger, hurt, and fear coming off him in waves.

"Why me?" he asks. "Why would you want me to teach you? You hate me."

"Perhaps," I say, my voice hushed, "but that doesn't mean I cannot use you."

He groans, scrubbing a hand over his face.

"If you want to make up for what you have done, you will train me to defend myself and keep myself safe. An innocent woman accused of witchcraft."

I am shocked at my boldness. What makes me think I can convince this soldier to help me? A soldier who owes me nothing, who dislikes me as much as I hate him.

But I see the moment he gives up.

"*Mierda*," he whispers.

I know I have won. I grin.

"On one condition."

I pause, waiting.

"You teach me, too," Diego says.

I stumble back in surprise. That's the last thing I would have imagined him to say.

"Pardon?" I ask, shaking my head. "Teach you what?"

"*Hechicería*. You said anyone can learn it, did you not?"

"Well, yes. I did, but—"

"Then let me learn it."

His face looks more confident than it had a moment ago. He folds his arms over his chest as he looks down at me with an arched brow.

Can I teach him *hechicería*? Though I do believe anyone can do it, I am unsure whether or not I will be able to train him in it.

But if I want to learn to defend myself, I don't really have a choice, do I?

"I will do what I can," I acquiesce. "And don't call me *brujita*."

As soon as I enter the dining room, Adanna catches my attention with a wave of her long arm. She motions for me to join them, pointing to the seat next to her.

I move toward her and see Preko sitting down at her other side, with Constanza across from him.

"I got everything in doubles, so you can just share off my plate, if that's alright," Adanna says to me.

I grin at her, slowly lowering myself onto the bench.

"*Gracias*, Adanna." I lean over and give her a kiss on the cheek. "You are a gem."

"Yes, it's true," she says. "If you could start spreading the word, that would be great. The people need to know."

"I already know," Preko says.

"Well, you're not people, honey."

Preko begins to argue, but Constanza cuts him off.

"There you are, Catalina," she says. It is not a question, but she doesn't say it with her usual haughty indifference. In fact, if I didn't know better, I might think she is concerned about me.

I never returned to class after I ran out and convinced Diego to train me. Instead, I took a walk around town, going in circles until I remembered how small the town really is.

Adanna doesn't say anything about my panic attack, just nudges her plate closer, offering the food she got for me.

I am about to ask about the rest of class when Marcos comes up to our table, setting a plate down on the opposite side of Adanna and next to Constanza.

"May I join you?"

Constanza stares at him, her nose wrinkling in disgust, and says nothing. Adanna feels me tense and studies me out of the corner of her eye.

"I don't know…" she starts.

"You know any cool stories?" Preko asks eagerly.

Marcos smiles and takes a seat. Constanza inches away from him, not so subtly. I can still feel Adanna's eyes on me, so I nod to her, and she finally looks away.

"What kind of stories?" Marcos asks.

"Like legends or myths, or gossip. Anything, really."

That lessens the tension. Adanna and I snicker, exchanging a look. Preko draws back, scowling.

"Preko must know everything. How do you manage to get everyone to tell you stories?" I lean around Adanna to see his face.

He grins, a little dimple popping in his left cheek. "I'm adorable."

Adanna cackles.

"I've got something," Marcos says. "Have you ever heard of the transporting soldier?"

Preko shakes his head. Marcos looks at the rest of us, but we shake our heads as well.

"Oh, it's a new one for everyone," Marcos says. "This is actually a true story."

"Of course it is," Constanza mutters.

"It happened more than twenty years ago in New Spain," Marcos begins, ignoring Constanza's skepticism. "One day, a Spanish soldier—a palace guard from the Philippines— appeared in the *Plaza Mayor*. Officials in the area noticed he was wearing the wrong uniform, so they confronted him, thinking he was a deserter.

"The soldier was frantic, panicked. He explained that he had just been in Manila moments ago. He said he was feeling dizzy and leaned against a wall, resting his eyes for a few seconds. But when he opened them again, he was here."

Preko leans forward, eyes wide, absolutely enthralled. I notice Constanza and Adanna have forgotten their food as well, concentrating on Marcos.

"Of course, the men did not believe him. Who would, with a claim like that? However, the soldier continued to argue, trying to make his case. He told the men about the assassination of Governor Pérez Dasmariñas that had happened the night before. The governor had been killed by Chinese pirates, and the guards of *Palacio del Gobernador* were awaiting the appointment of a new governor, which is why he was wearing the palace guard uniform.

"Nobody believed him, so he was arrested and thrown in jail for being a deserter, as well as a servant of the devil. But months later, a ship arrived from Manila, bearing news of the assassination of Pérez Dasmariñas. People recognized the story and realized the soldier had every detail right.

"They brought the soldier out of jail, and one of the ship's passengers recognized the soldier, saying he had seen him the day after the governor's death in Manila."

Constanza's eyebrows jump, and Preko's mouth falls open.

"With no reason to consider him a deserter, authorities eventually released the soldier and allowed him to go home. Some people still believed he was a servant of the devil, a witch, or a demon. That is how he must have teleported, or how he knew what happened. Others believed he was just lying, but no one could ever explain how the soldier knew of the governor's death," Marcos finishes.

"Is he telling you that teleporting soldier story?"

Pedro arrives with Alferez and Diego, just in time to hear the end of the story.

"It's one of his favorites," Pedro says with a laugh. He and Alferez take a seat, joining our group without a second thought.

Diego stands right next to Marcos, across from me, but he doesn't sit. He just holds his plate, staring at me. His eyes slowly move around my face, a line between his eyebrows in a scowl.

"Are you going to sit?" Marcos asks Diego.

Diego startles. "Oh, yes." He sets his plate down and takes a seat, not looking at me again.

"That is so crazy," Preko says to Marcos in an awed voice. It takes me a second to remember what he is talking about.

"It's not true," Alferez says, sitting next to Preko. "It is just a legend. The soldier was a deserter, and that's that."

Marcos shakes his head, a small smile gracing his lips. "I knew a man who knew the soldier. He was in New Spain at the time and says it really happened."

Pedro laughs. "You knew a man who knew a man."

"So you think it is true?" Alferez arches a brow. "Then how did he do it? How did a man just show up from across the ocean?"

"Witchcraft, maybe?" Marcos shrugs.

"That's not how it works, though," Preko argues. "We can't do anything like that. It is not natural."

"Sure, we can't," Adanna says, a mischievous grin on her face, "but we haven't sold our souls to the devil. Not yet, at least." Her eyes go wide, and she wiggles her eyebrows at Preko.

Preko and I laugh. I even see the corner of Constanza's mouth go up in a crooked smile.

"I do not know how it happened. I just know it did," Marcos says, leaning back in his seat with his hands behind his head. "What do you think, Diego?"

Diego freezes mid-movement, his cup halfway to his mouth. "What?"

"Do you think it's real?" Pedro asks him.

Diego's eyes flicker from Pedro to me. He clears his throat once—twice—then sets his cup down and shrugs.

"Anything is possible, right?" he says.

I hear Alferez groan. "No. Wrong."

Diego sticks out his bottom lip, giving Alferez an exaggerated pout. "Oh, did I not give you the answer you wanted?"

Pedro and Marcos snicker. Alferez rolls his eyes.

Every interaction between the four men gives me more information, but also more questions. It is clear that Alferez and Pedro are very familiar with Marcos. They know Diego, but not well. However, he seems to be well liked by all of them.

Diego and Marcos are quite obviously close. Of course, I already knew that they grew up together in some small town in Navarre. But it is even more apparent that Diego considers Marcos to be an older brother figure, while Marcos not only protects, but also trusts Diego.

There is something more there. They have experienced some-thing more than their childhood.

"If it had been a woman," Constanza interjects, "they never would have released her. Even after she had been proved right."

Sadness flickers on Adanna's face. "Probably."

"They would have called her a witch and burned her at the stake once the people knew she had been right about the assassination," Constanza adds bitterly.

"You think so?" Marcos asks.

"Most definitely."

Somehow, I have stopped paying attention to the conversation, staring forward, my eyes dazed. But I see Diego's eyes crinkle at the edges, silently laughing, and I realize it is him I have been staring at.

My cheeks heat, and I quickly turn my attention back to my food, taking a hurried bite. But my mouth has gone dry, and it is difficult to chew.

Adanna makes a sound in her throat, something between a laugh and a cough. When I look at her, she flicks her eyes to Diego and back to me while raising an eyebrow.

I haven't told her about my interactions with Diego—the one where he gave me the dagger and the one where I convinced him to teach me to fight. Yet she acts as though she is in on the secret. She knows something has happened.

I nudge her side with my elbow, trying to get her to shut up, but she just laughs.

Between Diego's unnerving gaze and Adanna's smug looks, I am eager to finish my dinner without further incident.

"Hey, Catalina."

I turn to see Juliana and Leonor approaching our table. Leonor slides onto the bench next to Preko and takes a bit of food off his plate, resulting in a cry of outrage.

"I was wondering," Juliana starts, "if you would come with me to visit that new family—the Estradas, the ones who came into town a few nights ago. The little girl has had a really bad stomachache, and it keeps getting worse."

I shake my head immediately. "Oh, I am not sure how much help I would be, Juliana. That's your area of expertise, not mine."

"Don't be a baby," Adanna says.

"Pardon?" I ask, turning to her.

"You heard me." She lifts her chin and levels me with a look, challenging me.

"Go on and help the girl, Catalina," Marcos comments.

Adanna narrows her eyes at him. "Shut up," she snaps.

Juliana smirks before addressing me once more. "Look, you wanted to get better at *curandismo,* and I could really use some help. Especially with your knowledge of medicinal herbs. You are like a walking apothecary."

"Except I don't actually have all those herbs in my pocket."

"No, but you know which ones do what," she argues. "So will you come with me? Please?"

"Of course, I will go with you, *prima.*"

"I will see you later tonight, then," Adanna says. "Good luck, you two!"

Juliana and I wave goodbye, and I follow her out of the *residencia.* We walk down the road toward the town's entrance, and it strikes me again how small this place is. With a main road that leads from one end to the other, I have found myself thinking of everything in terms of the church on one side and the entrance on the other.

Instead of going into a home, we enter the inn. It is small but welcoming. Cozy. Short tables and chairs are spread throughout the space, covering the wooden floor. Two men sit at one table in the corner, hardly glancing up at us, but the rest of the tables are empty. A warm fire burns in the large stone hearth at one end of the room. At the back of the dimly lit inn, a plain wooden staircase climbs to the second floor, disappearing above us.

"They haven't found a permanent place, yet," Juliana explains as we climb the creaking stairs.

We knock at a dark wooden door and hear shuffling behind it. Juliana absentmindedly pats her pockets. I assume she has brought herbs with her, but I realize I have brought nothing. I didn't even think to bring anything.

The door opens, and the man I met a few nights ago smiles at us wearily.

"*Buenas noches*, Señor Estrada," Juliana greets him softly.

"Thank you so much for coming," he says. He steps aside and motions for us to enter. "This is my wife, Margarita, and my mother, Lucia."

It is a small room with only one bed, barely big enough to fit two people. The space is cramped with the family, becoming even tighter with us in it.

"We have another room next door," the woman explains, standing from the chair next to the bed, "but we are all concerned about Rosalia."

"Come here, girls," Lucia says. "Come, come."

She ushers us to Rosalia's bedside.

The sight of the little girl in bed makes my heart hurt. Her pale face is wet with sweat, and she can hardly keep her eyes open. Dark, curly hair spreads around her head in a frizzy halo. It makes her look like a younger version of her grandmother.

"Hi, Rosalia," Juliana says sweetly. "My name is Juliana, and this is my friend, Catalina. We're here to help you, okay?"

Rosalia nods, licking her chapped lips. "I remember you," she says weakly, pointing at me.

I smile down at her. "I remember you, too."

Juliana gently presses her hand to Rosalia's forehead, pushing her damp curls back from her face as the little girl closes her warm brown eyes.

"She has a bit of a fever, but not too bad," Juliana mutters to me.

I nod but say nothing. I take a step back, letting Juliana do her thing, not knowing how to help.

"I heard you had a stomachache," Juliana says.

"Yes," Rosalia whimpers. "My tummy has been hurting for a long time."

"It started two nights ago," Lucia says.

Instantly, my mind begins filing through the herbs that can help with stomachaches and digestive issues: *artemisa, ajenjo, romero, saúco, hinojo.*

"Any suggestions?"

It takes me a moment to realize that Juliana is asking me. But before I can begin listing the herbs, she fixes me with a look.

"Not just a list of herbs. Try to sense what she needs," she says.

And then, to my horror, Juliana steps back and pulls me forward, right next to Rosalia.

Panicked, I try to decide what to do.

"Have you been sick at all?" I ask Rosalia. What else can I ask her? How else can I stall as I try to find the *curandera* power within me?

"Four times," she says.

Now what?

Inés told me that she just knows, but that isn't helpful right now. What else did she say?

She told me it was like when I know something is going to happen. She told me to follow my intuition. I try to clear my mind and find it.

Without any other ideas, I take Rosalia's hand and close my eyes. I focus on Rosalia's clammy skin, her tiny hand. I search her body, letting my spirit feel the energy around her. Though my eyes are closed, I can see her clearly: her hand, up her skinny arm to her shoulder, across her chest, and down to her stomach. I can see the unsettled energy swirling around there, making her sick. I keep going. Down her other arm and back up to her neck, her head. I sense a darkness there, too. I think it is her fear, her anxiety, the emotional and physical upheaval of being forced from her home with danger and violence.

Albahaca.

Just like that, the herb comes to mind. That is all.

My eyes fly open.

"She needs a tea infusion of *albahaca*," I say.

I look to Juliana for confirmation. Her brow is furrowed, her eyes trained on Rosalia. My stomach sinks, and I drop my hand, afraid I have done it wrong.

But then, she begins to nod slowly.

"I think that is a good idea," she says. She turns to the girl's mother and grandmother. "Tonight and three times tomorrow—with each meal."

Juliana pulls bundles of herbs out of her pocket, looking for the right one. Lucia stops her with a soft hand on her arm.

"We have *albahaca*. Do not worry yourself, dear," Lucia says. "Thank you so much for your help."

I did it.

But we are not done.

I motion to Lucia and Margarita, and they shuffle closer as I glance at the little girl lying in bed.

"The *albahaca* will help her symptoms, but there is a deeper issue here," I explain. But then I hesitate, feeling foolish. Who am I to tell this family how to act or heal? What could I possibly say that will fix this?

Lucia studies me, reading me like a book.

"Go on, sweetheart," she says softly. "Whatever you have to say, it will be helpful for us to know as we move forward."

I nod once, clearing my throat. "Rosalia is young. She is trying to deal with this trial as best she can. She is still afraid. She's keeping it inside, trying to be strong, but she is still in shock," I say with a shrug, unsure of what advice to give them.

"We understand," Margarita whispers. "Thank you for telling us."

"I wish I could help more," I admit.

"You have done more than enough. Both of you," Lucia says. The old woman turns to me with a smile, and I grin back.

She kisses our cheeks, and the family bids us goodnight.

"You will start to feel better tomorrow morning," I call back to Rosalia. "But you still need to take the tea all three times tomorrow, alright?"

The girl gives me a small smile, and my heart warms.

Juliana and I shut the door quietly behind us and make our way down the stairs, careful not to make too much noise. It isn't terribly late, but I am sure there are many sleeping already.

As soon as we make it outside, I fling my arms around Juliana.

"I did it!" I squeal, and she hugs me back with a laugh.

"You did so good," she says. "I knew you could do it. You're a natural."

We break apart and start walking back the way we came, taking our time in the dark.

"That was incredible," I say. "I know what my sister is talking about now. I looked around and just knew that she needed *albahaca*. I don't know how, but I did!"

"And you were completely right."

My body vibrates; my blood sings.

"Thank you so much, Juliana. For bringing me, for helping me, and for believing in me. All of it."

"You make it easy," she says. "You are a talented *hechicera*."

"So are you."

She slows to a stop, and I frown before remembering she lives with her father, not at the *residencia*.

Juliana gives me another hug.

"Thank you for your help, Catalina," she says. "Sleep well. I will see you tomorrow, yes?"

I watch her ease the door open, letting a stream of candlelight out into the street. She waves again and closes it behind her, leaving me alone.

24

Though the moon is only half full, it offers enough light for me to make my way through the dark streets.

I am not allowed to have a weapon, let alone be trained to use it, so Diego agreed to help me, but only under the cover of darkness.

When I quietly left our room, Adanna was still awake. She looked at me, her eyes filled with questions and lined with concern. I told her I couldn't sleep and was going for a walk. I know she didn't believe me, but she let me go, and I snuck out with my dagger hidden in the folds of my dress.

The town is quiet, but a few homes still have warm candlelight in the windows. Other than my own shadow, no one joins me in the street. But I see something out of the corner of my eye.

My heart races, and I freeze. Do I hide? Do I run? I cannot hear anything, but I know I saw movement.

Just as I begin to convince myself I had imagined it, I see a dark form streak across the street in front of me.

A black cat.

I snicker as my muscles release their tension. I approach the cat, and it watches me with eyes that reflect the moonlight.

"Hello, *diablito*," I whisper, bending over to pet its soft fur. She leans her head into my hand, and I trail my hand down her back before moving on.

I stay close to the walls and sneak around the side of the church. At the back, Diego leans against the building, his arms crossed over his chest, and one leg casually placed on the wall.

He looks more relaxed than I have ever seen him. He doesn't have his sword strapped to his belt, as he so often does, and the sleeves of his white shirt are rolled up, the bright fabric a contrast to the tanned skin on his forearms.

He stares down at his hands, one of them rubbing the palm of the other, and I can see the veins and tendons in the moonlight. His hair falls into his face, covering it in shadow, but his neck snaps up as I rustle in the grass.

When he sees me, he kicks off the wall and approaches.

"How did the healing go?" Diego asks.

I grin. "It went really well."

I am about to explain, but when I see his blank face, I close my mouth again. We are not friends, and he does not care about my successes.

"You brought your dagger?"

I hold it up, and he nods.

"Listen," he says, "I have never trained anyone to fight or protect themselves, alright? I will do my best, but I do not know how much I'll actually help you."

Diego watches me carefully.

"I understand."

He lets out a breath, almost disappointed, as though he were hoping I would change my mind.

"You need to be able to defend yourself and get out of bad situations," he says thoughtfully, almost to himself.

I don't mention that most of my bad situations have involved him.

"Let's begin with some basics. Put your dagger away for now."

I place it in the prickly grass by the stone wall of the building. When I face him again, he beckons me to stand in front of him.

"The goal is to never get to this point in the first place. Do everything you can to put distance between yourself and whoever is coming for you, understood?"

"Understood," I say, eager to get on with the lesson and grateful that we are wasting no time.

"Now," he says, a smile growing, "if I were to arrest you again and you were unable to run, I would get a hold of you and try to get your hands behind your back."

Before I have time to blink, Diego grabs my arm roughly, pulling it toward him. I try to rip my arm away, but his grip is too strong. Keeping his hold, he twists our bodies to come behind me. Within a second, he has my other arm pinned behind my back.

I let out a strangled cry.

Diego holds me there as I squirm against his firm chest, reluctantly noticing the way his strong arm feels so solid around my waist.

He lowers his mouth to my ear. His breath is warm, but chills erupt on my neck at his closeness.

"Let me remind you: it only takes a moment to catch you," he whispers. "Don't let it happen. Let's try again."

He releases me, and I fight a shiver, frustration rising—frustration and something else that has me shuddering. I am suddenly incredibly conscious of every inch of my skin. I can still smell him on me, woodsy and spicy, like worn leather. Yet with an underlying sweetness that is warm and pleasant.

I shake my head in an attempt to focus and grit my teeth, turning to face him.

Instead of attacking me again, he points to my feet.

"Remember to keep your stance wide," he says. "When your feet are close together, it is easier to knock you over or spin you around like I did. Make sure you have a solid foundation."

I move my left foot farther from my body.

"Good. Next, tell me what happened when you tried to pull your arm from my grip."

My skin burns where he grabbed me, and heat floods my face. "I couldn't get free." My pride is taking a bigger blow than I thought it would.

Diego tries to hide his smile, but I see his lips twitch. "Right, so clearly trying to pull free won't work."

"Then what am I supposed to do?"

He grabs my arm like he did before, but this time, his hold is softer, and his movements are slow.

"You need to twist my arm to loosen my grip." He guides my arm down and around in an outward circle. "Then, if your other arm is free, knock it into mine."

"Like this?" I punch his arm, but he doesn't budge. I growl at the smirk on his face. "Don't just laugh at me. Tell me what to do!"

He grins. "Use your forearm against mine," he says, still holding onto my arm. "Good. You want to use all your force, so twist your body into it and push."

I do as he says, bringing my left forearm perpendicular to his and smacking into it.

"Good, good. Now, put it all together. Loosen my grip and then break it."

With his hand holding my right arm, I bring it down and twist it outward with one harsh movement. I can feel his thumb bend as he tries to keep his hold.

I force my left forearm into his. As I hit him, I can feel it isn't enough. I throw my entire body into it, falling to the ground as I break out of his hold.

The dirt coats my palms, and I huff. But when I look back, I grin as I see Diego's eyebrows raised in surprise.

"I'm not going to lie, Catalina," he says with a quiet laugh. "I'm impressed. You were able to think on your feet and evaluate what you needed to do in the moment."

He reaches toward me, and I place my fingers in his palm, still smiling.

"Now, do it again."

Diego takes me through the same drill a few more times. He learns from my previous success and adjusts accordingly, as do I. His grip grows tighter. I throw my arm out farther. Then, we try the other side.

My forearms burn from Diego's hands and my repeated hitting. But it feels good to fend off a soldier as big as Diego, even in a controlled environment.

Diego holds his hands up and takes a breath. "Alright, let's try something different, okay?"

Since I fell to the ground, Diego's eyes have held the hint of a smile with every hit, every swing, every grab. A flicker of fire and excitement.

"I want to show you a few things you can do if someone comes up behind you," he says. He looks at me carefully, waiting for my approval. When I nod, he continues, "We will go slowly at first, talk it through. Let's see how much you have learned."

Diego makes a small circle in the air with his finger, motioning for me to turn around.

I hesitate, remembering the last time he grabbed me from behind. When he held me by the hair as I fled from Banyoles.

You will be easy to control.

But I asked him to do this. I want to do this.

As soon as I turn, Diego's arms wrap around my middle, pinning my hands to my sides. His hold is strong, but not too tight. It feels completely different from the day that seems like ages ago.

"Your arms aren't free," he says in my ear. "What do you do?"

I shiver.

Focus.

I think of what Diego said before. I'm not strong enough to break out of his grip.

"I need to make you loosen your hold," I say, talking myself through it.

I feel his smile, his soft lips brushing the shell of my ear.

"And how will you do that, Catalina?" he asks in a low voice.

Pushing my arms against his, I test his hold. Diego remains still as I struggle, letting me figure it out.

Finally, I decide to go for surprise, in the hope it will catch him off guard.

I stomp on his foot and hear him grunt in pain. He doesn't let go, but I lift my feet up from under me, using my entire body weight against his arms. He releases me, and I fall to the ground. I scramble away.

Diego recovers quickly. I hardly travel a foot before he captures my waist and hauls me against him once more.

His chest heaves against my back.

"Surprising," Diego says, breathing hard, "and rather effective. But not good enough."

I let out a frustrated groan, and I feel him laugh.

"This time, you need to have another move after you drop from my arms."

"Like what?"

"Keep your legs engaged, feet ready to land on the ground. Knees bent. Don't allow yourself to fall completely."

I do the same thing I did before. Diego is expecting it this time, but he lets me have this little win. I think he just wants me to get to the next step.

As I throw my body down, I stop myself with my feet under me. I try to run, but Diego is too fast.

"Better, but needs some work." He picks me up, and I kick my legs out in frustration.

"I am not fast enough," I whine.

"You need to gain a head start if you are going to run, so you need to knock me down or take me out. Instead of making a run for it, move to my right side when you land. Then move your left leg around my body until it is behind my right leg. Does that make sense?"

I nod. "Then what?"

"Use your leg to buckle my knee and bring me down. It shouldn't take much effort. Just push against the back of my knee. Every move should do the most damage to your opponent with the least amount of energy on your part."

I repeat our drill, following his instructions, but I lose my balance when I land and can't manage to get my leg behind him before he grabs me again.

We try again, but like before, I can't seem to move fast enough.

I scream in frustration. Diego slaps his hand over my mouth.

"We can't have anyone finding us," he chuckles. His other arm holds my waist, but his hold is gentle. "You can do this. Try it again."

This time, I'm able to get my left leg behind him. I bend my leg and push my knee into the back of his. He staggers, but doesn't fall.

"Much, much better," Diego says. "That was good, Catalina. I think we are done for tonight."

I collapse to the ground, tired and dazed. Yet I feel exhilarated, powerful, and excited.

Maybe I couldn't fight anyone, but I can do a lot more to protect myself than I could this morning. I know what weaknesses to look for and how to use my body.

I pull myself to my feet and spot the knife I laid next to the wall.

"Why did you have me bring my dagger," I say, out of breath, "if I wasn't even going to use it?"

Diego gives me a crooked smile. It lights up his entire face, making him look more like a young man rather than a weary soldier carrying the weight of the world.

"Because," he starts, reaching into his pocket. "I figured out a way for you to keep it on you."

I let out a quiet gasp. "Without anyone knowing?"

His smile grows as he nods. He holds his hand out and shows me a brown leather strap.

I look up at him, confused. "What is this for?"

"You will wrap it around your thigh, under your dress."

I laugh with delight. "That is brilliant." I take it in my hands and run my fingers along the smooth leather.

"Put it on now. Make sure it fits properly," Diego says.

I glance at him out of the corner of my eye, and he swallows, turning his head away stiffly to give me some privacy. I would laugh at how uncomfortable he looks if I weren't so eager to fit this dagger to my thigh.

I lift the hem of my skirt on my right side. Reaching down, I try to loop the strap around my leg, but my fingers fumble in the dark, and I can't get the buckle to hold.

"Done?" Diego clears his throat.

"I can't get it," I mutter. "It is an awkward angle, and I can't see in the dark."

Diego hesitates but slowly turns to me. "I can do it. If that is alright?" he says as a question.

Nodding, I hand him the strap and hold my skirt up for him, careful to keep it from going any higher than necessary. I blush, grateful that no one is out at this time of night. I should not be holding my skirt up for a soldier behind a church.

Diego kneels before me. I shift my weight, and he places his hand on my calf to steady me.

I thought I had caught my breath after training, but I must have worked harder than I realized. My heart is racing. My leg hurts from holding it taut in an effort to keep myself from shaking.

Diego moves his hand from my calf up to my thigh. He does not touch me, but I feel the ghost of his fingertips. He wraps the strap around my leg, his long fingers working quickly to get it through the buckle. He leans in closer to see in the dark, and his soft breath skates across my knee.

He gently takes the dagger from my other hand. I had forgotten I was holding it. I have forgotten a lot of things other than the man kneeling in front of me. He slips it into the sheath now wrapped around my thigh, moving so very slowly.

Diego glides his fingers around the length of the strap, ensuring it is properly buckled.

Satisfied, he looks up at me, his brown eyes shining gold in the hazy moonlight. On his knees with a pleading look in his eye, Diego looks like a devout disciple, intent on worshipping and praying to a mighty god. It makes me dizzy, but I don't know why.

"How does that feel?" he asks, his voice coming from his throat.

My breath catches, and I swallow hard. "Good," I say, letting the word out in a breath. I keep my eyes on him, my hands losing grip on my skirt.

The fabric falls and pools around his wrist, his hand still lightly touching the strap at my thigh.

His fingers trace the edges of the leather, and my skin erupts in goosebumps.

"Is it tight enough?" Diego's whisper is so quiet, I would not have heard it if I weren't completely focused on him.

Is what tight enough? What are we talking about again?

Mierda. What is happening to me?

I clear my throat and break the spell that held us captive. Diego pulls his hand back quickly. My skirt falls all the way back down to my ankles.

I straighten my leg, flexing my thigh underneath the leather. I reach down and brush against the dagger over the dress.

"Yes," I say, not looking at him, "I think it's tight enough. It won't be slipping."

I take a few steps just to test out the feeling.

"Wait, Diego. Can you see the dagger under my dress?" I ask, pivoting to face him. "Can you tell there is something under there?"

"Something under there," he repeats in a low voice.

I swallow hard. "Under my dress. The knife. Can you see the knife?"

"Right," he rasps. He clears his throat and shifts his focus to my legs, beckoning me forward. He bends down and watches me slowly put one foot in front of the other. His burning stare has me gripping my hands behind my back, forcing them to stop trembling.

Why do I feel so lightheaded?

"No," he says with a shake of his head. "No. As long as you wear those loose dresses and skirts, I don't think anyone will know."

I relax into myself again. I am hyperaware of the weapon, but it makes me feel powerful.

"Should..." Diego pauses. "Should I walk you back?"

I wrinkle my nose with a laugh. "I came here by myself, I think I can make it back on my own. Besides," I say, my voice dramatically quiet and conspiratorial, "no one can catch me now."

Diego looks down at the ground, rubbing the back of his neck with his hand as I have seen him do so often. His shoulders shake with a silent laugh.

"I certainly wouldn't want to cross you," he says. "Goodnight, Catalina." He turns his back to me as he goes to leave.

"Wait, Diego!"

He stops and looks over his shoulder at me, eyebrow arched.

"Thank you. For all of this." I motion to my legs and then spread my arms out, gesturing to the scene in front of us. He knows what I mean, doesn't he?

Instead of responding, he studies my face. He narrows his eyes, like he is looking for something. Finally, he offers a single nod.

"Tomorrow night, then?" I hate how small my voice sounds.

"Tomorrow night," Diego confirms. "Be ready to live up to your end of the deal."

25

I open the door as quietly as I can.

I'm not entirely sure what time it is, but it is certainly after one in the morning. Adanna should be asleep. I just need to make sure I do not wake her.

The room is consumed in a thick darkness, the only semblance of light coming through the small window. But even that is diffused by the curtains in front of it.

For once, the door doesn't creak, and I am grateful as I shut it carefully behind me. I look over at Adanna, heart in my throat.

She is lying on her side, her back to me and her breathing heavy.

I tiptoe to my side of the room and quietly remove my boots. I want to change, but it is too dark, so I just take off my stay and my skirt, leaving my blouse on.

As I do, I see the outline of the dagger on my thigh. Easing myself down, I sit on my cot and begin to fumble with the buckle. Luckily, it is easier to take off than it was to put on.

I look around for a place to hide it, but I think that under my pillow is still my best bet.

"Well, well," Adanna mutters. "And where have you been, young lady?"

Her voice makes me jump, my hand flying to my chest with a gasp.

"*Caracoles*, Adanna! Are you trying to kill me?"

She rolls over in her bed, now facing me.

"Why? Are you trying to get yourself killed?" she asks me.

"What does that mean?"

"Where were you? I've been worried about you, Cata," she says.

I am overcome with love and guilt all at once. I hadn't thought about what Adanna might think if she knew I hadn't come back.

"I am sorry, Adanna," I whisper. "I didn't think."

She sits up with a sigh, placing her feet on the floor to mirror my position.

"You are a grown woman. You don't have to answer to anyone. You can do what you want," Adanna explains. "But you also have people who care about you, okay? People who want to make sure you are safe."

"You're completely right. And I am so sorry."

"You're safe?"

"I'm safe," I say. "I won't do it again."

"Won't sneak out, or won't sneak out without telling me?" Her face breaks into a grin.

I laugh, but I do not answer.

"So are you going to tell me where you went?" Adanna's voice no longer sounds like a worried, disappointed, scolding mother. She sounds excited.

"Not sure if that is a good idea," I say.

"Come on," she whines. "It's not like I am going to judge you."

I roll my eyes. "I was out with Diego."

She jumps to her feet. "What?" Her voice is almost a yell.

"Hush!"

"You went off with Diego? The guy who put a sword to your throat not two days ago?"

"I can literally hear the judgment in your voice."

"Well, yeah!" She sits back down. "What is wrong with you?"

"It is not what you think, okay?"

"I don't even know what to think."

So, as with everything else, I tell her. I have learned that I can't keep secrets from Adanna. And I do not want to.

I tell her about the dagger, our training, and the thigh strap. I do not tell her about putting it on—that is not important.

"You could get in some serious trouble, *prima*," Adanna says, shaking her head.

"I know," I groan and drop my head into my hands.

"Hey, don't worry. I am certainly not going to tell anyone." She laughs. "I like this risky Catalina. You are even crazier than I thought."

"Crazier than I thought, too," I mumble.

We sit in silence. Adanna lays back down. So do I.

It is quiet for a long time, but I know Adanna isn't asleep.

"Does this mean you trust the soldiers? Diego, Marcos, and the others?" she asks in a low voice.

"No," I say hurriedly. But then I shake my head. "I don't know. I don't think so."

"You just trust Diego enough to meet him behind a church. At night. With weapons. And believe he won't kill you?"

"Well, when you say it like that, it sounds insane."

"It is insane."

I sigh. "I don't know, Adanna. When it comes to Diego, it's not clear. I don't know what I see."

"That must be frustrating," Adanna comments. "You are used to being able to read people pretty easily, right?"

"Yes. I mean, sometimes I'm off, and sometimes I can't see the whole picture, but this is different."

"Well," she says, voice trailing off, "we will just have to be cautious around all of them."

That much is certain. I definitely do not completely trust the other soldiers, no matter what Rafael says.

I fall asleep questioning my decision to trust Diego, and moments later, Adanna wakes me up in the morning.

I make my way to classes with puffy eyes.

I am tired but happy. And I certainly don't regret training with Diego last night, even if I did lose some sleep.

Our main class is taught by both Kosia and Rafael. We talk more about healing. However, this time it is less about the principles and the basic knowledge. Rafael tells us how to open our minds to seeing injuries and illnesses in others.

Although I have always been interested in healing, today I can hardly pay any attention. I didn't realize how much I was drained by last night's healing session with the Estradas until Rafael began talking. Of course, my late-night escapade didn't help, either.

But our main class isn't my high priority. Right now, I look forward to our study group after class. Leonor told me she would help me with etheric travel.

Once Rafael and Kosia end the class, Leonor and I hurry outside, rounding the corner to the back of the church. I shiver, knowing I was here only hours ago.

We are joined by Preko and Constanza—everyone else opted to study elsewhere.

"Let's start off with some grounding," Leonor says. She places one hand on her chest and the other on her stomach. "You guys know what you're doing, so if you have a specific way you like to ground, then do that. Do whatever is best for you. Like anything else, etheric travel is specific to you."

I press my palms into the ground, close my eyes, and breathe. I need to make sure my spirit is ready if this is going to work.

We sit in silence for a few minutes. Though I hear the breathing of the others and the sounds of the birds, it isn't long before I tune it out. Instead, I hear the rushing of my blood and sync my heartbeat with the energy of the earth.

"Now," Leonor says, her voice unusually soft, "just as we did with Rafael, move your awareness to the top of your head. When you are ready, look down on yourself from above your body."

It is extremely slow going today. I struggle to bring my energy up my body, and when I finally get there, I cannot envision myself from above.

"One thing that might help is to imagine a rope hanging above you. Reach up and grab it with your spirit. Let it lift you out of your body," Leonor says.

That is actually helpful.

Taking a breath, I follow Leonor's suggestion. I grab onto the rope and pull. I try again to bring my awareness above myself. But I hit a wall and can't get out of my body.

I keep quiet, but my frustration bubbles right below the surface. Why can't I do this?

My eyes snap open. Leonor still has her eyes closed, a peaceful look on her face. Preko's eyes are squeezed shut, and Constanza has a slight crease between her eyebrows.

But all three of them seem to be in some sort of etheric state.

Closing my eyes, I try again. I need to calm myself. Frustration will only take me further away from the energy I require.

But I'm getting angrier, and I start thinking about my family. After a while, I give up. I slowly lay myself down in the grass and stare up at the sky, like I did after the first etheric session. I hope this doesn't become a habit.

Out of the corner of my eye, I see movement. Constanza has returned and she leans back on her hands.

I give her a questioning look, but she just shrugs.

"It looks like we're all back," Leonor says. "How did it go?"

I sit back up. Leonor looks to Constanza.

"I think it went pretty well," Constanza says. She clears her throat. "I was able to get around the church and into the courtyard to see over the valley."

Leonor grins. "That is amazing, Constanza!"

"It was harder for me this time," Preko says. "Last time, I felt like I was floating. I didn't get far, but it was not hard for me to get out of my body. I couldn't do it today."

Leonor nods. "Sometimes it is easier when you don't realize what you're doing. Once you fully understand how important or powerful it is, you can psych yourself out. Maybe that's what happened?"

Preko nods. "Yes, I think I put more pressure on myself today."

"What about you, Catalina?"

I can see the hope and wariness in Leonor's eyes when she looks at me. She wants this to work. So do I.

"I couldn't get anywhere." I shake my head. "Couldn't even disconnect from my body."

Leonor frowns. She leans her head on her hand, her eyes narrowed and concentrated.

"I think some of your tips were helpful," I hurry to say. It's not her fault. She needs to know that. "I just couldn't do it. Maybe I'm too in my head like Preko?"

Preko nods with a seriousness so unlike him that it is almost comical.

I look down at my hands, unable to bear Leonor's scrutiny. How is this seventeen-year-old girl so wise and undeniably talented?

"Alright, Preko, let's go," Constanza says. She stands, brushing the back of her skirt. "This has been a productive hour, but I think we should join Adanna and Araceli."

Preko looks like he might argue, but with a glance to me and Leonor, he nods in agreement. The two walk off without another word, and I'm left with Leonor.

"You okay?" she asks.

I shake my head. "No, I am frustrated. And I feel heavy. I can't get out of my body."

"I don't mean the etheric travel." Leonor looks at me with a sympathetic look I have rarely seen on her. Not that Leonor isn't kind, but she is usually more lighthearted and fun-loving. She is seventeen, and most of the time, she acts seventeen. It makes me happy.

"I cannot stop thinking about my family," I say.

She scoots closer to me, and we both lay down on the grass.

"You are special, Catalina," Leonor says.

I let out a surprised laugh. "What?"

"I mean it. You are special. You are strong, powerful, and determined. And beyond that, you have a very unique energy. You are more in tune with natural forces than any of us have ever been."

"You are being too generous, I think." I shake my head on the ground, feeling the grass graze my cheek.

"No, I'm serious, Catalina. There is something about you. Juliana said the same thing about going to heal at the Estradas with you." Leonor sits back up and looks down at me. "Even though you are having trouble with etheric travel now, I have absolutely no doubt that you will figure it out fast. And you will be better than I am."

"Yeah, right," I scoff.

She shrugs. "I am just saying that if there is anyone in the world who would be able to help their family—who would be able to do the impossible—it's you."

Perhaps it is because my emotions were already at the surface, but Leonor's words bring tears to my eyes. I blink them away quickly.

"Thanks, Leonor." I reach out and grab her hand.

She uses it to pull me to my feet.

"But just because I believe in you, doesn't mean I won't do everything I can to help you," she says. Leonor begins to guide me in the direction of the *residencia*.

"Where are we going?"

"You are blocked. Let's fix that."

When we get home, Leonor takes us to her room, where she begins rummaging through a drawer in her nightstand. There is so much stuff crammed in there, I don't know how she ever finds anything: ribbons, papers, stones, herbs, a hairbrush. Though, to be honest, I would be more surprised if Leonor was organized in any way.

"Got it!"

She holds out a stone and waits for me to take it.

"Clear quartz," she says, struggling to her feet. "The best stone for pretty much everything, but I think it will help you right now. It can clear blockages, open spiritual and mental doors, and give you clarity."

"I have never used a stone to cleanse before," I confess.

Leonor smiles. "It's awesome. Just by having it near, it can do wonders on your energy."

I turn it over in my hand. It is different from the one Constanza showed me on my first day here. This one is smoother and it doesn't have such a clear shape. This one looks like any other rock, except that it is transparent.

"Here, try this," Leonor says. "Hold the stone in your left palm, face up. Then shut your eyes and hover your right palm over it."

I do as she says, swaying a little when I close my eyes.

"You might have to get really close to it, but try to feel its energy. The energy of the quartz."

I am about to argue, but I remember how Mamá taught Inés and me how to feel our own energy. My right palm heats, and a warm tingle lights in the middle of my hand.

"I feel it," I whisper.

"Of course you do," Leonor laughs.

I open my eyes to see her shaking her head.

"What does that mean?" I ask.

"It means," she grins, "not everyone can feel the energy of a stone that easily and that quickly. But I am not surprised that you found it so fast."

I look back down to the stone in my hand. It was so easy. The energy was so strong. How could someone have difficulty feeling that?

"Take the stone," Leonor says. She closes my hand around it. "You can give it back to me later, but for now, use it to cleanse your energy. Oh, and…"

She trails off, turning back to her nightstand drawer to dig through the mess once more.

"Have you ever used *romero* to cleanse?" she asks.

I am amazed at how my body reacts. My skin tingles, and my fingers twitch. I can't wipe the smile from my face. *Romero.* That is exactly what I need.

Leonor looks at me quickly, turns away, then looks back again. "I'll take your expression as a yes," she says.

I chuckle. "You would be right. Mamá had Inés and me cleanse every night," I explain. "I haven't used it since I left, though."

"Oh, then you definitely need it."

I agree with that. I had not thought of the repercussions of going from daily energy cleansing to none at all.

She stands again and hands me a small bundle of herbs. My fingers take hold of them, relishing in the feeling of the dry stems and the potent smell I know will stay on my hands.

"Alright. Go to your room and cleanse. Ground yourself. Do whatever you need to do, okay?" Leonor gives me a kiss on the cheek. "You can do this, Catalina."

I follow her downstairs, and we split up. Leonor goes back outside while I make my way to the kitchen. I retrieve a wooden splint and stick it into the fire, waiting for it to light. Once it does, I pull it out and hold the small flame to the end of my bundle of *romero*. It begins to burn, and I hurry back upstairs to my room.

As soon as I enter, I blow out the flame and let the bundle smoke. Emotion clogs my throat as I wave the smoke around my body.

The scent is home. It is the end of a long day. It is clearing and cleansing and sweeping with Inés. Even in this different place, I can almost feel my sister next to me, asking me to pass the herbs over the back of her neck.

I set the still-smoking bundle on a little metal dish sitting on the table by the window.

Part of me is comforted. I can already feel the difference in my energy and lighting the *romero* makes me feel connected to my family. But another part of me cannot get rid of the guilt and sorrow still sitting heavy in my stomach. I miss them.

Shaking my head, I sit on the ground beside my bed. Wallowing will help nothing right now.

I close my eyes, holding the cool quartz stone in my palm, and focus my thoughts on allowing the stone to cleanse. My energy flows into the stone while drawing on the stability of the earth until my body becomes a vessel for nature's power.

Eventually, I begin to hear a low, murmuring buzz. It starts quiet, barely making it into my consciousness. But I finally understand that the buzzing is coming from downstairs.

When I open my eyes at last, it is to a much darker room than I anticipated. It is already dinnertime. I hadn't realized how long I spent grounding, but it did the trick. My mind and spirit feel calm and strong.

After taking a few moments to breathe back into my body, I make my way downstairs.

26

L ike the previous night, the moon is still fairly bright, only beginning its waning phase.

I arrive at the same place, hiding in the shadows of the church. With no sign of Diego, I take a seat and lean against the wall.

It was much easier to sneak out tonight. Mostly because I did not have to sneak away from Adanna. Instead, she ushered me out the door with a grin and a wink before reminding me to be home by two at the latest. I think she enjoyed it a little too much.

A rustle echoes through the nighttime breeze, and I look up to see Diego rounding the corner toward me. I scramble to my feet.

"*Buenas noches*, Catalina," Diego says softly. He dips his head in greeting, almost like a tiny bow.

"*Buenas noches*," I say. "Thank you for meeting me again."

He eyes me. "Were you able to wear your dagger today?"

I pat my thigh with a smile. "It was perfect."

Diego grins.

My heart does a flip in my chest. His brilliant smile takes me off guard as much tonight as it did the first day I met him. And the thought of being the cause of that smile makes me feel... I don't exactly know. But it makes me feel a way that I like. And I don't like that I like it.

"Are you ready to teach me how to heal people?"

"Ha!" I let out a laugh.

He arches a brow. "You healed that little girl last night, right? You should be able to teach me."

"Diego, there is a lot to learn before you can heal people. I am still learning how to do it myself. I mean, I could make you a list of herbs and their benefits, but that is not the same as knowing how to heal someone."

"Fine. Make me a list then," he says. "What *can* you teach me?"

"We need to start with the basics. You must have an awareness—a relationship—with the energy within you and around you."

He shakes his head. "I have no idea what that means."

"Exactly," I reply with a sly smile. "This is the way my mamá taught us." I sit on the ground and gesture for him to do the same. He sits down across from me, both of us hidden from the moon in the shadow of the church. "Close your eyes and take a few deep breaths. In through your nose, out through your mouth."

He hesitates, but when I close my eyes and begin breathing, he follows my example. I can hear his breaths weave through the air and wrap around me.

"Now what?"

"Hush, Diego," I whisper. "Patience." I try not to smirk, but his irritation comes off him in a wave, hitting me even though I cannot see his face. I like this role reversal. I like making him wait, making him wonder. "Bring your hands in front of you and rub your palms together."

The soft shushing of skin brushing against skin comes from us both.

"Good. Now pull your hands apart, but keep them close together, so there is a small space between them. You will feel the heat from your palms, but if you focus, it becomes more than that."

I keep my voice quiet as I screw my eyes shut, trying to experience this as he is. My mother taught us to feel our energy from a very young age, so this is as easy as breathing. But for Diego, I am sure it is far more difficult.

"Push and pull your hands together, just an inch or two, in order to feel that energy. It might feel a little sticky, or like there is something stopping you from putting your palms together. It will be very subtle, so focus on the nuance of the movement."

Curious, I open my eyes to watch him. I am pleased to see he is focused and has understood my instruction. I watch his hands pulse, palms facing each other, in front of his chest. His dark eyebrows are drawn together, a line creasing between them as he tries to do as I say.

"It might help to move your hands in tiny circles," I say, remembering the first few times I tried this. I keep watching him, and when his frown deepens, I scoot closer to him. I take hold of his wrists, and he jumps. "Sorry, sorry. I should have said something."

"It's okay," he whispers. His eyes stay shut.

"Like this." I move his hands in slight circles. "See if you can feel the edges of your energy."

"The edges?"

I sigh and purse my lips. How can I explain this?

"Your hands will only move so much, especially when you are going in circles. It is as though your hands can feel the stickiness of your own energy."

I watch him for another minute, but I can see he does not feel it.

Finally, he shakes his head with a frustrated groan. He opens his dark eyes, hooded by his scowling brows. "I'm not feeling anything."

I give him what I hope is a reassuring smile. "That is completely normal. It is hard when it's not something you have experienced before. It will take practice. Try again."

He sighs, but obediently shuts his eyes and brings his hands into position.

"Take a deep breath," I whisper. I keep a loose hold on his wrists. "Focus on your hands and the space between them." I pull them apart slightly and push them closer together, pulsing them slowly before moving them in the same circle.

I can feel his concentration, and it makes me smile.

We continue like this for a little while longer before I can sense he's had enough.

"Open your eyes," I say. He opens his mouth to protest, but I cut him off. "You did a great job. Really. But like I said, it will take practice."

He nods. "I will practice again tomorrow."

"Good! I know this feels silly, but connecting with your own energy is vital in all other *hechicería*. Including healing."

"I believe you," he mutters. "And I still want that list of herbs."

I chuckle. "I can certainly help you with that."

He looks down at his hands, and I realize I am still holding his wrists. I release him and pull back, but he stops me.

"What is this?" Diego takes my right arm, inspecting it in the little light we have.

"I am a little bruised from our training session last night. You pushed me hard," I say with a grin.

His eyes widen, and the blood drains from his face.

"What is the matter?" I ask him, suddenly uncertain, suddenly feeling the need to hide my bruises and fold into myself. "Diego?"

He shakes his head. "I did this."

Confused, I take another look at my arms to see if I am missing something. I do not understand.

"Well, yes," I say slowly. "It is from our training."

"No, no, Catalina. I did this," he repeats. I still don't understand. "These bruises are from me grabbing you."

"So? They are from me hitting you, too."

He shakes his head harder, getting to his feet and stepping away from me.

"I never meant to hurt you, Catalina," Diego whispers, his voice pained.

I bark out a surprised laugh. He never meant to hurt me? The man who tried to arrest me for being a witch. The man who chased me out of town and held a sword to my throat the next time he saw me.

Diego frowns at me.

"I would have thought the chance to hurt me would be a plus," I say with a light-hearted smirk.

Instead of offering a retort, Diego leans against the wall of the church, sinking down with his head in his hands.

"Is that what you think of me?"

My stomach turns sour at his somber tone. I didn't mean to offend him, though I can't begin to comprehend why he is so shocked. Does my opinion of him really mean enough to disappoint?

I shrug, my mind searching for a response.

"I just, I mean," I stutter, "I don't understand. You are a soldier. You arrest witches—you arrested my family. You hate us."

"I do not hate you."

I want to laugh or scream or shake him. But after a pause, I repeat the question I asked him a few days ago. "Why are you here, Diego?"

I don't know why I ask it. It just spills out. I do not understand him, or what he thinks about me. What he thinks of witches. And now, I need answers.

He is silent for a long while, and when he doesn't respond, I duck my head as frustration and foolishness poison my stomach.

"Marcos and I grew up together, you know that?"

He isn't looking at me, but I can feel his energy warming, his soul opening up. So I stay silent and scoot over to sit next to him against the wall, carefully placing my skirt over my knees. When I nod, he continues.

"We grew up in Navarre, in a town called Zuggaramurdi. Have you ever heard of it?"

I think for a moment, but shake my head.

"It is small," Diego says, "but about ten years ago, there was a witch hunt."

The words alone chill my blood.

"The biggest witch hunt we have ever seen. It began in Zuggaramurdi, but it spread all through the region. As they always do, it started small, with a few accusations. But it quickly grew. Countless people were accused, mostly women. Thousands were arrested and tortured as well. Thousands."

He pauses to clear his throat, and I dare not speak.

"My mamá was one of the first accused. At least, that is how I remember it. But maybe there were more before her, I just didn't know. I was only ten." Diego's voice shakes. "She was arrested, taken to Logroño, and thrown in jail."

I place my hand over his, feeling a surprising sense of solidarity. His words and emotions are a mirror of mine. I know what it is like to have your mother accused and arrested for witchcraft. I try to shove my own fears down into my chest.

"They came to our house one evening, marching through the door," he continues quietly. "They took her. And I did nothing."

"You were only a child."

"But I should have fought. I could have hurt them, made them think twice about taking her. I could have done *something*." He shakes his head. "Instead, they just walked all over me."

His words take me back to the first day I met Diego, back in Banyoles. It feels like years ago, but I remember. *Violence is often necessary for our protection,* he'd said. *Without it, you are weak, vulnerable.*

"What happened to her?" I ask. I do not want to know. I wish I did not have to know.

He lets out a trembling breath. "She died."

My tears threaten to break through the lump in my throat. I squeeze his hand and slide my palm to meet his, weaving my fingers between his—as much for my own comfort as his.

He smiles at our hands on his knee, still not looking at me.

"She was not executed," he says. "She died in prison. Got sick, they said. I don't know if she would have been executed or if they would have let her go. I never got the chance to know." His voice trails off.

"What was her name?" I whisper.

"Aldonza."

"Aldonza," I echo. "And *was* she a witch? An *hechicera*?"

Diego shrugs. "Honestly, I do not know."

I think for a moment. "It was just you and her, wasn't it?"

He looks over at me. "Yes. Why do you say that?"

"Because she was an independent woman," I say, "and judging by the way you turned out, she was strong-willed, too. People don't like that." I laugh bitterly.

His eyes become unfocused, and he nods slowly. "I suppose you are right. She was very outspoken, very stubborn. Powerful in her own way."

My chest swells with anger at the thought that Aldonza may never have been a witch. Or anything even close. She had done nothing wrong. Neither did so many of the women and outcasts who have been targeted by the Inquisition.

I have to sit on my hands to stop them from shaking with fury. It is anger for Diego's mother, but it is also more than that.

Once I recognize it, I realize I cannot remember a time without it. This anger has always been in me, growing and festering, eating my insides and corroding my soul. It lies beneath every thought I have and every choice I make.

I don't want it. I do not want to live in this anger.

But I cannot wish it away. It cannot be assuaged by an apology from a soldier. Or a single moment of understanding from a man. I do not know how to soothe this anger within, and I realize now that I do not know if it will ever go away. For even if my family and I are made whole, there have always been—and there will still be—many who suffer for simply being who they are.

How can this anger ever be forgotten?

"When I chased you," Diego continues, unaware of the storm raging inside me, "I saw the same fear that my mamá had in her eyes. And I hated myself for becoming the person that did that to you."

He seems sincere. It does not make sense.

"But you became a soldier," I point out. "You are still a soldier."

I don't ask, but Diego knows my words are lined with questions. His choices confuse me. He *chose* to be a soldier. He chose to wear the emblem that took his mother from him, to participate in my family's arrest. He chose to chase me down.

His tragedy and trauma do not excuse him.

Diego nods in response, offering no answer. Perhaps he does not know the answer himself.

"Marcos lost his grandmother to the witch hunt. He understands the pain," he continues with a sigh. "After we made those arrests, the guilt was eating me alive. I don't know why it took me so long to realize I had become the same people who took my mother away from me. But that is when Marcos told me that he had been helping witches—or those accused. And, I don't know, I guess he thought I would want to help, too."

"And you did."

"He refused to give me any details. He did not even tell me where we were going when we came to Castellfollit. But I wanted to see what he had been doing. I wanted to help."

"Then you decided to threaten me, just to be helpful," I say with another smirk.

He sees the glint in my eye and offers a light laugh. "Just to be helpful," he repeats. But he sobers quickly. "When I saw you, it felt like I was facing the person I was trying to run from. The person who became a soldier and who arrested and hurt innocent people. The person I did not want to be. I wanted to get away from that, or make up for it, I suppose."

Without warning, he gets to his feet, pacing with his hands in his hair.

"I thought this might be my chance when you asked me to train you," he says. "But instead of making up for everything, I have hurt you again."

I follow and stand right in front of him.

"Diego," I say in a firm voice. He keeps his head down. I place my hand on his cheek to get him to look at me. His eyes meet mine in a pained gaze, filled with sorrow. "I asked you to do this. I asked you to teach me. If it were too much, I would not have come back tonight."

Diego stares at me, his eyes traveling the length of my face and searching for the truth. I let him see it.

"What do you think other soldiers will do if they try to arrest me? If they catch me trying to help my family?" I ask quietly. "They will have no problem hurting me."

His jaw ticks, and his throat moves as he swallows. He squeezes his eyes shut. With a sigh, he nods once.

His eyes open and find mine, holding them with a hard gaze.

"What?" I ask, taking a step back.

Diego catches my chin in his hand, his thumb in the dip under my lip. He tilts my face up at him.

"If I am too rough, you will tell me," he commands. It isn't a question, but he waits for an answer.

"I will."

"Promise me," he says.

I roll my eyes. "Actually, your grip on my chin is a little rough."

Instead of releasing me, his grip tightens. "Promise me."

"I promise, Diego," I say with a nervous laugh. I have never seen such intensity with his face so close to mine.

"Good," he mumbles. "Remove your dagger. It is my turn to teach you."

Just like that, the tension between us dissipates. He turns away as though he had never confided in me.

But he did.

I lean on the wall to balance myself as I take the dagger out of its sheath. I leave the strap on my thigh, but as I place the knife on the ground, I realize something.

"Why don't you bring your sword or gun or anything with you when we train? I would think you would need it more at night, no?"

He gives me a wry smile. "Fortunately for me, I have nothing to be afraid of. I am what people fear."

He is right. Diego is everything I have come to fear. He is a man. A soldier.

I envy him. I want to be what people fear.

"We are going to do the same drills we did last night," he says. "See if you can do it any better. Then, depending on how you do, we will learn something else."

We go through the first drill. I can see Diego hesitate when he grips my arm, but it's only for a moment.

I am able to get out of his hold every time. It hurts a little more because of the bruising and my sore muscles, but I don't let that stop me.

Next, Diego wraps his arms around me from behind. We are able to move more quickly this time. He doesn't need to explain it to me, I just need to practice.

I am unable to land on my feet the first try. By the second try, I land on my feet and move my leg into position to bring Diego down, but he stays standing.

"Good," he says. "Don't hold back, though. Give it everything you've got when you try to get me to fall."

I grit my teeth and turn my back to him once more.

Diego grabs me tight. Even though he expects it, he slightly loosens his hold when I step on his foot. I slide down and break his grip, pivoting on my right foot and moving my left leg behind him.

As I bring my knee into the back of his, I reach up with my left arm and grab onto the top of his head, forcing it back.

His knee gives out, his back bends, and he drops like a rock.

I gasp and bring both hands to my mouth. What did I just do?

Diego lays on his back, staring at me with wide eyes. I kneel beside him.

"*Ay! Dios!* Diego, I am so sorry," I say, my hands muffling my words. "I don't know what got into me. Are you hurt?"

He doesn't say anything. Did I break him?

Then he lets out a loud laugh. So loud, I am nervous a neighbor will hear him.

I cannot help but smile as he closes his eyes and lets out another deep laugh.

"Diego, hush," I admonish, though I chuckle with him.

I try to cover his mouth, but he grabs onto my wrist and removes my hand, taking me down with him.

I fall onto his chest, still shaking with laughter.

Diego quiets, looking at me with a small smile. He brushes a strand of hair from my face, smoothing his hand over my tangled tresses.

"Sorry," I whisper.

He shakes his head. "Don't be. That was incredible."

"Really?"

"Did you see me drop?" he asks. "You took me down, Catalina."

I should feel bad, but I grin. I did take him down.

He lays his head back down onto the ground and laughs quietly.

From where I lay on his chest, I can only see his chin and jaw, covered in dark stubble. I want to run my fingertips over it.

Dios. What is wrong with me?

I sit up next to him and scoot a little farther away, but I am still close enough to feel the heat of his body. Close enough to smell his warm, woodsy scent.

Diego eyes me.

"Thank you for telling me. About Aldonza," I whisper. "I am sorry. I'm sorry you lost your mother."

"I'm sorry, too." His voice is even quieter than mine, barely an exhale.

I don't know if he is agreeing with me or apologizing to me.

We sit there for a while longer before Diego says he wants to go over a few things. He shows me where to hit people and where their weak spots are. He shows me how to get out of certain holds by attacking specific pressure points. By the end of our training, I am worried he is more bruised than I am.

His body and his heart.

27

The next three days and nights follow the same routine:

Class in the morning—sometimes enjoyable, sometimes less so. Group studies and tutoring in the afternoons. Diego and I teaching each other at night.

I have tried etheric travel only once since that day with Leonor. I didn't succeed, but I definitely felt lighter. I consider it an improvement.

Adanna has been trying to help me with the whole talking to ghosts thing. She hates when I call it that. In each session, we start by meditating, as always. Then Adanna has me reach out with my mind in an attempt to be seen as available by the spirits we try to contact. She says that remaining open is key to communing with the dead—even for someone to whom it comes naturally, like her.

I have yet to see or talk to anyone, but the exercises we do are helpful for all areas of *hechicería*.

As for training with Diego, I get better each night. He has taught me more self-defense, along with a few offensive tips. Last night, we finally brought out my dagger. He instructed me on how to keep my grip on the knife when someone tries to twist it out of my hands. He also showed me where to stab people in order to create maximum damage, as well as places to stab if I am just looking to hurt rather than kill.

It was terrifying. I hate that I know this stuff, but I hate it more that I have very few qualms with actually using this knowledge. I do not want to look too closely at what I have become.

We normally start with a meditation or something. Diego says he's been trying to feel his energy on his own. I know he is telling the truth because I can sense the difference, and I am proud of him for practicing. I thought about bringing out some crystals, but I really want him to center himself first. In the meantime, I have started a list of healing herbs for him.

But we will not be training tonight. Tonight, the entire town is gathering to celebrate the wedding of Alonso and Mónica.

I find myself looking forward to it. I am excited to spend the night dancing, eating, talking, and laughing with all the friends I have made here. It is surprising.

Even in Banyoles, I never felt so eager to attend a town event or to socialize with our neighbors. But in Castellfollit, I feel seen and understood. Protected and appreciated.

"Stop moving," Constanza snaps at me. "This is already taking longer than it should."

She stands behind me, twisting my hair into plaits and wrapping them around my head like a crown. I was surprised when she offered, but Constanza must have seen the disbelief on my face because she explained that she always does the girls' hair.

She has already finished Leonor's hair—which ended up being two simple braids because she started whining about sitting for so long.

Next to us, Juliana works on Adanna's hair. It makes me smile. Adanna is always the one helping me and all the other girls. She deserves to have someone do her hair.

They have been working for twice as long as we have. Luckily, Juliana and Adanna have similar hair, so she has a better understanding and more experience when it comes to making the tight braids along her head. Adanna's look is nearly finished, tiny braids moving from her hairline to the back of her head, abruptly stopping to create a puff of curls and coils at the nape of her neck.

Juliana has had her hair done for days. She has a hundred little black braids cascading down her back, a stark contrast to the light blue blouse she wears.

"I have the flowers," Araceli announces, coming into the room Constanza shares with Leonor. She carries a small basket filled with pink, red, and yellow carnations, as well as some red roses.

"Finally," Constanza mutters. She snatches a few red carnations from the pile and gently fits them into my braided crown. "Oh, this is perfect."

I look at my reflection, turning my head from left to right to get a glimpse of the red flowers at the back.

Juliana lent me her red dress for the occasion. It is such a bright color compared to most of the clothes I have worn here in Castellfollit. The dress reaches Juliana's calf, but on me, it brushes the tops of my feet. The long, full skirt is flowy, and I am excited to see it twirl around me tonight.

"Thank you, Constanza," I say. "It looks incredible."

She looks smug, smiling at the back of my head to admire her work. "It does, doesn't it?"

Her hair is in one thick braid over her shoulder, reaching her waist. She flings it behind her and fans her face.

"Alright, up, up," Constanza says, shooing me out of the chair. "Is that everyone? Who's next?"

"Me!" Araceli hurries over to the chair and flops down, grinning at Constanza in the mirror.

"Fine." Constanza plants her hands on her hips. "But we aren't going crazy this time, okay?"

Araceli nods eagerly, happy that Constanza is about to do her hair, no matter the style.

I sit down on Constanza's bed and watch Juliana finish Adanna's hair. The way it pulls back from her face emphasizes her high cheekbones and sharp jaw. She looks like a goddess.

I shake my head with a laugh. "You are not of this world, Adanna."

"Right?" Juliana agrees with a groan. "She is just too beautiful."

Adanna chuckles, holding still while Juliana tucks a yellow flower into the side of her puffed ponytail.

She inspects the look in the mirror and turns to Juliana with a squeal. "It's perfect! Thank you, *prima*!"

Adanna stands. The two are nearly the same height, even though Juliana is four years younger. She wraps Juliana in a tight hug with a giddy laugh.

Adanna wears a dress similar to the skirt she gave me when I arrived in Castellfollit. The dark fabric hugs her waist before falling into a full skirt that features gold embroidery along the hem. The golden flower in her hair ties into her dress, making her look like a vision in midnight blue and radiant gold.

"Is everyone ready?" Constanza asks. She squints, wrapping Araceli's long braid into a bun at the top of her head.

Leonor sits up on her bed across from me. She wears a light blue dress with red flowers embroidered into it. It is the nicest thing I have ever seen her wear, and Constanza had yellow and red ribbons to weave into her braids to match her dress.

"I think so," Leonor says. "Just waiting on you two."

Constanza shoots her a look in the mirror, but she finishes Araceli's hair quickly, and the two inspect themselves in the mirror.

"Let's go!" Adanna opens the door and leads us out into the hallway.

The younger children are already in bed. The youngest attending tonight will be Preko.

Adanna falls back, letting the other girls go ahead of us.

"Are you looking forward to seeing Diego?" she asks, wiggling her eyebrows at me.

My face flushes. "What do you mean?"

She rolls her eyes. "Come on, *prima*. I know you like him."

"Like him?" I scoff at how wrong she is. She just smiles at me. "I can hardly tolerate him, Adanna. I suppose I see why someone might think that, with all the time we've spent training and—"

"I am not talking about training, Cata."

I frown. "I don't understand."

"I can see it," she says with a sigh. "But, clearly, you still can't."

We have slowed down enough that the rest of the group is far ahead of us.

I shake my head. "You are way off here. I am only using Diego, trying to benefit from whatever I can."

"And, as you have spent this time using him, you haven't softened toward him? You haven't had any sympathy toward him that changes the way you view him and his actions? You haven't begun to forgive him for what he did to your family?"

My mouth dries. Isn't this exactly what I thought when Diego told me about his mother?

"That doesn't mean I like him," I say quietly.

"No, I suppose it doesn't," she concedes. "But you need to stop lying to yourself. You are attracted to him. You are starting to understand him, maybe even relate to him."

"Wow, Adanna, tell me how you really feel."

"I am just here to help, *prima*. No judgement."

Deciding to turn this conversation back around, I question her. "What about you? Fancy any of Diego's friends?"

Adanna throws her head back and laughs loudly. We walk down the bustling street, voices and music floating through the air despite the late hour.

"No, definitely not," she says.

"None of them? Not even Alferez? He seems like your type," I say.

"My type, huh?" she asks, amusement shining in her eyes. "I can tell you that none of them are my type."

"What about that one guy? Um, is it Domingo?"

"Dominico," Adanna corrects. "No, not him either. And if you continue this line of questioning, you won't get anywhere."

I frown as we slow down, entering the square. At the eastern end of town, the area by the church is lit with a warm and lively glow. The lanterns flicker along the streets, and extra torches and candles have been set around the space.

Adanna offers a wry smile before I can ask what she means, and she skips off with Leonor toward two large tables filled with food and wine.

A band of five plays spirited music on one side of the square, near the big stone wall of the church. In front of them, the open space swirls with couples and friends dancing, colorful skirts spinning around them.

"Anyone want to dance?" Araceli asks quietly.

Constanza shakes her head. "Not yet. I want to talk to some people first."

Araceli looks at Juliana and me.

"I want to dance," I say.

"Perfect. Me, too," Juliana says, linking her arms through Araceli's and mine.

We leave Constanza behind and shuffle our way toward the music, laughing when Juliana refuses to release us.

The band plays an upbeat melody, and Araceli and Juliana take turns dancing with me while I lead. But it falls apart rather quickly and, soon we are simply spinning in and out of each other's arms.

I nearly bump into a couple and realize it's the Estradas.

"Oh! I am so sorry," I apologize, but the two of them just grin at me.

"No need, Catalina," she says. "It is wonderful to see you. And thank you again for helping Rosalia."

"Is she feeling better?"

"She's better than ever," her husband says. They pause their dance to speak with me. "She couldn't believe we wouldn't let her come out tonight."

I laugh, and Margarita reaches out to squeeze my hand.

"Thank you, *mija*," she says.

The song slows to a stop, and the crowd pauses to clap for the musicians. I turn away from the Estradas to find Araceli and Juliana.

But instead, I run right into a certain Spanish soldier.

He doesn't budge, and I nearly topple over, but his hands come to my waist to hold me upright.

"I thought you were getting better at staying on your feet, Catalina."

I crane my neck to see Diego's bright smile. His face glows in the warmth of the lanterns. The light and shadows make his jaw look even sharper than usual, and the need to reach out to brush my fingertips over the birthmark at his chin has me clenching my fist to stop myself.

"Don't worry," I say. "I can still bring you down."

He lets out a laugh, and I find myself grinning back at him.

"Wine?" Diego asks.

"I'll allow it."

He tugs me along behind him, and I try not to trip over my dress. We move toward the table of food, and as Diego pours a cup of wine for me, I spot Adanna. Her eyes move from me to Diego, and her face splits into a grin.

I roll my eyes and pull at Diego's elbow, moving us toward the side of the church.

"Wait, I didn't get—" He gasps as the cup spills over.

I don't stop until we have a wall between us and most of the party. This side of the church is darker, but still light enough from the fire and lanterns in the square. I realize Diego only has one cup of wine in his hand.

"What was that?" he asks, chuckling at my insistence.

I giggle back. "I just don't want to see Adanna right now."

"I thought she was your friend."

"She is. She is my best friend," I hurry to clarify. "But I'm not in the mood to hear her say *I told you so*." I sober. Why did I say that?

His brow wrinkles. "I told you so? What about?"

I shake my head. "It is nothing."

Every second I spend with him, with his hypnotizing scent in my breath, the more I think Adanna has a reason to say *I told you so*.

My heart races at the thought. And at the way Diego looks at me.

His eyes are dark and heavy, moving down to my mouth and back up to my eyes. I take a step backward, and he follows me, slowly backing me against the wall of whatever building this is.

"Have I told you how beautiful you look tonight?" he whispers. His tongue darts out to wet his bottom lip.

I shake my head. "Maybe you should."

Diego steps closer to me with a sigh. He brushes the fingertips of his free hand along my hairline, following the braided crown.

Somewhere in my brain, alarm bells ring out. But I can hardly hear them over the blood pumping in my ears.

Chills break out along my body, starting at my neck and moving down my arms. My eyes fall shut. It is all too much.

"You always look beautiful, Catalina. You *are* beautiful. Everything you do," he chuckles. "The way you fight. The fire in your eyes. The kindness in your heart."

His hand trails down my jaw. I feel his thumb brush over the corner of my mouth.

"Diego."

He tilts my chin up, and I slowly open my eyes.

I feel intoxicated, drunk. I have only ever gotten drunk once when Inés and I kept taking Mamá's wine every time she would refill her cup. So, perhaps I do not know, but it felt quite a lot like this.

"Let me kiss you," Diego pleads. "Let me taste you, Catalina."

I don't know what comes over me, but I find I cannot deny him. I do not want to deny him.

"Yes."

I hardly breathe the word, and his mouth is on mine.

I only have a second to be surprised before his hand cups the back of my head and he presses his lips to mine in a searing kiss.

Placing my hands on his chest, I return the kiss with enthusiasm, forgetting the scandal of kissing this soldier in this alley off the square. I feel a rumble in his chest when he groans.

His lips are soft, and his movements are gentle, hesitant. I feel sloppy and unpracticed, but he doesn't seem to mind. For a moment, his tongue slides over mine, and he tastes like oranges.

Goosebumps erupt from my ankles as a splash of wine tickles my legs. Diego has dropped the cup, forgoing the drink completely.

With his other hand free of the drink, his fingers weave into the hair at the base of my neck, and he grips it tight, sending a jolt of excitement down my body.

I don't get enough, though.

Two young girls round the corner, laughing loudly, and I pull away suddenly. I do not know how I didn't hear them earlier. We are shadowed enough that they pay us no mind.

But with this interruption, I finally have time to catch my breath—time to get enough oxygen to my brain. And I begin to panic.

What have I done? I just kissed the man who chased me from my town.

I glance up at him, but his eyes are still closed, his lips parted.

"We can't let anyone see you here, kissing an accused witch." I make a tutting sound with my tongue, feigning disappointment.

Diego finally opens his eyes, blinking slowly.

"Hmm? What?" he asks. His unfocused gaze is trained on my mouth.

I stare down at my hands and let out a nervous laugh. "What would people say?" I continue. "You wouldn't be able to keep your career, wouldn't be able to rise through the ranks."

It was meant as a joke, but it is all true, isn't it? Diego and I, we could never be together. Not really. No matter the way I am drawn to him, no matter the way I feel around him, our lives don't match up. They likely never will.

When I look back at him, Diego is finally back in the moment, listening to my words. He studies my face with a soft sympathy in his eyes. Like he knows what I am thinking. Like he knows that I am panicking.

"Dance with me," he says, holding his hand out.

I swallow hard and shake my head. His expression falls.

"Not here," I hurry to say.

He follows me back into the glow of the lanterns, and I walk to the middle of the square without looking back.

He pulls me close, wrapping his arm around me and taking my hand in his.

"You know, I feel like I have done this before," Diego comments.

"Really?"

"Yes," he says softly. "There was a young woman in Banyoles with whom I talked at a party. You remind me of her. But she didn't seem to particularly like me. She argued with me the entire conversation."

"That is not true!"

Diego grins down at me and pushes me out into a spin. When he pulls me back, he holds me with my back against his chest.

It looks so like the drills we have been doing. Yet his soft hands, his gentle hold, it feels different.

"It is true, Catalina," he whispers into my ear. "But I think I may have finally won you over."

My heart drops. Has he won me over?

I twist in his arms to face him again, shaking my head.

"I am not entirely sure you can win over a woman you chased from her town," I say. I try to keep my tone harsh, but I find myself breathless.

"What if that woman dropped you to the ground the other night? Surely, they are even."

The corners of my mouth twitch, and I suppress a smile. Is it so wrong to feel comfortable around Diego? He has taught me so much. He has taken time to help me protect myself.

What's more, he encourages and believes in me.

"Perhaps after a few more sessions, we can call it even," I reply.

He hums, sending a deep rumble through his chest.

"For the record, Catalina," he says, so softly I can hardly make out his words, "I want you more."

My stomach dips.

"More than what?"

"My career as a soldier. Rising through the ranks. Whatever other silly thing you thought to say." He pauses. "I want you more than I want any of that."

I want you more than I want any of that.

It is as though he read my private thoughts—the diary of my mind—and pulled out the exact words I wanted to hear. The words I had always wanted to hear. The words I had yearned for.

"You don't mean that," I whisper. My body hums with excitement, anticipation, and fear all at once.

"I think I really do." He sounds mildly surprised himself.

The music stops, and the couples around us clap. But Diego doesn't take his hands off me. I don't make him. We simply stare at each other, and his gaze jumps down, landing on my lips. My face warms, and I finally step away.

28

"Are you going to tell me what happened last night, or not?"

Adanna sits on her bed, staring me down.

I avoid her gaze as thoroughly as I avoid her question. She knows something happened between Diego and me.

And I want to tell her. But I am unsure whether I am ready to think about it. My chest is in knots, and my head spins every time I remember our kiss.

I slip my white dress over my head before lacing up my stay. I lean down to strap my dagger to my thigh, as I have done every morning since Diego buckled the leather around my leg. I have gotten better at it and can do it in seconds now.

"*Prima*," Adanna starts again. "I swear, if you don't tell me, I am going to lose my damn mind."

I roll my eyes.

"I am sure you will be fine," I say, smirking.

"Oh, but I won't," she says. Adanna stands up and begins gesturing with her arms, making her dramatic point even more exaggerated. "I think I might actually die. Truly, I may perish."

"Why don't you tell me what happened with you last night?"

She frowns. "Nothing happened with me last night."

Remembering what she told me, I shake my head. "That's not what I saw. You were talking to Teodora an awful lot."

"That is all it was, Cata," Adanna sighs. She flops back down onto her bed with a sad smile.

I shrug. "I don't know. It just seemed that Teodora liked spending time with you."

She presses the heels of her palms into her eyes. "She was engaged back home. Not every prolonged conversation means something, Catalina."

"Oh." I don't know what else to say. I try to turn away, feeling sheepish.

But Adanna grabs my hands and brings them to her chest. "So, would you please allow your loveless best friend to live through you and tell me what the hell happened between you and Diego?"

I laugh and yank my hands away from her.

"That was low, and you know it," I say. But she just grins. "Fine, fine. We may have... kissed... a little."

Adanna's eyes grow to an unbelievable size while her jaw drops open so wide I think it may be unhinged. She grabs her pillow and brings it to her face. And then she lets out a squeal.

"You are utterly insane," I tell her.

"Insane? *Insane?* I am not the one who kissed a handsome soldier and didn't tell her best friend until now!"

My cheeks hurt from smiling as I try to resist the urge to laugh, despite my internal struggle.

"I just don't know how I feel about it," I say.

"What do you mean?"

I sigh before sitting down on my own bed to face her, accepting that I have lost this battle. Adanna won't let me leave anything out.

"Well, it was amazing, right? I mean, the kiss was," I tell her. "But, I don't know. I'm just worried. This can't be a good idea."

"Why?"

"Because," I groan. "He is a soldier. He is the one who literally chased me from my town. I am not sure I should trust him."

"You're not sure you should trust him. What a comforting thing to hear after you have been meeting him alone, in the middle of the night," she mutters.

"Well, I trust him enough for that."

Adanna narrows her eyes at me.

"Maybe I am just overthinking everything," I say, massaging my temples. "I just got all nervous after we kissed. I don't know how I feel."

She nods. "It is normal to freak out a little after a first kiss."

"Really?"

"Definitely," she says with a smile.

I smile back, but I can't keep it on my face. The more I think about Diego, the more confused I become.

"You feel guilty," Adanna says quietly, reading me like a book.

"How could I not?" I whisper. "I kissed the man who helped arrest my family. My mamá and my sister are sitting in jail while I am flirting with a soldier. What is wrong with me?"

"Maybe he really has changed. He said he felt bad, right? He said he wants to help us?"

"I suppose," I say.

"Listen, your concerns are real, and we shouldn't forget about them. But for now, maybe wait it out. You don't need to make any decisions right now. You don't owe anyone anything. And hell, if you like him, just have a little fun."

I don't know if I agree with her, but I decide to ignore my doubts for now.

I scrunch my nose. "It was a really great kiss."

She lets out another squeal and taps her feet on the ground in front of her.

I cannot help but laugh. "Let's get going."

Less than an hour later, I am seated between Adanna and Leonor in the field on the outskirts of town, still struggling to smother my guilt.

Today, Rafael is taking us through another etheric travel meditation.

I glance at Leonor. She nods with a smile. *You got this*, she mouths.

I'm looking forward to today's session. Though I have only tried etheric travel once since that afternoon with Leonor, her tips were helpful. I think I can really use them today.

"I believe all of you were here last time, correct?" Rafael looks around the field while everyone nods in response. "We will be doing the same process, so let's start off by grounding ourselves."

Rafael instructs the group to close our eyes, breathe, and feel the energy of the earth. I tune him out, focusing only on the dirt coating my fingertips. The breeze blowing my hair onto my neck. The warmth of my inhale and the ease of my exhale.

"Now, envision the space around us. Picture it as clearly as you can, with every detail accounted for."

After Rafael's first lesson and my session with Leonor, it is easy to move onto the next step, with or without his instruction. Just like last time, I see the grass and plants around us. Leaves coat the ground, and some places are wet and muddy.

"When you are ready, lift your spirit out of your body."

Instead of lifting myself like last time, I follow Leonor's advice. I see a rope hanging right above my head, perfectly within my reach.

Without moving, I stretch my right arm toward the rope and take hold. It isn't hard to pull myself up. My spirit doesn't weigh much, it turns out.

I think Rafael is still speaking, but I don't listen. I am above my body. I can see my dark hair and my white skirt laying over my legs.

I go higher.

Rafael is in the middle of us all, walking in a slow circle. He's paused in front of Leonor. He pivots to the other side and looks at Preko. I can see it all.

I go higher.

To the west, the road to the town is lined by trees and shrubs. To the east, I see the sheer cliff drop off, leaving the town high above the rest of the valley. The river meanders through the landscape, the water bubbling over rocks. A subtle trail follows the river—the one I rode with Rafael. I can't see where it goes over the tops of the trees.

Curious, I go into the trees.

Following the dirt trail, I float along, moving quickly toward my home town. I know it's far away. I know I am nowhere close. But I cannot stop myself from being drawn to the place where I know my mother and sister are.

I pick up speed. I'm doing it, I'm really doing it. I go faster and faster, flying through the sky.

I have never experienced anything like this. It is amazing.

Just as I decide to dip down toward the ground, my stomach drops. I am so far from the ground. I am so high up. How is this possible? This isn't possible. What if I fall?

It's not physical, I try to remind myself. But that only makes things worse as I realize I have left my body. My body is back there. Unattended, unprotected.

I begin panicking in earnest. I have to get back.

Just as I plan to turn around, I feel my heart swell, my chest filled with warmth. Once again, Banyoles tugs at me. However, this time, I nearly feel Inés reaching out to me. It is as though the thin string connecting me to my family has snapped tight, growing stronger with every breath—as though whatever was blocking the link between us has disappeared.

As though my mamá and sister are free.

"Catalina!"

My eyes snap open to the sight of Rafael on his knees in front of me, his hands gripping my shoulders.

With a startled gasp, I shove him off me. He lets himself fall back away from me onto the ground.

"I am sorry, Catalina," he sighs. "I certainly never encourage returning from etheric travel in such a jarring manner. But you weren't listening to anyone." His voice trails off, and he brings his hand to his temple.

"You looked so scared." Adanna is on my left side, her eyebrows pinched together. "Are you okay?"

To my right, Leonor places her hand on my forearm, gently grounding me back to the moment. Her wide eyes flit around my face, waiting for my answer.

"Yes," I say quietly. "Yes, I am okay. I'm sorry. I just got scared."

"What made you scared?" Rafael asks me.

"Well, I started thinking about my family, but then I realized how far away I was from my body and, I don't know," I shrug. "It freaked me out."

"How far you were from your body," Leonor repeats the phrase slowly.

I nod. "I don't know how far down the road I made it, but it felt far."

After a moment, her face splits into a grin, and she lets out a single laugh.

"You traveled?" Adanna's question is hushed but hurried. Excited.

I sit and stare at her. Realization hits me. It only takes a second. Then I am smiling like an idiot.

"I traveled," I whisper back to her.

Adanna laughs and sweeps me into a hug.

"You did it!" Leonor squeals.

I pull away from Adanna to find the rest of the class has come closer. Juliana and Araceli start clapping. Constanza gives me a smile and a subtle nod of approval.

Happiness floods through my body. I did it.

"I am so proud of you," Leonor says.

"I couldn't have done it without you. I had no chance before you gave me those tips."

She beams at me. I debate mentioning the feeling I had—the connection I felt with my family—but then everyone is clamoring around Leonor, asking for the same tips and tricks she told me.

"Very impressive, Catalina. You are certainly an asset. We are glad to have you here in Castellfollit," Rafael says. His smile grows as he gets to his feet. "I think we have had enough excitement for today. Let's head back."

Juliana and Araceli pull me to my feet, Preko hurrying after them.

"What was it like?"

"How did you do it?"

"Why did it work this time?"

Constanza cuts in front of them, taking me by my arm and leading me to follow after Rafael.

"Calm down, you three," she says. We walk for a few more steps before she turns to me. "Was it amazing?" Her voice is hushed.

"It was weird," I admit. I pause. "Remember when you told me that I might be able to tell when my family was released? I think I may have felt something."

"What do you mean?" Adanna asks on my other side.

"I'm not sure," I say. "There was a change. Something is different. And I felt like my connection with my sister got stronger and... brighter, maybe. I don't know."

Adanna, Constanza, and I exchange glances as we re-enter the gates of Castellfollit de la Roca. The charged buzz of conversation hasn't ceased. If anything, everyone has taken it to the next level, talking excitedly with each other. A few people are milling about inside the town, each looking up to see the source of the excitement.

"What does that mean?" Constanza asks. "What is your next move?"

But before I can answer her, we notice Diego and Alferez walking toward us, amused confusion present on their faces. Alferez looks at Rafael with a questioning look.

But Diego's eyes find me immediately. He hurries forward, leaving Alferez and Rafael.

"What's all this?" Diego asks with a laugh, motioning to the group chattering around me.

"Your girl has done some next level *hechicería*," Adanna says. She smirks at me, but I hardly pay her any mind.

"I just did etheric travel," I say, looking up into his face.

He grins at me. "I have no idea what that means," he says. "But that is amazing!"

I giggle and take a step toward him, nearly throwing my arms around him. It only takes a moment before I realize what I am about to do. My face burns, and I hastily put some distance between us. But I guess I didn't act quickly enough.

Leonor's eyebrows jump up to her hairline, Constanza's jaw is nearly on the ground, and Adanna chuckles.

"Let's get a move on, *chicas*," she says, holding her arms out and ushering Constanza and Leonor away.

The three of them follow the rest of the group farther into town, leaving Diego and me alone.

"I am proud of you," Diego says in a soft voice.

I didn't think it was possible, but I blush harder at his compliment. "You don't even know what I'm talking about."

"Nope, not at all," he confesses with a shrug. "But I know it's a big deal. And I know you are amazing, so you will just have to explain ethery travel to me sometime."

"*Etheric*," I correct him with a snicker.

I look into his face, his full lips pulled into a warm smile, and I find myself wanting to reach out to brush my fingers along the straight line of his nose. His rich brown eyes seem darker as he lowers his lashes to study me.

His familiar face makes me feel as though I am almost in a trance. I don't know what I was so nervous about this morning.

He glances down, and—is he blushing? "I wanted to tell you something, too," he says. "It probably won't seem like a big deal after your travel thing, but I still wanted to tell you."

"What is it?"

"I have been practicing, like you told me. And this morning, I think I finally felt my energy. Like, I could feel that stickiness you were talking about."

My chest swells until I might burst. I beam up at him. "Diego, that is incredible!"

"I still need a lot of practice, but," he shrugs, "it was exciting."

"That is *so* exciting. I'm proud of you," I say.

His cheeks get a little redder, and it takes everything in me to stop myself from touching that birthmark on his chin.

"Diego!" Alferez calls out, his arms folded across his chest. "Let's get moving."

I open my mouth to ask where he is going, but Diego beats me to it.

"Alferez and I are about to meet a messenger," he says. "They will have more news about what is happening in Banyoles."

I freeze. Time slows. My blood begins to race. "News on people being arrested? People being released?"

"Exactly," he says. He grabs onto my hands and holds them softly in his.

I grip his fingers tighter. "Diego, I think my mamá and sister have been released." My words come out in a breathless whisper.

A small crease appears between his eyebrows, and he tilts his head, gazing at me before nodding with assent. "I will find out about your mother and sister," he says slowly, keeping his eyes locked on mine and making sure I understand his promise.

"Please," I plead, my voice breaking.

Diego leans down. "It was supposed to be just Alferez, but I won't leave anything to chance. I'll find out, Catalina."

He pulls me closer and presses his lips to my forehead without hesitation. My heart flips in my chest.

He doesn't say anything else. He just leaves me with a smile, motioning for Alferez to follow.

I squeeze my eyes shut, overwhelmed with emotion. I will know what my future holds soon enough.

29

The rest of the day passes in a haze.

At lunch, I tell Adanna about Diego and Alferez, and the imminent news. I cannot stop bouncing my leg. Every moment stretches into an eternity as I anxiously await the information that will determine my future. Though I want to believe what I felt, I also want Diego's confirmation.

In our afternoon study group, I cannot focus on anything. I spend the time working on the list of herbs I promised Diego. I write down the ones I know will help heal injuries: *hierba pincel, olivarda, jara, heliotropo, hipérico.*

Preko tries to bother me, asking about etheric travel, but Adanna has my back. She tells him to leave me alone, and Leonor offers to help him with another private session like the one we did before.

Before dinner, Adanna and I go back to our bedroom with Constanza. Where the other girls may pester me about Diego, Adanna and Constanza don't ask anything. In fact, Constanza doesn't even seem to care at all.

"Catalina, will you teach me how to make those flower crowns you were telling us about?" she asks me.

I lay on my stomach, my face stuffed into my pillow to keep myself from panicking about the fact I still have not heard from Diego.

"Seriously?" I ask. My voice is muffled, and I wonder if she can understand it at all. "Now?"

"I did your hair for the wedding last night," she says. Her voice sounds like a warning one would give a child.

"I don't know, Constanza," I say, trying not to whine. Or smack her. "Those are a lot."

"Catalina." Constanza's voice is surprisingly harsh, even for her.

I sit up, shocked at her insensitivity. Can't she see I am spiraling here? Constanza can be cold, stubborn, even mean sometimes, but I thought we were finally getting along. I wonder if this is her way of showing support. If it is, she needs to work on her people skills.

I groan but I motion for her to sit on the bed next to me. Adanna sits on her bed, facing us, with an amused look on her face.

Constanza pulls the basket of leftover flowers up into her lap. I had absolutely no idea she brought those with her. Sneaky girl.

"Alright," I sigh. "Start with three flowers. And try to use ones with the longest stems. The longer the stems, the easier it will be to braid."

I pick out three red carnations, and Constanza picks out three pink ones, laying them out on the bed and awaiting my instruction.

"Begin braiding them, but only do a few twists."

Constanza carefully braids her flower stems, eyeing my hands to ensure she does it exactly right.

"Then," I say, picking up another flower from the basket, "add in another stem and braid that for a few more twists. Just like you would do with your hair. Repeat that until you've got a long enough strand that it can wrap around your head."

She nods and we work in silence.

"Now what?" Constanza asks once she has a long braid of pink flowers.

"You cut off the end of the stems and then kind of stick it into the beginning of the braid. Like this." I demonstrate, struggling with the soft carnation stems. "When the end won't stay put, my sister and I used to just pull a bit of thread from our dresses and wrap it around to keep it in place. Mamá said we were ruining our clothes, one stitch at a time. But she never stopped us."

Constanza reaches to the hem of her skirt, breaking off a small length of thread and tying it around the crown.

"I did it!" she exclaims, placing the pink halo on her head. "What do you think?"

"It looks perfect," I say, smiling at her excitement.

"We still have flowers," Constanza says, picking them out of the basket. "I want to make some for the other girls. Adanna, do you want yellow?"

We decide on yellow for Adanna and Leonor, red for Juliana, and pink for Araceli.

As my hands move through the familiar motions, I feel as though I am sitting next to Inés at the shore of Banyoles lake, and my heart warms. No matter where I am, flower crowns will always connect me to my family. It may be silly, but my nerves slowly settle.

Constanza and I are both working on our last crowns when I start hearing chatter and laughter echo through the halls.

"What is happening downstairs?" I ask. I don't look up from my flowers. "It sounds like everyone is here."

"Probably because everyone is here," Adanna says slowly, confused by my question.

I finally look up and notice how low the sun has gotten and how the room has darkened.

"Is it dinnertime?"

Adanna laughs. "You didn't notice?"

Shocked, I shake my head. "No, I was so distracted, I didn't realize..." I trail off when I understand what Constanza has done. My jaw drops, and I shoot her a look.

Constanza sits next to me, looking smug as hell.

"You did this on purpose," I say, awed.

She nods. "You were going to drive yourself mad if you didn't have a distraction, Catalina."

"I can't believe how fast time passed," I comment.

Constanza's little smile grows. "You're welcome, *prima*."

I drop my flower crown and reach my arms around her, almost crushing the flowers in my show of emotion.

"Thank you," I whisper to her.

She laughs and pats my back, her embrace warm. But when I pull back, she looks concerned.

"Oh, no, no," she says. She reaches up and wipes her thumb across my cheek. "Don't cry. We're here for you."

After a day of an emotional pendulum, her show of kindness is apparently my last straw, breaking the dam holding back my tears.

I sniff and pat my cheeks with the back of my hands.

"Thank—"

Before I can finish thanking her again, there's a knock at the door, and Araceli pokes her head in.

"I think Diego is back, Catalina," she says.

I am out the door in a breath. I hurry down the hall and the stairs, my vision still a little blurry with tears. I pass by without looking back at the group still in the kitchen.

Pushing the door hard, it flies open, and I rush into the street. The sun has set, and the sky is colored with pastel hues, but the beauty is lost on me. It is still light enough that the lanterns are not needed, making it easy for me to run without worrying about losing my footing.

"Catalina!"

As I turn in the direction of the town gates, I find him running toward me, past the inn.

"What is it, Diego? What did they say?" I ask once he stands in front of me. I can't believe how fast I am breathing. I am hyperventilating, and he hasn't even said anything yet.

"Slow down, Catalina. Breathe," he says softly. He smoothes his hands down my arms in an attempt to calm me.

"Diego, please." My voice cracks. I wish it didn't.

He smiles. "Your mamá and sister—they have been released."

I almost fall over.

But he keeps going. "All witches have been released on the condition that they repent, commit to the Church, and cease all *brujería*. Whatever that means," he comments.

Diego gently brings his hands to the sides of my face, holding me still. His hands are wet and it takes a moment for me to realize it is from my tears.

"Catalina?"

His eyes search mine.

I let out a watery laugh. "They are free?" I ask.

He nods. "Yes, they are free. And you are free to go back to them."

I let out a sob. My knees buckle, and I lean toward the wall. But we stand right at the corner and my shoulder clips the wall, my weight taking me into the small space between buildings. I barely catch myself, stumbling with my hand against the cool bricks.

Diego matches my movements and wraps his arms around me as my knees give out. I am laughing, I am, but it comes out as sobs.

"Shh, *amor*," he whispers into my hair. "I've got you."

I let him hold me while I take in shuddering breaths.

Once I have my strength, I lean back from him and blink away the tears. I grin.

"I am leaving tonight," I say.

Diego's face falls fast. "What? Catalina, no, you can't."

But I cannot stop smiling. "I am leaving tonight, Diego. Now."

"No, no," he says, shaking his head vehemently. "That is insane. It's already dark." He reaches out to me, but I step back.

"I can't wait," I mutter.

"Catalina, please. You need to stay here tonight," he pleads. His eyebrows are drawn together as his eyes dart around my face frantically. "Listen, you can't leave at this time of night. It is too dangerous. You will be dead before you are halfway there."

"Diego—"

"Wait until morning. First light," he says in a rush. "I will take you myself, yes? We can take my horse first thing in the morning."

I pause. "First thing in the morning?"

"Yes, at first light. You will get there faster on horseback than if you leave on foot now."

That is not quite true, and he knows it. But perhaps I should wait. When I nod in agreement, he lets out a sigh of relief.

"Thank you," he whispers.

It hits me then that this may be a farewell to Diego. Will he stay in Castellfollit?

Last night, he said he wanted me more than anything, but that was likely the wine talking. The darkness, the romance—we were both caught up in the moment. If Marcos and the others are still here, why wouldn't he stay in Castellfollit? He might drop me in Banyoles and turn right around.

The late evening air around us thickens, the energy between us pulls tight, and I wonder if he has the same realization. I wonder if he will miss me.

My gaze lands on the familiar birthmark beneath his mouth. Beneath his beautifully full bottom lip that I tasted just last night.

"Catalina."

I meet his dark eyes, shocked by the need I see in them. Though perhaps I shouldn't be. I feel the same need in me, winding and burning through my stomach like the smoke of cleansing *romero*.

"Please."

I hardly breathe the word, and his mouth is on mine.

His lips are soft and warm, and I match every kiss, angling my head to reach him. This kiss is not like the one last night. This feels desperate, frantic. It feels like it might burn me alive.

He nips my bottom lip, and I gasp. It gives him the opportunity to slip his tongue into my mouth.

I grip the front of his shirt, worried I will fall over, even with this wall behind me. I will fall. Or I will float away. I'm not sure. All I know is that I want to be anchored to Diego in this moment.

He slides his hand down my neck and uses his thumb to press up on my jaw, tipping my head back. He drags his mouth from my lips, down my chin, across my jaw, and onto my neck. He sucks at the hollow of my throat, and I hear a sound that is a mix of a gasp and a moan. It takes me a moment to realize the sound came from me.

My head spins. I am grateful for this dim alley that hides us from the setting sun and the lanterns that will surely be lit soon. But even with the shadows dancing around us, I know this is wrong. I know that we should stop, that someone could walk by at any moment, that they might hear us. I just cannot bring myself to care.

I claw at him, trying to hold onto more of him. I reach his shoulders, wrapping one arm around his neck while I grip his bicep with the other.

Diego groans. "*Dios.*"

I slide my knee up his leg, and he grabs onto my thigh beneath my dress, hiking it higher and lifting me so I am on my tiptoes, barely able to balance on one leg.

His hand meets the leather strap around my leg and he pulls back from kissing my neck.

He looks down at it, fiddling with the leather as we both breathe hard, chests heaving.

"I'm glad you wear this," he whispers. "I need to know you will be safe."

I smirk. "Safe from what? The only one I need protection from," I say, "is you."

He grins at me. The way a wolf would bare its teeth at a lamb. But it only excites me.

"Then protect yourself. Press your dagger to my throat, if you must," he murmurs, his voice low. "I will give it to you willingly."

My hand cups his jaw, and I bring his lips to mine once more.

But this time, it is merely a soft press of a kiss. One that lasts long enough to burn through our history from the moment he picked up my *talavera* in the market. Long enough to surprise me with the depth of my emotions. Longing, desire, gratitude, and something dangerously close to affection swim in my veins.

I hope that only some of these feelings are mine. I hope he feels the same way.

We finally break apart, and I blink my eyes open, a small smile playing on my lips. Diego smiles, too, but it looks almost sad.

"Come on," he says quietly, taking my hand and guiding me back into the street.

We begin walking back to the *residencia*. We move slowly, taking our time to wander in the last of the waning light.

"I will have so much to tell Mamá and Inés. I have learned so much here," I say. "I'm excited to teach them!"

"You can tell them about your etheric travel," Diego says.

I chuckle. "You got it right this time."

"I pay attention."

"I guess you do." I scuff my boot along the cobbled stones of the street. "Oh! I finished your list."

"My list?"

"List of herbs. I think I'm just missing a few," I say. "It is harder than I thought, writing them all down. I have them in my head, and I can reach for them when I need to, but to put it on paper is different."

"I appreciate you taking the time."

"We had a deal," I reply.

The streets darken with every passing moment, and the sky is turning a deep blue. I glance back to see Felix lighting the lanterns, the flame flickering on the stone wall.

"I am going to miss Castellfollit," I muse.

I have been so focused on returning to my family that I haven't thought once about leaving my friends behind.

"This place, these people," I mumble, my voice thick, "they have changed my life. How am I going to say goodbye to everyone? How will I say goodbye to Adanna?" I stumble over Adanna's name.

I don't just mean Adanna.

Diego chuckles. "You won't have to say goodbye to Adanna."

"Why do you say that?" I look up to find a smirk on his face and an amused look in his eye. He doesn't just mean Adanna, either.

He hesitates, perhaps searching for the right words. "A friendship like yours and Adanna's? This isn't goodbye."

"I hope you are right." I could not bear to say goodbye forever. To anyone.

"Without a doubt," he says.

My heart swells.

We make it halfway between my *residencia* and the inn when Diego turns to me.

"I am going to find Marcos and tell him about the change of plans," he says. "You go on and gather your things. Tell your friends the good news."

I smile again, nodding.

The good news. I am going to see Mamá and Inés again.

Diego smiles down at me. "I will find you once I talk to Marcos," he whispers.

With that, he hurries off into the darkness.

My chest heaves as I take deep breaths. I shake my head, trying to get rid of the fog that has settled in my mind.

This isn't goodbye. It can't be.

I make it back to the *residencia* and am shocked when I find nobody there. Dinner has ended, but there is no sign of the usual lingering chatter.

I panic before I realize it is a clear night. Rafael or Kosia might have taken everyone out for some stargazing and astronomical study. I want to tell Adanna and the girls immediately, but I am sure they won't be gone long.

I race upstairs and begin gathering my things, noticing the other flower crowns have disappeared, leaving a few petals strewn across my bed. I smile at the thought of all my friends wearing floral halos beneath the starlight.

I am able to fit my belongings in a thin blanket that Kosia had given me. I bunch it up and tie it closed with one of my hair ribbons, creating a little sack of all my things.

Standing in front of our small bedroom mirror, I comb my fingers through my hair and begin a loose braid.

I weave only once before I hear a knock at the door. I drop my hair and open the door to find Rafael waiting patiently. The short facial hair on his jaw and chin seems longer and wilder than normal.

"I heard the news," he says, his brown eyes flashing. "You are going back to Banyoles tomorrow?"

"Diego said he will take me at first light."

"I am glad, Catalina." He grins at me.

"Me, too," I say, smiling back. "I'm just gathering my things now. Do you know where the girls are?"

"Of course," he says with a smile. "We didn't want to miss out on the opportunity to spend your last night with you, so I came to get you."

"Oh, good! Is everyone else with Kosia? Are we stargazing?" I grab my boots quickly and follow Rafael out of my bedroom door.

"Yes, that's right. For now they are out by the church."

As we reach the stairs, a black cat lies in front of the top stair, gazing at us lazily with no intention of moving. Its body is stretched out to block us completely.

"Move on," Rafael says softly, nudging it with his foot. "Shoo!"

"It's okay, Rafael. Let's just step over him."

I have to take a little hop to make it over safely, but as soon as I do, the cat gets to its feet and follows me down the stairs.

The cat begins circling me as I walk out of the *residencia*, and I can't help but laugh when an orange cat joins us, too, following Rafael closely.

"I don't think they are going to leave us alone," I say.

Rafael glances back and rolls his eyes, but says nothing when the orange cat begins meowing loudly. Over and over.

"Hush, now," I whisper, but it makes me smile nonetheless. That is, until she starts pawing at the hem of my skirt. I trip forward as my skirt catches on her claws. "Hey, get off."

The black cat moves over to Rafael, and I hear him cry out.

"Ow! It just scratched at my leg," he says, kicking at the cat.

"Rafael, don't," I admonish. "That won't help anything."

"Let's pick up the pace," Rafael says irritably, "and they will leave us alone."

He walks faster, and even if I didn't have a cat circling me, it is hard to keep up with his long legs and wide steps.

Just as we come within sight of the church, both cats hiss and run off.

"I suppose everyone went inside," Rafael says, gesturing toward the door of the church.

"I thought we were stargazing," I comment.

I stare up at the sky. The moon is waning, sticking lower to the horizon now. The clear night—rarer here than in Banyoles—offers ideal conditions for us to further our astrological studies.

It feels like only a few days ago that I gazed at the full moon, my heart aching, wondering if Mamá and Inés were looking at Mother Luna at the same time.

A sudden breeze sends a chill down my spine, and I shiver. Tomorrow morning, I will be on my way to them once more. On my way home.

Rafael shrugs. "Perhaps they decided to wait for us." He tries to hurry me along as I stop to look up at the heavens.

I follow him to the entry. The doorway seems darker than the rest of the shadows. A knot sinks in my stomach; a lump forms in my throat. The closer I get, the more anxious I feel.

Perhaps I am already missing my life here in Castellfollit.

As Rafael holds the door open for me, I walk past him into the candlelit building, eager to get out of the dark and start this final night with my friends.

It is warmer in here, but not by much. The stone walls only serve to block out the wind kicking up outside; however, the comfort stops there. The torches and candles do not seem as bright as they should be, and the goosebumps covering my arms do not dissipate.

At my feet, pink carnations are scattered across the stone floor.

I blink twice, trying to focus my eyes.

At the front of the chapel, I see Marcos and Pedro standing with their arms folded over their chests, watching me. They wear their full uniforms with swords strapped to their belts and vests buttoned up. They've not worn their uniforms since their arrival, and I forgot how aggressive they can appear.

I offer the two soldiers a small smile. But it soon drops from my face, and I choke on my next breath.

To the right of them, I see Adanna, Constanza, Preko, Leonor, Juliana, and Araceli sitting on the stone floor. Their hands are bound behind their backs, and they lean against each other, gags stretched between their lips.

They are all here. The younger children as well, their faces tear-stained. One of them hiccups on a sob.

Leonor is the first to see me.

She screams against her gag, trying to call out to Rafael and me.

Pedro crosses to her in two large strides and grabs her by the hair, his big form towering over her.

"Shut up!"

Leonor's scream turns into a primal growl as his grip tightens. She bares her teeth at him around the gag.

I watch Constanza twist around and kick him in the shin with the heel of her boot. Pedro releases Leonor with a yell, and he hits Constanza across the face.

I gasp, but she hardly even flinches. She just stares at him with a look that would make anyone wither, and her cheek blossoms with a red welt.

"Pedro, enough," Marcos commands in a low voice.

I whip around to Rafael who has just entered after me, desperate for support. His dark eyes go from me to Marcos, and he narrows them into slits.

I follow his lead and turn my gaze back to Marcos.

He stands tall, his feet planted in a wide stance. His broad shoulders bunch up as he folds his arms in front of him once more. Like always, his hair is pulled back away from his face, tightening his features, while his ice-blue eyes stab into mine. He lowers his thick eyebrows, making him look more threatening than I remember.

Then I hear Rafael speak behind me. "I brought the last one."

His voice is emotionless, but the words hollow out my chest.

Marcos's smile looks sharp and poisonous. I am not sure if it is his teeth or his pointed lips. His eyes are cold and dead, but he does not take them off me. "Grab her, would you?"

I see a flurry of movement to my right.

Alferez comes toward me with a length of rope in his hands. He reaches me quickly and grabs onto my arm, trying to put it behind my back.

Even through the panic, I know what to do. I hardly have to think about it.

In a jerking motion, I swing my arm in an outward circle, his thumb bending to keep a hold of me. I use my other arm to ram into his, causing him to cry out and let go of me.

Just like Diego taught me.

I spin away from him, ready to run, when I see someone else coming toward me.

His familiar eyes are dark and deadly, his full lips turned down at the corners. In distaste or determination, I am not sure.

My feet stumble with my heart.

And Diego is on me in a flash. I cannot move fast enough.

His large, rough hands take me from behind, and he wrenches my arms behind my back. He has a stronger hold on me than Alferez did.

I remember my training.

Unfortunately, so does he.

I slam my foot down, aiming for his, but he moves out of the way just in time. I try to drop my weight, but he is expecting it.

Desperate and shaking, I slam my head back. I make contact with his chin so hard that I see stars.

"*Mierda*!" he cries out in pain.

It is enough to get out of his grasp. I use his own training against him and shift my weight. This time, I move to the left instead of the right, in hopes I will take him off guard.

I do.

I am able to slam my leg into the back of his knee, and I can feel it buckle. I reach up to pull his head back, but my fingers barely brush his hair before they are ripped away.

Alferez grabs me and pulls me from Diego as he continues the fall I set into motion.

I had him.

But now, Alferez pushes me into the wall, and I nearly double over. As blood rushes to my head, dizziness hits me with full force. I do not know how hard I hit Diego, but my head is pounding.

I struggle against Alferez, but he pins my chest to the wall, his entire body pressed against my back. My arms are yanked behind me once more, and this time, he succeeds in tying them behind me.

I scream in frustration.

"Here, gag her." I think it is Alferez speaking.

He yanks me toward him, away from the wall, and he turns me to face the room. Diego approaches me with a strip of fabric, holding it up to my face.

He starts whispering to me. "Catalina—"

"Don't you touch me," I spit.

His face is stone. No movement, no expression. Nothing.

The man I kissed an hour ago is long gone.

The only one I need protection from is you.

He doesn't hesitate and reaches toward me. But I snap at him like a cornered animal, nearly catching his fingers in my teeth.

Marcos's laugh echoes through the schoolhouse.

"Come on, Diego," he says, still cackling. "Muzzle the witch."

You will be easy to control.

Diego grits his teeth, and I glare at him, refusing to break eye contact.

"I will have you begging for mercy before we are done." I throw his words back at him, the words he whispered in my ear the day he chased me from my home. The words that rattle around my head morning and night.

I see the shock register on Diego's face, and he hesitates. For just a moment. But it is enough to sprinkle satisfaction into my blood before it is washed away with the next beat of my heart.

He shoves the fabric into my mouth, wrapping it around my head and tying it tight.

"I am sorry, Catalina," he whispers.

My eyes burn, hot tears threatening to spill, and it takes everything I have to keep them at bay.

He tries to take me by the arm, but I pull away from him, and he backs off.

Instead, Alferez takes me forward and shoves me toward my friends. He forces me down next to them, my knees slamming painfully into the floor.

I turn away from Diego. My vision blurs with angry tears, and they finally fall when I blink, wetting the fabric gag tied around my mouth.

I think of the way Diego panicked when I told him I was leaving tonight. He made it seem as though he only cared for my safety. But this is why he wouldn't let me leave, isn't it? He knew.

What a fool he must have thought me to be. Did he laugh when he left me? Did he revel in my oblivious joy? Mock me for my heartfelt kiss?

The only one I need protection from is you.

I suppose he was right: I will not be saying goodbye to Adanna.

"We had a deal, Marcos," Rafael calls out. "Tell me where it is."

Rafael stands at the back of the schoolhouse, leaning against the wall to the side of the door. So casual. As I look at him now, I see the deception and betrayal surrounding him.

It swirls around him like an obscuring smoke, emanating from and covering his being. It seeps into the air, slinking through the room until it chokes me.

I think of the story of the Book of Blood. I think of the devil's changing appearance and of the transformation from handsome man to demon of darkness.

How did I miss this? Why couldn't I see this darkness before? Why didn't I see that Rafael is nothing but a self-serving traitor?

I was so hopeful, so vulnerable. I could only see the ways Rafael helped me. And I trusted that the rest of Castellfollit knew him better than I. I chose to leave behind my usual discernment, distracted by my own crisis.

I was a fool.

Before Marcos can respond to him, a small sound comes from the doorway. A meow.

Everyone pauses, listening. Rafael knits his brows together in confusion. Another meow, this one louder.

The cats that followed us never left me alone. I take a sad and strange comfort in the thought as the church door flies open, banging as it slams against the wall.

Kosia storms into the schoolhouse, her long red skirt flowing behind her like a flame of fury. Relief fills me, and I hear someone let out a sob that echoes through the stone chapel.

In less than a second, Kosia takes in the scene, and rage sparks in her eyes when she sets her sights on Preko.

She spins on her heels, locking her gaze on Rafael.

"How dare you?" Her voice shakes with anger. She whirls back around to face the soldiers. "What on earth do you—"

Rafael moves so quickly, I don't understand what is happening until it is done.

He has a knife in his hand. The metal glints against the candlelight. With inhuman speed, Rafael takes hold of Kosia from behind and slashes his knife across her throat.

Next to me, Constanza's muffled scream rings through the building.

Kosia brings her hands up.

The blood spreads through her fingers and soaks her white blouse. The dark red burns my eyes.

Her mouth open in a silent scream, she falls to her knees.

Kosia.

She topples over, and I cannot see her from my place on the ground, my sight impeded by the benches lining the chapel. But her rasping struggles for breath sound louder than my cries.

I cannot breathe. Adanna's gasping sobs pierce my ears and break my heart. I don't think it can get worse.

But then I crane my neck to see Preko.

Bound and gagged like the rest of us, he screams, tears streaming down his face. His agony echoes in the chapel. He struggles to get to his feet, clearly wanting to run to his mother. But he cannot move.

I notice then that the rest of the group is tied together, rope linking their bound hands to the other.

Rafael looks unbothered, even annoyed. He steps over Kosia without so much as a glance.

If I bend down, I could see her underneath the seats. But I don't.

Because the amount of blood...

If only I could get to her. I could use *milenrama* to slow the bleeding. *Hipérico* to help heal the injury. I don't have any herbs with me, but I'm sure I could find some somewhere. I wish I was prepared like my mother and sister. Like any smart *curandera* would be.

But I have to do something.

I am not tied to anyone else, and I slowly move my feet under me, getting ready to stand without catching attention.

"I will not remind you again," Rafael says to Marcos. He has crossed the room and now stands in front of Marcos, his face hard. "Where is it?"

Marcos smiles. It is a cruel twist of his mouth. "No need for threats, Rafael. I have no intention of going back on our deal. The book is in Banyoles," Marcos says in a low voice. He glances at me. "A *curandera* called Gonzalez Moreño."

The book is in Banyoles? What is he saying? A *curandera*? He can't be talking about my mamá.

But he is.

Soledad Isabel Gonzalez Moreño. A *curandera* in Banyoles.

Barely balanced with my feet under me, my jaw drops open, and my body falls to the side, brushing my shoulder against Constanza as my backside hits the floor.

Rafael studies me for a moment, and we lock eyes, my mouth agape. Time slows, and as it does, I finally see what he wants—what he is planning. I can see that he does not care that it is my mamá. I can see his satisfaction, his victory, his thrill.

He smirks.

But I manage to stay in this bubble, this strange connection we have forged between us. Narrowing my eyes, I glare at him, fury and fire raging through my blood, screaming and clawing their way through my body, smothering the fear I know will resurface.

My lips come together, and my skin tingles. I breathe out a soft rush of air.

Rafael sways on his feet and stumbles back, as though blown over. His eyes flicker, and before he can hide it, I see trepidation flash in his gaze.

He regains his balance and shakes his head slightly.

Then, he walks briskly out the door, stepping over Kosia once more. He leaves us to our fate, never turning back.

The moment our connection breaks, terror floods me, gripping tight. Rafael's betrayal knocks the wind out of me, and I squeeze my eyes shut, willing myself to wake up from this nightmare.

Perhaps I will scream, and Adanna will shake me by the shoulders to help me return to the land of the living. Perhaps she will listen as I tell her of this dream, and she can tell me that it means nothing. It is no premonition, no prophecy, no omen. It is just a dream.

But that relief never comes.

Marcos clears his throat. "Let's get moving."

31

Marcos, Alferez, and Pedro approach the group and begin forcing us to stand.

Everyone is tugged up as the person tied to them is brought to their feet and dragged out the side door of the church. One long line.

There are about fifteen of us. I can see little Tomasina and Ana Clara crying near the back of the line, and Ignacio is tied between Araceli and Constanza.

I watch them, left behind, when Diego approaches me, and I try to scramble away. But it is fruitless. I cannot make it far with my hands tied behind my back and my feet tripping over my dress.

He takes hold of my arm and pulls me to my feet, shoving me in front of him. We follow after them, Leonor at the end of the line with her back to me.

My vision tunnels, the chapel turning into a warped hallway that leads to the side door. The door looks like a black hole as I watch my friends get swallowed into it. Dread grips me at the thought of passing through that door. Once we walk through, there is no going back.

Kosia lies somewhere behind us, and I cannot hear her breathing. How can we leave her?

But we are not given the choice. They are forcing us to leave this community, this school of *hechicería*. Despite my plans to leave tomorrow, this is different. This is a horror.

I walk into the night, and hear Diego quietly shut the church door behind us.

The air is colder than I remember it being just a few minutes ago.

Minutes ago. It was only minutes that I thought I was meeting my friends for my final night in Castellfollit. That I thought Rafael was my friend, my ally, my teacher and protector. I swallow down the desire to let out a sob.

Marcos leads everyone around the back of the church, and my stomach clenches again.

Two nights ago, Diego was teaching me how to fight in this dark clearing. How can one's entire life change in just moments?

I suppose I should have learned my lesson when my mother and sister were hauled off in front of me and I was chased from my hometown. My life changed then, too.

And I cannot help but notice that both events involved these same people.

As if privy to my thoughts, Diego lowers his head to speak near my ear.

"Catalina, I am sorry," he whispers. "Listen, I can explain, alright?"

His deep, quiet voice resounds within me, and my body tenses. His voice used to bring me comfort and excitement, but now, I feel betrayed. I am furious.

Furious at him and furious at myself. I should have seen this coming.

Refusing to give him a chance to say another word to me, I bend my knee and bring my leg in front of me, using the momentum to kick at him. My foot makes contact with his shin in a hit so hard that it hurts through my boot.

He stumbles back, but he doesn't take his hand off my arm. "Ow! *Caracoles*, Catalina!"

I smile around the gag.

"*Vamos*, Diego," Marcos calls from up ahead.

Behind the church, I catch sight of two horse-drawn carts in the faint moonlight. The carts look like the kind used to take prisoners, like a big locked box—a cage.

Marcos and Pedro near the cart closest to us. It has an iron padlock that holds the wooden door closed, and the sight makes my stomach drop. Pedro takes a key from somewhere on his person, jiggling it into the lock before swinging the door open and loading half of the group into the cart.

Barely able to fit eight, Alferez cuts through the rope attaching the first group to the second. The first group ends with Araceli, the second starts with Preko.

Marcos and Alferez take the second group to the cart in the front, while Pedro reattaches the padlock.

The click of the lock rings in my ears.

Diego guides me past him, toward the second cart, his hand gentle on my arm. Once Leonor is inside as the last of the line, Diego helps me up.

He hesitates. He looks at me with knitted brows, almost apologetic.

But I do not want his pity. I raise my chin and turn away from him, squeezing into the cart next to Leonor and a little boy I vaguely recognize.

Out of the corner of my eye, I see him stare at me, as though waiting for me to acknowledge him. But he shuts the cart door on us, plunging the space into darkness.

The cart is dank, and the air is cool. It smells like dirt and death, almost like the shore of Banyoles lake. But this scent is darker, more desperate.

I hear a few sniffles bouncing off the walls of the cart, and the boy next to me shifts on the bench.

"Alferez, you go with Pedro," Marcos's voice penetrates the cart we are locked inside. "Follow behind Diego and me. And let's hurry, yeah? I'm not looking to be on the road forever with these damned witches."

Alferez grunts, and his footsteps fade away. Two other sets of footsteps sound on either side of the cart, rounding it to the front.

As my eyes slowly adjust, I can see a tiny slit at the front of the cart, large enough for me to tell Marcos and Diego have climbed up on the driver's bench, but it is too small to make out much else.

Without any warning, the cart lurches forward, and the horses take off at a quick pace. We are pressed against each other in the dark, falling into one another with every bump.

In minutes, we pass through the town gates, continuing down the road leading east and north.

I am barely able to use the slivers of moonlight to make out who is in the cart with me, but it is gradually getting easier to see. Our line started with Preko, followed by Adanna and Juliana. There are a few other children I know. Tomasina, Ana Clara, and the little boy, no older than ten years old, and, of course, Leonor at the end of the line.

The young children cry softly, and my heart twists. We have to save them.

It is time to put my plan into action.

I yell to Adanna, trying to form her name against the gag. It is incomprehensible, but I make enough noise that I get her attention. She looks at me through the dark, and I jerk my head downward.

Adanna shakes her head, brows drawn in confusion. I flick my eyes down to my legs and jerk my head again. I try to lift my leg, but it's too tight in here.

Finally, her eyes widen with understanding, and she motions to my dress with her chin. I nod quickly to confirm, praying she can decipher my meaning.

I see her forehead crease with determination, and she begins shifting around the cart, trying to get closer to me. Fortunately, it isn't a large space. Though it is difficult to maneuver with everyone tied together, the group must realize we are on a mission, and they try to move out of the way to make room for Adanna.

When she finally gets close enough, she turns her back to me so her hands can grab onto my leg. I twist my body to get it as close to her as possible while she yanks my skirt up and feels around for the strap.

Her long fingers press into the outline of the dagger before she figures out how to remove it from the strap. I feel it come loose. I twist in the opposite direction to take the knife from her.

Like she can read my mind, Adanna gives me the handle of the dagger, and once she can feel I have a hold on it, she removes the sheath with her hands.

I flip the dagger up and slide the blade between my hands clumsily. It slips in my wet palms. I realize I have cut myself with the blade, but it isn't bad. I don't feel any pain.

Sawing through the rope takes longer than I would like with the awkward angle of my tied and slick hands. I wish Adanna could do it, but without being able to see behind her, she may cut me or herself worse than I have.

I pull against the rope and feel it loosen. After a few more passes of the dagger, I can yank my hands apart.

Adrenaline rushes through me, and I let out a muffled laugh.

I reach up and untie my gag.

"I'm free," I announce quietly. "I'll cut through your bindings. It won't take long."

I turn around to take hold of Adanna's hands, but I find I do not need to cut through the rope. It is easy enough to untie her, and she's free within moments.

She wastes no time ripping the gag out of her mouth. "*Dios*," she whispers.

The two of us turn to those nearest. I untie one of the young girls to my left, while Adanna unties Preko.

A few minutes later, we are all untied and free of our gags.

"It is a miracle you had that knife, Catalina," Leonor says, rubbing her wrists. "Where did you get such a thing?"

My body burns at the reminder. I put my head down, focusing on putting the dagger back into the strap on my thigh. I swallow the lump in my throat and try to turn my thoughts away from Diego.

"That doesn't matter," Adanna says hastily. "We have to figure out our next move."

Without thinking, I wipe the sweat from my hands on my skirt. As the light fabric turns dark with my blood, I remember it isn't sweat.

"Where are they taking us? Does anyone know?" I ask.

Everyone shakes their head in response, muttering under their breath.

"What does Marcos want with us?" Adanna asks, almost to herself.

"I don't know," I admit. "But I do know that I don't want any part of it."

"But what do we do?" Preko asks. "We are locked in a moving cart. There is nothing we can do."

His voice is low and dark. His eyes look hopeless. I realize how unusual it is that he didn't speak the moment his gag was off, when the Preko I knew this morning could not be quieted.

My heart breaks. This is not the Preko I knew this morning.

"We could attack them when they come to get us. They don't know we are untied," Leonor says.

A few of the group nods, but I shake my head.

"No," I say firmly. "No, we cannot allow them to get us to wherever we are going."

"So we have to stop the cart," Adanna says, her eyes on me.

"How?" Leonor looks back and forth between Adanna and me.

I know the answer. I have known the answer since I watched Rafael murder Kosia in cold blood. But I also know the answer will not be a popular one.

"With a curse." My voice is deathly quiet.

A chorus of muted gasps sounds through the cart.

"We are not supposed to curse people," one of the little girls says. "We will be punished by the universe."

"She is right. It goes against the natural order. You know that, Catalina," Juliana says, her dark eyes wide. She anxiously twists a few of her little braids around her fingers over and over again. "Besides, I have never cursed before. Have any of you?"

I watch everyone shake their heads.

"I don't intend to start, either," she says, adamant.

I am not surprised. She is still young. They all are. I do not want them to have to curse anyone or deal with whatever repercussions follow. I want them to stay whole, but I cannot allow myself that luxury.

"And I don't want you to," I declare. "I don't want anyone to suffer for a curse. I will do it myself."

Leonor looks hesitant. "Catalina, are you sure?" she asks in a soft voice. I can tell she is afraid, along with everyone else in the cart with me. They are afraid of Marcos, but they are also afraid to curse.

Not that I blame them. We know the consequences of cursing—especially deliberate cursing—can be severe.

But I will not let Marcos win this. Give me the consequences. I don't care.

"I am sure. It is time to use every power I can. It's time to fight," I say. I roll my shoulders and set my jaw, drawing on every bit of strength I have. "If they want to call me a witch, then a witch is what I will become."

Her white teeth shine as Adanna's face breaks into a grin. "Oh, hell, yes."

I feel bolder with her unwavering support.

"If there has ever been a time to curse someone," she continues, "it's now."

I smile at her, and she reaches over to take my hand, nodding once. Her hand is warm against mine. I know she can feel the stickiness of my blood, but she doesn't waver.

Still, most of the group seems more than hesitant. I look around.

"I am the one who will be doing the curse," I repeat myself. "No one else needs to worry about facing the natural consequences."

We have all been raised to fear cursing to a fault. Even now, anxiety tingles down my arms at the thought of going against Mamá's teachings.

"I can help, Cata," Adanna says softly.

But I shake my head harshly. She needs to understand. "No, Adanna, if I can do it myself, it is better that only one of us..." I trail off, unsure how to end the sentence. Surely the universe will not punish me too severely, but who can know?

She nods. "What will you do?"

"I have never cursed anyone. At least, not knowingly," I confess.

"It should be something simple, but effective," Leonor says thoughtfully.

Adanna nods in agreement. "Something that will get them to stop the cart."

"You could blind him."

It is so quiet, so low. Preko's voice can barely be heard. But his words make me shiver.

He keeps his eyes down, and I shift my attention to Adanna. She stares back at me, the corners of her mouth tugging down as she considers it.

"It is a good idea," Adanna admits. "I think you will be more able to influence the body than the environment, and dimming his vision isn't really hurting him."

"That would certainly get him to stop the cart, one way or another," Leonor says.

Gritting my teeth, I nod once. "Okay, then that is what I will do."

Before anyone can say another word, I shut my eyes and put my hand up. The group quiets. I breathe deeply—in through my nose, out through my mouth—like any other grounding session.

But I know this one is different.

As I become more conscious of my own energy, I slowly reach out to the energy around me. The cart is filled with strong auras, but I weave through them, envisioning the front of the cart.

In my mind's eye, I see Marcos and Diego. Marcos with his hands on the reins, Diego sitting stiffly beside him.

With all the power I can muster, I cover Marcos's eyes with my spirit, trying to force his lids shut. But I feel no difference in his gaze, and the cart carries on.

Squeezing my eyes shut, I shake my head. I need to try again. This time, I take a moment to feel more of Marcos's energy in an attempt to create the connection I need.

His energy shocks me, causing me to flinch back, surprised at the chaos. He feels excited, yet panicked. As though he is in a frenzy, pleased to have two carts full of young witches and frantically eager to arrive at his destination. Wherever that may be.

His broad shoulders are tense, and his knuckles are white as he grips the reins. I move my attention to his eyes once more. I can feel him gaze ahead, utterly unblinking. Softly, I run my hands across his eyes in an effort to blind his vision.

But I feel nothing. I can't even manage to blur his sight.

Huffing in frustration, I open my eyes and look right at Adanna, too embarrassed to see the rest of the group when I admit I have failed.

"I can't do it," I mutter with a grimace. "At least," I hesitate, casting my eyes down to the floor of the cart, "not on my own."

From the edges of my vision, I see Adanna roll her shoulders back. I glance up at her. She pauses before she takes a faded handkerchief from somewhere in her skirts. She wraps it around her head, tying her textured hair up into a puff, like the day I met her.

"Good thing you are not alone, *prima*," she says with a grin.

I return Adanna's smile, and a weight lifts as I take a deep breath. She is right. I am not alone. Though I would like to save everyone and allow them to walk through life without needing to curse, I cannot.

"We can do it together," Adanna adds.

"Hang on," Leonor says, "I want to help, too. I would love to do some damage to those bastard soldiers."

"Language, Leonor," Adanna admonishes, covering the ears of little Ana Clara next to her.

Leonor widens her eyes, affronted. "You have sworn at least twice since we've been in this cart!"

I rub my hand over my face to hide my smile. Even in the depths of despair, Adanna cannot help but look out for everyone. And Leonor cannot help but call her out.

Before Adanna can tell her off again, Leonor asks, "Are we blinding Marcos and Diego, or just Marcos?"

At the mention of his name, I recall my first training session with Diego.

Bring me down. You need to gain a head start if you're going to run. That is what he told me.

"It needs to be more than that," I whisper as I realize Diego was right. We can't just stop the cart. We need to stop the *men*.

"We need to incapacitate the soldiers in some way," I say. I cannot bring myself to call them by name, my mind still lingering on the memory of Diego's face in the moonlight. "If we want any chance at getting away, we need to make sure they can't chase us."

"Are you going to hurt them?" The question comes from one of the young girls, the one closest to me. I cannot remember whether it is Ana Clara or Tomasina. Regardless, they both know enough about *hechicería* to understand the implications of hurting someone.

I refuse to say it outright, especially in front of the entire group. "We need to do something," I answer, but I know Adanna understands me.

"You are right," she says. "But what more can we do? You already struggled to blind Marcos."

What more can we do?

Every move should do the most damage to your opponent with the least amount of energy on your part.

How do we optimize our move of blinding Marcos? I am not alone anymore, I have Adanna and Leonor to help with this curse. Who else do I have?

I think of it all at once.

"Preko, would you be able to urge the horse to go faster?" I ask.

He looks up with a blink. He opens his mouth and closes it again, brows drawn. Slowly, he nods. "Yes, I think so. How fast?"

With his confirmation, I smile and turn to address Adanna and Leonor.

"We wait until there is a bend in the road, then blur or darken his vision," I say. "If the horse is going fast enough, he will lose control of the cart and won't be able to turn with the road. We will have to brace ourselves, as there is a good chance we crash. But I think that would do the trick."

I watch the three of them take it in, thinking on my plan.

Adanna nods. "We're in front of the other cart, so even if the second cart doesn't crash, there are enough of us that we should be able to get the horses to stop. We will rescue the other group, too."

"Then what?" Leonor asks.

"We run," I say. "The sooner we do it, the closer we are to town."

"Right," Leonor says with a stiff nod. She grits her teeth and lowers her brow, her classic tell of determination. "Someone needs to watch out front."

"I can do that." Preko sits closest to the front of the cart, and he is tall enough to get a good view through the narrow window, even among the dips and bumps of the shaky ride. "I want to see the horse, anyway."

He doesn't wait for a response. He stands in the middle of the cart, feet wide and hands braced against the wall to keep him from falling. Preko peers through the crack, blocking out most of the little light we have.

"Everyone quiet," he orders.

Adanna, Leonor, and I look back and forth between one another, barely able to see each other's silhouettes. We wait for a moment for one of us to speak, but the cart stays silent.

But then it gets louder, the wheels hitting dips in the road as we speed up. Faster and faster, jostling us in our seats.

I glance up to see Preko's eyes closed, muttering to himself as though communicating with the horse. Whatever he does, it works. We are going so fast that I hear Diego and Marcos say something outside the cart, their tones laced with concern.

"Take time to ground right now," Adanna says to Leonor and me once the cart has sped up. Her voice is quiet and hushed, already getting focused. "At Preko's signal, we will work together to dim, blur, and blind Marcos's sight, okay? Whatever works for you."

The three of us nod in succession, then shut our eyes.

This time, as I reach out, I feel Adanna almost immediately. Her aura is like the moon—comforting and loving, but terrifyingly powerful and vaguely threatening.

It isn't long before I become aware of Leonor. Her energy feels like one of the stray cats from Castellfollit, readying herself for a fight. Scrappy, feral, yet undeniably skilled.

I see the rest of the children in the cart, their energies swirling in colors. But it is Preko that gives me pause. His spirit contains only a fraction of the strength he usually possesses, suffocating the aura around him.

Shaking my head, I push past him. I see Marcos and Diego outside on the front of the cart, and I focus on Marcos once again, preparing to cover his eyes and throw him into darkness.

"Everyone brace yourselves," Preko whispers.

We collectively hold our breath, waiting for Preko's word. I steel myself. I'm doing this for myself, for my friends.

I can feel the thrum of power surging through my fingertips.

"Do it now."

By the time he speaks, I am so ready to curse Marcos that I barely hear Preko.

With my spirit, I run my hands over Marcos's eyes, leaving a muddy film in their wake. I do it again and again, supported by Adanna and Leonor, until his eyes are covered and he is blinded despite his open eyes.

The cart jerks.

"Marcos, what is wrong with you? Hold it, *tio*." I hear Diego's voice, exasperated.

Another jerk, this one harder.

"There's something in my eye," Marcos grunts.

We hit a rock or a ditch, something that jolts the cart and has the wheel creaking underneath us.

"Hey, Marcos!" Diego calls out to him. I can imagine Diego reaching out, attempting to take the reins from Marcos.

Marcos pulls the reins to the side as he tries to clear his vision. The cart tips, riding on one wheel for what feels like minutes.

I can feel when the road curves and when we don't follow it.

The wheel collides into something. Another rock or a bush, perhaps. Our bodies launch forward to the front of the cart while it falls the rest of the way to the ground.

But I do not open my eyes. I'm not done.

I know that if the crash isn't bad enough, this entire endeavor will be fruitless. We won't be able to escape. And we all may be hurt or killed in the process.

I shove Marcos, willing him to fly off the cart in a violent fall.

Time slows as I concentrate.

Every emotion—every bit of anger and fear and grief and betrayal—flow from my spirit to his body, pushing him with as much force as my spirit can muster.

Diego yells in surprise.

Marcos screams.

The wood of the cart splinters.

My body slams into the floor. My head hits someone's knee or elbow. I don't know what it is, but it hurts.

"Catalina!" It's Adanna. She grabs onto my shoulders.

I finally open my eyes.

"Didn't you hear Preko say brace yourself?"

I laugh, but wince at the pain throbbing in my head.

We are a bruised mess of limbs on the uneven floor of the cart. Leonor has her arms around one of the younger girls. Preko helps another one get into a sitting position in the tilted cart. As a whole, we are shaken, but uninjured.

"Look," Adanna whispers, her eyes focused behind me.

I turn to follow her gaze.

The door of the cart is splintered, letting fragments of light through the cracks and hinges.

Adanna squeezes past me, knocking me off balance, and I stumble into the wall.

She kicks at the door. It splinters further.

"Help me."

Preko steps around me, and the two of them shove their bodies into the door.

I watch the hinges dislodge from the wood. All it takes is one more kick from Adanna, and the door falls open, crookedly swinging on the top hinge.

Preko jumps out, followed closely by Adanna. She turns around, holding her hand out for me. I grab onto it and carefully hop down.

Even on the uneven earth, the ground feels solid beneath my feet. I look down to see the dirt smudging my boots, and I want to cry in relief.

"Marcos? Diego?"

I squint into the dark as I hear another pair of feet land on the ground behind me.

Pedro and Alferez have stopped the cart behind us. Alferez jumps down and runs toward our destroyed wagon. My throat constricts in fear, but he runs past us, completely ignoring our group as we escape the confines of the cart.

I can hear Alferez's worried voice slither its way across the dark ground. I dare not look in his direction.

Adanna has helped all the youngest children out of the cart. Leonor is the last one out, and her face blanches once she looks up.

"*Mierda*," Leonor whispers.

I turn around to face Pedro's cart.

Preko is low to the ground on Pedro's side, a large rock in his hand, raised as a weapon.

I gasp too loud, catching Pedro's attention. His eyes widen, and he turns to see Preko right next to him. He reaches out to stop him. But not soon enough.

Preko slams the rock into the side of Pedro's head with a sickening thud, and I watch Pedro's dark eyes roll back before he slumps out of his seat.

My own body feels cold, and I don't know how to react. How to move forward. Luckily, Adanna jumps into action.

"Key!" Adanna calls to him.

Preko climbs onto the seat, searching Pedro's body. Finding it in Pedro's pocket, he tosses it down to her, and Adanna rushes around to the back of the cart, with Leonor close behind her.

I hear screams and gasps as the girls free the second group. I want to follow them, but my feet pull me in the opposite direction, and my stomach sinks as I take in the scene.

The left wheel is shattered, and the front of our cart is broken. The horse has gotten free, and I see no sign of the creature.

Tripping through the brush and over stones, I walk off the path. Groans of pain and raspy grunts draw me to the shadows of two men: one lying on the ground, the other bent over him.

They hear me approach, and the one nearest me whirls around. Alferez looks at me with terror in his eyes, his skin pale.

I take a hesitant step forward, and Alferez trips back.

"Don't," he rasps. "Get away, *bruja*." He holds his hands out, palms facing me.

I stop, but he doesn't. Alferez begins taking wide steps to the side, circling around me as I twist toward him, never turning my back to him. His wide eyes flit around my face, and his fingers twitch.

I have nearly spun all the way back to the road when he makes a run for it, sprinting toward the horse still attached to the other cart. It is too dark to see, but I can hear the frantic neighing and hurried hooves as Alferez takes off with the only horse left.

I turn back to the man on the ground. He doesn't speak, but I can hear wheezing, labored breaths coming from his direction. I approach his silhouetted figure until I can make out his face.

And my stomach lurches, every organ racing up toward my throat. I may be sick.

Marcos lies on the ground, limbs bent underneath him at painful, unnatural angles. His clothes are torn, and his body is bloody and surely bruised.

But it is his face that haunts me.

A long branch has punctured his right cheek, piercing all the way through the thin flesh. The bloodied point sits inside his mouth, an inch away from the other cheek. Blood trails from both sides of his mouth and down his cheek where the makeshift spear has penetrated.

He sees me and stops breathing for a moment. I freeze.

Then, he tries to speak. His throat gurgles, choking on his own blood, and I cannot understand him as I watch his throat move.

He tries again. "Help. Me."

I swallow down the bile burning in my stomach.

Taking the same position Alferez had just moments before, I lean down over him.

This close, I see the dark red and purple bruise already appearing underneath his left eye and the deep cut on his eyebrow. His right leg is bleeding, the lower half of his pant leg torn off.

He would not have been this injured just from the crash.

This is my doing. This is because I shoved him off the cart. Because I cursed him.

His fingers shake as he tries to take hold of the branch stuck into his face.

I wrap my hand around his, squeezing around the stick.

"Why did you tell Rafael my mother's name?" My voice is a whisper, my face mere inches from his.

He doesn't say anything, just stares at me.

I pull. My hand yanks his entire face forward with my hold on the branch. It pulls at the skin and widens the hole. He howls in pain, but it doesn't drown out the squishing sound of tearing flesh. His rasping scream sprays flecks of blood all over my cheeks, my lips, my dress.

"Why?" I ask again.

Marcos shakes his head, hardly moving it, but shaking it nonetheless.

"What was your deal with Rafael? What did you want with us?"

"I can't— I can't—" Marcos breathes erratically. "Catalina, please."

I stare into his cold blue eyes, one painted red with blood. He blinks furiously, his entire body trembling.

I should be disgusted, disturbed. I did this. Yet it is still not enough.

I cannot help but think this is my chance to air my grievances. My chance to make him understand, to make him hear me. To make them all hear me. Because, for once, they are listening. They have to listen.

But when I open my mouth, there are no words. I have nothing.

I reach inside myself, clawing and grasping and wracking my brain to make my speech. I find only that familiar anger.

Anger for my mother and my sister. Anger for my friends, for Kosia, and for myself. Anger for our mothers who came before us and for our daughters who now suffer at the hands of these men, this country. It bubbles inside me and it makes me want to scream as it eats my soul.

So, I do.

I scream as I rip the branch out of his face. The end of it catches the raw gash in his cheek, but it does not stop me.

He shrieks again, and the sound cuts off when he passes out. I watch his body fall back. His head hits a stone.

And he lies still.

"Catalina!"

Adanna's voice precedes her footsteps.

"*Caracoles*," she whispers as she comes up behind me. "Serves him right."

She stands next to me as we look down on Marcos's unconscious form. His body is slumped on the ground, his leg still set at that awkward angle. Blood trickles down the right side of his face—from his eye, his cheek, and his mouth.

My ears ring with the sound of flesh tearing in his gaping wound and the cry of agony that followed.

I clear my throat, my voice thick. "Alferez is gone, but we should tie them up. Marcos and Pedro. Just in case," I add. After seeing Pedro hit by Preko, I am almost certain he is dead. And I do not know if Marcos will ever wake up, either.

Adanna hesitates. "Where is Diego?"

A shiver travels down my spine. I have used every extra ounce of energy to try to push any thought of Diego out of my mind.

"I'm here."

The low voice sounds from behind us, close to the cart.

We turn to see Diego, barely visible in the shadows. He is on the ground, his arm caught beneath one end of the large wooden cart.

His sharp jaw is clenched tight, and his face twists in pain—eyebrows drawn together and lips pressed into a rigid line.

I hear the breath catch in my throat. I try to stop it, but I can't.

"Catalina, please," he says quietly.

For a fleeting moment, I am reminded of the oath I swore to him, the one he swore to me.

I will have you begging for mercy before we are done.

"Please, listen. I can explain." He struggles against the cart, pushing upward in an attempt to free himself, but it hardly moves. He doesn't have the leverage.

Even in the dark, I can see Diego wince in pain as the cart places pressure on his injured arm. I cannot tell if it is broken, but it is bloodied.

"Catalina," Diego says again. His voice is pleading. He cranes his neck on the ground to face me. His burning brown eyes meet mine, and I have to look away.

I swallow hard. "Maybe we don't need to tie them up. It seems they are all a little indisposed."

The only one I need protection from is you.

In truth, I do not know if I can stand here looking at Diego for much longer. Seeing his earnest face breaks my heart all over again, his betrayal too much to bear.

You are anything but powerless, brujita. I want you more than I want any of that.

He had lied. Of course, he had lied.

Diego grunts with effort and tries again. "I had no part in this, okay? I did not betray you."

"I don't believe you." I turn away from him.

"Just listen to me."

"No, you listen to me," I hiss, whirling back to face him. I am shocked at the strength of my voice when I think I will break down in tears at any moment. Though, after ripping a branch from Marcos's cheek, I feel somewhat hardened, ready to push through my emotions, or at least push them aside.

I reach down and grip Diego's chin, wrenching his face up toward me. I see the blood on my hand from where I cut myself. It was the left palm that I cut, but my right hand is still red, the blood sticking to Diego's face.

"Don't you dare tell me you were not part of this. You stood by, Diego. Kosia is dead. My mother is in danger. And you tied us up and took us as though we were nothing but animals, ready to be shipped off to God knows where."

He doesn't blink, doesn't shrink away, though his face pales and his eyes hold a hint of fear. He may not have heard or seen every bit of my interaction with Marcos, but I know he saw enough.

I lean down closer to him. "If he ever wakes up," I whisper, my lips a breath from his, "you tell Marcos that this crash was our doing. This was our curse. And he would do well to remember this witch will not hesitate to harm him in any way I see fit."

I release his chin and straighten my back, looking down at him.

"I am not so easy to control, Diego."

He frowns for a second, but then his eyes widen slightly, and I know he remembers what he told me that day. The day he chased me. The day he caught me.

His gaze slowly sweeps up and down my body. "You have blood on your hands, *brujita*. And on your dress," Diego comments in a rough voice. "The girl against violence, covered in blood."

He shakes his head with a smirk, but it turns into a grimace as the movement jostles his arm. My stomach tightens, and I have to force myself not to wipe my hands on my dress again.

"The blood on my hands is my own," I bite out. "I cannot say the same for the blood on yours."

I see a flicker of emotion in his eyes. What I thought was fear is actually awe. He is staring at me with wonder, not terror. Almost like he is impressed.

I do not know which makes me feel worse.

The longer I gaze down at Diego, the more my heart hurts. It takes everything in me to take a step away from him.

"Goodbye, Diego Tremiño."

"Catalina, don't you dare!" Diego's cry is both angry and panicked.

I ignore him. I walk away on shaking legs, past the cart, and back to the road without looking back. Diego keeps calling to me. The farther I walk, the quieter it gets.

But his voice still winds in and out of my mind. *I want you more than I want any of that.*

And a fragment of my soul withers. The fragment that was naive and hopeful. The fragment that trusted Diego, that looked to him with admiration. With affection. The fragment that believed him.

It is a far bigger piece than I had expected.

There in the dark, a sob escapes from my throat. I clutch my chest, stumbling as tears flood my eyes. Another sob shudders through me, and I fall to my knees.

I want to be stronger. I want to not break because of a heartbreak and betrayal I should have seen coming.

I am not stronger.

Adanna is next to me in a moment. My hands covering my face, she wraps her arms around me, pressing my shoulder into her side before gently guiding my head onto her chest. I weep. She tightens her embrace, her strong presence a silent support. She doesn't say anything.

I do not know whether she disapproves of my relationship with Diego or whether she thinks me foolish to have fallen for him—and for his plot. And I do not know what she thinks of what I have just done, of the things I said to Diego. But I won't take it back. I meant every word. That doesn't stop my heart from breaking, though.

Once my chest has stopped heaving, I brace myself for another wave of tears. But Adanna grips my shoulders and pulls me in front of her.

"I'm sorry, Catalina," she says softly. Her face is full of sympathy, her expression twisted with sadness. She moves to wipe my wet cheeks, and I realize she has a matching set, her face shining with tears.

"Me, too," I whisper. My lip begins to tremble anew.

She shakes her head, wiping her own tears now. "We must go. You know we must go," she says. "I know your heart is broken. From everything. But now is not the time."

She is right, as always. I clench my jaw and nod in agreement, teeth grinding against one another. We help each other to our feet and make our way back.

When we approach the rest of the group in the middle of the dark road, I slow down, and Adanna moves past me.

I watch Juliana and Leonor embrace one another, ensuring that each is uninjured. Constanza grips Sofia's hands while talking to her in a low voice. Araceli and Rosa both wrap their arms around Preko, while Adanna kneels near the younger children and holds a sobbing girl.

Slowly, the group quiets, and Constanza whistles.

"Everyone," Constanza starts, "stay close to one another. We need to get moving now to make it back to Castellfollit as quickly as possible."

Agreement settles over the group with a quiet murmur. Adanna stands. Juliana releases Leonor. Constanza silently takes a head-count, ensuring everyone is present, and we begin to move down the road, back from where we came.

This time unbound and on foot. This time of our own volition.

We try to walk as quickly as we can, but the younger children slow us down. Leonor and Juliana lift Tomasina and Ana Clara onto their backs. Araceli holds the hands of Ignacio and Maria, hurrying them along.

I expect the journey to be longer, but we reach the end too soon. My end.

The road diverges, a small dirt path breaking off to the right. The path I know leads around Castellfollit and down to the river. It is the same road I took with Rafael when I first came to town.

They keep going, but I stand still, not joining the remainder of the group. I clench my fists as the lump in my throat grows, unsure of what to say.

But Adanna stops with me, immediately noticing when I don't continue with them. She turns to me with a small smile on her face.

"I am not going back," I say. It is a breath of a whisper, but Adanna hears me. "I'm going to Banyoles." My blood pumps with adrenaline, tainted by fear, and my chest aches.

"I know," Adanna says. She squeezes my hand.

I frown, confused.

"Come on," Adanna laughs. "You didn't think I would let you go by yourself, did you?"

More tears race down my cheeks.

Adanna wraps me in her arms in a brief, tight hug. I hastily swipe at my puffy eyes.

"What do you think he is after?" she asks me in a hushed voice.

"I'm not entirely sure. But I have an idea."

"Catalina." Constanza's voice calls to us. It doesn't quite sound like a question. She knows, too.

Constanza comes up to Adanna and me, taking one of our hands in each of hers.

"You get them back," Adanna says.

Constanza nods. "You be safe."

"I will miss you, Constanza," I whisper.

"Tsk, tsk," she says, "We will see each other soon enough, *chicas*. No goodbyes."

I laugh, and she offers us a warm smile before turning back to the group.

"Let's move," she says, waving her arm in the direction of Castellfollit.

The group begins shuffling forward. My sight blurs as I watch Juliana and Araceli follow Constanza.

"I'm coming, too."

Leonor moves in front of us with her hands on her hips. I open my mouth to argue, but she holds up a hand.

"I am seventeen," she says firmly, "almost eighteen. I can make my own decisions. And I want to help you, Catalina, okay? Both of you."

Strands of dark hair have escaped her braid, and they blow around her face with the breeze, making her look slightly wild. Dirt cakes the hem of her skirt, and her boots are covered in mud. Where the mud came from, I haven't a clue.

"We don't know what is waiting for us, Leonor," Adanna says. "We could die tonight, attacked in the forest. Who knows?"

Leonor nods. "So it may be helpful to have a practiced etheric traveler on your side, no?" Her face splits into a lopsided smile, and her eyes hold a cheeky mischief that begs us to argue with her.

But she doesn't even wait for a response. She just walks past us, untying her hair and freeing it from what remained of the braid.

"I want to come, too."

My heart stutters.

Preko's young face looks from me to Adanna and back again, his deep black eyes a reflection of Kosia's. His woven white shirt sticks to him, sweat and dirt making it appear gray. He's taller than I am, but at this moment, he looks small and subdued.

My ribs feel like a vise, constricting around my lungs at the thought of this thirteen-year-old boy joining us in the dark forest. I cannot allow this.

"No, Preko," I say. "It is too dangerous. You're too young."

He anxiously runs both hands over his hair and down his neck with a defeated sigh. "There is nothing for me there," he whispers. He doesn't have to say it. We know he is talking about Castellfollit. "I can't go back, Catalina. I can't."

His eyes shine with unshed tears, and my heart clenches once more.

I think of the Castellfollit everyone else is returning to. A Castellfollit without Kosia or Rafael. I know there are plenty of other people—other leaders, other families. But I cannot imagine an *hechicera* community without them.

Rafael is the one to blame for both losses.

"You're with us, Preko," Adanna says, her voice firm. She grabs him by the shoulder and turns with him to move toward Leonor.

The air brushes against my arms as they walk past me, but I cannot turn down the road. Not yet.

"Cata," Adanna says softly. "Let's go, *prima*."

From here, I can see the group Constanza leads fading into the town, their silhouettes getting smaller and smaller. The town gates are wide open, calling to me, welcoming us home.

The narrow street beyond it is scarcely lit by lanterns, but I know the stone buildings that line the road. I know how close together everything stands, clinging to the tiny space above the vast cliffs below. I know the smell of the field behind the church, the taste of Señora Ayala's *paella*, the creak of the door to the room Adanna and I shared.

Barely visible at the end of town, the church bell tower rises above the orange tile roofs. A white light lines the edges of the tower. I think it is the moonlight, but perhaps it is only my imagination.

I squeeze my eyes shut as I turn, refusing to look back in the direction of the overturned cart. In the direction of Diego. In the direction of Marcos's ruined face.

Once I face them, Adanna, Leonor, and Preko begin walking away from Castellfollit, their footsteps hardly lit by the moon.

I follow them, moving slowly on the rough and uneven trail. My left knee buckles, but I stay upright, a pain shooting up my leg. I feel it for only a moment, and it is gone so quickly I forget it instantly.

I hurry to catch up with my little ragtag group, and as I do, I pray I can leave this cursed scene behind.

EPILOGUE

Rafael leans forward, urging Caballo on as they travel the road south toward Banyoles. His horse is well-rested, and he had hoped to arrive before sunrise, but he had gotten stuck in Besalú, waiting for them to open the bridge once the sky turned into a dusky blue.

Now, the hazy morning light has brightened with the sun fully over the horizon as they pass through Serinya, the town just north of Banyoles.

It was between these two towns that he found Catalina not long ago. He remembers her careful, cautious expression. Eyes closed tight, eyebrows drawn together, hands trembling. She had been so afraid.

And once again, he cannot stop himself from remembering her face when he last looked at her. Thinking about it makes his stomach drop. It was something more than a hate-filled glare. She had seen inside his soul, she had knocked him over, and it felt like she had branded him.

He swallows hard, reminding himself that she is gone. He won't have to see her expression ever again. He will never see any of them again.

Marcos may think they are still partners, that Rafael will join him once he is finished in Banyoles. He thinks they have the same plan. Fool.

Rafael never cared about building some army of witches. He does not need an army. He has all the power he needs.

The sunlight glitters on the lake of Banyoles. The water is strikingly blue, and as he rides on, he sees the blur of green grasses and trees surrounding the lake. He spots several small boats on the water. Fisherman patiently waiting for the daily catch.

He has arrived.

He slows Caballo to a comfortable trot as he enters the city, the horse's hooves clapping loudly on the stone road and echoing off the houses and buildings that line the streets.

All he has to do is find this *curandera*. She shouldn't be too difficult to find. Most people will have at least some idea where the town *curandera* lives.

Chills dance up his spine in anticipation. Over a decade of studying, hunting, and bargaining has led him here. Now, he is so close, he can taste it.

Everything else pales in comparison. It makes it all worth it. All of it.

Rafael did not want to kill Kosia—he is not a monster. And of course, he did not fully agree with Marcos's plan of capturing over a dozen young witches. But it had to be done. If Kosia had put a stop to Marcos's plan, he never would have told Rafael about the *curandera*.

When he finally found Marcos five years ago, he knew the young man held the information he needed. He could see it; he could feel it.

The trail had gone cold when he discovered that the last known possessor had died. But a soldier had kept track of the man's family. And that soldier gave his secret to Marcos.

Now, Rafael knew it, too.

Soledad Gonzalez Moreño.

Rafael would never have known she was Catalina's mother if it hadn't been for her reaction. Perhaps Marcos had his suspicions, but it was Catalina's face when Marcos said her name that told Rafael everything he needed to know.

Of course, Marcos did not know the woman's first name either, just that it was a *curandera* named Gonzalez Moreño. But Rafael can recall Catalina telling him about her family: her mother, Soledad, and her older sister, Inés.

Unfortunately, they have recently been released from their arrest. It would have been much easier to get into their house with them out of the picture.

No matter. Rafael will do whatever it takes, and with Catalina out of the way, she will never have to know what becomes of her family.

Though it is still morning, Banyoles is busy and bustling. At least, busier than Castellfollit. Rafael forgets how small the mountain town really is until he is faced with a more populated place.

He rides only a little farther into the city before dismounting, choosing to lead Caballo by the reins in search of a stable somewhere.

The sun gets higher in the sky, breaching the roofs of the town and shining into the streets. Rafael closes his eyes for a moment, letting the rays warm his face.

When he opens them again, he sees a young boy right in front of him. He pulls the reins to stop Caballo.

The boy can't be more than eleven or so, walking with his head down, focused on the package of fish in his hands. He does not notice Rafael and Caballo, and if Rafael hadn't opened his eyes, he would have run right into him.

Caballo huffs, and the sound makes the boy jump.

"Keep your head up, kid," Rafael says. "Watch where you're going, or you will end up trampled."

"*Perdona!* Forgive me, sir," the boy says, his eyes wide.

Rafael waves away the apology and the smell of fish with one hand. "Can you tell me where I can find a stable? A place to water my horse?"

The boy nods. He turns around and balances the package on one arm, pointing down the road. "All the way into town. There is a stable one street over from the market."

Rafael pauses. "The market?"

"In the main plaza."

"*Gracias.*" Rafael smiles, moving past the boy with purpose and a new plan.

He remembers Catalina talking about the market in Banyoles. She said that she and her sister sell the *talavera* they made. Their mother rarely joins them, and he is unsure whether the family will be at the market so soon after being released, but perhaps he can find someone who knows where they live.

It isn't long before he comes upon the stable the boy mentioned. As he gets Caballo settled and pays the attendant, Rafael can hear the buzz of a crowd. He cannot see the market square yet, but it certainly won't be difficult to find.

He tries to ignore it, but an image of Catalina comes to his mind, unbidden.

He wonders if Catalina knew her mother's secret. Did she know her mother had something with the power to change the world? Did she know people had been searching for it for centuries? That he himself had been searching for years?

The Book of Blood.

And to think, the woman never used it. Well, as far as Rafael knew. Though, if she had, he would have probably discovered it. Besides, from what Catalina told him about her mother, he doubts she would have ever even opened the Book of Blood.

At least her husband used the Book. Rafael knows that for certain. Marcos would not have known where to find it otherwise. But the man has been dead for two decades.

He scoffs in the back of his throat. It isn't right that the Book has been sitting, rotting away, untouched. It is time to put it to use, and he will be the one to do it.

The power the Book can offer him will increase his strength and abilities tenfold, making the impossible possible. It holds secrets beyond imagination, the legends telling only a portion of its potential.

And Rafael never planned to hand it over to Marcos. It is his, and his alone.

He enters the square, weaving through the crowd that has already begun to form today. The borders of the square are adorned with stone arches that create a sheltered passageway, and Rafael ducks into the space to move quickly.

As he passes by merchants and booths, Rafael searches the plaza for sellers of *talavera* in the hopes that they will be familiar with Catalina's family.

The scent of fresh flowers wafts over to him, cutting through the smell of fish that still lingers on his person. To his right, a woman stands amidst a veritable garden of flowers. The booth is covered in different colors and species of flora, and Rafael slows his steps to take in more of the sweet scent.

He continues his search, walking by a group arguing in front of a table filled with embroidered textiles and clothing. The bartering becomes more intense, and when he hears the price, he understands why these customers are so aggressively adamant.

Then, he sees her.

Catalina.

The back of his neck prickles, his hair standing on end.

He swiftly shakes his head. No, not Catalina. It can't be.

But it is as though she has taken residence in the back of his mind, scratching at his subconscious and crawling along his skin. Tainting his vision and haunting him.

He turns his attention back to the girl in front of him. She is taller than Catalina, her skin slightly fairer, but she has the same long, dark hair and the same clear blue eyes.

Rafael approaches slowly, watching the girl offer small smiles to those walking by her table. Her table of *talavera*.

The girl runs her hands absentmindedly over the delicate design painted perfectly on the tiles in front of her. The pattern is one of yellow and green fruits, enhanced with blue borders and ornaments. It is beautiful and masterfully made.

Yet, no one stops. It is as though an invisible wall surrounds her booth, and shoppers swerve around the table to avoid her, casting glances as though suspicious of her.

Rafael knows for certain. This is not Catalina, but her older sister, Inés. When he nears the table, her face forms a lopsided half smile—one filled with mirth and mischief—and he sees the similarities in their mannerisms.

"*Buenos días*," she greets him.

He keeps his head down for a moment, picking up a few pottery pieces and examining them, turning them this way and that, holding one up to the sunlight to get a better look.

He finally returns her smile and lifts a blue-painted bowl.

"Did you paint this one?"

Glossary

Ajenjo: *(plant)* wormwood

Albahaca: *(plant)* basil

Amapola: *(plant)* poppy

Apatito: *(stone)* apetite

Artemisa: *(plant)* mugwort

Bruja: witch, or someone who practices witchcraft

Cuarzo: *(stone)* quartz

Curandera: healer

Escaramujo: *(plant)* blackthorn

Fluorita: *(stone)* fluorite

Hada: fairy

Hechicera: sorceress, or someone who uses magic

Heliotropo: *(plant)* European heliotrope

Hierba pincel: *(plant)* Montpellier Coris

Hinojo: *(plant)* fennel

Hipérico: *(plant)* St. John's wort

Jara: *(plant)* rockrose

Lino: *(plant)* Spanish flax

Manzanilla: *(plant)* Roman chamomile

Menta: *(plant)* mint

Milenrama: *(plant)* yarrow

Naranja: *(plant)* orange

Olivarda: *(plant)* woody fleabane

Prehnita: *(stone)* prehnite

Romero: *(plant)* rosemary

Rosa silvestre: *(plant)* wild rose

Saúco: *(plant)* elder

Serbal: *(plant)* rowan

Talavera: a type of handmade, hand-painted ceramic pottery originating in Spain

Tilo: *(plant)* big leaf linden

Toronjil: *(plant)* lemon balm

Vidente: seer

Acknowledgements

First, I'd like to give a shoutout to all my Spanish ancestors, whose names inspired these characters. Thanks—you guys are real ones for that. I could have done without you keeping me up at night, but fair is fair.

Next, to my sister, Tali, I cannot stress enough that this book would not exist without you. Thank you for your endless encouragement, excitement, and unwavering belief in me and in this story. Thank you for your input, your thoughts, and your help with the Spanish language and culture woven into this book.

To my editor, Lily Edgerton, thank you for your work in making this story far more legible. Thank you for your enthusiasm, your time, and for being my extra set of eyes.

To my mother and cover designer, Rhonna Farrer, thank you for the many hours you put into making this book something beautiful. Readers wouldn't have picked it up if it weren't for you.

I was only able to finish this journey with the help of countless friends and family. To my real-life *hechiceras*, Amy and Bailey, thank you for your love, friendship, guidance, and magic; many pieces of this story were inspired by you. To everyone who read this book while it was still under construction, I appreciate your patience, your feedback, and the love you showed to this piece of my heart. To Mom and Dad, thank you both for supporting me while I followed my dream and built my circus. Thank you for buying me that purple storyteller notebook at the Scholastic Book Fair when I was seven. I believe that is where it all began.

Last but not least, I want to thank you, dear reader. Thank you for being part of this little bit of *hechicería* magic.

About the Author

Jaya Farrer is a historical fantasy author and lifelong writer. She is currently living in Scotland for her Master's degree in Comparative Literature. When she isn't thinking of all the reasons she would have been burned as a witch hundreds of years ago, Jaya enjoys spending time in the gym, baking bread, and perfecting her paint-by-numbers skills. *Book of Blood* is her debut novel.

www.ingramcontent.com/pod-product-compliance
Lightning Source LLC
Chambersburg PA
CBHW020351010826
48973CB00005B/1364